From Higher Places

From Higher Places

Roger Curtis

Matador
9 Priory Business Park,
Wistow Road, Kibworth Beauchamp,
Leicestershire. LE8 0RX
Tel: 0116 279 2299
Email: books@troubador.co.uk
Web: www.troubador.co.uk/matador
Twitter: @matadorbooks

ISBN 978 1788035 132

British Library Cataloguing in Publication Data.
A catalogue record for this book is available from the British Library.

Printed and bound by CPI Group (UK) Ltd, Croydon, CR0 4YY
Typeset in 11pt Aldine401 BT by Troubador Publishing Ltd, Leicester, UK

Matador is an imprint of Troubador Publishing Ltd

BY THE SAME AUTHOR

Murchison's Fragment
and Other Short Plays for Stage and Radio

HIGHTOWER

May 1987

1

It was the click of the car door that lodged itself most vividly in her memory. Not the knife, not the footfall on the stair, not even the imagined expression of hate behind the stocking mask: just a simple everyday sound that would have been multiplied in innocence a dozen times during the course of that warm May afternoon.

In reality Sarah-Jane – for that's what she was called then – had heard nothing, being content with herself before the dressing table mirror. But when the police came she had overheard Marguerite's casual remark to them, and during the days that followed her mind had worked on this benign observation and the image had come to assume terrifying significance

Marguerite had been in the room to place her mistress's laundered clothes in the stacked white drawers on either side of the king-size bed. It might have been the sound of the car that caused the girl to turn towards her mistress. More likely, though, it was the urge to compare her pert Latin features side by side in the mirror with Sarah-Jane's more delicate profile: to savour and scorn the ten years or so that separated them, yet at the same time to envy a quality of beauty that years alone could not efface.

Sarah-Jane saw the girl's reflection in the mirror and

patted the red-gold curls that just caressed her own bare shoulders.

'Tell me honestly, Marguerite, should my hair be up or down this evening?'

'What dress, Miss?'

'The black one, with the lace collar.'

'Then up, of course, so we can see the lace.'

Sarah-Jane smiled, reassured. Not by the advice – the reverse of what she had already decided – but by the hint of jealous disdain that her question had elicited, and her own flush of self-gratification that resulted from it. She could afford to be intimate again with her outspoken domestic. Still, there was a subtlety about the girl that she found oddly, and unexpectedly, attractive.

'Would you please unfasten me?'

The olive hand touched the skin of her neck, and lingered for a moment before pulling down the fastener. The gesture was worth a response: a crumb, at least, from her well stocked table.

'Mr Preston will be at home this weekend,' Sarah-Jane said.

'That will be nice!'

'For me or for you?'

'For both of us I think.'

Sarah-Jane glanced towards the younger woman, seeking evidence of a developing conspiracy, but finding none. Marguerite turned her back and resumed packing the drawers with a vigour that threatened the integrity of the exquisite lingerie.

From somewhere near the gate to the road Sarah-Jane heard the scrunch of gravel. Until the week before the surface of the drive had been grey tarmac, cracking but undeniably serviceable. For Sarah-Jane it had simply not been right. It didn't fit, for example, with the keeping of her three horses – Gemma, Pitta and Pasta – in the red cedar stables behind the house. Only when she – or rather Mark under protest – had changed it did she think to look more closely at the other houses in the Dell, each with its pristine approach between manicured lawns. As Mark agreed later, theirs had not been consonant. That was partly why she remembered the footsteps on the gravel.

Sarah-Jane angled her body to the window and thought for a moment. She saw Marguerite pause in anticipation; she would know from experience what kind of morsel might be coming her way.

'If you like you can ride with us on Sunday,' Sarah-Jane said.

What a barbed hook that was! There was a long pause before the girl replied, 'I would like that very much.'

Sarah-Jane knew that Marguerite disliked animals, and horses in particular. They didn't come naturally to a girl raised in the back-streets of Marseille, and from a family whose macho males thought nothing of tossing an errant cat – or so Marguerite had led her to believe – through an upstairs window. Determination and the language school in Cambridge had done something to dispel the effects of such influences, but the residues were hard to shift. So she knew the inner conflict that her invitation had caused. Marguerite would consider the possibility that Sarah-Jane might have one of her migraines and withdraw at the last minute. There were certainly precedents for that.

Had she not seen it from the beginning? Did it not begin one Sunday a year back when she and Mark had taken their new charge to Hever Castle and Sarah-Jane had responded to the flame of a young photographer claiming to represent *Vogue* magazine? But although her eyes had flashed with the thought of gracing that illustrious cover, they had not failed to notice the touching of fingers as her husband and the girl receded stealthily into the background. And that, like the crunch of the gravel, she would never quite forget.

Sarah-Jane pushed these thoughts aside, following with her ears the footsteps up the drive. Suddenly, inexplicably, she was concerned.

'Are you expecting someone, Marguerite?'

'No, Miss.'

'Then why has the door just banged?'

'Perhaps it's Mr Preston…'

'He always drives the Mercedes to the door. Besides, he rang from town only an hour ago.'

'Then I don't know!'

'Then go and look, for goodness' sake!'

Marguerite pressed heavily on the clothes in the drawer, pushed it shut and marched out, slamming the door behind her.

The duty delegated, Sarah-Jane relaxed and smiled at herself in the mirror. Then she looked out of the window.

It was still, at that moment, a perfect day.

On the golf-course beyond the trees lining the road she could see figures motionless around the final green, their shadows like black torpedoes. They peered at the hole with the devotion of the couple in the hand-crafted reproduction of Millet's *Angelus* on the chimney-breast in the drawing room. No duty weighed more heavily upon them than the execution of the final putt. Some days she would look for Mark amongst them. She could easily pick out his angular frame and sense in the set of his shoulders the same strength and purpose that he brought to his business dealings. Or, as Brian had once put it, the vanquishing of his adversaries.

Brian. There was an enigma. He was her husband's friend. Once he had been her friend too, almost. But that was five years before, after she graduated at St Catherine's. When she married Mark and left medicine, Brian had said, 'He may have stolen you from me but I have gained the ambition you have shed to add to my own.' And at the time that seemed strange. Ambition was something that both men had in common and in abundance. As with like poles they should have repelled one another, but they did not. Mark, the more transparent of the two, had said jokingly, 'You never know when we might need a really good medic.' But, looking from the other side, she could see no similar advantage for Brian. It was a subject to which she had given much thought. Still, he would be at the dinner tonight, probably without Alice, as usual. After dinner, for amusement, she might pair him up with Marguerite. Perhaps even arrange a double act with the horses on Sunday. That could be amusing.

Then she thought again and wondered if that was really what she wanted.

It seemed that at this moment the sky had darkened and the birds had stopped singing.

The silence was broken by Marguerite's scream from somewhere on the stairs.

Sarah-Jane became frightened. She stared into the mirror – this time not at herself, but at the reflection of the solid oak door with its gold plated handle, willing it not to open. Her hand reached desperately for the squirrel pendant that had once been her sister's. Pots and bottles crashed to the floor, spewing their contents.

She turned her face to him as he came, making everything easy.

The blade of the knife entered her cheek half an inch from the corner of her left eye and continued downwards in a gentle curve, taking in the extremities of both lips and emerging just above her chin. There was no pain, then; just a taste of iron in her mouth.

It seemed that for a moment he stopped to inspect his workmanship. That was before the blood began to flow, but by then he had gone.

ST CATHERINE'S

April 1981 – July 1982

2

Sarah thrust the gear lever into third and put her foot down to take the gradient. At the brow the trees on either side gave way like parting curtains to the pasture-green vale of Oxford. On a bright day the city would be shining in the distance to cheer her. Today though, under a squally April sky, it was an ochre smudge.

She drew into the picnic area set there for tourists to admire the view before continuing on to spend their cash in the city; but the coaches of summer were still weeks away and the place was deserted. She angled the car so that she could look along the line of trees to the north and switched off the engine. Across the valley, at a similar elevation, the village of Peverell Hessett peeped through greening trees that would soon obscure it. A handful of rooftops nestled around the squat tower of St Peter's Church. Beyond them rose the bare dome of Beacon Hill, incongruously prominent for the northern edge of the Chiltern Hills.

From the glove compartment she took out her cosmetic case. Then lowered the mirror, dabbed powder on her cheeks and patted a few stray hairs into place. None of it was necessary. Replacing the mirror and the case, she folded her hands in her lap and stared again at the village. This was a ritual that took place whenever she returned home, a delaying tactic to give space to prepare; and to reassure herself that she would be back in London by nightfall. Except that today – the occasion of her father's funeral – things would be different.

A week before she had sat at this same spot, guiltily savouring a new-found sense of freedom that she couldn't quite explain. That morning her mother had telephoned the hospital and it had taken an hour for the message to reach her that her father had gone. Ignoring the ambiguity and guessing the worst, she had high-jacked her friend Alice's car and sped up the M40 to do what was needed for an ailing woman confused – grieving would be too strong a word – after the death of her husband from cancer. Now, as the rain-clouds rolled in from the west and drops spattered the windscreen, that sense of release had gone. In its place was an irrational foreboding. Closure – but against what? – would not come quite so easily.

Could she bring herself to think of him kindly? It was difficult. Her thoughts drifted back to the clamping down of the coffin lid. Not that she'd witnessed it, of course. She did not regret ignoring her mother's entreaty to take one last look. 'He's peaceful now,' Betty Potter had said. Was that an idle throw-away or an insightful realisation that her daughter was now safe? No, that was an exaggeration; perhaps beyond influence was a more charitable way of expressing it. Whatever, she had to press on. Her mother would need protection from well-meaning helpers assembling right now at Laurel Cottage.

The engine started fitfully, as well it might given Alice's lack of empathy with anything mechanical. Sarah took one last look across the valley. In its depths a blanket of mist obscured the ancient stone bridge over the river. How symbolic that bridge had become: a kind of Check Point Charlie separating her London life as a medical student at St Catherine's from what had gone before – and rumbled on since. One day, returning home, she had taken her pulse before crossing it, then again in the lay-by on the other side. The magnitude of the increase had surprised her.

Across the bridge the road led upwards towards the village. The turning into Tippett's Lane – an evergreen tunnel leading to Laurel Cottage – appeared on the right. On an impulse she ignored it and continued on, past the ironmongers and the butcher's shop, to stop at the village store a hundred yards further on. They sold newspapers and there might just have been time for an obituary in the villages edition of the local rag. It seemed sensible to be informed. The young woman across the counter eyed her warily. 'Not yet, Sarah, I looked,' she said, handing her the paper. The steel blue eyes fixed Sarah's. 'Quite a stranger these days, aren't we?'

'Not really, Julie. I get back when I can.'

'And finals soon, your mother was telling me. Then we'll have to watch our Ps and Qs.' She turned to occupy herself with the shelves behind her. ' Sorry I won't be with you after the funeral, with the shop to think of – it's the post office bit, you see. He was such a lovely man, your father.'

'Yes, wasn't he.' She hadn't intended it to sound sarcastic and maybe that was only in her mind. But just in case she added, 'The village will miss him.'

The woman looked round, half-hiding a wry smile, saying nothing.

Sarah had known Julie Bradwell since primary school, where they had been in the same class and inseparable. Then Sarah had gained a place at the grammar school in the city, leaving Julie – to some the brighter of the two – to fester (her words) in the local comprehensive. The problem for Julie was that her elder brother Jonathan was already there: to greet and, in her eyes, be exploited by Sarah. The girls' friendship dissolved in a single night of acrimony, leaving a permanent aftertaste of mistrust. For Sarah, the relationship with Jonathan – now an accountant in Aylesbury but still living in the village – had smouldered on after they left school. She'd tried to extinguish it, but not hard enough, because there had been times – admittedly not often or recently – when she'd found herself short of male attention. He was likely to be at Laurel Cottage after the funeral; it amused her to think what his excuse would be, having had no regard for her father.

The annoying tinkle of the bell as she left the shop made her pause and look round. Julie had come from behind the counter to stand behind her. In as flat a tone as she could manage the woman said, 'It's nice they'll be buried close together, don't you think?'

Sarah did not have to think. The realisation came with a flood of frustration that might have expressed itself physically if Julie hadn't retreated to the safety of the counter. How could this woman know of Sarah's insistence that the grave should be where all recent burials had been, in common ground with nothing to single it out as special? Her mother had shown no wish for it to be otherwise when they'd seen the vicar together. Julie's words had one meaning only: that he was, instead, to be buried next to Elizabeth, her sister. Not in the open, sunlit area east of the chancel that now served the modern village, but in the ancient leafy enclave at the foot of Beacon Hill that for Sarah had become a place of seclusion and reflection. It was the only place where she ever cried. Her instinct was to go there now, but they would be waiting for her at Laurel Cottage, and she was needed.

She tossed the paper onto the back seat, alongside the hatbox, whose pink stripes seemed more appropriate to a birthday cake than a funeral. 'Make sure it's a nice one,' her mother had pleaded. She'd gone along with that, and bought a simple round confection in straw, uniformly black, with a wisp of a veil. The night before, setting it at a rakish angle, she'd assured the figure in the mirror that come what may her behaviour would be above reproach. Stay calm regardless of how you might feel, then get away with no-one the wiser, once the duty's done. At any rate, that was the intention.

The line of cars drawn up outside Laurel Cottage caught her by surprise. She'd expected a few ageing relatives and Albert Potter had had a couple of brothers and a sister she'd not seen for a decade. To her knowledge none of them drove a Mercedes or a BMW. She pulled in behind the last of the vehicles, put on her hat, got out and cautiously approached the house. The group of men around her mother opened up to absorb her like a predatory crustacean claw. No one smiled. One continued talking, ignoring her. Another looked pointedly at his wristwatch. 'You'll be going in the car with your mother,' he told her, 'and we'll all follow.' What right had he… but she kept her peace. She had never seen him before.

But some she did know, because from time to time they'd come to the house. She knew them as voices behind her father's closed study door – deep sullen voices habitually used to being held low. A few were local, like Tom Sharp, the butcher, and Julie's father from the shop; a couple were churchwardens, as her father had been before cancer of the throat took hold.

Thankfully, Jonathan was nowhere to be seen.

From time to time during the service she took her mother's hand and squeezed it. Each time the returned grasp was exaggerated, then limply forgotten. But suddenly, as the coffin was borne up, they were joined by a sparking filament of mutual understanding. The word burst from Betty Potter as a bolus of anguish from deep within. 'Elizabeth!' she whispered. Had her mother only just realised the connection?

For Sarah, her dead sister's presence was everywhere, like a vast tender glove holding the church and all it contained. She half-closed her eyes until the departing coffin was just a shadow passing by. The years peeled away. Tears pricked at her eyes and rolled down her cheeks as they had then, when her father had barred her way in the aisle with an expression telling her to pull herself together and not make a fool of herself. That was when she began to question the circumstances of her sister's death, caused by a never-to-be-found hit-and-run driver as she emerged onto the Oxford road on her bicycle. With her father dead, how could those questions now be answered?

An usher took Betty Potter's arm to lead her into the aisle. Sarah followed, in time to see the coffin depart the church into the wan April light. Of the six bearers, two she had seen at the undertakers, and Tom Sharp she knew. 'Who are the others?' she asked her mother.

'Your father's friends,' came the reply.

'Do you know them?'

'Not really.'

Sarah watched the bobbing heads of the bearers, puzzled. Instead of turning right, as she expected, they took the left-hand path beside the chancel. Linking her mother's arm with hers and patting her hand she led her down towards the flower-speckled patchwork of recent graves. There, already, the dark-suited mourners were impatiently gathered. The newly dug pit came into view from behind an excavated pile of chalky earth. 'But this *is* where we agreed,' she said, confused.

'That's right, Sarah, alongside Edina's.'

'Who on earth is Edina?'

'His foster mother.'

'You never told me.'

'You never asked.'

Resentment – this sense of exclusion – welled up against her mother. She felt an intense urge to race to her sister's grave, as if events might be happening there as in a parallel universe. All week, since her father's death, she had felt in control. Now her thoughts became confused. She looked down into the valley, towards the stone bridge, portal to a more secure existence, now crisp and beckoning in the shifting light. What was this place she was in? Who were these people, who seemed to be conspiring against her?

The vicar's drone was lost to her until it hit a final cadence. A gentle unseen push from behind propelled her towards the heap of earth. Against her will she found herself grasping some and tossing it into the grave, hearing it clatter onto the wooden coffin. Someone took her shoulders and eased her back, as if she could not cope with the presumed emotion. Take that, you bastard, had been the reality.

The violence of the thought shocked her into realising she was neglecting her mother, who was standing inert, staring down at the coffin. Not in grief, Sarah knew, but simply because she did not know what to do next. She put her arms around her mother's shoulders. 'It'll be alright, Mum, look at all the friends you have here. They'll look after you.' Betty Potter turned towards her. 'But will you, Sarah?' she replied. Sarah looked down into the black void, unable to speak, admitting to herself the accusation implicit in what her mother had said.

'We'll take Betty back, if you'd like to stay awhile, Sarah.' She recognised the vicar's wife, a friend.

'Thank you. I think I will for a minute or two, if that doesn't sound neglectful.'

'We all understand.'

The mourners eased away from the grave, taking paths of least resistance between the tombstones. They reminded her of oil finding its way over paving stones to a sump hole that was the lych-gate to the road. From somewhere amongst them her mother's voice carried back in clear untroubled tones. She thought she heard the words 'time for lunch.'

Men with shovels began to attack the earth pile. Standing back, she tripped as her heels struck the low granite surround of the adjacent grave. Spinning round to save herself she came face to face with Edina's headstone, rising barely two feet from the ground. In small red letters under the deceased's name someone had written with a felt pen: *Find ASAAW*. A clue in an ill-conceived treasure hunt, perhaps? It must have been there all the time; curious, then, that no-one else had noticed.

The church had never attracted her as a place of refuge. When she was at primary school the family had come here every Sunday morning. She had watched her sister become absorbed into its ways, then confirmed into the faith. But what had started for Elizabeth as innocent exploration turned into an obsession. By the time of her death at seventeen the relationship with the church had become intense, as if an unrelenting need had to be satisfied. It was something Sarah could not begin to understand. It represented, bar one other, the only barrier that ever existed between the two sisters. That it was not breached could be laid squarely at Sarah's intransigence; that she knew.

Without people to warm it, the interior of the church had again assumed the same cloying dampness that Sarah had found repellent from an early age. She shivered as the massive door swung to behind her. Taking the nearest pew she sat and looked about her, sensing nothing that others so readily recognised as spiritual. The rituals had never attracted her as they had her sister. Perhaps the difference between them lay in their genetic make-up, and she lacked whatever gene it was that her sister had. Was that what had set Elizabeth on an altruistic path towards medicine while she, Sarah, was alive only to the wonders of the physical world? Surely that was all too simplistic.

And where had her father fitted in? As a parish councillor and churchman, would he have been embarrassed by a younger daughter's pig-headedness scorned within the community? It was possible, though hardly likely to be significant given his forceful personality and ability to brush aside adversities far greater than this. Moreover, would Elizabeth's adherence to the church have explained his favouritism, to Sarah's detriment? Even in early childhood Sarah had considered herself the plainer of the two sisters. In some twisted way was he ashamed that it was she who seemed to attract boys while Elizabeth, the favoured one, always kept herself distant? There were occasions when this became the focus of her father's wrath. Once, finding Sarah curled up with a boy on the sofa – no more than that – he had called her a precocious bitch and Elizabeth, fearing violence, had fought to draw him away. There were other examples. She reflected that at the beginning, besides her sister, it was only within these relationships with boys that she could open her heart to someone. The problem was that it was always a trade-off; when things became only physical, as they always did, so she became resentful. By the time she entered medical school she had come to accept that you got nothing from men in return, and should expect nothing.

A spear of sunlight through the medieval glass of St Michael the Archangel pierced the gloom and as quickly faded. She needed to return home, but there was one more duty to perform: to visit her sister's grave, as she sometimes did when things got difficult. No-one knew this: how, just before nightfall, she would drive to the village not via the stone bridge but through the lanes from the direction of the city, parking well away and entering the graveyard using the path through the undergrowth skirting Beacon Hill – the same path, no longer used, that once led through the trees behind the buildings along the street. As young children the sisters had come to this spot from time to time to escape family conflict; but in the months before Elizabeth's death the visits had become more frequent. After her death and with hindsight the significance of the place seemed to intensify, as if in life Elizabeth had been trying to impart something she could never quite articulate. Gradually, during Sarah's years of study, such dark thoughts brought on a feeling that in some obscure way Elizabeth had engineered her own death. That was nonsense, of course. She looked at her watch. But wouldn't it be better to come back later, when all was quiet at home?

She raised her hand to lift the latch of the door, then froze. Pinned there, at eye height, was a card bearing the letters she had seen at Edina's grave. There was no reason to think it was intended for her but she knew it was. There could be only one meaningful destination.

The footprints on the sodden path didn't surprise her. She saw it as soon as she rounded the corner of the tower, on the gravestone, in red, as before, but this time in an irreverent scrawl. Beneath her sister's name she read:

A SISTER AND A WHORE

She looked around, her mind in turmoil, sensing eyes watching her, but seeing nothing.

She had to expunge the obscenity. Somewhere inside the church there must be cleaning materials. She found a brush and a bottle of kitchen cleaner in the vestry. Using water from a butt against the tower wall she rubbed until the letters were illegible. Then she scraped away the surrounding lichens so that there was no ghost left by the brushed stone. Angry now, with filthy hands, she returned the materials to the vestry.

Beside the sink lay a clean towel and a bar of soap. She did not remember seeing them there before.

It began to rain again. Sarah sheltered in the church porch and put the card that had been pinned to the door into her coat pocket. She needed to think, but the refuge of her car was a quarter of a mile away in Tippett's Lane. That removed the possibility of her getting away from the village, if only for a while. The only option was to walk back to Laurel Cottage. They would be scoffing sandwiches for a while yet; to delay her return would only attract more attention.

It was a not unfamiliar predicament: to perceive herself to be the target of the malice of others unknown. She thought back to beyond the grey years of her grammar school days. It was the worst of her memories there, when the children would surround her in the playground, chanting, 'We know something you don't know.' Miss Jenks, her teacher, would smile at her, insisting that they knew nothing, but Sarah never believed her. The worst thing was that the insinuations were never substantiated; they drifted away in the wind – until it occurred to the children that she might once again be fair game. Did the fault lie in her imagination – or with real issues she knew nothing about? The pain was in not knowing which. She shivered to think that back in Laurel Cottage some of those same children, adults now, might be waiting for her still, just to see how she might react. She resolved not to give them that pleasure.

As she walked the ambiguity of the defaced stone grew in her mind. At first it had seemed just an insult to herself: she was the sister in question. There were certainly aggrieved boys in the village, now men, who might once have had some justification for thinking themselves hard done by. But that was long ago and surely just part of the rough and tumble of teenage life. Or was it a reference to Elizabeth, written in the sure knowledge it would hurt her. That seemed more likely. Then came a third possibility – that it referred respectively to both Sarah and her saintly sister. She found she had stopped walking. It was as if a damp restraining hand had been placed on her forehead.

When she reached the post office Julie opened the door. Was she waiting for her to pass by?

'Sarah, your lovely hat's getting all wet. It'll be ruined.'

'Then it's a good thing fathers only die once, isn't it.'

'You've still got your mother to think of.'

'By then, I'll be able to afford a new one.'

She had allowed herself to be drawn. She told herself there would be no further skirmishes, and walked on.

To her surprise, many of the cars – the more prestigious ones – had gone. Unaccountably, she felt disappointed. Moffat, the family's ageing Jack Russell terrier, trotted up wagging his trail. 'Why do you think that is?' she asked him. I don't know either, the bright eyes seemed to say.

The rain stopped as she approached her car. She tossed her wet hat onto the rear seat, removed the card from her pocket, took off her coat and adjusted her hair in the mirror. Then she got out, breathed in deeply and walked up the drive with the dog padding at her heels.

Betty Potter spotted her first and stepped forward. 'I'm so glad you could come, Sarah, but the funeral's over.'

'Mother, I've…'

Dr Hislop, Betty's doctor, stepped in briskly. 'Your mother's had a trying day, Sarah. We're a bit tired, aren't we Betty?'

'I don't know what I'd do without him, Sarah. Look, there are cup-cakes over there, the ones you like.'

At the food table there was no alternative but to engage with Jonathan, who obviously had similar tastes. Crumbs were already nestling in the fork of his lapels. She didn't wait for him to swallow what he had in his mouth.

She held his gaze as she produced the card with the cryptic letters, watching for his reaction.

'I wouldn't let it worry you, Sarah. I really wouldn't. It's just that some people round here have long memories.' He looked at his watch. 'Now, I must fly – unless, of course, you feel like a bit of fresh air.'

'Why would I want that?'

His eyes drifted down to the card, then re-united with hers.

'Okay, then,' she said.

The house had been named with good reason. Laurels enclosed the garden, as if planted densely to exclude prying eyes. In winter dreary, in spring the two acres became transformed as the herbaceous beds came alive, creating a network of walkways. It was a natural place to exchange confidences.

'With your father gone, your mother will struggle.'

'You're offering to help?'

'Only if I thought…'

'There was some mileage in it with me?'

'For God's sake!'

Sarah bit her lip. 'Sorry.'

He seemed amused. 'I gave up that idea a long time ago.'

She had initiated that separation, but his words were still uncomfortable to hear. She produced the card. 'And this?'

'No idea.'

'Then why…'

'In this village odd things happen, Sarah. My advice is, take no notice. Now, I really must go.'

'If ever you're in town...'

'Well, yes, I suppose I would be safe enough there. Goodbye, Sarah.'

Back in the living room, her mother said, 'Such a nice young man.'

'I don't think he's quite got over you, Sarah.' It was Pauline, Tom Sharp's wife, who had overheard and stepped beside them. 'You need to be tactful.' She was one of those women who, on first acquaintance, brought to mind the word 'mouse.' For her, fashion was an irrelevance, gardening clothes the norm; her rimless glasses did nothing to enhance an undeservedly plain face. Yet behind that façade Sarah had found integrity and kindness unique in the village. The possible exception was the vicar's wife, but Sarah's atheistic credentials had blocked that particular conduit. The odd thing about Pauline was her choice of a husband brash and loud. It had sometimes crossed Sarah's mind to enquire how their marriage had come about. The surprising thing was that it seemed to work, outwardly at least.

'I don't see Tom around, Pauline.'

'He had to rush off after the interment. Apparently sausages were missing from this morning's delivery and he went to the wholesalers. When we lost you we thought you might have gone with him.'

'You're not serious?'

Pauline's hyphen mouth widened into a mischievous grin. 'Actually no. But I live in hope. Listen, I think I hear our car.'

Through the window they saw Tom's white MG Magnette draw up close to the door just as Jonathan was leaving. The sturdy figure eased itself carefully onto the gravel. With dark suit and carefully knotted tie, hair smoothed and parted, the butcher in him had given way to a creature of the city, or big business. It struck Sarah – probably, she realised, for the first time – that he was not uncomfortable with this image. He glanced towards her, then looked away without apparent recognition. For a few seconds she struggled to divine his motive, before realising that he might not even have seen her. He and Jonathan spoke together, moving further and further from the house, onto the lawn, out of earshot. After a couple of minutes Tom came in and joined their group. It seemed a cue for the half-dozen remaining mourners to put down their plates and leave.

'All sweetness and light, are we?' Tom said, to no-one in particular.

'Meaning me, I suppose?' Sarah pinched herself for having taken the bait.

'Meaning you, sweetheart, if you insist.'

'It's been a sad day for all of us.'

'I'd have thought more a red letter day.'

'Tom!' Pauline looked horrified.

An innocent remark – or had he given too much away to score a point?

'I'll get some more tea,' Betty Potter said, walking away, confused.

'Look, Pauline,' Tom said, 'you know they never got on, so let's not pretend. Hurt by that, Albert was, after all he'd done for her.'

'Like what?' Sarah asked; but cautiously, afraid of where these exchanges might be leading.

'Like keeping you on the straight and narrow. Getting you into medical school. My wild child, he used to call you. True, isn't it, Pauline?'

'I'm sure he didn't mean it that way.'

Sarah had never credited her father with any positive contribution to her career. If she'd strayed into dissolute ways in her sixth form years she'd got out of it unaided. Getting into medical school with mediocre grades had been fortunate, just that; and, God knows, hadn't she made up for it since? Did Tom and Pauline not know how her dancing lessons had been stopped to make her study, how she had the longest and dowdiest skirt in the class, how her friends were selectively barred from Laurel Cottage? And then the most galling thing of all, when he'd torn up her photoshoot pictures after she'd been talent-spotted on Brighton beach that last summer holiday before medical school; and that he'd only managed by getting her out of the house to search her room.

She was on the point of asking what business this was of Tom's. But that would only prolong the acrimony. Besides, a look at Tom's pursed lips told her he knew he'd gone too far. There were things afoot that didn't quite make sense and somehow they concerned her; she would need time to think them through. So she said, 'I'm tired and we've been here before. Let's just call a truce, shall we?'

'Ah, here's Betty with the tea,' Tom said. 'A cuppa should put us all back on track.'

She flinched as he put his arm around her shoulders.

The house had emptied. Down the lane the last of the cars was drawing away. In the living room Sarah sat listening to the bustle in the kitchen, where two elderly aunts were helping Betty with the washing up. She had volunteered but been ushered away, probably to allow them to catch up on several years' worth of gossip. In that, she was sure, her exploits would figure prominently.

Her mother appeared at the door, as if pitying her daughter's isolation. She crossed the carpet to sit in the chair opposite. This was the point reached sooner or later in every visit home, when they would sit staring at one another, having exhausted common ground, clutching at things to say.

'Enid and Margaret have decided to keep me company tonight, Sarah. Enid was wondering if she could have your room.'

It had been Sarah's intention to stay for a couple of nights. A tutorial had been cancelled and her clinical sessions swopped with Alice's. That didn't matter now. Her spirits rose. She could use the time for revision instead; but she knew that was not the reason.

'Are you sure you won't need me? Aren't there things to sort out?'

'Like what, Sarah?'

Sarah had rung the family solicitors before she left London. Were there issues to be sorted? Nothing that we know of, Sarah, beyond what we've discussed, but should you come across a will you might let us know. She hadn't, neither had Betty, though both had looked. She would be back anyway at the weekend, so there seemed no compelling reason to stay.

Driving away from the house she fought off an urge to return to Elizabeth's grave. She'd thought of removing flowers from one of the arrangements that had found their way to the house and taking them there, as an apology for the desecration. But the connection with her father rendered the idea useless. In any case, what other traps might have been laid for her in the churchyard? She would go secretly next time she was near the village, with no one the wiser.

She knew that, once across the bridge, her mind would again flood with thoughts of student and hospital life. There was a fleeting moment of not wanting to leave the village because, for all the hostility, there were issues that held grim fascination. Was there really a tangible line passing through the bridge that separated her two worlds so absolutely?

She had long been attracted to the theory that within an individual there are separate entities corresponding to different parts of the psyche: one for thinking, the other for allowing an autopilot to assume control. As the car approached the bottom of the hill her will to cross the bridge, strong as it was, faltered. The robotic entity took charge, pulling at her hands on the wheel and lifting her foot from the accelerator. The car slewed into the lay-by. She got out and walked the twenty yards to the centre of the bridge.

A fan of yellow luminosity had begun to penetrate a lightening sky that an hour earlier had delivered rain. Slowly the oncoming clouds parted, giving way to washed blue. Another minute and the bridge was in sunlight of that strange and uplifting quality peculiar to the month. Below her the fast scintillating water swirled around the central piers. It was as it had been one other April evening, lodged in her memory because, in a niggling way, it still troubled her. Was this why she had stopped?

Julie had been beside her, leaning on the parapet. Both wore the red and grey uniform of St Peter's Primary School, still covered, at that moment, by hooded plastic macs so that only their faces showed. There was a feeling of carefree expectation, the school day forgotten; above all they were friends, equals. They had picked twigs from the willow tree on the bank and now pruned and selected them, one each, for their dynamic potential. They shouted ready, steady, go in unison and dropped the sticks into the water, then ran to the opposite parapet and looked down.

The two sticks emerged exactly together. Sarah remembered how Julie's face had lit up, delighted because their friendship had been symbolically cemented, in need of nothing more. But for Sarah it was not enough, there had to be a result. That bush down there, that's the finishing line, she cried, leaving the bridge and running alone along the bank. Finding her stick ahead, exalted by the gain, she looked back, shouting I've won, I've won. There were now two figures there on the bridge: Julie, still staring at her, and her brother Jonathan, sent to take her home. Without sign or word the pair turned and walked from the bridge, back up the hill.

Her dalliance at the bridge had resolved nothing.

Traffic on the Oxford road was heavy. Sarah waited impatiently at the junction, ready to squeeze into the London flow. Almost opposite was the black waste of the car park where, that morning, she had contemplated the potential traumas of the day ahead. Something was worrying her, holding her back, but she couldn't quite identify what it was. Wouldn't it be sensible to stop there now, to reflect a little, before leaving this place that troubled her so? Gaps appeared simultaneously in the flows in both directions, making her mind up for her. She put her foot hard down, shot across the road and pulled up in her usual position facing the village across the valley. There, the lights of the houses shone faintly through the trees. The lamp set to illuminate the church tower came on. Instinctively she looked at the dashboard clock. It was the time, exactly, when her mother would be switching on the television to look at the news. Wasn't that once a time in happier days when the family would gather together, the four of them, with trays on their laps and soup and bread, maybe, and her mother alive to the events of the day, years before the dementia had set in and their relationships had begun to crumble? There was love and mutual affection then, and she remembered cuddling up to her mother before they went upstairs to bed to read a story. Had it all gone – what she had felt then? She knew today that she had acted as if it had, and to her shame had done for a very long time. But if that was so why were there tears streaming down her cheeks and a lump enlarging in her throat. How could she have used her aunt's commandeering of her room to justify her premature flight back to London? Could these two ancient aunts possibly give her mother – who in daylight she'd thought indifferent to her husband's demise – the comfort she most likely needed in the darker hours? She could sleep on the sofa, or in the great chair in her father's old office; tomorrow's boring lecture on jurisprudence could be safely missed. She put the car into gear, re-crossed the road and descended the hill to the old bridge and on into the village.

3

A shaft of sunlight impaled the pillow next to her face. Sarah rolled her naked body away from it into the hollow beside her. For a moment she was confused. Then she explored the depression with her hand. But the sheet was cold and yielded no more than her memory.

She had not even bothered to ask his name. Perhaps she would see him at next week's gig. Perhaps not. She didn't really care about that. What she did care about was the voice in her head – her mother's voice – telling her to be careful. She thought she had been.

Beside the defiantly mute alarm clock was a sheet of paper headed *Consultants' Rounds*, where she had placed it the evening before when still in control. She glanced from one to the other in disbelief, then leapt out of bed. How could it be one of Stricker's? He'd had it in for her last time she was late and grilled her unmercifully. Did she not think the patient was jaundiced – just a little, perhaps? Look carefully, Miss Potter, and don't speak again until you are sure. But she'd held her ground and said quietly, no. It had earned her, if not the respect of the surgeon, then at least the admiration of her fellow students. They had all been coerced into pronouncing otherwise. She had vowed to herself never to risk being late again. So much, then, for her resolve.

She skipped her usual toast and margarine and her customary descent to the front door three floors below to pick up the *Mail* ahead of her flatmates. But she didn't skimp on her make-up, discreet as it was, and no-one seeing her emerge from the front door and swing confidently down the steps to the street would have suspected the pain in her head or the void in her stomach. Two labourers on the building site across the road whistled in unison. She waved back at them.

Through the glass doors to the ward the others were gathering around the first bed, stethoscopes dangling from their necks like the proboscises of alien insects. Their long white coats looked grubby even at this distance. She put on her own freshly laundered one, thrust her instrument into her pocket and walked purposefully towards the group to stand behind the slender figure of her friend Alice.

'Stricker not arrived yet?' she whispered.

Alice put her finger to her lips and rolled her eyes. Then Sarah saw him – and he her.

'Sir Edwin is unfortunately indisposed. I'm Brian Davison, senior registrar in maxillofacial surgery.'

She had taken him to be just another student. No logic in that, of course; surgeons did not have to be vertically advantaged, though most seemed larger than life. He was neither. Nor had he renounced the white coat. But when she looked at him there was no doubting what he was destined to become. The deep-set eyes were fired with endeavour and conviction, moving precisely from one object of attention to another. Sarah wondered which avian species he most resembled and settled on a crow. He was much as Alice had described him.

'I'm sorry I'm late, Mr Davison,' she said.

'No matter. We've only just started. So let me ask *you*, Miss Potter, what do you make of this patient?'

She was surprised he knew her name, but set the thought aside.

She already knew the history. 'A forty-five year old male, heavy smoker, with a swelling of the left mandible, firm, probably bony, developing steadily over the past nine months, as yet painless but already impeding mastication and swallowing.' She smiled at the patient, whose eyes had not left her since she entered the ward. 'That's right, isn't it, Mr Gordon?' As he mumbled agreement the lump on his jaw was plain for all to see.

'And your diagnosis?'

'Probably osteosarcoma.'

'And what are the consequences for the patient? You can speak freely. The patient is aware of the situation.'

'Operable but with a strong likelihood of recurrence, depending on local spread. Burns and Stavin have reported that only forty-five per cent of cases survive to beyond two years.'

Brian Davison did not look overly pleased. 'That's good, very good, but haven't you forgotten something?' The hostile eyes scanned her face, as if for some sign of contrition.

Sarah blushed, searching her mind for information unsaid. 'There is a possibility of certain immune factors influencing the outcome.' It was the best she could do.

'Immune factors? What immune factors?' He was angry now. 'What I was expecting, Miss Potter, was a proper and thorough examination of the patient, not a rehash of his notes.' He turned to Alice. 'Miss Pardoe, may we please have your assessment of this case?'

Sarah stepped backwards, hurt and angry. She had not examined the patient because she had been present when the history was taken and had done so then, thoroughly, to her satisfaction. Eric Gordon looked at her in astonishment,

33

seeming to tell her to stand up for herself. But she had learned enough to avoid a dispute in front of a patient and held her tongue.

She did not speak again for the duration of the round. When it was over she waited until the others had left before approaching him.

'Mr Davison, I should tell you that…'

'Yes, I am aware. But that doesn't absolve you from observing the niceties of the ward round.'

'Did Mr Gordon tell you?'

'Miss Pardoe whispered it to me. We know each other slightly through her friend, Dr Ellis. So she was brave enough to speak up for you. I share a flat with him.' A shadow of concern – or was it embarrassment? – crossed his face. 'Since we were students, you see. We hardly ever bump into one another these days.'

It was not Sarah's nature to bear a grudge. She let her smile descend on Brian Davison, just as it had upon the luckless Mr Gordon. 'Then thank you for an interesting round.'

She had gone only half a dozen paces when he called after her.

'Miss Potter. That paper by Burns and Stavin. You know that there are demographic differences between their study and our situation here?'

'I know,' she said over her shoulder. 'I would have told you if you'd given me the chance. Goodbye, Mr Davison.'

She caught up with Alice at the door to the tea-room. 'Some friend you are! You didn't tell me you had a relationship with Jeff Ellis.'

'Did Davison tell you that?'

'I'm afraid so.'

Alice bit her lip. 'Look, I don't want to talk about it, right? It's getting a bit messy.'

'Right then. Changing the subject, how did you get on after we split up last night? If it's any consolation mine wasn't up to much.'

Alice looked full into Sarah's face. 'That's the problem. Mine was.'

Sarah went ahead in the queue and paid for their teas. They sat opposite each other at a window table. Sarah rested her chin in her cupped hands, waiting for the information she considered was now rightfully hers. She knew Alice couldn't keep a secret for long.

Someone had once said, in a quiet and not unmotivated aside, that there was something of the cat and mouse about their relationship. Sarah had denied it, but the incident came back to her now. She looked around to see if anyone was watching them at the table together. Sarah was conscious that Alice, although intelligent and attractive enough in her own right, to others always seemed the lesser figure, whatever the criterion.

They had got to know one another when both had elected to do a BSc course after the second year and had joined forces at the bench. Alice had done most of the work, but it was Sarah who had the better commendations at the end. When they resumed their clinical studies Sarah had cultivated the relationship, needing a foil for her own critical and capricious nature, and Alice did not have the strength of character to break away. It was not that there was no affection, or even mutual respect, between them; but Alice, as if to keep her end up, did not always allow Sarah access to her private life. This, she surmised, was why Alice had put off telling her about Jeff Ellis.

'It's a funny thing,' Sarah mused, 'that after five sterile years – socially I mean – here you are, just before finals, tossed into a whirlpool of conflicting desire.' Suddenly she felt earnest and caring. 'Are you sure you can handle it?'

'And you, I suppose, never get committed.'

'I try not to.'

'A predatory she-wolf, biding her time.'

'Alice!'

'I'm sorry. It just got to me. But don't you think it's time you became serious about someone?'

Sarah leaned back in her chair. 'You might just have a point. I don't exactly see myself as a spinster-surgeon either.'

Alice stared gloomily out of the window. Opposite, the lights in the library were coming on, illuminating rows of students cramming for finals. 'I can already feel the post-qualification depression coming on. It'll be like being launched into space, not knowing where you're going to fall.'

Sarah knew that Alice had never really thought hard about doing medicine. It had been a simple matter to follow in her father's footsteps and overcome the academic obstacles as and when they arose. Mindful of her own complex reasons for making the choice she was sympathetic. 'Maybe you do need the strong arm of Jeff Ellis.'

'And always be looking beyond the next hill?'

'It doesn't have to be permanent. You're not committed to anything.'

Alice looked aghast. 'You mean string him along?'

'At least till finals are behind you. It just needs a bit of discretion, that's all. By the way, what does he do, the other one?'

'Classics student.'

'And not very well heeled? Well then, there's no choice. And you can't afford an emotional crisis, not just now.'

Sarah had failed to disguise a concern that was a shade too intense.

'Sa-rah!'

'Alice?'

'I'm getting the feeling that this conversation is leading somewhere.'

'You do?'

'Definitely. Now let me guess. Last night, remember, at the Travellers Bar. Your life was a blank sheet waiting to be written upon.'

'I don't remember. Perhaps I was a little merry.'

'You'd only had three Merrydowns at that stage. The merriment came later.'

'So?'

'So what, one might ask, has happened since, if last night's stand wasn't up to much? New admirer on the way to the hospital – at 8.00 a.m.?'

'Two building labourers, actually. Would need both, though, to satisfy me.'

'Be serious!'

'I'm not sure I want to be.' Sarah suddenly felt disconsolate. 'You might just be on the right track.'

It was a long time since their usual roles had been reversed. Alice was going to make the most of it.

'Then let me guess. Brian Davison. Now I begin to see where Jeff Ellis fits into all this. Ha ha ha, so you want us all as go-betweens.'

'Don't you think he's interesting?'

'Interesting certainly, but hardly glamorous.'

'That depends on your level of sophistication.'

'Come on, Sarah, he's not your type.'

'Maybe not, but we shall see. At worst he could be useful.'

The final exams, when they came, presented no great problems for Sarah or Alice. Sarah approached the board on which the results had been pinned content to stand back while others in her year jostled themselves into elation or despair. She waited for them to allow her space, and quietly noted the expected. Alice, wide-eyed at her own success, was puzzled.

'You don't look very pleased.'

'Oh, I am. Really.'

'You're a deep one sometimes, Sarah.'

Back in her bedroom, Sarah reflected on Alice's words. Yes, she told herself, you were expecting more, but it never happened. Why? Flat on her back now, she let the thoughts tumble in her head, ridiculing her for a choice of career that could not, at least at that moment, inspire. The answer, in spite of its simplicity, took a long time coming. She never really, deep down, wanted to do it. Why, then, did she? Her father? No, surely he only went along. The pointing finger of her dead sister then, for whom medicine was an unquestioned aspiration, not doubted by anyone? Well, possibly. Rather, it was the way things seemed to have been smoothed for her – mediocre A-level results that turned out to be no barrier, a grant from the council in spite of her application arriving late, and so on. On the other hand, during the course she regularly gained satisfaction from whatever she was doing at the time, and from time to time she achieved ahead of her peers. And towards the end, increasingly so.

The phone rang – Alice reminding her about the evening celebrations in the Travellers Bar. Of course she was going, she agreed brightly, knowing inwardly that at some point during the evening her well-intentioned restraint would weaken, that she would turn a blind eye to the topping up of her glass by over-attentive males and regret it bitterly the following morning. Funny how alcohol, in its aftermath, unlocked a door to a chaotic inner world of twisted memories, through which things that repulsed her could be glimpsed but not grasped. The waking moments were always the most difficult. But that was too far ahead, and – what the hell – she deserved to celebrate. 'Elizabeth, stay with me,' she said to herself in front of the hall mirror, before opening the door to descend the stairs.

The idea to celebrate Alice's engagement with a dinner at Brian and Jeff's was wholly Sarah's. Having made the suggestion she withdrew from all responsibility, save that of being a guest. 'It must be your show,' she had said to Alice. It happened a week later.

She walked from Bermondsey station and threaded her way through the complex of streets and decaying alleys flanking the river. The gaunt edifice of Lightermen's Mansions stood out as one of the few ailing repositories that had not been replaced by modern apartment blocks. The dilapidation explained why the two men found the rent affordable.

The balcony of the living room hung like a pulpit over the dozen or so boats drawn to the river by the promise of fine weather. From it, in the distance to the west, the square aperture of Tower Bridge was slowly capturing the setting sun as if it were the sighting mechanism of an enormous cannon that was the steel-blue river.

Sarah was one of the last to arrive and exploited the mêlée in the living room to examine the items on the walls. There seemed to be two distinct themes. An automotive one, clearly Jeff's, linking the dog-eared copy of *Performance Cars* on the coffee table with a comic porcelain replica of a popemobile on the top of the bookcase which made her think, rightly, that Jeff was a lapsed but repentant catholic. What she supposed was Brian's theme was altogether darker and occupied her thoughts for longer. There was a print of Dali's *Metamorphosis of Narcissus* which she liked for its repetitive geometry. But then – wow! – there was a series of five small but exquisite portraits in acrylic. One was of Stricker, another of a medic she had seen in casualty. The others she didn't know.

'Good, aren't they?' Jeff said at her shoulder. 'Have you deciphered the signatures?'

She peered more closely. 'Brian's? I didn't know he was that gifted.'

'I wouldn't know. They're not my cup of tea. Which is why he won't do one of me. Takes him ages to do them though. Uses photographs, the lot, but not to copy. Can't see what the object is myself. Why not just frame a photo?'

'You don't paint yourself?'

'Only when I'm decorating. But I've got an original Rolf Harris in my bedroom. Want to see it?'

'No thanks. Not interested and in any case don't trust you.'

'It's my engagement party, for Christ's sake!'

Had he misunderstood her well-meaning sarcasm or was he responding in kind? It was difficult to tell with Jeff.

She resumed her scrutiny of the portraits, then murmured quietly to herself, 'Achieving perfection, I would think.'

'Yeah, yeah, you might be right. That just about sums him up.'

Sarah turned to face him, now serious. 'Is he like that with other things?'

'Come to think of it he's pretty meticulous in most of what he does.'

'Like his surgery?'

'Yeah, that especially.'

There were too many people crowding around the dinner table and Sarah wished she had suggested a seating arrangement to Alice. She found herself next to Stricker. The steady pressure of his leg against hers set her thinking. Well, let him if it gives him pleasure. It had the makings of a debt to be repaid.

'Would you pass the wine, Dr Potter.' The right hand

which wafted in front of her face gave cover for the other to grasp her wrist. The touch was dry. Was he used to doing this sort of thing?

'Has Brian spoken to you yet, Dr Potter?'

'No. Should he have done?'

'Well, I thought he might have. Perhaps you ought to speak to him. One of the first things you must learn is to cultivate your colleagues.'

'I do, Sir Edwin, but so surreptitiously they never notice.'

He swivelled in his seat to look at her face-on, eyes staring, rubicund cheeks puffed with approval. 'I'm almost inclined to believe you, young lady. But we digress. The art of the surgeon is so open to inspection, often far too open, that... in short, Surgical Unit needs to be more... progressive. We're rather short of people equipped for that at the moment. You understand what I'm saying?'

'I think so. So what might my credentials be?'

'Take yourself back, Dr Potter, to your preclinical days. The Anatomy Prize for dissection, for example.'

'I'm surprised you know about that?'

'Why are you blushing? You don't believe that we had our scouts out, even then?'

'I'm beginning to believe anything.'

'That's grand. Now listen. This is not the place for detail. I'll leave that to Brian. Suffice it to say that we need new blood in the Unit. New approaches, new techniques, publications – lots of them. Will mean weeding out dead wood, of course. Attract young blood. Hear what I'm saying?'

'I think so. I'm flattered you think of me in that light.'

'Ha, think of you in all sorts of lights, Dr Potter.'

Sarah became aware of the circle of eyes converging upon them. Alice would tell her later that Edwin had reminded her of a dog that had gained possession of a choice bone. Jeff saw only a colleague sinking condescendingly to the level of the gathering. Only Brian, more sober and with greater insight, saw in him an ageing lion at bay, his only defence the protection of younger and abler men raised in a more competitive world than he had known.

He grasped Sarah's wrist for the second time. 'Take what is offered, Dr Potter, and see where it leads.' Then he rose from his seat, congratulated Jeff and Alice, and left the room.

Alice was cringing into the cushions of the sofa, pretending to be mesmerised by a tall, flaxen-haired young man swaying above her, dangling some sort of medallion before her eyes. The shining disc was connected to a chain around his neck and its short excursions were so rapid as to be unfit for purpose. Some in the group gathered around were laughing, but one – Jeff – was clutching the sleeve of his jacket, trying to pull him away. Sarah, seeing the threadbare cloth over the elbow, felt fleeting pity, in spite of knowing that Alan Murphy's background was one of wealth and privilege.

Alan had begun his medical studies in the same year as Alice and Sarah but went ahead when they did their intercalated science course. Seldom seen in lectures, he failed his preclinical exams and had to repeat a year; in the end they all graduated together. While qualification as a doctor had erased the worst student tendencies in almost everyone else, Alan, true to himself, had remained a loose cannon, needing little provocation – and usually not very much alcohol – to descend into unruly and objectionable behaviour. Sarah wondered how he had made it this far but, like his teachers, she knew him to be one of the more intelligent and potentially able in her year; and that had got him through. Most of his female peers saw him as a charmer and a minor Lothario, but for Sarah there was something about his attitude to women that had repulsed her from the start. She had never succumbed and had an uneasy feeling – and in this she would be proved right – that in Alan's thinking she still remained a target.

Sarah, deliberately, had kept herself sober. She made for the balcony, slipped off her shoes and stretched out on a chaise longue with Tower Bridge trapped between her big toes. There was a gentle lapping of water far below. Her eyes lazily traced the wake of a pleasure cruiser full of tourists who had waved at her a minute before when the boat had turned in mid-stream.

The city lights began to twinkle. For a minute or so they seemed in perfect harmony with the embers of sunlight in the glinting water. For the first time in many weeks – it could even be months or years – her mind was able to discharge itself. She felt at peace, with the delicious privilege of time to think her life out and build it as she wished, as yet untroubled by the burgeoning pressures of hospital life.

So although she had anticipated it, Brian's appearance on the balcony was an annoyance as well as an objective partly attained. Looking back in later times she would see this opportunity to be alone with him as the key for what was to follow.

'Dr Potter, I've not yet had the opportunity to congratulate you, in private at least. Yours was a very creditable performance. More so than you may realise.' He offered his hand and grinned. 'Welcome to the profession.'

She squeezed his hand and returned the smile. 'Hello Brian, I'm Sarah.'

'Yes, of course you are. How silly. Old habits are difficult to break.'

He sat on a chair beside her and gazed into the distance. 'I well remember this time. Perhaps the greatest crossroads we come to.' He paused. 'Which leads me to ask. I saw you two talking earnestly back in there.'

'He's hinted that I might like to join Surgical Unit for my first house job, if that's what you mean.'

'And would you?'

'I said I'd consider. I was just doing that when you appeared.'

'Mercury, the bringer of fortune?'

'And an artist, I see, as well as a winged messenger.'

'I'd hardly say that.' He looked flustered. 'Changing the subject, how are you getting home? Alice is in no fit state to drive and Jeff... well, let's say Jeff is poised to take advantage.'

'Then yes, I'd be grateful for a lift.'

He rose and made to go, shyness overcoming his better judgement. 'Be ready in twenty minutes?'

Sarah nodded and smiled at him quizzically. You fool, she thought, to waste what is left of this magical evening on the balcony. She sighed and looked along the river to where, against the fading sunset, the twin bascules of Tower Bridge were beginning to open for a three-masted schooner whose forward motion alone seemed to determine their stately rise. I must be like that ship, she told herself, and went inside.

Brian's VW Beetle sped eastwards along Jamaica Road and round the black void that was the northern end of Southwark Park. For a moment, the light of the street lamps gave way to moonlight thick and bright through the windscreen. She caught him dragging his eyes from the road to search her face. They seemed not just to light up, but to burn, whatever they touched. It occurred to her that this was not an active, positive thing, but a defence, a barrier through which gentler but unseen communications might come and go. She thought of doves emerging from the recesses of an ancient brick dovecote in her village. 'I wonder if they can be caught,' she said to herself.

'What did you say?'

'Your thoughts. I was trying to get behind the facade.'

'And probably succeeding, I imagine,' he said, looking fixedly ahead. 'But why would you want to do that, even assuming there is such a structure.'

'Some things fascinate, others don't. Difficult to explain.'

'Wouldn't you rather I told you what you want to know?'

'And spoil the fun?'

There was a long silence. Then he said, 'I was keen on astronomy once. It was an alternative – but medicine won.'

'That's because you can't get your hands on the stars.'

'That's right. Exactly right. I'm impressed.'

'So where's the point?'

'In those days we lived in a basement flat near Greenwich. One summer evening, out cycling after exams, I discovered the observatory in the park and the astronomer Flamsteed's old house. From the hill you get a wonderful view of the city. What you saw from our balcony is a magnified image, but the feeling's the same.'

'You want to take me there? To see the stars?'

'Or the city. If… if you'd like to come.'

She felt he had transcended a self-imposed barrier of propriety. He had always seemed to her – though admittedly without evidence – a chaste man, different from the usual run of medics she had known. Did that make him more or less interesting to explore? Was it that which was driving her first shimmers of arousal? She did not know, and not knowing was a powerful incentive.

They passed an amorphous block rising above a row of dingy shops selling goods and services one could not imagine anyone wanting – grimy electronic components, car parts, insurance advice, a newsagent with sodden evening papers left on a rack outside; some were boarded up. Midway along their length was a once grandiose entrance, with graffiti on its sandstone columns, its windows papered with advertisements for long-defunct musical productions and plays. There was something familiar about the monogram in stone above the door, but it was too far to decipher and Sarah could not place it. Only when they had driven far beyond the building and she looked back could she appreciate its great height. She saw that Brian had noted her interest.

'Have you heard of the Massingham Tower?' he asked tentatively.

'No, should I?'

'Oh, no reason. I'll tell you sometime.'

They drove up the avenue of Greenwich Park and left the car beyond the buildings so that they could walk up to the observatory, now dark against the lights of the city. She grasped his hand, but even when they reached the balustrade there was no hint of the expected arm around her shoulders.

But it was Brian who spoke first.

'What were you thinking about earlier on the balcony?'

'Oh, I suppose the future. Where the balance lies between taking charge of one's life and being manipulated.'

'That's radical thinking when you're just starting out.'

'You weren't sitting next to Stricker.'

'Did he frighten you?' He chuckled. 'The whole room was watching.'

'No. It's a question of how much one has to give to get something worthwhile in return.'

She felt his body stiffen, as if he were deeply troubled. But it was medicine itself she had offended, and he was its proud guardian.

'For a houseman to do anything other than immerse herself in her subject is a travesty of six year's effort.'

'I accept that, Brian. But, you see, some of us can divide ourselves in that way.' She linked her arm through his. There was no response.

'Why do you hold back?' she said.

She felt him weaken and draw towards her, an amalgam of misery and desire, his great plan, his strategy for the evening – for she knew there was one – perilously close to failure. After a minute he drew away, she thought to ponder whether his resolve could ever be restored. She knew this, for it had happened before, with others. She gently touched his cheek. 'Now tomorrow, when I start on the wards, this experience will not even cross my mind.'

'So it means nothing to you?'

'I didn't say that. It's just that I can switch off when I need to.'

'And you think I can't?'

'I don't think you can.'

'Perhaps we should go.' He sounded bitter and forlorn.

'Just like on the balcony?'

'Yes, just like on the balcony.'

His frustration with himself angered her too. Then, suddenly and unaccountably, she was sorry, and guilty. It was how she had felt when she had once slapped her sister in temper and happened to touch her eye and hurt her; the remorse was terrible.

Brian had turned to go but she stayed at the balustrade looking far into the distance.

'What was it you said about a tower? That building we passed?'

'Nothing much to tell, except that it seems to have been a brainchild of Stricker's – or at least he invested money in it.'

'So what is it?'

'It's many things – apartments, offices, shops; but what it's best known for is that it houses a highly exclusive club. Beyond that I know little about it. One hears tales, of course, but I'm inclined not to believe them, still less repeat them.'

'Could you join?'

'Hardly. Entrance is astronomical, and highly selective. Stricker once said that if I became a consultant he might just consider sponsoring me, but in any case I probably wouldn't get in. I remember being hurt at the time. He was quite resolute about it. Strange, when he's usually so easy-going.'

'That suggests something to hide!'

Brian cast her one of his burning glances. 'You might just be right.' She saw him pause, debating whether to say more. 'You know, you can see it from here.'

He took hold of her shoulders and rotated her body. She pressed her cheek against his hand.

'You see that pinpoint of light, midway between here and the city, where we passed?'

'But how do you know?'

'Sometimes I bring my telescope up here. It's not always the stars that are interesting.'

'And what have you seen?'

'Just the top floor, all lit up. That's all. There's a kind of translucent dome. If you look carefully there's sometimes movement inside, as if there's a party going on.'

'Do you have it now?'

'What?'

'Your telescope, of course.'

'It's always in the car.'

'Then let's get it.'

They set it up in a small leafy alcove beneath the balustrade, facing the city, where the ground sloped away, invisible from above and protected from pedestrian intrusion from below.

'You've always been here alone?' she asked, squatting beside him.

His embarrassment was palpable in the darkness. 'Yes.'

Her response was a wearisome sigh born of experience. Surprising him, she grasped his arm tightly. This time the lifeline she knew he ached for was not repulsed. It was a long while before they again gave their attention to the telescope.

Below them, across the river, the red lamps of cranes heralding the development of the docklands drew the eye westwards over the glowing tapestry of the city. Sarah saw the metropolis from a perspective she had not appreciated during all her student years. It was like the day she had grasped the human form anew, placing within the grace and vigour of its shell the tissues and systems that previously had been meat on the dissection table, or dull pages of physiology text. So the city could be seen to live, breathe and pulsate. Was this what Brian had seen, helping to shape his destiny so young? She thought she could glimpse her own life-course establishing itself before her eyes.

Then, by chance, she saw it: the pinpoint of light transformed through the lens into a vibrant, quaking spectacle. She could hear in her mind the frenetic beat of unseen rhythms and see in the shadows that flitted back and forth behind its pearly shell the workings of spirited decadence.

4

The dusting of snow on the rooftops opposite Sarah's flat glistened in what remained of the afternoon sunlight. She paused to look as she pulled at the curtains. Then, with a flourish, she snapped them shut and turned to Alice, who was lying on the sofa. 'Three,' she said. 'Isn't that impressive?'

Alice looked up from her book. 'What was that?'

'I expected one, two maybe. But three!'

'Sarah, I can't imagine what you're talking about.'

'If you'd received just one you'd know.'

Alice rolled onto her side to face her. 'OK, you have my attention. What are you on about?'

'The first was your friend, Dr Murphy.'

'What makes you think he's my friend?'

'Confidant, then. Come on, I've seen you exchanging glances. Definitely not my imagination.'

'Quite right! And I'm surprised your ears aren't burning.'

'What?'

Alice seemed reluctant to reveal her secret. 'That's for later,' she muttered to herself. 'So what about Alan Murphy?'

'He's asked me to the Christmas ball.'

'That doesn't surprise me. He seemed to get good value last time. The Travellers Bar, remember?'

Vague and troublesome images she could not quite place crossed Sarah's mind. 'Anyway, he was the first to ask.'

'And the second?'

'Guess.'

'Davison – and you accepted.'

'Yes… well no. I mean, I don't intend to accept.'

'No? Strange. I thought that's what you were angling for.'

'Guess again.' Sarah said, hinting at the ultimate prize.

'Could it possibly be Sir Edwin?' Alice asked, with as much sarcasm as she could muster.

Sarah had not met him socially since the dinner party at Lightermen's Mansions months before. It surprised her that there had been no follow-up, although she had got to know Brian well. It had even seemed that Stricker had tried to avoid her, in clinics and on the wards, and their exchanges were of a strictly professional kind. But, thinking about it, it was a tactic she had seen in others: the withholding of favour, like depriving a child of sweets so that later they could be used with intent. It was no surprise when he telephoned, but she was curious about the motivation.

'I think you're playing with fire,' Alice said.

'Why?'

'You don't remember Dr Shalambani?' Alice had been to the last Christmas ball, when the young intern had graced the celebrated arm. Sarah, being ill, had not gone, but was aware of the rumours.

'So he ditched her and she left.'

'Could happen to you.'

'Alice, you are naive. How little you know me. What have I to fear from a mere surgeon? And an ageing one at that.'

'Plenty,' Alice said, getting up and leaving the room.

The anatomy room at the hospital was suffused with a pale fluorescent light that coated the livid green drapes with the rime of a winter landscape. Most of the students had already left for the weekend; only a handful of tables remained active. Under burning lamps the still exposed, half-dissected relics of human flotsam could just as easily have originated from a knacker's yard as from the mortuary. But for Sarah, recalling her preclinical days, the cadavers that were invisible held the greater menace. One could never quite be sure what they were up to under their drapes.

'Have you seen Mr Davison?' she asked the nearest of the students. The girl flicked a piece of formalin-fixed tissue from her forefinger and pointed to the far end of the room.

Sarah studied the hunched figure from a distance before drawing closer. It was curious how his motionless body, even from the rear, could convey the same coiled-up energy that was ever present in his expression. The fine instruments picked and poked at the grey flesh with the deliberation of a blackbird dispatching a worm.

'If you put your nose any closer you'll get it pickled,' she said into his ear. 'What can be so engrossing, for goodness' sake, at quarter to five on a Friday afternoon?'

He did not look up. 'You see that nerve,' he said, pointing with his scalpel blade. 'How it veers away from the vessel. It's a favourite for surgeons to cut when they don't remember their anatomy.'

'And you do?'

'I do now.'

'You always practice before an op?'

'I always aim for a perfect result, but it's rare to go this far. By the way, how did you know where to find me?'

'Alan Murphy told me.'

'You've seen Alan?' His face darkened; realising it, he

thrust it even closer to the wormlike complex of vessels and nerves. 'I suppose you've been considering our respective invitations?'

'To the ball? Well yes, I have actually.'

'And?'

'And, in the interests of equanimity within the Unit, I'm going to disappoint you both.'

She tried hard to tell whether the twitching of his facial muscles was an expression of disappointment for himself or relief at Alan Murphy's similar dismissal. Maybe it was both.

'So you're not going then?'

'I didn't say that. I said I'd go with Edwin, as the standard bearer for you all.'

'That won't be how he sees it.'

'There'll be conditions.' She paused. 'You could always take Alice, as Jeff's away. Want me to arrange it?'

'Can I stop you?'

'I'll see you on Monday morning, seeking perfection in the theatre. Goodbye Brian. Enjoy your weekend.'

'Goodbye, Sarah.'

She walked towards the exit, knowing that his eyes would be following her. Behind her an instrument clattered on the tiled floor. She felt a pang of guilt, but did not look back. As she approached the door, Alan Murphy appeared at the other side, pressing his face against the glass. She knew beyond reasonable doubt that Brian would not be enjoying his weekend but, seeing Alan's grotesque image, she wished it could be otherwise.

They sat together at a table in the Travellers Bar. For the first time Sarah was able to appreciate the extent of the material advantage that enabled Alan to transgress so freely within a wide framework of social responsibility. It explained the shabbiness of his suit and the looseness of his tie – and accounted for his certainty that such things did not matter. He might have been a navvy dressed for an occasion; until, in other circumstances, one noted the assurance with which his wallet was withdrawn and the largesse enjoyed by those purporting to serve him. What people thought concerned him not at all. Sarah wondered how he would fare in a profession still conservative in such matters. It seemed to her he would not remain in it for long.

'You're his exact opposite, aren't you,' she said.

'Who, Davison?' He leaned back in his chair. His raucous laugh seemed to bounce back off the ceiling. Everyone in the bar turned to stare. 'Could *you* take your professional life that seriously?'

'Part of me can,' she said softly, watching his eyes widen in mock astonishment. 'But then part of me is a whore, as you well know.' In teasing him she realised she'd overstepped the mark. She felt her cheeks burning.

'Whew. I never thought I'd hear a filly admit to that!' He leaned across the table and leered into her face. 'Does Davison know that's what you are?'

'Yes, but for the moment he chooses not to see.'

'Tell me something,' he said. 'How do you square that with your patients – what you are I mean?'

'They see a pretty lady wearing a starched white coat and smile to match.'

'Lucky them.'

'Actually, yes. I do my best for them. And that's something I have in common with Davison.' She copied Alan's movements aggressively across the table. 'Now you tell me. What do you suppose I have in common with you?'

'Heh, heh. Bitch. Licentiousness to be sure. But mine is all irresponsibility and gay – or not so gay – abandon. Yours is calculating. But the bottom line is physical. Would you settle for that?' He was suddenly thoughtful. 'What are you doing this weekend?'

'Nothing doing.'

'Champagne dinner at Lovatt's. Roadster back to Chartwood. Get up just in time for lunch in the orangery, where there's also a pool. Needn't set eyes on me if you don't want to.'

'It's tempting, but no.' She smiled at him. 'Some other time perhaps.'

Sarah saw Alice emerge from a knot of people gathering at the doorway and snake towards them between the tables. 'She's coming to tell us something. She's got that look. Do you think Davison's invited her already?'

'Then she ain't got nothin' to fear.' Alan got to his feet. 'I must go. Still time to pick up a nurse or two at the hostel, if I'm lucky.'

Alice was now beside him, taking the vacated seat. 'Where are you bound this weekend, Alan? St Peter's? House of the Blessed Virgin?'

He looked at her blankly as she bent her head towards Sarah. 'They're our local convents,' she whispered. 'The inmates are noted – no, prized – for their chastity.'

'Well, there's a contradiction in terms.' He bowed low to each of them in turn. 'Bye girls.'

'So, Alice. Back to Brian. Did he fall or was he pushed?'

'Brian? Oh definitely pushed. I don't usually wear your cast-offs, Sarah, but on this occasion…'

'Changing the subject,' Sarah said, 'how well did you know Dr Shalambani?'

'Jazreel? We were friends, sort of, in the second year. Then she went ahead when I did the BSc. We lost touch after that. Look, Sarah, you're not checking up on Edwin, are you?'

'Stable character?'

'Why, yes. Why?'

'I thought I'd visit her this evening. Want to come?'

'To Brixton? You've spoken to her?'

'Not exactly. Only to her boyfriend, I think. Said she was asleep. So I said I'd arrive at five and then hung up before he could say no. He sounded hostile!'

They parked around the corner and walked the fifty yards or so to the front door. The wasted elegance of the three-storey terrace house frowned upon bare earth bespewed with rubbish from a split bin bag. There had once been a gate, but the rusting hinges now shared only a single fragment of rotten wood bearing traces of black paint. A cat sitting on the step hissed at Alice as she bent to stroke it, then slunk away across the street.

'God, Alice, is this mess really necessary?'

Alice shrugged. 'Rachmanism lives on.'

They were taken to the first floor by a tall, softly spoken Eurasian whom both women recognised but could not place. At first he seemed reluctant to acknowledge a connection, then gave way and offered his hand.

'Ali. Technician in Anatomy. No reason for you to remember.'

'But I do, of course I do,' Sarah said. 'You've shaved your beard.'

'She's in here,' he said, opening the door to the front room and rubbing his chin as if rueful of a lost manhood. 'But I must tell you that you won't be welcome.'

The curtains were drawn against what remained of the evening light but didn't quite meet in the middle. The window was closed, against common sense, preserving the stale atmosphere. Jazreel was lying on a double bed in the far corner of the room, propped against a pile of faded oriental cushions.

'Jazreel?' Alice looked horrified.

'Why have you come?'

It was a question Alice could not yet properly answer, in spite of quizzing Sarah on the way. 'Just a social call,' she replied lamely. 'We heard you weren't well.'

'Isn't it a little – how would you say – late in the day, to be concerned?'

'I'm sorry,' Alice mumbled, 'but I don't remember us being that close.'

Jazreel jerked her head towards the wall. 'No-one was, when it mattered.'

Sarah's resentment welled up inside. At that moment she saw in the woman's demeanour not her true mental state but only self-pity. She strode towards the bed. Then, as their eyes met, she stopped short, her urge for confrontation dissipated. She bit back the words sharp on her tongue and said simply, 'You need help, Jazreel.'

Jazreel twisted rapidly to engage her fully. 'You're all cheats and liars!'

Sarah could not reconcile the haggard face with the photos she had seen of an alluring and beautiful woman.

A baby began to cry in the adjoining room. The cries turned to lusty screams. Jazreel banged her fist on a cushion. 'You see what you've done?'

'We've done nothing!' Sarah cried, losing patience. She made for the door but again something – that recurring prick of remorse – held her back. She turned and spoke softly to the woman, who was now sobbing into the cushions. 'Jazreel, is the baby yours?'

'Yes, mine, all mine! So now you know. Now go please!'

Alice looked in desperation towards Ali, who seemed to be blocking the doorway, as if their continuing presence there offered a lifeline. There was despair in his eyes.

'The baby is not well. It keeps crying. It will not stop.'

'Are you the father?'

57

'He is Jazreel's, and therefore mine.'

At the bottom of the stairs they looked back to see Ali holding the baby at arm's length while drops of urine fell to the floor like a ribbon of tinsel.

As they reached the car Sarah threw Alice the keys. 'You drive. I think I've got a migraine coming on.' She slid her bottom forward in the passenger seat, resting her knees on the dashboard.

'Then you bloody well deserve it.' Alice thrust the key into the ignition. 'You were not nice to that poor woman. In fact I've half a mind to go back and apologise. What possessed you, for goodness' sake?'

'Something I needed to know.' Sarah, now contrite, said softly, 'We can go back if you want.'

'And get another earful?' Alice sniffed into her handkerchief. 'So, did you get it?'

'Perhaps.'

'What?'

'Did you see the baby's colour? Pale, not like its mother at all.'

'Or Ali.'

'Certainly not Ali. You can be sure of that.'

They were surprised to see Alan Murphy pacing up and down outside Alice's flat. Sarah slid hastily further into her seat, but too late. He came over to the car.

'To be sure you must have changed your mind.' He turned to Alice. 'Thank you, kind lady, for bringing her back to me.'

'The answer's still no, Alan,' Sarah said, 'and I don't go in for drunks.'

Alan swayed on his feet and pointed a finger that was constantly seeking its target. 'You go in for ponces, and queers and… fornicators.' The last word was spoken in rich booming tones.

'I am a normal girl wanting a quiet weekend.' She swung across to the vacant driving seat. 'Get Alice to drive you home. See you, Alice.' She drew away, leaving Alan gaping on the pavement.

'Isn't she gorgeous,' she heard him call to Alice.

Drifts of snow lingered amongst the laurels that edged Tippett's Lane. The dog Moffat appeared fleetingly at the bend before Laurel Cottage, then vanished, confident that she would meet him at the gate. How did he know she was coming? Betty would have told him for sure, but to what effect she couldn't judge. Or perhaps he appeared for every car, just in case. All he understands, her father used to say, is a good boot up the backside. With the words came the dull didactic voice, as unsolicited as the fleeting image of grey suits, masonic cummerbund and the smell of beery breath.

Her mother was waiting at the door with the dog smug at her side.

'I'm glad you've come, Sarah. It could have been sooner but I'm glad to see you all the same.'

'Mother, you know I couldn't leave my patients. How would you feel if Dr Hislop were to abandon you?'

'He's a good man. He wouldn't abandon me.'

'Well then.'

She grasped her mother's hands. The prominent joints made her feel she was clutching a handful of hazelnuts. Had the arthritis worsened or was it that since Sarah had qualified her clinical perception had changed? Whichever, it did not bode well for the future. Back in London the publications on latest treatments were piling up on her kitchen table.

Tea and cakes were waiting on the coffee table in the living room. 'I've changed the pot twice,' her mother said. The remark was devoid of criticism. It was what she would have done for her husband, unquestioningly, had he still been alive.

Sarah sank deep into her armchair. Her mother sat opposite, waiting for her to eat. There was pride in the woman's eyes that sent a shiver of guilt up Sarah's spine. She was relieved when her mother went into the kitchen to fetch the sugar.

And suddenly there was an all-pervading silence above which the ticking of the clock on the mantelpiece was louder than she could ever remember. The house at last seemed at peace with itself. Sarah began to drink in this new experience with child-like wonder. 'It's quieter since your father went,' her mother said from the doorway.

Later that evening Sarah found herself wandering about the house to savour distant memories. She opened an old school book and found a love-note from her very first boyfriend, pure and delightful because it dated to her period of innocence. Objects – so many of them – that had acquired a glaze of neutral indifference over the years became new again, like blackened paintings after restoration. Halfway up the stairs a framed photograph showed her with her parents and sister in deckchairs on Brighton beach, all four smiling. Why had it passed her by during all these years?

Her mother found her back in the armchair with her eyes closed. 'Sarah, you're not asleep, are you?'

'No Mum, just thinking how peaceful it's become.'

'It's become a lonely place, Sarah.'

'It'll take time to adjust.'

'He did everything, you see. Shopping, money. Everything in the house. I was a bit of a cabbage, I think.'

Sarah laughed. 'Even cabbages flower. Actually they do it rather well, when they're allowed to.' She patted her mother's hand.

'Will you come home more often, Sarah?'

'I'll come more often. I promise I'll come.'

'You'd like that, wouldn't you Moffat?'

The dog lifted his chin from Sarah's foot and to her surprise looked at her rather than the speaker. Then he replaced his chin exactly where it had been and closed his eyes.

'It's nice to know I haven't been forgotten,' Sarah said solemnly.

'That reminds me,' her mother said. 'People have been asking after you.'

'Like who? They only saw me at the funeral.'

'Well. Tom Sharp, for one. He's been good to me, Sarah, since your father went. When he's not busy with the butcher's shop. He's even started to paint the windows.'

'That explains the ladder outside.'

'He said they couldn't wait another season. He was about to help your father with them anyway.'

'Extraordinary! Did my father ever tell you that?'

'Why do you say that? No. Tom's a good, kind man. Made your father bearable at times.'

Sarah turned her face to the wall. 'And unbearable at others,' she hissed to herself.

Already she could sense that the charm of the place was being compromised by worms emerging from the woodwork. There were others besides Tom Sharp, and some she feared as much. 'I'm going outside,' she said.

'He left a note, you know.'

The remark had the effect of a billhook through the shoulder, dragging her back through the doorway.

'Can I see it?'

'Tom has it. I said he could show it to Pauline. I'm sorry, Sarah.'

'What did it say?'

'How he would miss us all. How proud he was of you.'

'You were taken in by that? God, Mother, how can you be so blind?'

'It was written fifteen years ago, Sarah.'

An unwelcome mass formed in her throat. She turned her face. 'I see. I'm sorry.'

Later that evening Sarah set about reclaiming the bedroom she had known as a girl. A mountain of cardboard boxes full of school books and A-level notes soon appeared on the landing. 'Tom will take them away for you,' she told her mother, realising as she said it that the sarcasm was wasted. 'Get him to burn the lot.' To the pile she added torn-up fragments of pop-idol posters. The bespectacled left eye of John Lennon peered at her from the edge of the box and she poked it out of sight. 'Why are you doing this, Sarah?' her mother asked. 'You loved your posters.' 'Yes. I did,' Sarah replied, 'but not enough.'

There remained only a series of framed prints of Beatrix Potter characters, with Squirrel Nutkin in pride of place above her bed. They, along with a squirrel pendant, had been her sister's most significant possessions before she died. Elizabeth's favourite – Sarah never quite knew why – had been the one showing Old Brown the owl grasping the errant squirrel in its talons. Sarah took it down, idly turning it over. There was a small fragment – possibly part of a visiting card – stuck to the back. The letters MF of the logo looked vaguely familiar, but she couldn't think why. Then her mother called her down for supper and she put it from her mind. Only when she was lying in bed that night, and prompted by other thoughts, did an explanation – far-fetched and untenable – occur to her.

For years Betty Potter had gone to bed at nine-thirty, just after the television news. The timing had less to do with current affairs than the historic refusal of the church wardens to allow the church bell to sound after ten. Since childhood, so her mother had once told her, the chimes had been a signal for her eyes to close and the balm descend upon the rigours of the day. For ten minutes each night she would lie in delicious anticipation of the familiar sonorities. And when at last they came she would simply roll over and sleep, cleansed of troubles magnified by a lonely and idle existence.

For Sarah too the bell was a kind of signal, but dating far back to a time almost beyond memory, and for reasons still obscure. It tolls for thee, she had once overheard her father tell Elizabeth. She had not understood the allusion or the context, but the resonance of the words had lodged in her memory and always returned with the sound of the bell. Whenever, as a child, she heard it she would grasp the crisp white sheet and cover her head. Usually she would pull it no further than her nose, in case it became untucked at her feet, and she would have to endure the terrible indecision of whether to repair the damage or live with the discomfort. Then, as her mother slept, so her own perception would sharpen and she would await the moment when the random tapping of the branches against Elizabeth's window seemed to surrender to a more measured and less wholesome beat.

When her mother woke her with tea and toast long after the sun had risen she still had her thumb firmly in her mouth, and the string of her sister's squirrel pendant entwined around her fingers.

'Sarah!' Her mother stared at her in alarm. 'I haven't seen you do that for years!'

The morning was spent in aimless wanderings, first to the village shop on the pretext of fetching the Sunday papers and then in the vicinity of the house. In the herb garden she brushed away the snow from dead stems and popped the pods of black and lustrous seeds like tiny pearls. At the bottom of the garden something – it must have been a rabbit – ran into the undergrowth. She followed, without thinking, into a dark laurel-green tunnel that had once sheltered a path. Then she stopped, repelled by the gloom, and withdrew to the safety and indifference of the lawn. She could not comprehend why, wherever she went and whatever she did, the tranquillity of this old cottage and its garden was becoming so easily compromised.

In the distance the telephone rang. Her mother came to find her. 'It's a Mr Seredwin,' she said.

'Tell him you can't find me,' Sarah replied, knowing that the lie, when relayed, would not convince.

The present as well as the past were reaching to her, even in this secluded place. She was grateful she had no choice but to return to London.

With each mile closer to the city Sarah's thoughts became more organised around the work of the coming week, in the theatres and on the wards. With each set of traffic lights her professional responsibilities assumed greater ascendency over other areas of her day-to-day existence.

There was no need to go there.

Outside Lightermen's Mansions Jeff, angry at Brian, was loading a suitcase into a taxi.

'Bugger wouldn't take me to Victoria.'

'And neither would I.' Against her better judgement she was beginning to enjoy baiting Jeff. 'Where are you off to?'

'Paris conference. Thought you knew.'

'Then watch out for culture. It bites!'

'Resisted it so far.' He shut the door and wound down the window. 'By the way, if you're going up to the flat – which I don't advise – you might try to cheer him up. Last night him and Murphy damn near finished my lager. Commiserated with themselves until two, can you believe?'

Brian did not seem pleased to see her. 'Can you please explain why it is that my heart pounds and sinks whenever I see you?'

'It's the Thatcher government. People call it the sinking pound syndrome.'

He didn't even smile. 'Why are you here?'

'Because I didn't want you to go into theatre tomorrow after a sleepless night.'

'Thinking about you? That's bloody arrogant, if I may say so.'

'But true?'

He turned away, refusing to answer.

'Believe me,' Sarah said, 'I'm not here to preen myself or crow. I just wanted to ask if I could assist you tomorrow, with the op.'

'You mean that?' He looked fiercely into her face, then relaxed. 'Actually, I'd be glad of your input.' He moved to the table where several sheets of surgical scribblings were scattered. 'Here, let me show you what I want to do.'

After half an hour Sarah got up to go, wriggling to free herself from the arm placed hastily around her shoulders.'

'Please stay,' he whispered.

She pushed him aside. 'It would spell disaster for tomorrow. After the ball, take me out for dinner sometime. I promise I'll accept.'

'Done.' The relief was tangible.

She kissed his cheek and ran down the stairs, leaving him to ponder what possible business she could have at the hospital on a Sunday evening.

It was quiet in casualty and she walked to the staff lift without being seen; but before the doors had closed she was out again, remembering that sometimes patients found their way there. She didn't want a confrontation, not on a Sunday evening. At least on the stairs you could keep your distance.

On the third floor ward Sister Barrington had just begun her night duty. Through the glass the little office reminded Sarah of one of those museum exhibits depicting a room of long ago. The nurse was a waxwork figure bent over the light of a desk lamp with a book in one hand and an apple in the other, absorbed and still.

Sarah tapped on the open door. 'I'm here to see Mr Gordon. Dr Murphy asked me to look at him if I was passing.' That was a lie. Alan Murphy wouldn't have given a damn. But to visit another doctor's patient unannounced might have raised questions.

'Fourth bed on the left. Just had his medicine so he'll be a little dopey. Otherwise stable.'

Sarah pushed up her collar in case her own patients might recognise her.

The bright eyes within the disfigured face were directed at the ceiling. Without a word Sarah pulled the curtains around the bed and sat beside him.

'Hello,' she said quietly. It was not her usual voice, but came more naturally, soft and musical, without an edge. 'Are you able to speak to me?'

The jaw was misshapen and enormous, but that was the lesser of his problems. Only the drugs were keeping him alive.

'I'm nearly ready. There's only one thing now to keep me.'

'Yes? What's that?'

'My daughter from Canada. Coming with her baby boy, on Thursday.'

'Your grandson? You didn't tell me! That's great, Mr Gordon.'

He nodded vigorously, then stopped suddenly. 'Tell me I'll still be here, doctor. It's all I'm holding on to, you see.'

'There are no promises in medicine, Mr Gordon. But with the drugs you're getting, and your will-power – that's important too – you should just make it.'

She left the ward without a word. Her heels striking the bare stone stairs must have sounded to Sister Barrington like distant gunfire.

5

Why hadn't Stricker arranged to call for her? One explanation came to mind: there was something he wanted to impress her with. As soon as she'd negotiated the security desk at Atherstone House she knew what it was – an opulence seldom found outside the demesnes of the seriously rich. The concierge accompanied her to the lift; then, sizing her up and without attempting to hide his uncertainty, travelled with her in silence to the tenth floor. Stricker was waiting at the door to greet her.

'Dr Potter!'

She resented the avoidance of her first name. Retaliation was impossible to resist. 'Dr Stricker,' she countered.

'Ah, you think that is one of my weaknesses, to mind being pushed from my pinnacle. I can tell you, Sarah, that I wouldn't mind in the least if we were to exchange our identities, here and now. Sit yourself behind that desk over there, become Dame Sarah Potter, and tell me what you would think of me if I were to come through that door as a mere houseman.'

'You wouldn't even have got that far.' She giggled like a schoolgirl, realising she had been stupid.

'Then I will tell you, my girl. You would envy me from the bottom of your heart. And why? Youth and choice. To be able to turn on the spot and look in any direction at the vistas that are yours for the choosing. Drink?'

'Cinzano and lemonade.'

'You're not driving?'

'You're supposed to be driving me home.'

'Home, surely, is wherever the heart happens to be. But we can discuss that later.'

Under Edwin's surprised stare Sarah seated herself at his desk. She could sense his bemusement as her eyes travelled from one object to another, neglecting his attention. She touched a photograph with her forefinger. 'Your wife?'

'She died. Many years ago.'

'You loved her.' It was a statement, not a question.

'Why do you suppose that?'

'And you loved your daughter. But not, it seems, your son.'

He stood behind her and placed a hand gently on her shoulder. 'How did you deduce that? It's true, I'm impressed.'

'It's how I would have arranged them – the photos – on your desk.' She turned to look at him with a smile sweet and open.

'My dear Sarah, this will involve us in much time, much pleasure and much pain. But it's for a rainy day, not now.' He looked at his watch. 'We have to go, or the youngsters will beat us to it.'

'Before we do, tell me one thing.'

'Ask.'

Sarah's mind raced, then she said, 'It had better be later.'

Brian and Alice were ahead of them in the queue for the function rooms at Cutlers' Hall.

'You can almost feel the tension between them,' Edwin said, squeezing Sarah's arm.

'That's cruel!'

'Cruel, but true. He was – indeed still is – my most

brilliant student, you know. Single minded, intent on one goal and skilled. A perfectionist but – unusual for that class of person – quite capable of achieving perfection.'

'And innovative?'

'Ah, we'll have to wait and see, won't we? That's the real test, to go where no man has been before. And in surgery that's quite something. Nothing like surgery for putting your career on the line – results are so bloody obvious.' He rolled his eyes, then looked into her face. 'You respect him, don't you?'

'And I'm grateful to him. He's helped me.'

'The ultimate accolade.'

'And Alice?'

'Nothing to say about Alice Pardoe. My God, did you see that!'

From out of nowhere Alan Murphy had materialised behind Alice and pinched her bottom, then leapt to Brian's other side as if he had joined them from that direction.

'What *did* you do to her?' he said to Brian, in response to Alice's scream.

Sarah's attention was caught, not by Brian's protestations of innocence, but by the scowl of Alan's neglected partner, still standing in the doorway where he had left her.

'Poor little soul,' Edwin said.

But she's pretty, Sarah thought.

In the hall the decorations were more reminiscent of a children's Christmas party than an adult gathering at thirty pounds a ticket. The place reeked of cigarette smoke because, it was said, no-one had bothered to open the windows since the night before. Gradually the thickness of the atmosphere was augmented by the smell of cabbage from the kitchens, a peculiarly academic smell, Edwin said, that took him back to his student days at Cambridge. Sarah puckered her nose and was rebuked with a frown of disapproval.

Surgical Unit had a round table for twenty. There was a vast confection in the middle with representations of the abdominal viscera, distended, as if they were about to explode. The liver, its red lobes drooping, bore an uncanny resemblance to Edwin's pink jowls.

To Sarah's surprise, Edwin began the evening by ignoring her; but he was the first to ask her to dance. He held her close and whispered into her ear, 'The others would have sat there all night, not daring to lay a hand on you until I fired the starting pistol. Now just watch the fight for succession.'

'Surely you won't abandon me to them, Edwin?'

'Ultimately no. But it would be fun to let them think that. Let's let the evening take its course, shall we?'

There was something different about him and it took Sarah a while to decide what it was. A faint mustiness about his person. Not perspiration or an odour, rather an envelope of air one associates with a falling barometer before a storm. And the hand she remembered so clearly as dry was now perceptibly damp. He was weakening.

Edwin was wrong about his protégés. They were beaten by a final year student called Tim, whose presence there no-one could quite explain and who seemed blissfully unaware of the hierarchy. His eyes hardly ceased to wander between Sarah and Alan's new girl. They had four dances in succession, finishing with a waltz and a parting just short of a kiss. Tim returned to his table in a crab-like sideways shuffle which drew more, rather than less, attention to what he was seeking desperately to hide.

If nothing else, Alan had a sharp eye for an opportunity. There were tables still to be turned.

Alan said, 'Guess what happened on the ward today.'

Alice rounded on him. 'No, Alan, you're not to tell her,' she hissed, hoping that Sarah had not overheard.

'Tell me what?' said Sarah.

'She's a brave wee gel. She can take it.'

'No, Alan. It'll spoil the evening,' Alice was pleading in earnest.

'You have to tell me now,' Sarah demanded. But she could hear the wariness in her voice.

'Your friend with the cricket ball in his mouth. He died this afternoon.' Alan reached across the table for the wine bottle.

'Oh, no!' Sarah thought for a moment. 'That surprises me. He seemed so stable.'

'But in pain, great pain,' Alan said, lowering his voice to a whisper. 'So I exercised my clinical judgement.'

'You did what?'

'Took him off medication, apart from upping the morphine. What's a day more or less? Probably made no difference. That's between us, mind.'

'Between us nothing,' Sarah cried. 'You're a bloody murderer! Did you know what he was waiting for?'

She felt an intense pain in her forearm as Edwin lifted her abruptly to her feet and led her like an errant schoolgirl to a space on the dance-floor, his face red and contorted. 'You will never again, ever, question a colleague's judgement in public. Do you hear me?' She could tell he was itching to shake her violently.

'If you knew…'

'I heard the whole conversation and know precisely what the score is. You must learn to control yourself.'

Faces throughout the hall turned. A lover's tiff, and involving Sir Edwin. That was worth watching.

The band started up again. Edwin put his arm around Sarah's waist and with the other pushed her backwards into the quickstep. It took half a dozen paces before they were in step. A ripple of laughter spread across the tables, then died almost as quickly as interest waned.

But the Dean was still clapping as they sped past his table. 'Not as subtle as last year, Edwin.'

Eventually the music stopped. 'I have to go to the loo,' Sarah whispered, walking briskly away. Edwin marched back to his seat with the bearing of a field-marshal returning empty-handed from the battlefield.

Alice found her leaning into a mirror with her body pressed hard against the basin edge. Black streaks ran down her cheeks.

'I'm not cut out for this game, Alice.'

'What Alan did was inexcusable.'

'To Mr Gordon or to me.'

'To both.'

'Ah well.'

'Are you coming back?'

'Pour me a glass of something strong and have it ready. I'll be a few moments longer. To tidy myself up. Tell them I'm okay now.'

The contingent at the table had regrouped. Edwin had changed places with Alan, who patted her vacant seat in invitation. If it had been Edwin's crude attempt at reconciliation it failed miserably. Alan was still intent on exploitation, and Sarah ignored him. For two hours he studiously topped up her glass each time she was dragged onto the dance floor or whenever she wasn't looking. But unwisely and against his better judgement he kept pace. As he would tell Alice later, it softened the pain of witnessing her favours to all but himself; and Alice half-believed him. Towards the end of the evening the pain surfaced.

'I've been meaning to ask you, Sarah, what was the subject of your anatomy prize?'

'The innervation of the human penis,' she replied. 'What else could enthuse a pubescent teenage fresher?'

'And your conclusions? Were they... innovative?' So Alan had overheard her conversation with Edwin.

'Very. They marked the beginning of the new science of psycho-anatomy. Clever, don't you think?'

'Too bloody clever by half.' Alan's speech was slurred and threatening. 'It's sickening to see women so bloody cocksure of themselves.' He looked round for approbation, but none came. 'Sometimes they need to be taken down a peg or two. Let the error of their ways be their downfall.'

'Hoisted with their own petard,' remarked Alice.

Alan looked at her with approval. 'Hoisted with...' he repeated slowly, rummaging in his pocket. 'Now's the time, now's the place. Voilà!'

Sarah recognised her panties, unaccountably missing after a celebration in the Travellers Bar months before had got out of hand. She lunged wildly towards them. Alan, waving them high above his head, stepped backwards and tripped. The pair fell sprawling under the table. Disinclined as she was to get up, Sarah was just aware that Edwin had turned his attention to the girl Alan had brought. 'What did you say your name was?' she heard him say.

'Christine.'

'Well then, Christine, it seems you are going to need a lift home. I'm sure it's safe to leave the others to clear up the mess. Come child.'

Brian was trying desperately to persuade Sarah to get up. 'I'll have to take Sarah home,' he said.

'*We'll* take Sarah home,' Alice said grimly.

What was the expression Elizabeth had once used, lying on the bed in Sarah's room that first Sunday morning after the world had somehow turned grey? Inner fear, that was it. You sometimes show it, Sarah, without realising. Just occasionally it seeps through that tough hide of yours and

I can tell. That was when, without explanation, Elizabeth had stretched out her closed fist and dropped the squirrel pendant into her waiting palm.

Why had she not questioned her sister? Then, when the opportunity was there and they were so close? Was Elizabeth, through her silence, shielding her from something? Inwardly she had known that whatever the confidence might have yielded, the truth would be hard to contemplate. When Elizabeth was killed on her bicycle two summers later Sarah regretted with an indescribable intensity that she had never brought herself to ask. Her own sister! Had she not cared enough, for God's sake?

In periods of despondency it always came to occupy her mind before she was fully awake. There it was, like a face at the window, rain or shine. There were times when it seemed malevolent, and it had taken her years to realise that there was a pattern: that the sharpest bite of pain was when the autumn chill touched the last of the summer mornings – for that was when Elizabeth's demeanour had changed.

The exuberance and abandon of a Saturday night never seemed to translate into the satisfaction that was promised. On such mornings even the telephone, a normally steadfast lifeline to a less troubled world, held no promise of relief. So she would return to bed and turn her face to the wall, as she had done as a child, so as not to see who it was the owl held in its talons.

But that afternoon, the day after the ball, the telephone did ring. The encounter with Jazreel in Brixton was still vivid in her memory.

'It's Ali.'

'Hello Ali. What do you want?'

'To talk. Can we meet?'

'I suppose. Why?'

He seemed to be groping for words.

'We lost the baby.'

'Ali, that's awful! Yes, of course we can meet, if that would help.'

'Can I come round? Like now?'

'Of course you may.'

For once Sarah took her clothes from a drawer that had remained closed since she moved into the flat. She chose a black-buttoned grey cardigan to take the edge off her youthfulness, then stuffed a handkerchief into her sleeve, as if anticipating tears.

'You look different,' Ali said, ill at ease in the doorway.

'For the better or worse?'

'More beautiful still.' His face became flushed. 'I'm sorry, I should not have said that. But, well, you see, it's really why I'm here.'

She had not understood. 'You're here because I'm beautiful?'

'It is because of your beauty that you are… vulnerable.'

'Very enigmatic and I'm flattered. But you have something else to tell me surely? Tell me about the baby.'

'It was an infection. Very sudden.'

'Or not so sudden?'

'Please, it is a book closed. There is a saying where I come from that evil must be absolute for no good to come of it. That is sometimes difficult to understand.'

'You are older than your years, Ali. And Jazreel, how is she?'

'She was nearly broken, but she will mend. She has gone home. For how long I do not know. I may join her.'

'Then why…'

'Jazreel, too, was a beautiful woman. Maybe her beauty will return, maybe not.'

'You've come to warn me, haven't you?'

'To tell you to be careful.' He searched in his pocket for a packet of cigarettes, then lit one, inhaling hard. 'You will ask me what of. In truth I cannot tell you. Jazreel was so shamed she would not reveal it, even to me. It was before I knew her well, you see. I think then I would not have interested her.' He pulled a wry smile. 'You see, for me good may have come from evil.'

'Go on.'

Ali tapped his cigarette packet nervously on the table. Sarah watched the muscles of his mouth organise themselves into an utterance of contempt.

'Your friend, the surgeon. I think he was responsible.'

'Edwin, you mean? But for what?'

'For her pain. Beyond that I cannot say.'

'Then why accuse him?' Sarah's frustration was mounting. 'Stricker's just a harmless old buffer.'

'Because of the depth of her hatred for him. It was without parallel.'

'I'll go and make us some coffee.'

When she returned Ali had gone.

This time the concierge at Atherstone House waved her through with hardly a glance. She wondered to whom he reported and what instruction he received in the art of discretion. She tried to guess how he classified her. More to the point, what others had earned the same weary and sanctioning nod, devoid of interest and respect.

And the residents, players all! One read it in the oils of hounds and huntsmen that lined the corridors, in the darkly framed notices of long dead cabaret artists and in small-group photos taken at garden parties at the palace. The opposite corridor on the tenth floor was devoted to falconry and camel racing in some Gulf state. For these people the science of taking pleasure was as serious, almost, as the art of generating wealth.

Edwin's door was already open. She saw him in the far corner of the room, framed in the window, gazing across the Thames and South Bank to an arbitrary point on the horizon. There was a long silence, as if he were receiving instruction from a presence far away. The clock of a church somewhere below struck six.

'I was expecting you, Sarah.'

'Then you know me better than I know myself, Edwin.'

'How is that?' His voice was bland and empty. 'Ah, you mean you had considered not coming, is that it? I would have thought that an apology in person was the least I deserved.'

Beyond his hostility she sensed a hurt pride that was quite capable of expressing itself to her disadvantage. She saw in him instruments to manipulate and cajole, nurture and torment, but which, for the moment, would be used to pacify. Only later, and prompted by others in different contexts, would she realise that behind his behaviour might have been a true element of affection. She gripped the hairy fist clenched over the chair-back. It drew no response, yet she was certain of the impact.

'You do deserve one, Edwin, and you are right to reprimand me for my behaviour when I should have been contrite. Well I am and I apologise for spoiling last night. Alice rang to tell me I'd behaved rather badly. Tell me what I can do to put it right.'

'You can show me the real Sarah, not an automaton engineered for sensuality that blows its fuse at the slightest provocation.'

'Is that what you think?' She had underestimated his capacity to retaliate.

'A harsh judgement, I'll admit – perhaps. I will give you some tea, young lady, and while we sip it we can contemplate our respective positions. See if there's common ground. Mutual advantage even. That sort of thing.'

'I would like it very much if we could begin again.' She didn't care if he saw she was being less than truthful.

'That's splendid.' He led her by the shoulders to a door next to the fireplace which he opened with a flourish. Beyond was a smaller, more cosily furnished room with curtains drawn and a crackling coal fire. Before the fire a low table covered with an embroidered white cloth bore more cakes and delicacies than they could eat in a week. To each side were cavernous armchairs with rich oriental cushions, oblique to each other and to the fire.

She sat and Edwin took his place opposite her. 'We should each begin at an appropriate landmark in time. Choose one for me.'

'The death of your wife, perhaps.'

He looked at her sharply, as if a cut had been intended; but there was no premeditation or malice on her part.

Then she asked softly, 'And your daughter?'

'In a car accident, both.'

'The emptiness you must have felt.'

'You speak with experience of such a thing?'

'Once. My sister, on her bicycle.'

But she could not bring herself to exchange remembrances of a common grief. She bit her lip, wondering what inner demon prevented her seeking the way of friendship instead of denial. 'It's still too painful to talk about.'

'I understand.' He reached across and patted her hand. 'After it happened I could no longer live in the family home and wanted to sell. My son Alex would not hear of it – and I should have seen in him then the manorial tyrant he's become – so I let him have it in exchange for this. What do I need with acres of grass to mow when I have my surgery?'

'And other things?'

Again the questioning look that was becoming habitual.

'As you say, other things.' He had been looking above her head but now his gaze descended hard onto her face. 'Now how about you?'

She was prepared. 'You remember my father died some months ago? Before that just a conventional upbringing in the country, quite devoid of interest. Good at school but could have done better, lucky in exams and reached medical school, somehow. The rest you know.'

'Something tells me…'

'That there's a reason I sometimes go over the top?'

'My goodness me, no. I'm a surgeon, not a shrink. I only dabble around on the surface, where I'm happy with everything in view.'

'Something tells *me*…'

He became serious, appearing to sense a battle he might not win. 'We all have skeletons, Sarah. Large benign ones, small threatening ones, ones that rattle, and well-oiled ones that creep up on you when you least expect it. Sometimes it's best to let them rest, don't you think? The superficial pleasures of life can be quite intense. Why should we not content ourselves with those?'

Edwin rose and walked behind her chair. He rested the palms of his hands on each side of her neck with the tips of his fingers entering the front of her dress. She closed her eyes as he explored between the cotton and the skin. Funny how that approach always seemed to work, the battle lost before it had been joined.

She felt the soft radiance of the fire as his cupped hands expressed her breasts. The warmth spread through her body, a surging force sectioning and extinguishing the part of her that wanted to offer reason as a defence.

What happened next was as unexpected as it was perplexing. Edwin called a name, his voice barely rising, as if to someone already present in the room. 'Maia,' he repeated, 'come!'

A small door near the fireplace that Sarah had taken to be a cupboard swung open without a sound. A young woman of Asiatic caste in a clinging white gown stepped from the subdued light of another chamber. She was of medium height, with dark shoulder-length hair that framed an oval face of great regularity, without blemish.

'Maia is from northern Thailand,' said Edwin. 'You can see how the Malaysian and Chinese influences each combine to obliterate the lesser characteristics of the other. She is beautiful, is she not?'

Sarah had never thought of her own attractiveness as a subject for comparison. It was a given right, to be used to advantage or as a tool when occasion demanded, but never to be called into question. Now she was confronted with a beauty that at least rivalled her own. For the first time that she could remember she felt a need to fend off a perceived disparagement. Edwin, to his credit, tried to allay her discomfort.

'She is beautiful, Sarah, but she is also mute. Have you any idea how that changes things?'

The girl made no further move. She stood looking directly at them, a faint benevolent smile on her lips, passing no judgement.

For several seconds Sarah held her breath in anticipation. The unexpected relief she now felt was translated into a series of deep and involuntary inspirations that suddenly made her an accomplice to Edwin's encompassing hands. It was a situation she had never encountered, even in dreams. Forgotten was her planned manipulation of Edwin's attentions. Under the steady calming eyes of this slight girl the last thin veils of inhibition peeled away. A path had opened for the sensual enjoyment of the flesh, without guilt, without thought, for the future or for the past.

'You will find it pleasurable to let Maia help prepare you – indeed us – for the evening. Assuming, that is, you wish to stay.'

The thought of flight had not occurred to her. But his remark opened a faint crack in the completeness of her abandonment, letting in for a moment the light of the outside world. She thought of Ali and Jazreel, and of a moment long past when Brian had alerted her, almost unwittingly, to Edwin's darker interests. She glimpsed a means to pursue her own mounting fascination with whatever it was that seemed to link these diverse characters.

The sensual freedom engendered by the girl's unswerving gaze had not lessened, but once again Sarah felt in control. She rose from her chair, twisting her body out of Edwin's grasp so that she could see his face.

What she found there hardened her resolve, for Edwin's eyes were pleading with her to remain. Only now did she appreciate the gamble he had taken in setting up this scenario to entrap her.

'Edwin, I want so much to stay, truly, but it's probably better if I leave now before something happens that each of us might regret.'

'Sarah, you know that we can both live for the moment, without anything spilling out into our other, more conventional lives. I, because I have learned how. You, well, because it seems to be your nature.'

'Edwin, the truth is… I wish to stay, really, but…'

'But you are unsure. Let me suppose, it is still negotiable, is it not?'

'Yes, yes, it is.' She placed her arms around his neck so that her still bare breasts brushed his chest.

'And what must I do? I believe there is little I would not do at this moment.'

'Then you can promise to show me the Massingham Tower.'

Conflicting expressions of anger and resignation crossed his face. 'That's impossible. You don't know what you ask.'

'Edwin, nothing is impossible, and nothing is at risk. You know that I'm discreet.'

'Yes, I believe you are but it worries me that you may just have a motive.'

Sarah squeezed her arms about his neck and laughed.

'Nothing so sinister! Once Brian took me to Greenwich Park and we happened to see it through his telescope. What I saw fascinated me, Edwin, and curiosity is something I find difficult to live with.'

Edwin shrugged. 'Then so be it.'

She saw him nod to the girl and closed her eyes. She was tired, with the helpless, delicious weariness of achievement. There was no obstacle now to the enjoyment of what was to follow.

She scarcely noticed that her dress had fallen to the floor.

6

Alan Murphy was standing just inside the tea-room door when Sarah swept in from a session in theatre with Brian. He fell in behind her in a wild parody of her quickstep at the ball, not noticing Alice cutting across on her way to the coffee machine.

Alice picked herself up from the floor. 'Damn you, Alan.'

'That wasn't funny, Alan,' Sarah said. 'You could hurt someone doing stupid things like that.'

'Then you shouldn't provide me with the material, should you? By the way, I've got a present for you. Sort of an exchange, you see, if you get my meaning. It's on my desk next door.'

'Intriguing,' Alice said.

'Then you get it for me, there's a sweetie,' Sarah said wearily. 'If we don't humour him there'll be no end to it.'

Alice came back clutching what in other circumstances might have been a small round tin of sweets wrapped in pink tissue paper and tied with a red ribbon. Both women recognised the items as surgical packaging. Alice was curious. 'May I open it for you?'

'You won't deprive me of any pleasure.'

'You're right about that.' Gingerly Alice handed her a glass pot containing some sort of pathological specimen, pinkish-white and ragged in the fixative.

'What's that?'

'Read the label.' Alan sounded like a child at Christmas.

'Gordon. Died… ' Sarah thrust the pot into Alice's hands. 'Sick, sick, sick!'

Alice glared at Alan. 'Won't you ever stop?'

Fleeing into the corridor Sarah nearly collided with Brian returning from the theatre. 'That man's not fit to be a doctor!'

'Oh, really? I thought we were turning him into quite a useful surgeon.'

'Not if I have anything to do with it. You'll see!'

Brian cautiously entered the tea-room.

At lunch-time Brian found Sarah alone in the cafeteria, gazing at the far wall. In front of her was an untouched bowl of soup. He set down his tray opposite her.

'May I join you?'

'The others haven't, so why should you?'

He sat and began eating, all the time looking down at his plate. Then he said, 'It seems that little fracas with Alan has left you somewhat isolated. They think you over-reacted.'

'The clown seems to think he's impressing me and can't get it into his head that he's not.'

'Maybe it's the only way he can think of to establish a relationship.'

'Balls.'

'Sarah!'

It was not the first time she'd seen him embarrassed by indelicacy in women. Could she never control herself, think ahead sometimes? 'Sorry. Look, changing the subject, you promised to take me out to dinner, remember?'

Brian looked puzzled. 'I thought you'd taken up with Edwin.'

'Oh, not in the way you think. We're only friends.'

'You are? Well, yes, then why not. I'd like that. How about Thursday. The rota says we're both off that afternoon.'

'Sorry, going shopping. Well, sort of shopping.'

'Surely you can put that off.'

'Perhaps I don't want to.'

'What's so special…'

'Well, if you must know, Edwin is taking me to the Massingham Tower. There, I've said it. Now you know.'

Brian whistled softly. 'How did you persuade him to do that?'

'Blackmail!' No, that was too extreme. 'A kind of blackmail, anyway.'

Brian looked worried. 'I'm sorry to say I find myself believing you. Be careful, Sarah. I know you think you can take care of yourself, but be very careful.'

'Funny. You're the second person to tell me that.'

'And the first was Ali.'

'How on earth did you know that?'

'Because he came to see me after your meeting. Said he could see destruction in your eyes. You know he's something of a clairvoyant?'

'I didn't even know you knew him.'

'I… um… treated his child once. Or rather Jazreel's. You see, a year ago she was quite a close colleague. Until she flipped.'

Sarah grasped his wrist and stared at him, forcing him to look up. 'Do you know the reason?'

'I wish I did. I don't believe anyone does.'

'Except Edwin?'

He looked at her sharply. 'I really wouldn't know.'

It was the first time Sarah had seen the building close up, in daylight. From the pavement the dull chequers of red brick and black glass rose in regimented columns to terminate many floors above in a low balustrade. It was only when she crossed the road and walked backwards for many yards down a side street that she realised the building continued upwards as a jumble of brick structures and aerials. Behind them she could just make out the top of a vast bluish-grey dome.

You will meet me in the vestibule off the street, Edwin had told her, though I might as well tell you that members normally enter by car using a hidden tunnel beginning some blocks away. Unfortunately the members only rule is inviolable and guests are no exception.

She had expected some compromise once within the miserable entrance. There was not even a hint of sophistication. Anyone remotely curious about the building would have had their interest stifled by the slate-grey matting carpet and reception desk in cheap teak laminate. The negativity seemed calculated. The role of receptionist had been usurped by two black-clad security guards, one reading the *Mirror*, the other the *Sun*. At first they ignored her. Then one looked up and pointed behind her.

She turned in time to see the elevator light click on. Before the doors had opened even an inch a shiver of anticipation passed up her spine. And there was Maia, quite motionless, looking at her with that same giving expression and benign smile that was still lodged in her memory. The clinging white gown had become a smart beige suit that might in other circumstances have set her apart as a successful business woman. Sarah suppressed an urge to hug the doll-like creature.

Maia held out her left hand: not for Sarah to grasp, but so that she might see what was written on a tiny conversation pad attached to the wrist by a fine gold chain. She recognised Edwin's spidery hand: *I am unwell and hope to see you later. For the moment go with Maia and she will introduce you to Preston, who manages the business side of things.*

Inside the lift only the possibility of a hidden camera prevented Sarah from touching her. But Maia, apparently sensing this, laid her hand lightly on Sarah's arm. Sarah wanted to grasp the little pad and write upon it – anything to establish some sort of dialogue. But she could think of nothing that was not banal. It saddened her that, in spite of their previous closeness, they had yet to share a single conceptual thought.

At the tenth floor Maia indicated the way with a motion of the hand that was as perfect in its geometry as the opening and closing of a fan. Mindful of her own relative clumsiness, Sarah held back from going ahead and walked beside the girl.

They came to a short flight of semi-circular stone steps more in keeping with an Italianate garden than a southeast London interior, and climbed up into... daylight? It seemed strange that in the two minutes or so they had taken to get here an overcast sky had given way to what seemed to be bright sunshine.

Maia stood aside to let her go ahead. Just before she reached the top Sarah looked back and was disappointed to find that the girl had disappeared. A sign on the far wall at the foot of the stairs caught her attention: *It is suggested that Friends might not wish to pass beyond this limit of pleasure.*

There was no choice but to go on. As her eyes drew level with the topmost step a wonderful scene unfolded before her. What at first had seemed to be open sky was actually the vast translucent shell of the dome she had glimpsed from the road. This finding was based more on deduction than observation. The only evidence was the join at its periphery just – and probably only – visible from this particular point of vantage. The light was of that rare luminosity she associated with Provence or the Greek islands. Beneath it, sparkling blue water lapped against stone terraces, wooden quays and sandy coves, all laid out with consummate taste; and surrounding all that a lush green swathe of palms and all manner of other tropical plants. Here and there small and isolated cabins, some in wood, others of stone, were festooned with purple and red bougainvillea. In the far distance a limestone cliff was peppered with steps and terraces and mysterious entrances. There were human figures too, but so well did they blend into the surroundings there was no suggestion of intrusion into the sense of peace and tranquillity. It was an island paradise inverted upon itself and so perfect in concept that the constraints of space were dispelled by the most subtle illusion.

At her feet irregular steps in the simulated rock-face led precipitously to a paved patio. Below her, pots of geraniums of that essential Mediterranean hue that was neither orange nor red surrounded a small round table in white and gilt with two matching chairs. The figure seated there looked up and rose to his feet.

'May I help you down, Dr Potter? I'm Mark Preston.'

She almost stumbled and he grasped her hand. She wondered if the grip was exaggerated to impress. His face was wide and open, with blue eyes and an expansive guileless smile.

'Edwin would not have thanked me for losing you so early in our relationship, Dr Potter.'

She did not speak until they were seated at the table.

'Thank you, Mr Preston. Do you lose many visitors that way?'

'Well, actually, visitors are as rare here as some of the birds and butterflies you see flying above you. And members wouldn't think of using it. Their entrance – far more grand – is on the other side of the lagoon. I consider we would be failing them if ever they felt the need to wander.'

Sarah's face must have shown she had not yet come to

terms with the incongruity of being in a London street only minutes before.

'I have lots of questions, Mr Preston.'

'Mark, please. And you are?'

'Sarah. Sarah Jane.' She had no idea why she had volunteered her middle name. Later she would come to marvel at the ease with which he used his relaxed manner to draw people out of themselves.

'Sarah Jane.' He said this condescendingly, as if rewarding a child by exaggerated approval. 'Let me welcome you formally to the Massingham Foundation. I will be as open as I can, because Edwin has assured me of your discretion, but you must realise there are certain things I cannot tell you.'

Two tall glasses of a light straw-coloured liquid appeared on the table. She looked up just in time to see Maia disappear into a cleft in the rock-face.

He continued, 'The Foundation includes diverse business interests, and is itself part of a larger enterprise about which even I know little. The headquarters are here in this building, and I am a senior manager responsible for… well, what you now see. It's only a tiny part of the whole, in capital terms, yet the return on investment here has been quite exceptional. Perhaps you can guess why.'

'The affluence of your customers, I suppose.'

'Not just affluence, Sarah. Extreme wealth. Our mission here is to provide facilities for recreation – in a qualified sense of the word – which in terms of sophistication are unsurpassed, at least in this country and probably anywhere in the world. You can see the lengths to which we have gone to create this.' He swept his hand towards the lagoon.

She was beginning to find the assurance of the man overpowering. There was a need to redress the balance.

'I see a glorified boating pool. There must be a limit to what people would pay for that?'

'Yes, surely. But let me give you a harmless example, in confidence, of course. There are friends – that's what we prefer to call our members – who have paid a fortune just to have these rare birds that you see flying overhead. There is one – as a matter of fact a household name – who has paid considerably more for the option of being able to kill them, without fear of retribution or criticism. I hasten to say that he has not done so, and indeed is unlikely to, but to possess the *power* to render a species extinct appears to be exquisitely pleasurable to him. Can you imagine what it costs to set up that particular scenario? It is our willingness to do such things – to go to extraordinary lengths when it is required of us – that makes us quite unique.'

She was tempted to ask about the legality of such enterprises, but decided it was wiser stay silent. Then darker questions began to enter her mind. Mark Preston had anticipated them.

'Then there are the pleasures of the flesh. I make no bones about that since it must be in your mind to ask. Again we cater for extreme subtlety. Another example, to you trivial beyond measure but to one other most definitely not so. A friend recently commissioned a study – study note – of the conditions under which the simple scratching of his back could be made more pleasurable. Eventually we found the combination of device, technique, person and material – I refer to the cloth worn against the skin – that satisfied him. And he rewarded us most magnificently with his gratitude.'

'Extraordinary!'

'Extraordinary, yes. But there are countless other examples.'

'Including some far closer to home?'

'Excuse me?'

'Closer to the needs of – how shall we say – more conventional men and women?' She paused. 'Incidentally, are all your friends men?'

'Well not exactly. Yes and no.'

'You don't seem very sure.' She grinned at him impishly.

'Perhaps it's because there are so few seriously rich women. But it's true that at the moment all the friends are men. On the other hand we cater for women as companions. That is what we call them – companions.'

'And what might you offer them?'

'Whatever a particular friend will pay for. But there are also social occasions when they – the companions – can participate. The last was a masked ball. They're very popular.' He looked at his watch. 'Oh, the demands of business. I will have to leave you now, Sarah. When we next meet perhaps I can tell you a little more, if you're still interested.'

'There's just one more thing I would like to know now. How can you be sure that one man's gratification is not another man's displeasure?'

'We are constantly mindful of it. It is a condition of friendship that friends will show consideration towards one another and under no circumstances make moral or even ethical judgements on others. There's a small committee that considers new proposals, specifically to obviate such eventualities. In practice there are never problems. Friends tend to be very private and civilised people.' He rose from his chair, 'Goodbye, Sarah Jane.'

For the first time Sarah could appreciate the stature of the man, and not only physically. She wondered how his natural dignity might survive the negotiation of the flight of steps under her gaze. But he did not go that way and instead seemed to dissolve into the rock, as Maia had done.

She had been left alone deliberately to reflect; of that

much she was sure. She began to appreciate the pure isolation of this sky-bound paradise. She listened for the sound of London traffic, which she knew penetrated to the tops of the highest buildings; but there was none. All she heard was the plop of a gay-plumed diving bird at the far end of the lagoon. A butterfly she did not recognise alighted on the table beside her glass, its wings trembling in a breeze so gentle that she could not feel it upon her own skin. The scene assumed a dream-like quality. Her body throbbed with the sense of well-being that follows the first few sips of a potent spirit, when troubles of the mind and life's responsibilities drift away like bubbles in the wind. She looked at the empty glass. Could it be...? But it did not matter. The wisps of cloud that had formed above danced in a sky that seemed more, not less, than real.

When at last she looked back there was Maia smiling at her, arms held out in invitation. Join me, do not fear, do not think; above all, do not resist.

Sarah took a taxi to Lightermen's Mansions to see if Brian was home. Jeff appeared at the door, dishevelled, reluctant to let her in. 'He decided to work after all. He'll be at the hospital if you want him.'

Edwin, Brian and Alice were examining radiographs against an illuminated screen when Sarah walked in. The three heads turned towards her in unison. She was surprised to see Alice; in that moment a supposition of naive innocence seemed to give way to the less wholesome charge of complicity. Edwin broke the silence.

'Ah, the traveller returns!'

'How was your afternoon's shopping?' Brian asked, with no particular expression. Sarah looked at him hard. Was he being sarcastic or just covering for her in his usual simplistic way.

'She's been to see the Tower, Brian,' Edwin said. 'It's no secret and we're allowed – indeed entitled – to ask how she got on.'

Sarah felt she was being tested. Would she or would she not commit an indiscretion? Much might hang on that.

'It was quite fascinating. Mr Preston was most kind in explaining things, particularly how one makes money in business today.'

'And how does one?' Edwin asked.

'By finding a niche in a specialist market, it seems.'

'Did he take you to the roof garden?'

'I saw the swimming pool and the tropical vegetation, if that's what you mean.'

'Could you see Greenwich from up there? The observatory, perhaps?' He said this looking directly at Brian.

'It wasn't the day for that, Edwin, as you well know.'

'But you've satisfied your curiosity?'

'Oh, quite, thank you.'

'That's good. Topic closed. Now, have a look at that.' He pointed to a lab report in a file open on the bench. 'What do you make of that?'

She read through it. 'Intermittent abdominal pain, but not much there to support a diagnosis. What's special about it?'

'Only that it's one of our nurses,' Alice said. 'Debbie, from the theatre team. They've admitted her.'

'Remarkably, she asked to talk to you, Sarah,' Edwin said. 'Perhaps you'd look by and have a few words when you have a moment. It seems to be a gift you have, to be trusted by patients. Make sure you hold on to it.'

Brian, who had left the room during the last exchange, now returned looking anxious. 'Sarah, there's a call for you, a Dr Hislop.'

'Oh my God. Something's happened to Mother.'

It was less of a crisis than she feared. Betty Potter had been found wandering in Tippett's Lane in pouring rain and had been taken in by the Sharps to dry herself out and rest. Only later did she think to tell them that she had locked herself out and was on her way to fetch help when the rain came down. Dr Hislop's tone was judgemental. 'My other reason for ringing, Sarah, is to remind you that you haven't visited your mother for a month now. Don't you think that's rather a long time?' She returned to the others humiliated; she knew that her forced smile had failed to hide the downwards pull at the corners of her mouth .

'Alice, I need to go home tonight. Can I borrow your car – mine's in the garage.'

'Sorry, I promised Jeff a lift.'

'I'll take you,' Brian said. 'You don't look fit to drive. In fact, you didn't look too good even before that call. I'm sure you can get an early train back tomorrow. Better still, we can cover for you over the weekend.'

They drove in silence for most of the way. Sarah's feeling of guilt slowly abated, giving way to sombre reflections on her bizarre experiences earlier in the day. There were more questions than existed before. Mark Preston's abrupt departure had caught her unawares; it had also left a disturbing after-image that kept returning. She wanted to tell Brian, but something in his taciturn manner advised against it; maybe he wouldn't want to hear.

'That's the lane leading to mother's. The Sharps are a bit further on, after the shops and just before the church.'

They were expecting her.

Sarah looked for a reaction in Brian's face as he shook Tom's hand, but found none, then tried to avoid Tom's leering glance towards her. She knew they were sharing the same thought: evaluation of a point scored.

Pauline waited her turn, hands meekly by her side, then kissed Sarah's cheek.

'Nothing to worry about, Sarah,' Tom said. 'She panicked a bit, that's all.'

'Where is she?'

'In bed, asleep. I think it's better to leave her there, don't you?'

'I'm going to her.'

There was a smile of contentment on her mother's face. Another stormy day successfully weathered. Sarah looked at her watch. Ten past ten. The church bell would have rung. It would be a pity to wake her now.

'I'll collect her in the morning.' Sarah looked at Brian, realising she would have no car.

'Sarah, I really have to get back. I've a full list tomorrow.'

'We'll bring her back. No problem,' Tom said. 'About ten?'

'Nice people,' Brian observed when they were back in the car. He'd obviously developed a relationship with them during her absence upstairs and looked surprised when she didn't respond.

Then it struck her. 'Oh my God,' she exclaimed, sitting bolt upright. 'I'd forgotten about Moffat.'

But the dog was there at the end of the lane, patient in the headlights, waiting for her.

The ladder was still against the house, apparently untouched.

She fumbled with the door key, giving herself extra seconds to think. Then she relented. 'You'll stay for some coffee, Brian?'

'I'll need something to keep me awake.'

'Your father,' he called from the living room, 'what sort of man was he?'

Sarah shouted back from the kitchen. 'Local figurehead,

moderately successful businessman, neglected the family a bit. Why?'

'Because there's absolutely no trace of him. I'd have expected at least a photograph or two.'

Sarah returned to scan the walls. 'You're right, they've gone. Whatever's she done with them?'

She sat next to him on the sofa, then looked away, aware that she was biting her lip. She got up to switch on the electric fire and put on a Sinatra record; almost in silence they made their coffee last until it had finished. It was difficult not to be nervous. Only later would she realise she had given Brian the impression of a kindling desire that was not there.

'Brian, would you stay here tonight? I'm sorry, that must sound awful. The truth is I've never been alone in this house at night. Can you believe that? Besides, it's getting foggy and I don't want you to drive back in that.'

'That's thoughtful of you, Sarah, but how can I get back for nine-thirty?'

'The odd times my father went to London he left at six-thirty to beat the traffic. I promise to get you up. I'll even cook you breakfast if you like.'

'I only ever eat corn…' He checked himself in time and put his arm around her shoulders. 'Sarah, I'd be pleased to stay.'

'And share my bed?' It was difficult to keep her face expressionless, obscuring purpose.

'I shall be perfectly comfortable here on the…'

'… lying awake all night wondering why you said no. That would hardly be in your patients' best interests, would it?'

'Does being trapped absolve me from responsibility?'

'Absolutely.'

Looking back, as she would one day do, she would

realise the significance of this moment. It was when the future pattern of events began to be woven around Brian's resolve, from what, until then, had seemed random skeins of circumstance.

They moved away from one another and simply held hands. Brian's breathing became regular and Sarah was glad for him. Temporarily, at least, his mind would be untroubled. But she could not sleep.

The house was quieter than she had ever known. By straining her ears she could just hear the ticking of the clock in the hall and Moffat's sporadic restlessness in the kitchen. One o'clock struck and a gust of wind rattled the shutters of the bedroom window. She got up to check the fastness of the catch and pulled the curtain aside to look out into the all-concealing blackness, pure save for a shimmer where the tops of the tallest trees emerged into stifled moonlight. *On such a night as this...* Why now should her father's words come to her, and from a story told so far back when image and fantasy had no connection with reality? And life was about love, and protection, and feeling secure. She brushed away a tear with the back of her hand.

She was back in bed when it came. Not, this time, a sound imitating the light tap of branches upon the window, increasing in insistency and impatience. It came from downstairs: at first a click, then a faint scuffle as Moffat set out from the kitchen to investigate. Her mind raced. She had not expected this, but should she not have guessed? And then, surely, the awaited creak of the third riser; was someone or something mounting the stairs?

'Brian, Brian. I think we have an intruder.'

He woke abruptly, and almost as quickly rolled away from her, asleep. She shook him by the shoulders.

'Help me... Please!'

He got up, walked mechanically to the door and opened it.

The silence remained absolute.

'Are you sure you're not imagining it, Sarah?'

'Please check downstairs.'

'If you say so.'

Five minutes later he returned. 'There's no one. I've checked everywhere. It must have been the wind, or Moffat, or your imag…' She was grateful he stopped himself in time.

'Thank you Brian, thank you, thank you, thank you.'

She was as good as her word. Brian was woken by the smell of frying bacon and percolating coffee. He found his clothes folded neatly on the chair by his bed, together with a toothbrush, shaving tackle and a towel. When he left her on the doorstep she kissed his cheek and for the next two hours he became a commuter dreaming of a state of matrimony he had temporarily left behind. It was this sentiment, in Brian's rash aside to Alice during the morning clinic, that would be conveyed back to Sarah.

Tom delivered her mother precisely at ten, thankfully staying no longer than was necessary to bring her to the front door. Sarah had already arranged for the locks on the doors to be changed and left at the end of the afternoon as soon as it had been done, and after she had cautioned Betty to tell no-one.

She arrived at the hospital in time to find Brian dictating his reports to GPs on referred cases. His rarely seen smile radiated goodwill. Then she noticed the several empty sherry glasses on the table.

'Tell me then, who's come into money?'

'I have,' he replied. 'Well, indirectly at least. I've got an appointment at Tommy's. In reconstructive surgery. And Sarah – and this is for you only – I've also got a Harley Street consultancy.'

That night, alone in bed, Sarah reflected on what a relationship with Brian might mean. On the plus side were status and security. Not that, as a doctor, she could not achieve both, but there were limits, and her awareness of potential obstacles in her own career was becoming ever clearer. And the downside? Well, what were men but ephemera? And Brian lacked the strength to constrain her. She recalled her advice to Alice about Jeff. That had seemed to work. Alice was enjoying herself, but Sarah knew – because Alice had told her – that she could be out of it in the twinkling of an eye. And that from Alice! There was only one snag: Alice had developed a crush on Brian and Sarah was loath to lose her as a friend. Edwin had told her that you can have a man as a husband, a friend or a lover, but you have only one chance and if it goes sour the other options are emphatically closed; so choose carefully, which it is to be?

Besides all that, there was something about medicine that was beginning to gnaw at her self-confidence. She loved it and was potentially good at it, but there were things she couldn't handle emotionally. Like poor Mr Gordon, and the children who came into casualty and, worst of all, the grief of friends and relatives. You must detach yourself, Edwin had told her, but she knew that however hard she tried the doubts about her chosen career might always be with her. Brian offered a kind of compromise and that consideration over-rode her regard for Alice.

She lifted the telephone and dialled his number.

'I just wanted to thank you for protecting me, and for...' She managed to stop herself in time.

'I've thought of little else.'

'In spite of your other windfalls?'

'Yes.'

'Then let's take it from there.'

The character of the silence – his inability to respond in the face of emotional challenge – told her all she needed to know. She said goodbye and put down the receiver.

The following day the team was busy in the clinics. The weather had turned; the sun that had coloured the leaves with coppers, reds and gold in the morning had been displaced by low sullen cloud and wraiths of mist drifting in from the river. Out-patients in their thick coats and all-weather gear filled the reception areas; what little space was left seemed occupied by the dampness rising from them. Sarah was glad when the natural darkness of early evening restored everything to normality. 'You haven't forgotten Debbie, have you?' Alice reminded her. Sarah hadn't.

It was still too early for there to be many visitors on the wards. Sister Barrington was nowhere to be seen, which allowed Nurse Trubshaw to feel sufficiently uninhibited to apply make-up in the mirror hanging behind the office door. There was a five-pound note lying beside her handbag on the table. She scooped it up when she saw Sarah.

'You'd best wait a moment, Dr Potter. Dr Murphy's still examining her.'

'At this time of day, whatever for? I thought she was only under observation.'

'He… thought there might have been some… complications.' The words were mumbled and unconvincing. They did not sound her own. She returned her attention to the mirror. In it, from behind, Sarah could see the agitation on her face.

'Then I'll look for myself.'

The nurse turned to face her. The smile was authoritative and under control, but the eyes were pleading. 'Why don't I make you a nice cup of tea while you wait?'

'Nurse, what are you trying to tell me?'

'Just to hang on a minute, doctor.'

'You'd better come with me,' Sarah said.

They walked together to the far end where there was an annex hidden from the main body of the ward. It was normally reserved for surgical patients whose post-operative features might have alarmed others, although such a policy was never openly admitted.

'Why was she put in here?'

There was no answer.

The curtain was drawn tightly around the only occupied bed. There was no sound from the cubicle, but a barely perceptible tremor of the whole construction.

Nurse Trubshaw said in a loud voice, addressing the bed rather than Sarah, 'This one's Debbie's.'

Recognising it as a warning, Sarah grasped the edge of the curtain and flung it back.

The warning had been insufficient. Alan Murphy, naked, had only managed to set one foot on the floor. Debbie had drawn the sheet over her head.

'Coitus interruptus,' Sarah muttered.

Nurse Trubshaw turned furiously on Alan. 'You said you only wanted to talk. Now look what you've done. Bastard!'

The occupants of the bed seemed frozen into position. The scene reminded Sarah of the birthday cakes made by her mother that her father used to decorate with bizarre family figures in icing. Why should she think of that now, for heaven's sake? That was years ago.

Sarah took the trembling woman's arm and led her away from the bed.

'A pity you had to see that, nurse, as it ties both our hands. Now we have no choice but to report it.'

'But we'll all lose our jobs!'

'I daresay.' Sarah engaged Alan's vacant, unbelieving

eyes, forcing them to travel with hers towards a patch of dampness on the sheet.

She walked back into the main body of the ward, the nurse a pace behind. Most of the other patients were asleep. It seemed doubtful if any had heard, still less understood, what had happened. 'You would be wise to say nothing to anyone, nurse,' Sarah said. 'Leave that to me.'

On the pavement outside, with a sudden sharp prick of remorse, she realised she still did not know why Debbie had wanted to see her.

7

There was a slip of paper deep in Sarah's pigeon hole, and a similar one in Brian's. It invited them both to meet Edwin in a room off the stationery store on the tenth floor of the medical block.

A distant church bell chimed seven as Sarah opened the door. The two men were seated across a desk lit by a single table lamp whose yellow glow barely included the three chairs around it. Brian held a sheet of paper between his hands, nervously, as if it were burning his fingers. They rose together with a politeness that suggested complicity. Edwin pulled at the third chair, inviting her to sit. On the desk two near-drained tumblers and a whisky bottle showed they had been talking for some while. Already she felt excluded: more like an interviewee than a close colleague.

'Sit down, Sarah.' Edwin did not offer her a drink, neither was he smiling. He snatched the piece of paper from Brian and held it to her face. She recognised her complaint against Alan Murphy.

'First, Sarah, I must ask if others, besides ourselves, have seen this letter. Alice, or Miss Trubshaw, for instance, or even Alan himself?'

'Nobody has, and I have spoken to no-one.'

'And the other patients on the ward? Would they have seen anything or understood what they might have heard?'

'I'm sure they didn't.'

Edwin leant his elbows on the table and exhaled in relief. He returned the letter to Brian. 'Then we have nothing to fear.'

The light of the lamp threw into relief the lines in his face. The thin emerging smile exaggerated the wrinkles around his mouth. For the first time Sarah saw him as old.

'You were quite correct to draw this matter to my attention. I am grateful to you for doing what you obviously saw as your duty. As a result I shall – in fact I have done so already – reprimand Dr Murphy most severely. He is, as you can imagine, quite devastated and wholly repentant. I have also told him to take a few days off to consider his position since clearly his behaviour of late has been unacceptable. He has to mend his ways. I believe he accepts that and will do so.' He drained the last few drops from his glass. 'I hope you will agree that I have acted appropriately under the circumstances.'

Out of the corner of her eye Sarah could see Brian nodding in agreement. 'It's for the best,' he said.

Sarah felt her chest tighten; but for the moment she could control the germ of rage. She said quietly, 'You mean you're going to take the matter no further?'

'To what purpose? To risk destroying a man's career and, worse, blackening the name of our unit at the point of just recognition of its labours. That would be an unacceptable price, Sarah. No-one gains and the losses could be incalculable.'

'I don't think I can accept that.'

'Not accept it? What do you mean not accept it? I'm telling you, my girl, you don't have any choice. Forget your stupid grudge against Alan. When you've thought about it further, you'll thank me.'

Earlier in their relationship the change in Edwin's

demeanour would have alarmed her. Now, to her surprise, she found herself almost euphoric and mildly amused, confident for the moment she would not be the first to weaken.

'Edwin, first of all I don't hold a grudge against Alan. And even if I did that would be irrelevant. Secondly, if I forgot it – as you so conveniently put it – I could not live with my conscience.'

Edwin's eyes narrowed to concentrate his disgust. Then lights appeared there, of a battle engaged. 'Conscience? You have no conscience. You are a cheap little tart who has absolutely no right to cast stones.' He had begun to shout.

Brian, sensing a lost cause, attempted to intervene. 'Edwin, Edwin!'

But Edwin was in full flight. 'A cheap little tart who thinks nothing of hopping into bed with anybody. And now you pillory a colleague for doing something that is at least natural.'

'That's unfair, Edwin, and untrue. And you demean yourself and your profession by using such language. What I do in my own time is my own business and nothing to do with my professional life.'

'So I am not part of your professional life? Brian is not part of your professional life? Where do you draw that particular line, might I ask?'

'Where patients are involved.'

'Patients? There are patients and patients, Sarah. You have still much to learn about patients.'

Brian's fingers were drumming on the table. 'Edwin, you need to calm down. Let me talk to Sarah for a moment.'

Edwin looked at his watch. 'I have to go to a meeting anyway.' He glared at Sarah. 'It's in your court to see reason. Fail me and you fail us all. Goodnight!'

'Oh dear, Sarah. Did you have to antagonise him?'

Sarah barely heard him. She had already prepared her strategy. 'Go after him, Brain. Tell him that if he doesn't come back a copy of my letter will be delivered to the Dean. At his home, tonight.'

Brain left the room without speaking, believing her.

Now alone, she began to cry. There was only so much pressure her will could contain. She was still crying when Brian returned. He found her at the window, gazing out over the city.

'The blessed damozel.'

'Oh, Brian. There are no lilies, and no seven stars either. Not for me.'

'We'll see.' He paused. 'He's coming back.'

'Why?'

'To contain the damage. He knows you won't give way, not without reasoned argument.'

'Do you think I should?'

'Sometimes loyalties cannot be reconciled. I share your view that our first consideration must be for our patients. But the alternatives are frightening, particularly for Edwin.'

'Why Edwin?'

'Because he is not himself a model of virtue, as no doubt you've found. There are others poised to pounce on any new misdemeanour or indiscretion. The Dean is one of them.'

'I see.'

'And the consequences of that could be the disbandment of the unit as we know it. Then where does that leave your patients?'

They could hear footsteps in the corridor.

Brian said, 'Try to bury your pride, because he won't be able to do that with his.'

They resumed their seats, out of the darkness, like participants in a TV chat show. Sarah could see fear behind the tension in Edwin's drawn face. There was an urge to go for the kill, but Brian had set her thinking.

Edwin spoke first. 'It is possible, Sarah, that I underestimated the import of what Alan has done. I would ask you this: could you agree that a solution – if we can find one – without reference outside this unit would constitute an acceptable course?'

'What do you have in mind?'

'To ask Alan to resign.'

Sarah rose and went to the window. It was not enough. Really not enough. She wanted Alan expunged, not just from the medical stage… Arguments and counter-arguments fought to a standstill in her head. Then the tears began to flow again. She returned to her seat, not minding that they saw.

'I would accept that,' she said quietly.

'Then I'll see it's done.'

She knew it was the end of their relationship.

When Sarah took Brian to meet her mother the following weekend Tom Sharp was there, waiting for them.

'I thought Sarah would like an update on her mother's progress,' Tom explained casually. 'It was an adventure, wasn't it, Betty, when you got caught in the rain?' He spoke loudly, as if she were deaf, which she certainly wasn't.

'It was more than that, Tom,' she replied. 'More like I was nearly a goner.'

'Nonsense. You're a tough old bird and you know it.' He gave her a gentle push.

This banter was foreign to Sarah. Tom had shown nothing but respect for her mother when her father was alive, however contrary to his nature.

'Have you started on the windows yet, Tom?' she asked. 'That ladder's been there an awfully long time. Will need painting itself soon.'

Tom lay back in his chair, lazily letting his eyes wander over her face and body, with all the time in the world to pick off her features one by one, mentally digest them and spit them out. She saw in his behaviour the intense enjoyment of a situation rather than satisfaction from what he drew from her. You can be as sarcastic as you like, but I have the upper hand: that's what it suggested. 'We don't change, do we Sarah? My goodness we don't.'

He stayed for a cup of tea; then, in his own good time, got up to go.

She must have surprised Brian by walking with Tom to the car. He may or may not have been sympathetic to her cause had he heard Tom's final remark from the seat of his white Magnette: 'Your mother gave me her keys to copy. It seemed a sensible thing to do, just in case anything happens to her again.'

'Bastard!'

Tom put his foot hard down on the accelerator. A shower of gravel struck her legs. She bent to pick up a handful to throw but the speeding car was already out of range.

The following morning they wandered in the garden and around the lawn, reaching a point where the laurels, there most densely planted, divided slightly to reveal a dark cavernous vacuity. Sarah said, 'They say there was once a path from here to Beacon Hill. I think this must be where it left the garden.'

'Didn't you children ever go that way?'

'I… don't think so.'

'You don't seem too sure. Why don't we try?'

Sarah's mind clouded, groping for a reason not to go. 'It'll be far too overgrown and muddy.' She could feel her heart beating in her chest, but couldn't think why. Wasn't she safe with Brian? Of course she was.

But Brian had already found a stout stick and disappeared

into the bushes. He called back, 'It's an adventure! Let's try.'

She caught up to find him swinging his stick against the nettles and making good progress.

'Not bad at all,' he said. 'I'd say it's been in use until quite recently.'

She followed reluctantly. The heavily filtered light drew her eyes to the dense canopy above. She shivered. Had she really never been here with Elizabeth, or by herself? That cannot have been true, yet she had no recollection of it; strange, with hindsight, when such mysterious places are normally magnets to children. Why had the sisters always reached their sanctuary at the foot of Beacon Hill by bicycle, leaving their machines hidden behind the church wall? Was it Elizabeth, then, who had been afraid?

Brian was out of sight now, but she could still hear the swish of his stick, and his call. 'Come on Sarah, stop dreaming!'

Within sight of the church tower the path forked. Sarah stopped and looked along the narrow earth track to the left that led on to the church and the houses nearby.

'Are you alright, Sarah?'

'I'm fine, really.'

Their path continued through decaying stands of bracken, then tearing brambles as the gradient steepened. Near the summit the undergrowth stopped abruptly, giving way to springy grass kept short by rabbits. They sat on an ancient plank bench at the top. Looking back, far below, they could see Laurel Cottage, set apart from its neighbours and surrounded by the deep green of oaks and sycamores. The seclusion seemed to impress Brian but to Sarah the house looked isolated and vulnerable.

'You can just make out the path we took through the trees, Brian said. 'And isn't that your butcher friend's house just beyond the church?'

Sarah had chosen to look in another direction. 'On a clear day you can see the spires of Oxford,' she said. 'Sometimes, in the summer, one of us – my sister or me – would come up here and the other would stay at home looking out of the window. And if we could see them – the spires – we had a special signal with a mirror; and another if they were glowing in the evening sunlight. Then it was magical. That link between the house and Oxford was something special.'

'You didn't think of going there – to study?'

'Elizabeth did, to do medicine. And would have. She was the brighter one, you see. After she died, well, somehow I couldn't bring myself to go in that direction.'

Brian looked puzzled. 'That's strange reasoning. You must have been very close.'

'She died when I needed her most.' Sarah got up, brushing the lichens from her jeans. She had said more than she intended. Then she turned and smiled.

'They say there was once a real beacon up here. Can you imagine the excitement, sitting here in the blackness with just a small flame, waiting for a fire to appear miles away? Now no-one comes. Not even children these days, with them glued to their televisions. For us it was a step to heaven. And you know, in all those years we never met another person up here.'

From the working of his lips Brian seemed to be toying with a question he found difficult to ask.

'After your sister died, did you come up here then?'

'Alone, you mean?' She faced him squarely and put her hands on his shoulders. 'I never have, till today. Is that what you want to know?'

Sunday lunch at Laurel Cottage was a ritual that had stretched back unbroken as long as Sarah could remember. That first Sunday after Albert Potter's death there had been

110

no need and her mother had made herself a cup of soup; she was still gazing at it when Sarah came in. After that, visitors were welcomed, mainly as an excuse to revive the practice. Betty's bustling between the kitchen and the dining room seemed to amuse Brian, but Sarah, who had seldom lent a hand in the past, felt guilty. For the first time for a long while she helped with the cooking.

After the meal Sarah got out her long neglected board games. Her favourite, called *Barricade*, involved thwarting the movement of her opponents' pieces up the board. She remembered how competitive she'd been against her sister, then wondered why she was untroubled when Brian won twice in a row. The threesome, like a newly constituted family, laughed the afternoon away in front of a coal fire. 'It's time for crumpets,' Betty said, her face flushed in the firelight. 'You amaze me,' Sarah replied, 'I didn't know you still made them.'

In the car back to London Sarah said, 'Do you know, we haven't discussed medicine once.'

'I've thought about it,' Brian admitted. 'Actually, if you can stand some supper with me after today's gluttony I'd like to bounce some ideas off you. Jeff may be home, though. Your place okay?'

'Fine by me.'

They turned the last corner before her flat at precisely eight-thirty. Sarah could remember that detail because her face was suddenly only six inches from the dashboard clock and her head firmly into Brian's lap. 'Drive past,' she hissed. 'Don't stop, for God's sake.'

'Whatever's the matter?'

'Just do it. Stop around the next corner.'

Brian brought the car to a halt. 'Now please explain.'

'Alan Murphy's car. It's outside my flat.'

'So?'

'I don't want to see him.'

'You'll have to sometime.'

'It'll spoil a lovely weekend.'

Brian saw the logic. 'Then you'd better come home with me.'

They sat on either side of the kitchen table, with the light out. Reflections of the city speckled the walls like distant galaxies.

Jeff had left a note to say he was with Alice and would Brian put the coffee on for breakfast.

'He will get hurt, Brian.'

'I know. And he knows. There's nothing to be done, except let it run its course.'

'Hm. Perhaps that's what people would say about us.'

'Well, it's a course full of obstacles, Sarah.'

'Why?'

'Oh, because of the demands of medicine, mainly.'

'We're both doctors, for goodness' sake!'

'Yes, but there's something else.' He was forcing himself to look at her. 'This… drive I have.'

'The quest for perfection?'

'That's part of it, but it goes further.'

'I don't understand.'

'A need not just to meet challenges, but to seek them out. That's why I took the Tommy's job. It's one of the most demanding there is.'

'And Harley Street?'

'To give me the flexibility to do things my own way. No health service. No hospital managers. Patients prepared to go the whole way, accepting the risks. Trusting in me.' He coughed nervously, as if unused to laying bare such inner motives. 'It's not the money. That doesn't interest me.'

'So where's the problem?'

'I could be difficult to live with.'

It sounded banal. Suddenly he was looking at her with startled eyes. Sarah saw that, true as his admission might have been, he had realised the danger of compromising the satisfaction of other needs, emotional and physical. And those needs concerned herself.

'I'm an independent sort of person too,' she said. 'Freedom on both sides would not be such a bad thing.'

'You think that? You really think that?'

'Yes. But I must tell you that I'm not quite ready to commit myself.' She laughed. 'I too have dreams, but they're not nearly so easy to understand.' She looked at her watch. 'I must go. A heavy day tomorrow and Alan must have gone by now. You'll take me home?'

'Reluctantly, yes.'

'But no coffee this time, agreed?'

He dropped her at the corner of the block. She waved once, then didn't look back.

It was Alice, not Alan, waiting outside her door. Beneath her eyes, moon crescents of smudged make-up told of genuine grief. 'I rang Brian, but there was no reply. Can I come in?'

Sarah could see Jeff pacing the pavement further along the street.

'You'd better both come in.'

They climbed in precise military steps, without speaking. Alice's platform shoes echoed around the concrete stairwell. The main light at the bottom threw Nosferatu-like shadows on the walls, turning Sarah's sense that Alice had no ordinary message to deliver to one of dread.

'Sarah, you'd better sit down.'

She obliged, clasping her knees between interlocking fingers fighting with themselves to achieve rest. 'I'm sitting down. What now?'

'We've lost Debbie.'

'Lost? What do you mean lost?' The fatuity of the remark hurt her because she knew what was coming.'

'You don't understand.' Alice's cracked words were little more than a whisper. 'They found her this morning. She'd been to the drugs cupboard during the night. She had access, of course. No-one thought about that.'

'But why?'

'You won't like this, Sarah.'

'Too bloody right she won't,' Jeff said.

'She blamed herself for Alan's sacking. They were close, apparently. I didn't know that.' Alice went to the drinks cupboard and poured each of them a whisky. She set a glass at Sarah's feet 'Here. Not sure you deserve it though.'

Jeff said, 'Isn't there something else she should know?'

'What?'

'Debbie was pregnant,' Alice said, 'Alan believes the unborn child was his.'

'Then it will be awful for him not to be sure.'

'Ah, but he still might.'

'How?'

'He asked for a sample from the foetus. He has a friend at Leicester researching DNA testing for paternity. Apparently it's possible now.'

'So?'

'Either way the result's going to hurt him.'

This was becoming a monumental assault on Sarah's integrity. She could feel her brain begin to compartmentalise, as it always did when faced with conflict. Guilt was uppermost, for she had been the cause, no doubt. But, against that, had she not been forced into an action that was ethically justified? In fact she'd been put in a position of no choice at all. If anyone was to blame it was Alan himself, with his daft and irresponsible attitudes. Alan, who had all along held a blade to her side, seeing through her as no one else seemed to, relishing her discomfort. Her response was a long time coming but she was powerless to stop it. 'Good.'

'Sarah, what did you say?'

'Good. Bloody good show! It's the lesson he deserves.'

'Sarah!' Alice screamed.

'I can't believe what I'm hearing,' Jeff said.

He had been standing by the window, thoughtful, apart from them. Suddenly he leapt across the room, grasped Sarah by her lapels, lifted her clear of the chair and hurled her backwards onto the sofa. 'Little bitch! He's still a friend to some of us!'

It was not within her to deviate now. Quietly she lifted herself to her feet. With as much force as she could muster she slapped Jeff's cheek. The nails drew blood.

Alice switched on the main room light and stared at them wide-eyed.

Within her chest Sarah's pounding heart found new excursions. 'You think I've taken leave of my senses, don't you. But I warn you, he's not the only one who'll suffer!'

'You're insane,' Jeff called, as she raced towards the bedroom. The ice-cold novelty of the remark stopped her dead. She turned and stood in the doorway, watching them, her defences melting away.

Alice reached for the telephone. 'I'm going to call Brian. Maybe he can do something.'

The call was answered immediately. Perhaps he was expecting one. 'Brian, can you come over? Sarah's not well. Yes, straight away please.' She put the phone down.

'Why so abrupt?' Jeff asked.

'Can't risk him prevaricating and not coming.'

Brian arrived ten minutes later. Sarah, flat on the bed, could hear them through the half-open door. 'She's in the bedroom,' Alice told him.

He stopped within the doorframe, uncertain what to do. She saw he was carrying a bouquet of roses, the blooms numerous and large, the colours subtle. The sentiment seemed out of character. She heard herself say, 'Ooh, they're lovely. Thank you, Brian,' then cringed within herself at the stupidity of her predicament.

Brian stepped forward sheepishly. 'But they're not from me, Sarah. I picked them up from the hall table on the way in.' As he gave them to her the card bearing her name flicked open. 'They're from a Mr Preston and there's a note with them.'

8

At the time, Edwin's retirement from St Catherine's passed without much notice: his age was about right, his achievements substantial enough. There was a suggestion of impending ill health, but those close to him thought he'd seeded the idea deliberately in the staff common room. His medical colleagues wished him well and that should have been the end of it.

A well-intentioned reporter from the Bermondsey Gazette, living locally and in touch with the hospital community, decided to write a piece about him. All might have been well had the investigation stopped with the man himself: the story would have flickered brightly, then died. Instead he started with nursing staff and patients, including two who had been on the ward when Sarah discovered Alan with Debbie. It was only a matter of time before the tabloid press got wind that something was amiss. The *Sun* had a first page headline: *Nurses Having Sex – Your NHS*, with photos of a nervous Nurse Trubshaw and a grinning Alan Murphy taken out of context. The *Mail* ran a longer piece chastising the hospital administration and calling for the Dean's head. Sarah found herself lauded as a whistle blower, then ostracised by her medical colleagues. Only Brian seemed to have benefited: he was needed to run the unit. Alice, swallowing hard, cultivated Brian from a

117

respectful distance. Alan, meanwhile, had gone to ground.

The end of Sarah's house job was approaching at alarming speed. Two applications to other London hospitals had already been turned down. Without Edwin as a reference the task had fallen to Brian and she had no idea what he had said. She asked him: could she stay at Catherine's? 'Difficult with Edwin's shadow still hanging over the unit, Sarah. Besides, you need to widen your experience.' As he said it he turned away from her, but not before she had seen the curious sideways glance that told her the decision had not been easy.

It wasn't difficult to explain Brian's equivocation. He'd failed her when she flipped, that night six weeks before with Alice and Jeff, after which the claw marks on Jeff's face had been an embarrassing reminder to him until they – but obviously not the inner scars – had healed. But that was not all that bugged him, as he let slip to Sarah over the theatre table: this man Mark, who knew Edwin, seemed to be constantly hovering in the background. Brian, who seldom visited her at home, happened to be there delivering a research paper when Mark rang.

'Sarah-Jane, it's Mark.' She motioned to Brian that the call might take a while; to her relief he picked up his papers and left. 'I'm wondering why I've not heard from you.'

She was fairly sure the ball had been in his court after their lunch together at L'Atelier Jean-Jacques. One day she would realise that this was a ploy and second nature to him, this casual passing of responsibility, and blame. But now, momentarily clutching the receiver to her chest, the light in the room was already becoming brighter and the flowers outside the window a little more colourful. Stay in control, she told herself.

'Good to hear from you, Mark… yes, very busy… doing what? Well, applying for house jobs for one thing.'

'Yes, that's something I wanted to talk to you about. Are you free this evening?'

She knew she was. 'Let me just check… yes, any time after five.'

'Six, then, for a ride in the country.'

'A magical mystery tour?'

'Exactly that.'

'Six, then.'

She threw herself backwards onto the sofa, grabbed a cushion and hugged it. The plaster ceiling decoration above the grubby beige shade, why hadn't she noticed it before? Her eyes followed its radiations and whirls, absorbing its intricacies. It reminded her of a clock-face and then the time: heavens, it was three already, what on earth to wear. Why hadn't she asked where they were going? It should still be warm enough for a light blouse, not out of place with the grey trousers, and the matching top if things turned formal. And the amber brooch like the ceiling pattern: that would look great.

She was standing back from the window as the plum E-type drew stealthily into the kerb. She watched him get out, purposefully, without hesitation. A jacket, but no tie. Informal, good. Clattering down the stairs she felt the euphoria of release. The front door opening was like a prison gate promising freedom. The light flooding around him had a Mediterranean quality she had not experienced for a very long time. He was holding something out to her, but not the expected flowers. 'From a grateful client this morning, and I thought…' 'He's lovely,' she said, cradling the toy bear in her arms. She smiled at him and saw that he was watching her reaction with interest and amusement; and something else?

'The thing is, Sarah Jane, a recent sad event has resulted in something quite the reverse. You wouldn't have known

Matthew Bridges, a long-standing business associate. He and Myra, his wife, had a passion for hunting – and for collecting zoological specimens. You remember the rare birds in the Tower, for example. In Tanzania a month ago he was killed by a charging elephant. His shot missed and, well, to come to the point, Myra isn't coming back and has offered me first refusal on her house at Shirley Hills. You know Shirley Hills, near Croydon? I thought we'd take a look. 'Ah, I see from your face you were expecting dinner.'

'No, not at all!' She laughed. Was he being serious?

'So I've made provision.' He raised the lid of the boot, revealing a large wicker hamper. 'Fortnum and Mason's finest. The terrace overlooks a lake. A perfect setting.'

'And the weather? You've fixed that too?'

'The weather as well.'

The Dell was a quiet lane lined by chestnut trees, leading nowhere in particular, separating the houses on one side from the golf course on the other. Mansions, villas – she didn't know what to call them; grand, anyway, set far back, their lawns sloping gently to the road.

'Here it is – Hightower.'

The name was on a brass plate embedded in the brick pillar. She felt a tingling at the nape of her neck. 'Is that significant?'

'A connection, yes,' he replied. 'Of course.'

They stood at the door while he felt in his pocket for the key. She thought it might be in his mind to carry her across the threshold. He didn't, but it wouldn't have surprised her. Minutes later, sitting on one of the red velvet sofas in the drawing room, she wondered why she had allowed herself to think that. So much was opening up to her. Was it sensible to let her thoughts race ahead?

Mark returned from an inspection of the garages. 'Myra

never mentioned a vintage Bentley. Maybe we should keep quiet about that.'

'Definitely part of the contents.'

'I'll check the inventory.' He sat beside her. 'I've taken the food to the terrace and found a bottle of *Château Pétrus* in the cellar. Before we eat, though, a little business.'

'Please don't spoil anything.'

'No, I promise. Sarah Jane, let me first be blunt, I know your situation.'

'That I shouldn't have blown the whistle?'

'No… no, not that. It's more that – and don't take this the wrong way – I'm not sure that a busy London hospital is the right environment for you.'

'How could you possibly deduce that?'

'Through Edwin, and latterly through your friend Brian.'

'Brian?'

'He hasn't told you? Well, from time to time medical services are required at the Tower. He seemed an ideal choice. Only yesterday one of our companions – you remember companions? – happened to trip and fall. I believe Brian benefitted greatly.'

'Then good luck to him.' He looked at her sharply with raised eyebrows, querying what he had heard. She changed her tone. 'I'm pleased for him,' she said simply, and with relief saw his features relax.

'But we're digressing. I think… I know, that you may have difficulty finding another appointment. But I also know that you are a caring and potentially competent doctor.'

'Fair so far.'

'To come to the point, I serve on the board of the Beckenham Hospital, where a part-time job has come up in vascular surgery. He took a sheet of paper from his jacket pocket. 'Here are the details. Would you think about it?' He got up, as if to minimise what he said next. 'There would be strings.'

'Oh?'

'I'll tell you later.' He held up his palm against her enquiring smile. 'Let's go to the terrace.'

The light was beginning to fade. There were frissons in the creeper trails falling from the trellis above. Stepping onto the sandstone flags Sarah was unprepared for the flickering lamps on the walls and the already laid table with its crisp white cloth, silver cutlery and crystal glass. She was startled to find they were not alone: far back in the shadows, visible only because of her long white dress, stood a girl of oriental caste. Was it Maia? Sarah walked towards her, smiling, and was disappointed that it was only a clone.

'Don't worry. Jamela will serve us and then retire,' Mark said. Was it possible that he knew of... no, surely Edwin would have been discreet. Wouldn't he?

The girl came forward to light the oil lamp on the table. The flame was curious: its multiple orange components glowed independently in the gentle air, moving this way and that like a miniscule bonfire in the wind. 'It's the combination of oils,' Mark said, 'chosen so that they don't mix properly, always in conflict.'

'A bit like me,' she volunteered.

Sarah became absorbed by his face in the shifting light: one moment reserved and stern, the next benevolent and impish. It was as if he had set up the lamp to profile himself for her. But wasn't the reverse more likely: that he was scrutinising her? She began to feel bold in his company, capable of holding her own. 'Mark, what is it you want to know?'

'Gracious, am I that transparent? Or is it just feminine intuition?'

'Maybe I just worked it out.'

'Then a bit of background, perhaps. For example, Edwin once said you had a sister.'

'Elizabeth, yes.'

'Older, younger? More beautiful... no, that's impossible.'

'Three years older, cleverer and, yes, more beautiful.'

'Then you must have envied her.' He leaned forward and gazed at her, as if to discover why her expression had changed.'

'I admired her. Worshipped her sometimes. But envied her, no. She was a very unhappy person. I've no idea why.'

'Perhaps your parents favoured you.'

'We can definitely rule that out.'

'You were persecuted? As a child?'

'A bit, but I think I was more an irrelevance.'

'So what made your sister... relevant?'

'I've never thought about it in that way.'

'Maybe you should. Didn't she confide in you?'

'We shared a room, when I was very small. Later we had our own, of course, next to each other. She made up for what my parents lacked: the ability to channel any affection they had for me. My father because he didn't know how, my mother because she was weak and seemed to copy him.'

'But it was not you they resented.'

'Resent? That's a strange word.'

'But strikes a chord?'

'There was always an atmosphere. They seemed for ever to be on edge. I've no idea why.'

'Really no idea?'

For the first time that evening he smiled the wide captivating smile with which he had first greeted her at the Massingham Tower.

She barely noticed Jamela topping up the wine glass in her hand. Mark raised his. 'To our future.'

'That's rather vague, but okay, to our future.' They clinked glasses and suddenly she caught his meaning. 'You mean our future *together*?'

'Sorry. Deep down I'm a simple, shy man.'

She should resist, get up and demand to be taken home. The ride here, this house, the balmy evening no doubt deliberately chosen – how long had he been waiting for that to come along?

'I ought to be getting back,' she said. 'A busy day tomorrow.'

'Tomorrow is your day off.'

'Really? I see I can't win.'

'Look around you, Sarah Jane. This could be yours. You need want for nothing.'

'But you mentioned strings.'

'One is that you disentangle yourself from London hospital life. Beckenham would be a pleasing backwater.'

'And two?'

'That we would allow each other…' For the first time she saw him blush. '… a certain… latitude. You have cast your net wide Sarah Jane, everyone knows that. It would be difficult for you to… Which brings me to the purpose of this evening.'

'We don't yet know one other.'

'Exactly that.'

The meal over they wandered into the conservatory. 'Myra had a deft touch. To me this is a glasshouse worthy of Kew. And all this in only ten years. These rare *Attelea* palms, see how they've reached almost to the roof. I'll find it difficult to cut them back.'

'Extend the roof upwards, then.'

It raised a small smile. 'The Massingham solution, you mean?'

From the glass door to the house the marble floor of the conservatory widened into a central area with cushioned benches and tables; from there wide doors opened southwards onto the lawn. In the centre, as the focal point of the whole structure, stood a fountain, or, rather, a perfect dome of water, seemingly motionless and barely identifiable as such until you touched it. 'You have to listen hard to hear it, so precise is the engineering,' Mark said. 'But watch.'

He had taken from his pocket a leather box a little smaller than a Rubik's cube. He inserted his hand into the flow so that the waters parted, forming an aperture. Then, with his other hand, he placed the box on what must have been a shelf inside. 'That's secret,' he said, savouring her fascination and forestalling her question. Withdrawing his hand the waters closed, becoming immediately perfect.

They sat together on a bench above the lake, under a bright moon in a sky dabbed with wispy cloud. Scents of jasmine and honeysuckle, and others Sarah did not recognise, wafted from the pergola behind. Mark placed an arm around her shoulders. It was the first time he had touched her, properly touched her. It was the moment she had longed for since the day they had met. He said, 'You asked what I wanted. What I want is you, Sarah Jane, and have done since you came down those stone steps in the Tower and I willed you to stumble so that I had an excuse to hold you.'

Back in the house she was surprised to find Jamela waiting for them at the foot of the stairs.

'I haven't brought my…'

'You will have everything you need,' Mark said. 'I'll join you when you've made yourself comfortable. Jamela will tell me when.'

She followed Jamela's sinuous progress up the stairs. The girl stopped on the landing, full in the moonlight flooding through the window. She raised her arms above her head and rotated her body, slowly, in a complete circle. Her eyes widened in invitation. What did she know, this girl? But this time Sarah's thoughts were wholly elsewhere. The test passed, Jamela lowered her arms, smiled and walked on into the bedroom. 'It will be wonderful,' her expression said. She left Sarah contemplating a complete collection of her favourite toiletries neatly arranged on the dressing table surface.

She awoke. There was no-one to pull the curtains or bring her tea. But there was an envelope on her pillow. She opened it with trembling fingers and read the note:

My Dearest Sarah Jane

Do not be alarmed that I left early for town. I thought you would wish to have time to reflect without being under any pressure. The house is yours for the day if you need it and no-one will disturb you. There are no longer doubts on my side.

If you decide that the future is for us you should retrieve the little box from the fountain. If not just press the blue button on the phone and a taxi will be at the gate in twenty minutes.

Affectionately,

Mark

There was a perfect stillness about the house that had bitter-sweet resonance. She'd felt something similar the day her sister was buried and she'd returned home ahead of the others to prepare the food, though actually to grieve. The clock chiming – as the longcase clock in the hall at Hightower did now – seemed then to mark off a period of existence that could be put behind, telling that whatever came next could not possibly be as difficult. The difference now was the element of choice. The future was for the taking. But could she just throw herself upon fortune?

In the morning room breakfast was laid out for her. She poured herself some coffee – food could wait for later – and wandered with it into the kitchen. Gone were any signs of activity, as there must have been, in clearing up from the night before. She smiled at Mark's deception with the hamper. No picnic basket could have included the dishes that Jamela served. The girl, too, seemed to have gone.

Out in the garden the warmth of the sun had brought myriad insects to hover over the richly coloured beds of acanthus, canna and ligularia. At the lake dragonflies skimmed the clear water. She saw a tiny rowing boat moored there and climbed in. Lying back with her arms over the sides, she paddled it to the centre with her hands. Lazily turning the boat in the water she took in the woodland beyond the paddocks, then, nearer, the cedar stables, silent and empty. Between them and the house lay the rose garden. She paddled to the shore, tied up the boat and made for it, hoping that new sensations there might inform her decision.

Was there really a choice? Did she know enough about him? Enough to know that he was unlikely to be physically threatening, for he was not alone in doing his homework. Given safety, there was a promise that her freedom would not be too harshly limited. Saying goodbye to Catherine's would be no hardship after all that had happened. And while patients were important to her, she was no altruist, or so she thought. The Beckenham hospital would be an ideal compromise. Shouldn't she ask someone, just to be sure? But there was no-one, was there? She had no friends, not even a functional mother. So, then, what the hell. She marched into the conservatory.

The perfect dome of water shimmered in the sunlight

filtering through the palm-fronds above. She sat on one of the benches and stared at it, knowing that she had reached a landmark in her life. Then she thrust her hand in and with the other extracted the little box. It contained the expected diamond ring, which she placed on her finger; there was also a set of car keys.

She drove back to town singing in her own brand new, flame-red Lamborghini. She hoped that Elizabeth – wherever she was – would be happy for her.

SHIRLEY HILLS

May 1986 – May 1987

9

The years of her marriage – her time at Shirley Hills – had been squandered; that she now knew. The paradox was that she'd taken refuge in the very things that, deep-down, repulsed her. The allure of an affluent suburban lifestyle had been a kind of safety net when her contract at the Beckenham hospital had ended and she'd chosen not to renew it. The decision had been reinforced by her friends – or perhaps more likely Mark's, especially those whose husbands were not succeeding – for whom such a lifestyle was the pinnacle of ambition. Their dictum – 'you're so lucky' – could have been the motto for the group that surrounded her.

One day she had glanced down before sitting at her dressing table. She saw the embroidery of the seat was becoming threadbare. Sitting there, day after day, month after month, she'd peered into the mirror with ever increasing frequency and closeness at the tiny valleys that were beginning to cross her forehead and the arrow heads pointing to the corners of her eyes. She would never admit to herself that it was only she who saw them, though she was right in thinking that her friends – such as they were – did from time to time have her face under surveillance.

Stretching back over the five years since her marriage were those three-weekly rituals that were Mark's social gatherings: lunches in preference to dinners; barbeques rather than buffets indoors. And here was another paradox: for all his charm to the outside world as a *bon viveur* she knew now that he had the makings of a recluse. She saw it in little, trivial things: undue attention to the integrity of the perimeter fences and hedges; his switching of the telephone to automatic answering when he was sitting by it; an extravagance in his ordering for the wine cellar, as if some alien force was about to lay siege.

But to outsiders they were still the same privileged couple, wanting for nothing.

The first dent in that outward image came when Mark was asked to be godfather to the Simpkins' second child. Against her better judgement, Sarah-Jane had accompanied him. It was the fact of being a second child that had struck home, and she had felt the eyes around the font all asking, 'And why not you?' The 'why not' she had never previously thought to address. Whatever the reasons for her childlessness were, they seemed to reside in the preservation of her figure and a temerity towards disturbing a non-challenging, if dull, existence. The christening had forced her to think about eventualities.

Did Mark want children? Had they ever discussed it? In not discussing it she had assumed not, and perhaps he was as scared as she about introducing a factor that might break the fragile shell that contained them both. But the idea of a child must have taken root, for more than once, in a bookshop, she had found herself drifting towards the maternity care section; and on another occasion, at the doctors', she'd leafed through the pregnancy pamphlets on the rack. Yet in spite of that, she had not once suggested to Mark that they should not 'take precautions,' as he called it. Why was that? Perhaps she knew that infidelity – his, not hers, in this instance – could present a real hazard to her; and she didn't need to be medically qualified to appreciate the risks of unprotected sex in their particular social stratum. That, she knew, was not the reason, but she was at a loss to say what was. Alice had once hurt her by saying – as if innocently, but she could not be sure – 'I don't really see you as a mother, Sarah' and holding her gaze just long enough to see whether she had been stung by it. These thoughts – which came and went at all sorts of odd times – were like dancers around a totem pole; their origin was obscure, but they were becoming more persistent.

It was not long after such thoughts began to surface that Mark suggested they take on an *au pair*.

'Whatever for?'

'Just that you've been looking tired lately.'

'Too much sitting and staring into the mirror.' The sarcasm of her self-criticism was usually lost on him.

'Exactly,' he said. 'A companion would get you out of yourself.'

'And how do we go about that?'

'Girls are always writing for work with the Foundation. I'll bring back a selection of their letters.'

She knew what to expect: a choice already made from a handful of letters passed to her over the breakfast table. Only one deserved a second look, and then only because the English was just intelligible. Marguerite Renard, eighteen years old, six weeks at a Cambridge language school after her *baccalauréat*. And not much else apart from liking the English.

At the top of the letter, Sarah-Jane noticed, was a discoloured spot that might have been dried adhesive gum.

'No photo with it?' she asked.

'I expect it fell out when I gathered them up. I'll check my desk.'

'You do that.'

From this exchange Sarah-Jane deduced that the girl

was at least pretty. Then something curious happened: an unexpected shiver of excitement passed through her body. It was inexplicable because the first thought of another woman sharing the house should have been of flashing red lights.

They drove together to fetch her from East Croydon station and found her absorbed in the billboards extolling the night life of Croydon. As she turned, the dark hair blew across her face. She parted it with her hands, revealing a pair of brown eyes that simultaneously expressed amused boldness and timid uncertainty.

Sarah-Jane looked instinctively towards Mark and the girl for signs of mutual recognition but could find none. The two kisses that should have been perfunctory were held just long enough for Sarah-Jane to feel the warmth of her cheeks. Mark carried her rucksack to the car. You must sit in the front, she told Marguerite; then, from behind, she scrutinised the pair carefully for portents of things to come.

In the weeks that followed, to Sarah-Jane's immense relief, the girl proved adept at establishing her own work patterns around her new mistress. The question of why she was there gradually receded from her mind. In spite of Marguerite's occasional flights of Gallic ebullience the two women became, if not exactly friends, then at least sympathetic towards one another. At times they were even glad to be in each other's company.

It seemed to be the arrival of Marguerite that re-invigorated Sarah-Jane's relationship with Alice. No matter that it was probably prompted by curiosity on Alice's part. After all, Sarah-Jane had nothing else new or of particular interest to offer.

When Alice had married Brian some four years before – and about a year after Sarah-Jane had left Catherine's – the couple had bought a dilapidated Georgian house in Putney.

She remembered stomping around the echoing rooms while Alice relayed Brian's grand plan for restoration.

Almost a year later Sarah-Jane and Mark were invited to see the outcome. Remembering Brian's meticulous attention to detail, Sarah-Jane was not surprised at the result. What did surprise her was Mark's apparent familiarity with the house: for example, how he approached a certain armchair in way that could only have been habitual; how his attention was drawn to a particular painting that Brian told her afterwards was the only one that was new. But then he and Brian were friends, so why should that not be so? 'Yes,' said Alice, 'Mark's here quite often, but usually when I'm out.' When she thought about it afterwards the visit told her as much about her relationship with Alice – whom she sometimes met in town – as it did about her husband.

Events arise in life that, with hindsight, are turning points. The Prestons' first encounter with Mrs Adams was one of them. Mark – how well she would come to remember it – was leaning against the mantelpiece, boring her with his latest business venture. They watched her coming up the drive, in measured and determined tread, collecting box in hand.

Tell her to come in, Mark had shouted to Marguerite. The woman paused in the doorway, a brown-grey figure of middle age and above average height. Her body had an angularity begging to be set off by uniform, because the features had horizontal elements, like the wide firm mouth, the short fringed hair and even the flatness of the uppers of her brown leather shoes. Mark would later brand her Salvation Army; Sarah-Jane likened her to an ageing Julie Andrews with chronic indigestion. She greeted them with uninvited shakes of the hand and an unwavering smile.

She had a grand-daughter with cerebral palsy, Clare, her widowed son Jack's girl. That's how it had begun. Now she spent most of her time collecting for medical charities; this one happened to be for a scanner but there were three or four others whose committees she chaired.

Mark must have liked her, otherwise he would not have asked.

'I will put a golden guinea into your box for five minutes of your time,' he said, writing a cheque for a hundred pounds for the Beckenham Hospital Scanner Appeal and waving it in front of her nose. 'I have a distinguished medical colleague who is on his way to establishing a new plastics unit at that very hospital. Is that the sort of thing you and your friends might be interested in? My own involvement, I must tell you, is strictly on the construction side.'

It was some while before he told Brian of their new accomplice: it had taken time to check her out through his police contacts. By then the fundraising committee had been established. When Brian came to address the inaugural meeting Sarah-Jane was amused at his astonishment at finding sixty or so like stalwarts packed into the local community hall.

Outwardly the dutiful wife in public, Sarah-Jane began to dust off her abandoned medical credentials and take an active interest. For a while the two women worked amicably enough together.

Even Mrs Adams was at a loss to explain the torrent of donations. There were cheques, each for many thousands of pounds, from the most fashionable addresses in the capital. She confided that, partly out of curiosity, she had tried to call on the donors but had not once managed to get past security. They are private people, Sarah-Jane told her, repeating Brian, and best left that way if you want their help.

The new wing was completed in March and opened in April, with a ceremony at the hospital to be followed by a lavish reception at Hightower.

It was then – just over a year before the assault on her face – that Sarah-Jane's difficulties really began.

Bunting in stabbing triangles of white and liver – Sarah-Jane's suggestion, her only one, as lip service to the surgical theme – fluttered between pennants at either end of the concrete and glass mass appended to the western wing of the hospital. The lintel of the central portico bore the words *Khasoni Centre for Surgical Endeavour*. Beneath it, ushers in beige jackets and black bow ties herded in the remaining stragglers from the terrace, then closed the doors behind them. Unlike them – though she didn't realise it then – Sarah-Jane was still only dimly aware of who Khasoni was. But she was sure he had visited the house. Or at least she had, one dark evening, seen a Rolls with the registration number KHA1 parked discreetly between the trees, the plate momentarily visible when the chauffeur, standing guard, happened to light a cigarette. And she, by less chance, was walking back from the stables.

She was shown to a seat in the front row bearing her name. Besides Mark and Brian, sitting together, she recognised none of the half-dozen dark-suited, expressionless figures sharing the podium. Somehow their sobriety was at odds with the extravagance of the floral displays. It seemed that the act of taking her seat was the cue for Mark to rise. She became the uneasy focus for his delivery.

'My dear colleagues and friends,' he began. 'Today is one of those rare occasions in the development of medical science when we are able to put our names to something new and exciting to set against the contraction, compromise and defeat that has characterised medicine in London for the past decade. When Brian Davison first came to me with plans for what has now been realised, I have to say I was sceptical. No, worse, dismissive. Then one day he said to me, Mark, if you don't have faith in the scheme, at least let me show you…'

Shuffling in the row behind Sarah to admit a late-comer ended in the harsh scraping of chair-legs on the teak floor. A frown of recognition crossed Brian's otherwise inscrutable face, but there was no corresponding blip in Mark's delivery, which was curious. His eyes were still fixed on her.

'And so,' he continued, 'I met some of his patients in the clinics before and after treatment, and some, even, during their procedures. Financial questions remained, certainly, but the goal was no longer in doubt. Looking about me now I see faces glowing with satisfaction because you, too, made that same right judgement. I can tell you that there are people here…'

'Bullshit!'

The quiet expletive came from just behind Sarah-Jane's left ear. She rounded on the offender, ready to mete out brimstone in defence of her husband. But she could not.

Alan Murphy was looking straight at her with an expression that was no expression at all. Write on my face what you want to see, it said, and I will take it from there. But be careful, get it right, because it's important. For you I mean.

Brian was on his feet now. Sarah-Jane turned to the front, seeking refuge in what he was saying. She felt her face burn. Try as she might, she couldn't turn her head again. She imagined the thoughts that impelled themselves towards the back of her head. They hurt her, because their origin was in a hurt. But she would not, could not, look back. Try. No. Try. No!

Brian was talking in that clipped precise way of his, targeting faces in the audience, one by one, impaling them with logic and reason and the justification for his vision. Then he looked at her. She felt as if her head were being squeezed in a vice, from back and front. Are you ill, she asked herself, that you can be so weak? Pull yourself together, take control.

Mrs Adams was on the platform now, amid an orgy of mutual congratulation. One by one the dark figures slipped away. Glasses were raised. Sarah-Jane found one had been thrust into her hand and joined the toast, thankful for the distraction. Then the audience dispersed, groups hiving off to look at the surrounding sleek displays of equipment and microscopes, and posters red with carnal expositions of surgical practice. When finally she mustered the courage to look for him, Alan was no longer there.

Mrs Adams materialised from out of the departing crowd. 'Why did you not join us on the platform? We were calling for you.'

'I think I must have felt a little faint. It's very hot in here.'

'Yes, yes it is, and some fresh air you shall have.' She led Sarah-Jane through the door to the wide stone terrace overlooking the descending expanse of bare earth that would soon become lawn.

Sarah-Jane could see Alan Murphy talking to Jack Adams, who was idly pushing Clare's wheelchair back and forth in front of him. The child's presence there was unclear, but no matter, she and the child were good friends. Clare's head was to one side with the palsy, as it always was. Alan bent down beside her and inclined his own head at a similar angle. Without hearing a word it was obvious to Sarah-Jane he was offering to push the chair. Jack, laughing, let go of the handles with a thrust of his wrists and Alan took control.

A voice came from behind, deeply authoritative and resonant: 'Hello Sarah.'

'Edwin? I didn't know you were coming.'

'Why ever not? Your husband and Brian are still colleagues, in a manner of speaking. That was one thing at least that was not destroyed.' His voice seemed to carry no bitterness, and was at odds with his words.

Sarah-Jane had felt no regret when he lost his position at the hospital and the press had picked over his remains. Perhaps he had accepted it with grace, as he had once accepted the loss of his wife and daughter. When the story broke she had already left the hospital, although marriage to Mark was still to come. She had not seen Edwin, nor thought much about him, since. She had even forgotten that he had once been her husband's business partner. It came as a surprise to think that he still might be.

'Edwin, you brought it upon yourself. I had no hand in it.'

'My dear child, you misunderstand me. I was speaking of our relationship. It had such potential, though you could never see it.'

'Let's make the most of today, shall we? I've severed my links with that part of my life.'

'Have you, Sarah? Have you really? It's such a pity if you have. Besides, I would have thought it not to be the case.'

Sarah-Jane became aware of Mrs Adams at her elbow. The alignments of her square face seemed less rigid. Sarah-Jane felt relief. Here might be a friend, after all; but exploring that was for later.

'Come on you two! It's no good reminiscing about old times. It's the future we must look to.' She turned to Sarah-Jane. 'Shouldn't we be getting these people back to your place? It will be just marvellous in the garden if the weather holds.'

'You're right. I'd better go on ahead to check on things.' To Edwin, sweetly, she said. 'I'm sure someone will show you the way, if you've forgotten.'

'Don't worry your pretty head about it. I still have some influence, I'm pleased to say.'

Along the terrace Alan Murphy was making little charges with the wheelchair. The wheels rumbled on the flagstones. With each thrust the child screamed, though whether in terror or delight was difficult to tell. Nobody took much notice, except Edwin, who was looking on thoughtfully from a distance.

Sarah-Jane made her way down the steep flight of steps and along the road to where her car was parked behind a dense cluster of trees. She went slowly, recalling Edwin's remark of long before about skeletons from the past. Yet was it so remarkable to see him here with Alan? She realised how isolated from her former life she had become, and from the responsibilities it had bestowed. She had taken the route of leisure and idleness as if of right, and it had not until now occurred to her to question whether it should have been earned. Certainly there was little on the slate to mark her early promise, although that had always been the opinion of others, not her own. Did she really need three horses growing fat in their stables because she rarely rode them, or two gardeners to tend land on which neither she nor Mark set foot, or Marguerite… She had often told the image in the mirror that she was content, but could never bring herself to use the word happy. Possibly it was not so and her present skirmish with medicine was really a beckoning finger. Let's see where it leads. But no pressure, no urgency. After all, there was that little bit of modelling she did; that could still grow into something.

A faint dizziness as she reached the tarmac of the car park made her wonder about the punch. Otherwise she felt relaxed and confident. She had met those two relics from the past and weathered the experience. Perhaps they'd been with her all the time, deep in her subconscious, like rough garments unnoticed until the moment of taking them off.

Her Porsche was where she had left it, straddling the white line of the parking bay. A note on the windscreen suggested she should be more considerate in future. She tore it up, not bothering to read the signature. The car started with a roar. She pressed the accelerator with the clutch down, once, twice. The throaty sound of the engine gladdened her. She would be ahead of them all on the open road. She might even go via the lanes where she could work up a passable turn of speed.

She was glad she had persuaded Marguerite not to come to the opening, in spite of Mark's protests. At least everything would be ready. Later there would be a small band, with dancing on the terrace if it stayed fine. The attention would be more than she had experienced for a long time – well, of that collective kind anyway. Perhaps she would dance with Edwin, certainly with Brian. She would even allow Mark a little more rein, so that Marguerite might enjoy some competition for once.

It was not to be.

With hindsight it was a pity for her that those on the terrace had heard the revving of her engine. It left in some an impression of irresponsibility that would prove difficult to shift, in spite of other evidence in her favour.

As the car emerged from the trees the wheelchair was already gaining momentum down the flight of steps leading from the terrace. The contraption lurched from side to side, scraping the stonework. The child it carried resembled a rag doll with its head swinging wildly. A second figure just behind tumbled over itself in a desperate attempt to stop the flying chair.

The first sound, other than the squeal of brakes, was of the metallic crushing of the chair under the nearside front wheel. The second was of Alan Murphy's body slamming against the rear door. The brakes slewed the car round so that it was pointing at the two figures sprawled on the tarmac like abandoned, spilled luggage. It seemed to Sarah-Jane that some malevolent force had manhandled the car just so she should see the destruction she had caused. An extrusion of frantic activity at the bottom of the steps formed itself into a ring around the stricken figures. The worst of it for Sarah-Jane was that they ignored her, even when she got out of the car.

That was not to last.

'It was an accident.'

'It was no bloody accident. She could have stopped if she'd wanted.'

'Blame that idiot medic, if you have to blame anyone.'

'At least he's sorry. Look at him, poor sod. But there's nothing he can do for her.'

'She was going too damned fast.'

'Doesn't everybody?'

Sarah-Jane looked around desperately for Mark. She must have called his name.

'He'll be coming, Sarah. Just keep calm.'

Brian appeared. She flinched as he put his arm around her shoulders. 'It wasn't your fault and there's nothing you can do.'

'She was so helpless, Brian.'

'But you're not, so pull yourself together. We'll stand by you.'

It seemed to her that an accusing finger had never been pointed more directly.

Her dry lips stuck to the white tube she had to breathe into. When the colour changed Mark looked grim. 'That's a great help, but never mind.'

'I tried to say I was sorry,' Sarah-Jane said. 'I tried. He wouldn't listen.' With her handkerchief she dabbed at the muddy brown rivulets coursing down her cheeks.

'Did you expect anything else?' Mark said.

'Jack loved that child.'

'Yes he did,' Brian said. 'It gave point to their lives, to the whole family. And to the fundraisers. She was a cult figure, that girl.'

Mark said quietly, 'That's enough, Brian. Let's get some coffee and organise a clear-up at home, before it rains.'

The evening Jack Adams called Sarah-Jane was alone in the darkened drawing room, curled up in her now characteristic position on the sofa. The world was marking time around her, waiting for the result of the inquest in two days' time. Until that was over she could settle to nothing and had no appetite for anything except profound reflection. In her mind images of her past life were becoming increasingly vivid and intrusive.

Mark was not expected back until ten. 'We're draining the lagoon,' he'd said. 'I need to be there to stop them flooding the building.' Marguerite had the evening off and could be there or anywhere. That didn't matter now.

She led Jack into the dark room. He asked if the light could be switched on. She obliged with a little shrug of the shoulders, resentful of being told what to do in her own home, though the request was reasonable enough.

With him standing precisely where his mother had once stood it was impossible not to compare them. Here was none of Marjorie Adams' authority that achieved its ends by marshalling the efforts of others. In its place she saw an aggressive sullenness that she was unable, then, to dissect into its components of tiredness and grief. There was weakness where his mother had strength; and for Sarah-Jane that perceived defect became the focus for the inner poisons that sought escape. The best course was to take command. 'You may sit if you want to. Can I offer you anything? Some tea?'

He looked bewildered, expecting from her compassion and sympathy. 'Sarah-Jane, I need to talk to you.'

'I don't see what there is to talk about. I told you at the time I was not to blame and that hasn't changed.'

'Sarah…'

'Look, I know you're upset and you're entitled to be. Clare meant something to me too, you know, in spite of what people have been saying. Actually I'm finding the whole blame thing difficult to take.'

Jack had been holding his cap to his side, but now clamped it between his knees. 'Not from me!'

'That's what I've heard.'

'Not from me. But from the way you're behaving, Sarah-Jane, I can understand it if people doubt your word.'

'What? What do you say?'

'A normal person would feel remorse and a wish to put things straight. You seem to want neither.'

'What is there to put straight? Your daughter was propelled under my car because of an infantile prank by someone who had hardly more sense than…'

Jack looked incredulous. 'What are you saying, Sarah-Jane, what are you saying?'

She had stepped into a morass from which it would be difficult to extricate herself. The options were now extreme contrition or a more violent thrust still that would carry her through and to hell with the consequences.

'You've gone too far, Sarah-Jane. What you are saying hurts me beyond endurance. I came here so there would be no rancour at the inquest to spoil Clare's memory. Instead her death has spawned… I don't know… some demon within you. Where it's come from and what you're to do about it… that's your problem. I want nothing more to do with it.'

Sarah-Jane said nothing.

'But I'll tell you something,' he continued. 'When I hear

the revving of that engine, every night, in my head, and see the car lurching from those trees…' He lowered his face into his hands.

Impelled by feelings over which she had no control Sarah-Jane crossed the carpet to stand above him, not knowing what she should do. But as he looked up her anger was forced from her. Something of the pain in his eyes jarred her body. She thought of her dead sister. An ethereal hand seemed to grasp her wrist, guiding her own to Jack's shoulder, where it rested limply, impossible to withdraw. 'I'm sorry,' she whispered. Nothing else would come into her head. She stood motionless, tears springing to her eyes. Jack rose slowly, gently removed her hand with a flicker of a smile, and left the room.

The dining table was set for five. Whether to include Marguerite had occupied Sarah-Jane's thoughts for much of the morning. To her surprise the decision, once made, had brought a measure of relief, if not pleasure. Precisely laid cutlery gleamed blue-grey under high tapering candles. In the centre low vases were bursting with cornflowers that the two women had picked and arranged together. She was still experimenting with the background lighting when the Davisons arrived. Marguerite, in simple white skirt and blouse chosen from her mistress's wardrobe, went to let them in. Sarah-Jane caught Mark's glance towards the departing figure, wondering what part he had played in that choice. Was the intention a considerate contrast with her own embroidered one-piece, or to emphasise the girl's dark complexion? Or was she just being paranoid?

Brian, avoiding eye contact, simply shook her hand. Alice was less inhibited.

'Mark tells me you've been able to put it behind you. I'm so glad.'

'Why shouldn't I? Sarah-Jane replied, mildly irritated. 'The coroner said I was not to blame. Nor Alan either, amazingly, but there it is.'

'It seems that the flagstone at the top of the steps had still to be cemented in.' Mark turned away from them to fill the sherry glasses. 'Funny no-one noticed it at the time.'

'Damn fool behaviour though, all the same,' Brian said. 'Nobody's seen him since, but Alice got a long letter from a village up north that no-one's heard of. He's obviously keeping his head down.'

'What puzzles me,' Sarah-Jane said, 'is why he was there in the first place.'

'Ah, you don't know?' Sarah-Jane saw in Alice's face a fleeting expression that brought back student days: it signified possession of knowledge that could be traded. 'It's simple enough really. I think it's because his name had just been restored to the medical register. It was a kind of coming out opportunity, do you see?'

'Then he certainly put it to good use.'

Brian said, 'What puzzles me is why there was no mention of the breathalyser test at the inquest.'

Mark stared at him. 'It seems the police made a mistake, Brian. It's easy to do.'

Alice said, 'I wondered that.'

'A mistake, okay? Let's leave it at that, shall we?'

Alice lowered herself into a chair, hands between knees, face blank but for a wisp of a smile, like a naughty child.

Sarah-Jane slid into the role of hostess. 'Now, I want to tell you about Mark's plans for the conservatory. Shall we all sit?'

The perfect meal drew to a close with Marguerite bringing in a platter of wild strawberries on a bed of aromatic leaves, the whole speckled with minute crystalline berries that Sarah-Jane had never seen before.

'Courtesy of the Massingham Foundation,' Mark said, as Marguerite excused herself and left the room.

Alice was impressed. 'You're so lucky, Sarah, to have a husband with that connection.'

'Well, perhaps.' Sarah-Jane hesitated, wondering how best to respond. 'We made an agreement, you see, when we were married, that home life and Massingham wouldn't be mixed. And mostly we've kept to it. This is an exception.'

Mark seemed anxious to change the subject; though, as they would shortly find, that was not what he had in mind. 'I wonder if you two ladies would excuse Brian and me for a few minutes. If we get our little business over now we can all relax for the rest of the evening.'

'Take your time,' Alice said, 'It will be nice to gossip with Sarah alone for a change.'

The awaited click of the door to Mark's study at the end of the corridor had the effect on the two women of a nail being driven into an over-inflated tyre. Sarah-Jane slumped forward over the table and buried her face on her folded arms. Alice lay on her back across two dining chairs, below the level of the table top.

'It's not that great, is it Sarah? I can tell.'

'Nope.' Sarah-Jane placed her chin on her arm. 'You know the worst thing? The assumption that I was somehow against Clare: as if there'd been some intent in what I did. And… and to give me no credit for having feelings towards the child. I have not slept, Alice, but not because of guilt.' She picked up a knife and began toying with it. 'One evening – and I haven't told this to a soul – Jack came round. I think he expected me to fall at his feet and beg forgiveness.' Sarah-Jane grasped the handle of the knife and Alice, who had raised her face above the level of the table at Sarah-Jane's sudden change of tone, watched her knuckles whiten. 'I can't repeat what he said to me.'

'Isn't that understandable, under the circumstances.'
Alice thought for a moment. 'You didn't taunt him, did you Sarah? You know how you can sometimes.'

'Perhaps. Anyway, there's something I want to show you.'

Sarah-Jane jumped up and walked to the writing desk in the far corner of the room. From beneath a mass of papers she withdrew a single sheet and handed it to Alice. 'This was the first of the hate letters. There have been others since, but this one's – how shall we say – different.'

Alice scanned the few typewritten lines. 'Tell me then.'

'Whoever wrote it was involved. It's not written from a distance like the others.'

'I wouldn't take it too seriously, Sarah.'

'And the bit about him watching me?'

'A crank, a nutter.'

'That's what I thought until yesterday.'

'So what happened yesterday?'

'There was a knock at the door. It was that woman three houses down, Mrs Fowler, who's always complaining about horse droppings in the road. Apparently she'd been walking the dogs on the golf course and come across a bloke with binoculars.'

'Bird watching, I should think.'

'Possibly, but from where she said she'd seen him in the bushes the only thing visible is this house. I walked up there later. You could even see where the grass had been flattened.'

'Sarah, you must be careful! What did he look like?'

'Cap pulled down, beard she thought, scruffy mac. No one she knew.'

The men's voices sounded in the hall. Sarah-Jane thrust the letter back into the pile. But the footsteps continued past the door, in the direction of the conservatory.

'I'm glad your marriage has worked out, Sarah. We all wondered about it at the time.'

The two women had not found themselves in so intimate a situation since the Davisons had bought the house in Putney after their wedding and invited the Prestons to what turned out to be, overall, a stilted evening. It had puzzled both women that a friendship had later developed between their husbands, and more so that it had evolved independently of their own, so that Mark hardly knew Alice in spite of Brian's frequent presence at Shirley Hills. As for the women, they met in town occasionally, but that was all. Alice's observation on Sarah-Jane's marriage seemed to invite an exchange of confidences. Sarah-Jane, needing a friend, was receptive to the invitation.

'It's played to pretty strict ground rules, Alice, so don't be misled.'

'Meaning?'

'Oh, basically my comfort for his freedom. Not that he neglects me, you understand, but there's a quirkiness about the arrangement I could sometimes do without. Like my crazy public name which – God knows why – he likes. That was part of the package.'

'I did wonder. But why leave medicine?'

'I've thought about it often. Responsibilities I couldn't face up to, I suppose. I was tempted to go back and probably would have if it hadn't been for the accident. Mark wouldn't like it – dutiful wife and all that – but couldn't exactly stop me.'

'We'd love to have you back.'

Sarah-Jane smiled to herself because Alice could not have guessed that the freedom she had grudgingly bestowed on her husband was hers also in equal measure. By unspoken agreement the daytime hours were hers and only Marguerite, who was regularly despatched on a variety of spurious errands, had any real inkling of what that entailed. And Marguerite knew well enough on which side her bread was buttered. But such things were not for Alice's ears, at least not yet.

So she just said: 'Yes, I gather so. Brian has asked me a number of times.'

'Has he? He never said.' Alice hesitated. 'In fact he doesn't tell me much really.' Another pause, as if she were gathering herself to jump a hurdle. 'It's not a very happy relationship, Sarah. He's so wedded to his work. You'd think, as a fellow medic, I'd be ideally placed to keep up – but I can't. There's some hidden agenda, and I don't know what it is.'

'Fame? Fortune?'

'No, they're incidental. It's something much more inward looking. The way he looks and acts. It frightens me sometimes. But he's kind enough when he thinks about it.'

They heard the men returning. Mark appeared in the doorway, grinning broadly. 'Sarah-Jane must leave the room for one minute, because we have something to show her.'

Sarah-Jane dutifully obeyed and Mark stood aside to let her pass, brushing her cheek with his fingers. On the minute she returned.

On the wall facing the door was an exquisite portrait in oils. It showed her siting demurely, wistfully, on an armless chair, her long legs drawn up under her body and one side of her face illuminated by the light of a table lamp. On the table – and the subject of her rapt attention – a silver bowl of red roses. The artist had captured every nuance of her face and figure.

'It's beautiful!' She couldn't control her delight.

'We thought it would help to cheer you up. You recognise the artist, of course.'

She was reminded of the miniatures she had once

seen at Lightermen's Mansions. 'Brian?' she said. 'Brian, you really did that? For me?' She kissed his cheek, which immediately flushed pink. Then she turned to Alice, 'Alice, did you know about this?'

'No, I'm afraid I didn't,' Alice said, looking away to hide her anger and hurt pride. 'He's good at keeping things secret.'

Sarah-Jane's response was a half-smile that said don't begrudge me this little pleasure. Alice returned it with one which answered, sorry, for the moment I got my priorities wrong. Mark appraised the situation in a second. 'You come with me,' he said to Alice, 'while Sarah-Jane is doting over her own image. I'd appreciate your advice on revamping the conservatory. She tells me yours is looking quite superb.'

Alice followed forlornly, no doubt regretting she had not invited Sarah to see it.

Sarah-Jane's eyes had hardly left the painting. 'Brian, it must have taken you weeks.'

'No, Mark only asked me at the inquest. He gave me one or two photos to work from. I… um… cancelled a clinic to finish it.'

'That's praise in plenty!' Sarah-Jane took a step backwards. 'You know, if it was anyone else I'd say the artist was in love with his subject.' The remark was casual, without implication, but Brian's response made her turn sharply to look at him.

'Perhaps he is.'

'Poof, don't be ridiculous!'

'Why ridiculous? Artists can express emotion in their work.'

'It was just a way of saying I was pleased with it. Sorry.'

'Then I'm glad you like it.' He was ill at ease, fumbling with his cuff links, unable to say more.

Sarah-Jane thought it prudent to change the subject. 'Brian, may I ask you something?'

'Of course.'

'How well do you know Jack Adams?'

'Reasonably well. He was very helpful with the fund-raising. One of the few people who could understand the project and explain it to laymen. That was vital.'

'But personally. Does he harbour grudges, for example?'

'Why? Has he tried to contact you?'

'He came here one evening, yes.'

'My advice would be to keep out of his way for a while, until the dust settles. He'll come round eventually. After all, it was hardly your fault.'

'It wasn't my fault at all!'

'No, no, of course, but not everyone saw it that way.'

Sarah-Jane manoeuvred the subject back on course. 'Would you say he could be... well... threatening?'

'He has a bit of a... no, that's not right... can get a bit agitated sometimes. But vindictive, no. Why? Has he threatened you?'

Sarah-Jane fetched the letter she had shown to Alice. 'Have a look at this.'

'That's not his style, Sarah. You can discount the thought. But the letter's interesting. I have a psychologist friend who's into this sort of thing. May I show it to him?'

Sarah-Jane shrugged. 'If you think it's worth pursuing.'

'I promise I'll return it.' He refolded the letter. 'You haven't, by any chance, shown it to the police?'

'No, why?'

Brian appeared not to hear as he stuffed the letter into his wallet.

10

Winter passed and with the coming of spring Sarah-Jane's altercations with Mark increased. It was a pattern she had noticed, although to a lesser degree, the previous year when Mark's mood swings seemed to reflect the cycles of rain and shine. Once again the focus of his agitation was Marguerite, whom he claimed was becoming ever more bored with the monotony of life at Hightower. Actually, Mark had become aware that Marguerite's social life now extended well beyond Croydon and their own circle, and he had seen off a number of admirers from the city bold enough to call at the house. In short, Sarah-Jane thought, he was scared of losing her. Couldn't she, Sarah-Jane, find something new to occupy her? Like the horses, for example, which in any case were hardly earning their keep.

Marguerite's misgivings were tempered by the alluring prospect of being kitted out as a clone of Sarah-Jane. The two women drove to New Bond Street, where a full morning was spent trying on riding jackets, jodhpurs, hats and boots. Sarah-Jane had even to persuade Marguerite to put on her original clothes for the journey home. The following morning, both appropriately attired, they led the most docile of the horses – Pasta – into the paddock next to the rose garden.

Horse and rider had the rigidity of a statue of an

erstwhile general, except that Marguerite's lips quivered with frustration verging on panic.

'Move on!' Sarah-Jane called.

Marguerite's heels pounded the flanks of the confused animal but still it did not move.

'Loosen the reins.'

Pasta shot forward, moving rapidly through its gears until it was heading at a gallop for the fence bounding the paddock.

Sarah-Jane ran after, willing it not to jump. But the alternative was almost as bad: an abrupt halt with Marguerite grasping desperately at the animal's mane before sliding across its neck into the long damp grass .

'You said that on purpose!' Tears were running down Marguerite's cheeks.

'Of course I said it on purpose! How else did you expect the thing to move?'

Sarah-Jane grasped Marguerite's hands and pulled her to her feet. But, as their eyes met, the movement, initially abrupt, became gentle. Keeping hold of the girl's right hand she released her own to wipe a smear of dirt from the wet cheek, allowing her fingers to linger there for a moment longer than she intended. Now at the centre of the paddock Pasta paused to look at them, then continued grazing. 'We'd better go and retrieve the wretched animal,' Sarah-Jane said.

Marguerite wiped her hands on her less than pristine jodhpurs. 'Get it yourself,' she said, but her resentment was already dying.

As the two women advanced, Pasta retreated hoof behind hoof, in a passable display of dressage, maintaining a constant distance from them. Eventually the trio were back where they had started twenty minutes earlier.

'Try again.'

'No!'

155

'You will!'

Neither woman had seen Brian enter the gate and walk up behind them. 'Patience, patience, Sarah. Fighting with her will achieve nothing.'

Marguerite, calmer now, grasped the opportunity. 'I'll be going now, Miss. I'm sure you two want to be left alone.'

Sarah-Jane glared at her, then at Brian. 'If that girl so much as smells a blade of grass she's reduced to a gibbering idiot. She'd be happy living in a concrete bunker.'

'Quite. As it looks like rain why don't you put the poor beast away and make me some coffee?'

'Marguerite will…'

'You will.'

Once in the kitchen Brian spooned instant coffee into mugs. Sarah-Jane took an opened carton of cream from the fridge, sniffed it and set it beside him with a thump. Then she sat at the table with her head in her hands.

'Country life too stressful for you?'

'Probably.' She stared at him, not trying to conceal her antagonism. 'Why are you here? You usually only come when Mark's around.'

'I'm lecturing at Oxford on Thursday, at the Radcliffe. The treatment of facial tumours. I wondered if you'd like to come?'

'Not really, Brian, thanks.' Her spoon turned the cream in her cup over and over. 'But thinking about it, I do need to go home. I haven't been for ages and yesterday Mum's solicitors rang to ask me to call in. Heaven knows why. I suppose we could combine the two.'

'Easily.'

A niggling obligation potentially resolved, she suddenly felt relaxed. The cloud that had its origins in Marguerite's riding lesson lifted. 'I still like the picture, Brian. So does everyone who sees it. I think you cheated, though, in not making it full face.'

'Perhaps that one's still to come.'

She looked up in surprise: there was a darkness in the tone of his voice that shouldn't have been there.

Sarah-Jane was relieved when the taxi arrived to take her to High Wycombe. Bentley and Carruthers had offices near the centre of town, where a little regency terrace had become an anomalous enclave in a sea of concrete. There was something reassuring about its creeper-clad brick facade that attracted clients; and the partners, without trying too hard, had lived up to the image. They had served the Potters well for many years and one of the Carruthers brothers had been Elizabeth's godfather.

The narrative of Lionel Bentley's life included public school, profligacy, ruin and a clawing-back of respectability. That aside he was almost, but not quite, the perfect solicitor. The not quite part explained both why she was there and why she did not know why she was there.

'I'm going to leave the room, Sarah. Do you remember when you used to come here with your father and we would play I-Spy while he was talking to boring Carruthers? Well, I'm going to leave the room now and the clue is something beginning with W. Suddenly he looked sad and old. I should add that the game becomes more serious with the passing of time. I'm sure you will understand why.'

Window, wall, wicker basket... will! It was poking out from a neat pile of papers on a desk remarkably clear of the legal detritus that littered the rest of the room.

Sarah-Jane pulled out the copy of her mother's will and read: *To my daughter Sarah I bequeath my house and all its contents and all my jewellery and personal effects together with the sum of five thousand pounds.* And lower down: *To my dear friend Thomas Sharp I bequeath the residue of my estate.*

It took only a second for the significance to sink in,

confirmed by something she had at first thought odd: a single teetering stack of one pound coins precariously near the corner of the desk.

Bentley had re-entered the room without her hearing. 'Don't let them fall, Sarah; they are too valuable to lose.'

'I think I understand.'

'It's quite a relief if you do.'

'Mr Bentley, I'm sure I can ask you this. When my father died intestate...'

'That is our understanding, Sarah. Go on.'

She couldn't see where this was leading, but continued, '... why was his true financial situation not revealed?'

'Surely because it all went to your mother. A few years back she was in control. The house was in her name also, as were various accounts held jointly with your father. The rest happened to be insufficient to attract death duties, so nothing was ever publicised. You are not aware of the sums involved?'

'No.'

'Then perhaps you should raise the matter tactfully with your mother. The emphasis is on tact, Sarah.' He touched the side of his nose with his finger and winked. She could picture him with his back to the fire in a prim London club, communicating with the bar waiter behind the back of a demanding and obstreperous colleague.

Back in the general office he offered his hand. 'It was nice to meet you again, Mrs Preston. Do call again to see us.'

Brian arrived earlier than she had anticipated; her taxi followed his car into the drive. He walked back and offered to pay but she would not hear of it.

After they had eaten, Brian said, 'You remember that game – what was it? – that we once played? It would be jolly to do it again.'

'But Brian, you've got to get back to London. You must be exhausted after your paper.'

'I'm as right as rain, really. Though I thought perhaps I might ask if I could...'

'Mum,' Sarah-Jane called to the kitchen, 'Is there any more coffee left?'

She turned back to him, knowing that her words would hurt. 'Look, Brian, before you say anything. Five years is a long time and things change. I'm Mrs Preston now and we're in my mother's house. There are things you can't take for granted, or expect.'

'But you're not exactly a changed woman are you, Sarah?'

'Meaning?'

'That from what I've heard you're not too... well... discriminating, in your choice of...'

'Of men? Is that what you want to say?'

'I didn't say that.'

Sarah-Jane hunched her shoulders with the petulance of a small girl. 'If you just knew how trivial it's all been.'

'Then is there not an opportunity now for something better, more meaningful?' He waited for a response which did not come. 'You saw in the painting the depths that can be reached.' It was a bold card to play, but the timing was wrong.

'So I *was* right!'

'You were right.'

'But it still doesn't change anything. I'm grateful to you for bringing me but I'm not sleeping with you. It's probably better if you go.'

Betty Potter came in with a steaming pot of coffee on a tray.

'Brian miscalculated, Mum. He's got to rush off after all.'

At the gate she intercepted his car. Angrily he wound down the window.

'Stay friends with me, Brian. One day perhaps I'll have sorted myself out.'

Sarah-Jane took the precaution of drawing all the downstairs curtains, carefully closing any gaps.

'Mum, there's something we have to talk about urgently.'

'Can't it wait until morning?'

'No, it can't. Here, sit down and have some of Brian's coffee.'

'You know, he hardly said goodbye to me, Sarah. Dr Hislop wouldn't have behaved like that.'

'Never mind. I want to ask you something important.'

'I go to bed after the news.'

'And you shall.' Sarah-Jane grasped her mother's hands, steeling herself for the task. 'Mum, why did you change your will?'

Betty Potter looked puzzled, as if unable to recall what had been asked. Then she smiled. 'Oh, that was just after Christmas. I can remember Mr Carruthers bringing it for me to sign.'

'But what made you ask for it to be changed?'

'I didn't need to ask. Tom said he'd arrange it for me.'

'What did Tom have to do with it?'

'It was such a little matter. I can hardly remember. He was kind to me when I was laid up with flu – nursed me like a son. He didn't want any reward and I said I'd leave him some little thing if I went, and he said he'd arrange it. Then Mr Carruthers came. It was only a little thing, Sarah. Nothing to get het up about.'

'No, of course it isn't. But probably a better way would be for me to put it back how it was, all cut and dried, so that I can make sure he gets something reasonable. How it was left was a bit vague.'

'I'd like him to have something reasonable, Sarah. Do you think a hundred pounds is too much?'

'And some little personal thing, perhaps?'

'You can be thoughtful sometimes, Sarah.'

As soon as her mother had gone to bed Sarah-Jane telephoned Carruthers at his home.

'By all means bring your mother in tomorrow morning. Not a problem at all to change it. It will be delightful to see you, Sarah. How did we know she wanted to change it? She wrote to us. I remember the letter was typewritten, so I suppose someone helped her with that. I assumed that was you.'

'Well that's right, Mr Carruthers. You must think I'm becoming quite senile.'

'I hardly think that, Sarah. Bentley had quite a spring in his step after he'd seen you, but don't tell him I said so.'

Just after ten Sarah-Jane climbed the stairs and opened her mother's door; the breathing was laboured but regular, promising sleep till morning. She went down the corridor to her own room and stood still in the doorway, listening. But for what? The curtains at the closed window were apart. Through it, in the distance, the treetops were the plumed helmets of warriors marching against a leaden sky. She wondered if a ladder was still propped against the wall.

She got down on her knees and crawled to the window. Feeling with her hand she found with relief that the catch was locked. Then she withdrew as she had come and crawled backwards out of the door, which, deliberately, she left wide open. She took a blanket from the hall cupboard and switched off the light, leaving the house in darkness.

She made first for the windowless toilet. Having closed the door she put on the light and stood motionless, staring into the mirror, her hands gripping the basin. With little adjustments of her position she inclined her head, letting the hair fall from her shoulder. Slowly her reflection became Brian's painting, perfect in its execution; yet there was a discrepancy that, try as she might, she couldn't identify. Then she sprinkled water on her face and hands and rubbed them briskly with a towel. In darkness once again she picked up the blanket and went downstairs.

Her father's study had been left untouched since the funeral. She sat in the high-backed armchair with its tapestry fabric and draped the blanket across her body. As a final precaution she got up and locked the door. She reasoned that anyone approaching the house would assume she had left earlier with Brian in the car. Not until the following morning would she ask herself why she was doing these things.

Her dreams – if the thoughts compressed into the minutes when she was not awake could be considered as such – were of a packed courtroom in which she was counsel for both the prosecution and the defence. In the dock was a child of about twelve or thirteen but she couldn't be sure about its age as the face bore no expression. As the trial proceeded the blank features became painted in according to the force of her eloquence; but changingly, so that the beginnings of a smile could move to a frown and back again as the thrust of her argument shifted. One moment there was the joy of innocence; then, in its place, fear and despair, and worldliness, and finally a plea for love and understanding, all in an recurring cycle. When she had finished the judge climbed down from the bench and drew from his gown a bejewelled mirror which he handed to the child. Look, child, he said, look carefully, and give me your verdict. Then he took the mirror with its imprinted image and handed it to the jurors, who passed it from one to another, nodding gravely as they did so.

As the foreman rose to deliver the verdict a yellow band from an opening door at the back of the courtroom became a sliver of grey between the closed curtains. Grasping for wakefulness, Sarah-Jane imagined torchlight playing across the window. She shrank further into her chair and did not sleep again until the room was suffused with the light of dawn, and filled with melancholy birdsong.

She awoke to taps on the door. 'Are you in there, Sarah? It's nearly ten o'clock.'

Graham Carruthers was the antithesis of Joshua Bentley. Closer though he had been to the family, to Sarah-Jane he was a more distant figure, and much more the product of a conventional education and apprenticeship than his more flamboyant, but fallen, colleague.

The two women sat side by side in chairs set equidistant from the desk. Sarah-Jane would have preferred Bentley's less formal style of the previous day.

While her mother had prepared breakfast Sarah-Jane had scribbled frantically on a piece of paper, which she now handed to Mr Carruthers. 'You will see that it's much more specific now. I hope it can be incorporated as it stands.'

Carruthers stared at it. 'I can see you would be equally at home in our profession, Mrs Preston.' His head swivelled. 'This is your wish, Betty? Your late husband's stamp collection to Mr Sharp? You will be content to sign this?'

'You must do whatever Sarah says.'

He peered at her over half-moon spectacles. 'I assume that means yes. I will deliver it personally for your signature on Monday, as soon as it's been typed. Would you like me to send Mrs Preston a copy?'

'I would appreciate that,' Sarah-Jane said. 'Oh, by the way, Mr Carruthers, you will have on file my mother's last instruction. Would it be an awful bother to run me off a copy of that too?' She lowered her voice. 'I think my mother has mislaid the file – it's just lucky the will was kept separately.'

Without looking at it, Sarah-Jane folded the sheet and put it in her pocket. 'I've asked my mother to involve me if any further changes are to be made. I'm sure you will understand why.'

'I'm beginning to, Mrs Preston, I'm beginning to. You may have every confidence in the firm – its reputation is founded on absolute integrity.'

The taxi bumped its way back down Tippett's Lane. Pleased as Sarah-Jane was at having resolved the matter of the will, her relief – she was slowly realising – related as much to having survived the previous night without incident. But now, in bright daylight, that notion of threat seemed unfounded and ridiculous. She looked forward to returning to Shirley Hills as soon as her mother had settled back into her routine.

The absence of a particular feature from a familiar situation is sometimes more difficult to identify than the simple perception that all is not quite as it should be. As the taxi neared the house Sarah-Jane's mood changed to one of alarm. For several seconds she struggled to understand why. Then it came.

'Mum, I thought we left Moffat outside.'

'We did, Sarah. We left the conservatory open for him in case it rained.'

'Then why isn't he waiting for us?'

Her mother's fingers dug deeply into her arm.

The taxi driver was still rummaging in his purse when Sarah-Jane set off at a brisk walk towards the house. There were more important things than waiting for change from a twenty pound note. After a few paces she turned with an apologetic smile and a shrug to wave him away.

Betty Potter circled the garden shouting for the dog,

then disappeared indoors. Sarah-Jane's feet crunched on the gravel path around the side of the house. She stopped at the corner before the conservatory, holding her breath. Are you psychic, Sarah-Jane, that you know what it is you're going to find, you who believe in nothing beyond the physical world?

Later, with hindsight, what worried her most was that the conservatory door was closed. April is a strange month for weather, but the morning had been still and the afternoon calm. The catch of the heavy door was difficult at the best of times. It would have taken a violent gust to have closed it.

Moffat lay stretched out along the centre aisle, his head in a pool of blue liquid that appeared to have spilt from a large can on its side on the shelf above. Upset flower pots and spattered liquid surrounded the body. Whatever had happened, the dog had not died swiftly. She set the can upright and read the label: *Weedestruct Concentrate*. And under that: *contains 10% paraquat*. She stroked the dog's head and wept. Seeing her stained fingers she looked around for a cloth, unable to bring herself to wipe them on the hair of the dog's chest.

Her mother said, 'Sarah, I think you've lost your only friend, as I've lost mine.'

When the vet came Sarah-Jane held Moffat's hind legs to lower him into the gaping orange bag, like the ones the hospital used for clinical waste. The indignity of it appalled her. She stopped and rearranged her hold so that the hind feet went in first, as gently as she could manage. She kissed the dog's nose, mumbled an apology and left the kitchen to be sick. When she returned the vet said, 'You must not draw premature conclusions, Mrs Preston. At least wait for the pathology report.' Through the window she followed the tail lights of his car before it disappeared into the lane. 'What possible good can a vet do now, Sarah?' her mother asked. 'He can tell us what happened,' she replied.

With an arm about her shoulders Sarah-Jane guided her mother to the living room sofa, puffed up the cushions and eased her down into them. At the kitchen door she looked back at a woman clasping her knees and rocking to and fro, suddenly old through grief and loss. There was, too, a frailty she had not seen – or did she mean noticed? – before. Years must have elapsed since they had last had physical contact of a similar emotional kind.

She stayed until the following morning to keep her mother company. The night was silent, without incident. Of course it had been; what else might she have expected? She smiled, thinking to herself that it would have taken a reckless intruder to have approached the house on that occasion.

In the taxi to the station she caught her reflection in the driver's mirror. Instinctively she patted her hair, as she often did when driving herself in stationary traffic. It was her expression that caught her attention. What could she see there? Anxiety? No, not really. Incomprehension? That was more likely. 'It's still weekend, why can't you stay?' her mother had asked. She couldn't answer, only admit to herself that she was drawn back by a sense of expectation that had not been with her when she had left London with Brian on the Thursday. It occupied her thoughts for much of the train journey back to Paddington and another taxi ride across London to home.

There were two envelopes waiting on her desk. One, in Alice's scrawl, like stretched springs, was without a stamp; the other, typewritten, bore a local postmark. She fixed herself a drink and had poured another before deciding which to open first. Alice had written:

My dear S-J. I had hoped to call on you this afternoon as there are things to tell you, but Brian arrived back so

166

*exhausted from his visit to Oxford that – against all the odds
– I've persuaded him to take a break. So we're heading off to
the Norfolk coast for a couple of nights. What I really wanted
to say was that Jeff Ellis – remember Jeff? – has heard from
Alan Murphy. It seems that after Clare's death he got very
low and tried to end it with an overdose. Three deaths on
his conscience were just too much. He's now staying with Jeff
at Bermondsey. You may – but probably won't – want to do
anything about it but I thought you ought to know. I should
add that all this happened a week or so ago so things might
have changed since. Wish us a tolerable two days. Love, Alice.*

The second letter resembled the one she had given Brian.
It was, if anything, more threatening, promising physical
harm. She regretted not having the first for comparison but
the typeface looked the same. She hid it among the papers
on her desk where the earlier letter had been and resolved
to contact Brian as soon as he returned.

The following Wednesday Sarah-Jane telephoned St
Thomas' but Brian had cancelled his clinic for that day.
Then she rang the Harley Street number. He was consulting
and couldn't be interrupted. She left a message asking him
to ring back.

The next evening he telephoned. In the opinion of
his friend, the psychologist, the letter had been written
by a psychotic and should be taken seriously. It would be
sensible to take it to the police along with all the others; he
would put it in the post. He was interested to know if she
had received any others. She said no without thinking and,
having said it, could not account for why she had done so.
When the first letter arrived on the Saturday morning post
she took the whole collection to the police station.

It was beyond doubt that the two threatening letters shared
the same typeface and were presumably written by the same

person. It was both a relief and, strangely, a disappointment that the typeface did not match that of the letter of instruction from Betty Potter to her solicitor concerning the will.

The next post included a letter from the Hillfield Veterinary Hospital at High Wycombe. It enclosed a copy of the pathologist's report confirming, not surprisingly, that Moffat's death was consistent with paraquat poisoning. It also mentioned abrasions and bruising within the mouth and pharynx. Why had she not thought to look for herself, she wondered. A yellow sticker on the letter bore an unsigned message which read: *It seems your suppositions were well founded, but they do not constitute proof. Please be careful.*

It took Sarah-Jane an evening to compose the letter to Tom Sharp and the whole of the following day to decide whether or not to send it. Copies in sealed envelopes were sent to Mr Carruthers and to her bank, in both cases for safe keeping and with precise conditions under which they were to be opened. When they had gone she felt exhausted but reasonably satisfied that her mother would not be troubled again.

When May came it seemed to Sarah-Jane that her life had become bland beyond description. Her existence was that of a ship setting sail, with all the recent happenings, good and bad, becoming fainter and fainter upon the shore. One by one the memories of them ceased to trouble her.

There had been no recent contact with Brian or Alice, no further news of Alan Murphy, no word from home. Jack Adams and his mother were said to be on a cruise in the Caribbean, but no-one seemed to know exactly where. Mark left early each day and returned late, with a perfunctory kiss for her if she happened to be awake – or there. She never thought to question his movements, nor, it seemed, he hers.

Whole days were spent whiling away the time: talking

horticultural nonsense with Abel and Jed, petting the horses when she should have been riding them and sniffing flowers whenever she encountered perfumes she didn't recognise. She avoided contacts outside her defined geographical domain, in which Marguerite buzzed around and came and went like a robotic bee.

Although she could not bring herself to acknowledge it openly, the girl had become essential to her well-being. They had little in common and did not even particularly like one another, but Marguerite was the only friend that Sarah-Jane had – in the sense that the relationship was honest and direct.

But compared with her physical exertions, her brain was far from idle. It had seized upon the imagery of the sailing ship; with no coast in sight, it had begun, in the quietest of ways, to exploit a freedom characterised by total absence of distraction. Her thoughts coursed over her brief adult life. Suddenly, unaccountably, her ship was heading with stately purpose up the great river, with the twin bascules of Tower Bridge giving way in salute as it made its way towards the heart of the capital. Should she listen to Brian and Alice and return to medicine, or please Mark by staying as she was? She did not know, but the germ of opportunity had vitality still. Perhaps, for a second time, she had found herself at Brian's crossroads.

The telephone sounded on her bedside table: Mark ringing from town to remind her about the arrangements for the dinner that evening. 'It would really please me, Sarah-Jane, if you were to wear your little black dress. You know, the one in Brian's portrait, with the lace collar. I'm sure the guests will appreciate the connection – at least the more observant ones.'

She got out of bed and went downstairs to check that the arrangements were in hand. The kitchen was still full of steam, but the women who had prepared the meal were about to go; those that were to serve it would return later. In the dining room the table set for twenty people glistened with their finest dinner service, cutlery and crystal.

She went upstairs again and sat looking at herself in the dressing table mirror, pondering what to do with her hair. Marguerite entered with an armful of freshly laundered clothes and fussed about in the drawers and cupboards in her usual irritating way.

Between the softly billowing curtains, over the tops of the chestnut trees in the Dell, golfers moved upon the rich green swards. Birds sang in the late afternoon sunshine.

It was still, at that moment, a perfect day.

AFTERMATH

May – September 1987

11

From the speed of the responses it seemed that Marguerite must have dialled the emergency services. But then and later she claimed to have no recollection of it, in spite of the police assurance that a young woman with her name and sounding like her had made the call. This at the time trivial inconsistency became a worry that would grow in Sarah-Jane's mind.

The police were first to arrive, followed by an ambulance. A young constable raced up the stairs to find Sarah-Jane frightened and trembling above the washbasin, a bloody towel clamped to her cheek. Marguerite was standing behind, clasping her shoulders, weeping against the bare skin. Sarah-Jane tried to speak, but the air from her mouth forced red bubbles from the wound. The noises sounded obscene.

The paramedic tried to be comforting, but his face bore the expression of an antiques dealer contemplating a smashed Ming vase. 'They'll soon get that sutured, love,' he said, without conviction.

It was the 'they' that caused Sarah-Jane to look at him in disbelief. She tried to say that she didn't want just to be sutured up, but the words came out as a bloody mess on the white porcelain. They led her to a chair and the paramedic held a gauze to her cheek to stem the bleeding. With some voice capability restored she felt calmer. Strangely, the searing pain in her cheek was helping to focus her thoughts.

Here was a consideration of immense importance. She thought of patients from her days at St Catherine's, how their outcomes so often mirrored the skills of the surgeon, how it was accepted within the surgical fraternity – but seldom admitted – that for the best cosmetic result it was critical who you got to do it. Hadn't she herself confided this to patients, those with the rare luxury of choice?

I want Brian, she told herself. She waved to Marguerite. 'Paper.'

'Comment?'

'Allez! Get me paper and…' It was wise to say no more.

Her first message was to Marguerite to telephone Mr Davison. The girl accepted the sheet bearing the number and trotted off like a bookie's runner. The second was to the paramedic, saying thank you, but she could manage to get help. If all else failed Marguerite could drive her to St Catherine's.

His look of bewilderment unnerved her. 'I suppose that's your right, but are you sure it's sensible?'

She followed Marguerite to the telephone.

'He's not there,' Marguerite said. 'It's Alice Davison.'

'Tell her what's happened.'

Replacing the receiver, Marguerite turned to Sarah-Jane. For the first time their eyes properly engaged. Sarah-Jane, seeing the girl's concern, felt a desperate need to be hugged by her. She drew close, then stopped as red drops from her cheek began to speckle the girl's white shirt.

Marguerite smiled and Sarah-Jane realised she wouldn't have minded. 'Mrs Davison's coming right away,' she said kindly.

Outside, another police car arrived, spewing up more gravel. A man not in uniform strode into the room holding out a hand. 'Guthrie, Mrs Preston. Inspector Guthrie.' She offered her own and was surprised at the fleeting squeeze that couldn't, surely, have been her imagination. His first few questions seemed formulated to need no more than nods or shakes of the head; then he led Marguerite aside and stood talking to her at the window. Sarah heard him say, 'Think hard. Time may just be on our side.'

When Alice arrived she assured the police that, as a doctor herself, she could secure treatment for Sarah-Jane. Against their better judgement the paramedics drove off. The police promised to return later with more questions.

Alice tried Brian's number; there was no reply. Then she tried St Thomas'. Yes, they'd seen him only a few minutes before, but he said he was just leaving. Five minutes later they rang back to say he had definitely gone, but he'd left a message to say he was returning to his private clinic in Putney.

Slumped back in the rear seat of Alice's car Sarah-Jane felt guilty that they had driven away before Mark arrived, then relief that she'd been spared his reaction to her plight, his trophy wife destroyed.

They made straight for Brian's clinic at the Davisons' town house. It was only the third time Sarah had been there, which said something about her friendship with Alice. The intense regularity of the manicured lawn and shrubberies against the sullen, perfect façade of the building only heightened her sense of impairment. Their echoing steps in the uncluttered hallway confirmed what she had already anticipated: Brian had not reached home. 'You've really got to get yourself stitched up,' Alice said. 'I'm taking you to casualty.'

The registrar was young, black and kind. Sarah-Jane remembered the inevitable misjudgements and uncertainties of her own days as a houseman, but wisely stifled an urge to seek a surgeon of higher status. She was thankful there were no students around.

'Did you say a Stanley knife, Mrs Preston?'

'Yes. It had a red handle.'

'Then it must have had a blunt blade.' She could see he wished he hadn't said it.

'You mean it's not a clean cut?'

He patted her hand.

For Sarah-Jane, with her privileged knowledge, that information was as frightening as the act of violence itself. She could hear her old lecturer, Dr Ponsonby, and how curious it had sounded when he had spoken for the first time of healing by first and second intention. And it was fear of the latter, with its implication of scarring, that frightened her now.

What intention lay behind her mutilation? she asked herself. Until that moment she had felt no anger towards her assailant. Somehow it had all seemed inevitable and ordered, like the appearance of the man to read the electricity meter. Now, suddenly, she was angry. She grasped the nearest object, a vase, and hurled it across the room. The glass shattered against the floor. The two pink carnations followed through the air like maimed parachutists.

She was still there, her face stitched and bandaged, when Brian walked in.

He took both her hands in his; his eyes pierced her through. 'Oh, Sarah, who did this to you? Your lovely face!'

She tried to hold his gaze, seeking the pity that that must surely be there. But, like in former days – and it came back to her like a push in the back – whatever emotion there might have been was unreadable behind a glassy film of concealment.

Alice's car snaked through streets full of pedestrians set there only to peer at Sarah through the hyper-transparent windows. Billboards seemed to have been placed just so that the arrogant unfocused eyes of mindless celebrities clutching cans of energising liquid or shaking lustrous locks could spring into life to follow her progress. Cringing on the back seat one thought occupied her mind: 'Who, Brian, who? Alice, who?'

'The police will go into all that,' Brian said. He peered at her around the head-rest, subjecting her face to the same critical scrutiny she had experienced at the hospital. She returned the stare, seeking compassion, then had to look away, uncertain of what she had found. 'It would be helpful if you could give a lead,' he said.

'Try to think,' Alice said. 'Try to cast your mind back. Is there anyone…'

'I don't know!'

'But there's one possibility, isn't there,' Brian said.

'Jack Adams, you mean?' Sarah-Jane turned her head away. She could no longer stem the tears.

'You must tell them,' Alice said.

The few guests Mark had not been able to contact were turned away at the gate. Marguerite handed each of the women a bouquet of lilies hastily cut from the garden. Sarah-Jane, having just reached home, wanted to do it but Mark had insisted she did not. From behind the net curtain of her open bedroom window she strained to hear their speech. Were these really expressions of concern for her – or for a lost social opportunity?

Sarah-Jane wandered about the house and found herself in the conservatory, sitting in front of the fountain. Its silent bell-like cascade was continuous and perfect. Without knowing why she thrust her forefinger into the glistening film, and shrank back as a savage vertical gash disrupted the pattern of the flow. When she withdrew her hand the waters closed, and everything was perfect again.

The light was fading when Marguerite found her, still gazing at what she could make of her reflection in the water.

In the ceiling mirror above her bed the length of barbed wire connecting her mouth to her left eye seemed to flex menacingly with the forced grin. She shivered. You'll have to keep your nerve, girl, or you'll be lost, she told herself.

The demons that had assembled around her as she'd drifted into sleep had taken their pleasure. One had undone all the stitches like bootlaces and retied them in random order; another had poked his pink mushroom head through the gaping wound, shrieking at her because he was in the wrong place. But the worst was the continuous trickle of fire that flowed from her mouth into her throat. When Mark woke her in the morning with a cup of juice to sip the relief was blissful but short-lived as the dream faded into reality.

'You're alive and that's all that matters,' he said.

'But it's not, Mark. You know it's not.'

There were separate calls from Alice and Brian, and from others who would have come to the dinner. The last were relationships unlikely to survive the present crisis and she expected little sympathy there. Not that the women had shown no previous interest in her – just the reverse in fact. There were times when it had been intense, like when she had once permed her hair in curls and they had all, consciously or otherwise, copied her. But how had she responded to this quasi-adulation? Why, by flirting with their husbands, just as Mark had flirted with them. What gloating there would be behind these sanctimonious expressions of concern.

To get up or not to get up. To wander down to the beautician at eleven, as was planned, and suffer the... No, that would not do. That crazy Booker novel, maybe she would give it one more try. Or cook herself something, like eggs and bacon, but bacon was sliced and… Besides, she had almost forgotten how. Perhaps Marguerite…

But there was a sobering thought. Didn't her influence over Marguerite reside in the edge that her appearance gave? She rolled over in despair; the filament sutures brushed the silk pillow like stubble against the sheets when she'd forgotten to wax her legs.

Problems. But come what may there was no choice but to get up.

Later that morning Alice found her in the conservatory, at the far end, away from the fountain, sitting so that only the right side of her face was visible to anyone approaching. Drawing close, it seemed to her that Alice couldn't quite disguise that familiar twist of the mouth that Sarah-Jane had come to interpret as envy. But how could that be, now, given the changed situation? Alice said, 'It would have been silly of me to have brought you flowers, with you surrounded by them.'

'Just you is enough,' Sarah-Jane said. Her response came with a tiny jolt of surprise, because it ran counter to what she was thinking. It was like momentarily catching an exotic perfume on the wind. It seemed to come from a previously forgotten cache of affection somewhere deep within.

A butterfly, uniformly orange with black veins and twitching antennae, settled on Sarah-Jane's wrist. She rotated her hand as if showing off a new bracelet. The insect was one of several Mark had brought back as chrysalides from the Massingham Tower the week before.

'That's pretty,' Alice said.

'I touched one for the first time today! Can you believe that until yesterday I hardly ever came in here? Now it's become a refuge created just for me. Aren't I lucky, Alice?'

Alice was at a loss to answer. 'Sarah, did you know that Mark had rung Brian?'

'He didn't tell me. What did he want?'

'An assessment of the damage, I guess.'

'Yes, I suppose I'll have to accept I'm a commodity of dubious value. Did he ask if Brian could do anything?'

'Yes.'

'And?'

'He said he couldn't. I'm sorry, Sarah. I asked him myself again and again, till I was blue in the face. He says what's done is done, and even if he could do something, he couldn't steal another doctor's case. And he says he's got complete faith in Dr Ransome.'

Sarah-Jane looked her full in the face, unable to control her anger. 'I thought they did that all the time.' Perhaps it was the contortion of the black and crusted line that made Alice turn her head away. 'Alice, don't! Please don't!'

'Sarah, I'm sorry. I'm sorry. It wasn't deliberate.' She began crying and groping for Sarah-Jane's outstretched hand.

Sarah-Jane saw the door to the house open. Marguerite was standing there, uncertain whether to come forward, until the looming figure of Inspector Guthrie brushed past her.

'I'll come back later,' Alice said, sniffing into her handkerchief and making for the door to the garden.

There was a succession of well-wishers – against her expectation and, to her disappointment, all women – whom Sarah-Jane classified as nosey-parkers, do-gooders or malcontents; none of them did she recognise as a friend. She was polite, and glad to see them go. But having lost one advantage over them she had, unexpectedly, gained another: an aloof indifference that negated the effect of whatever platitude took their fancy. She told herself that she no longer cared.

There was to be one exception.

By late afternoon she had moved to the drawing room and lay stretched out on one of the two crimson sofas, contemplating the plaster ceiling rose above the confection in crystal that Mark had bought at Sotheby's. She wanted Mark to come home and comfort her with assurances that he had enlisted Brian's help. It was inexplicable that Brian had not come to see her; but then, as Alice had explained, he had his patients to consider.

Around five o'clock she heard Marguerite answer the door bell, then the girl's protestations as another, more forceful, voice gained ascendency. Brisk footsteps sounded on the polished oak floor of the hall. It was the least expected of all her potential visitors.

'It's kind of you to come, Mrs Adams.'

The woman seemed taken aback, eyebrows arching, as if it were not the greeting she expected. Then her face reassumed its usual angularity.

'There's no kindness in it, Mrs Preston, as you well know. Nor will there be, leastways not for a long while to come. I take pity on you because I would wish that on no-one, and I hope your face heals, in spite of what you've done.'

After all this time the pang of remorse for Clare's death was sharper than Sarah-Jane might have anticipated. But it had to be countered; she knew no other way. 'Done? Will you never let the matter rest? Haven't I done penance enough for you and your family?'

'Maybe you have, maybe you haven't. God will be the judge of that. But I think you know that's not why I've come. Let's be straight about it since you seem not to understand.' Marjorie Adams' eyes seemed to want to tear Sarah-Jane's wounded cheek apart. 'Why have you accused my son?'

'Accused…' At last she understood.' I have accused no-one! I have no idea who it was.'

'But you told the police.'

'They asked who might have a grudge against me. That's a different matter. You're not denying your son once threatened me?'

Until that moment the woman had remained standing. Suddenly her composure evaporated. She removed a cushion and lowered herself into the far end of Sarah-Jane's sofa.

'You know they've searched our house? Rooms, garage, attic, workshop, everywhere.'

'No, I didn't know.'

'And they've taken Jack for questioning.' She opened her handbag, took out a handkerchief and sniffed into it.

Sarah-Jane had her own problem to occupy her. There was no room for another's. 'Then events are going to have to take their course, aren't they?'

'You'll regret saying that, Mrs Preston. You mark my words you will.'

'I've expressed enough regret, Mrs Adams. I think you'd better go, don't you?'

'You know my boy's not capable of such a thing.' She was crying now.

Sarah-Jane thrust her injured face towards the woman, jabbing her forefinger at the wound. 'With this I no longer care. Now please go!'

Brian arrived at nine forty-five, just as the hall clock struck the quarter. Mark had sent her to bed and she lay imagining Brian on the doorstep looking at his watch to achieve a precisely timed entry; she'd seen that before. Whatever it was that Mark has slipped into her drink – as he admitted later – it had not quite taken effect. Through the haze in her head she heard them climbing the stairs. The bedside light was still on. She shifted her position so that it illuminated the damaged side of her face, then closed her eyes, pretending to be asleep. She sensed Brian's feline scrutiny of the lesion, taking his time, as he did with his patients, his face almost touching hers. The minty medicinal breath forced her to stay still. The back of his hand brushed the angle of her jaw.

'He's done a good job, that young man of mine. I could hardly have done it better.' He drew himself away. 'There's nothing much to be done, Mark, at least not in the immediate future. When it's settled down we can consider other options.'

'Like grafting?'

'Perhaps.'

'My poor Sarah-Jane!'

'It'll become less obvious with time. You must be patient if you're to help her. I'll call by tomorrow and talk to her if you like.'

'Would you? You're a good friend, Brian. I appreciate that.'

Mark switched off the light. She felt his dry lips brush her forehead; would that it had been her damaged cheek. Then they tiptoed from the room. She opened one eye and watched the door close after them.

12

Although the attack had happened on the Friday, in Sarah-Jane's mind day one began on the following Monday morning. She remembered that when her sister – but not, it must be said, her father – had died a similar thing had happened: the flurry of actions by those purporting to be concerned and the inner turmoil that made time pass in a kind of emotional high. Now, there was even the dubious excitement of not knowing where it all might lead. It was still there, that feeling, when she went to bed on the Sunday evening, cheered by the television, a bottle of Mark's finest claret and those around her wishing her well. When she woke it was gone and in its place lay a featureless, grey wasteland stretching into the future.

Marguerite, with a cup of tea, tip-toed into the room so as not to wake her until the last moment as the curtains were drawn back. But the already open eye above the wound had seen her enter. For a second a little flame flickered – the girl didn't usually do this – but then was gone.

'How's your face, Miss?'

'Still painful, thanks, but at least I slept.'

'That's good.' There was a moment's silence. 'I wanted to ask. Could you take me to the station again, please?'

'I thought you were here with me today.'

'Mr Preston said I could.'

'What did you do to earn that?' The week before it wouldn't have mattered; now it did.

The girl looked away. Her request had not been made without conflict. But the balance between what you want for yourself and what you can reasonably expect from others is difficult to set at that age.

'Can you be back early, then?'

'I'll try my hardest.' She meant it.

Brief though this exchange was, it seemed to tell Sarah-Jane more about Mark and his priorities than about Marguerite.

There were flowers downstairs. Not, this time, roses, but there was a note attached: Jed and Abel had cared enough. Now there would be reason to get to know them better. That cheered her a little.

She began to realise that the killing of time – which until now had only occasionally pricked at her conscience – would become a burden from which she might not extricate herself. This was partly in the mind, but it was also a sensation exacerbated by the knowledge that little time-filling packages – like going to the shops for no real purpose other than to be seen, or picking up the telephone when you still hadn't decided who to phone – might no longer be available to her. Time, she could see, could become her greatest enemy. In the past it had been a friend and an asset, but it had been squandered. She knew that now.

Surely the secret was to plan ahead, so as never to be left with nothing to do.

Gingerly sipping her coffee at the right commissure of unobliging lips – she had thrown away the sodden straw in disgust – she watched the postman on his bicycle ploughing through the new gravel, before giving up and pushing for the last few yards. The post fell in a cascade. Still at the door, she opened each item, glanced at it, then tossed it onto the hall table. It took her a while to realise that what she was seeking was word from her assailant. After all, a relationship had been established between them; wasn't it likely it would be pursued?

On the table beside her lay the pad she had used to sketch the outline of her attacker. The police had taken the sheet, but the imprint remained on the next. She angled it to the light, following in her head his reflection in the mirror. She judged that he could not have been very tall. Why, then, had she not tried to defend herself? To have stood up, struck out at him or screamed were options she had seemingly and perversely rejected. Why?

At eleven Inspector Guthrie called to tell her that the raid on the Adams' home had yielded nothing.

'I didn't think it would, Inspector.'

'Oh, why's that?'

'Because the man's basically a wimp, and harmless.'

'Jack Adams? You surprise me. I thought he was held in high regard. Like for his charitable work.'

'A vested interest, wasn't it? Clare's condition, I mean.'

'Not in all that he did. If you'll forgive me, Mrs Preston, off the record I would strongly advise you against taking that particular line.'

Sarah-Jane shrugged.

Guthrie was staring at the pile of cards and letters. 'May I look?'

'Help yourself.'

'Any suspicious, like typed ones for instance?'

'A couple. Did you get anywhere with the letters I gave you?'

'We're still working on them.'

'Do you think there's a connection?'

'It's the only lead we have. What puzzles me is the total

lack of witnesses. Outside in the lane, I mean. Further away, even.'

'Did you try Mrs Horsedung – Mrs Fowler I think she calls herself – three houses down?'

'We've visited all fifty of your neighbours, all the golfers, all the local public services, buses, taxis. Nothing even slightly suspicious.'

'Inspector?'

'Yes?'

'Will he try again, do you think?'

'The deliberation in his case suggests to me that he won't, but who can tell. We have an officer near the gate. In fact we've had one there since Friday.'

'I didn't know.'

When he'd gone the whole house became silently, unbearably oppressive. It had the feel of one of those grey mornings long, long ago when the house at Peverell Hessett was given over to her mother's Monday wash and cheerfulness was not allowed back until the wretched business was over. Only then was the sun permitted to filter through the dank clouds to restore her spirits. Here, now, today, it seemed the sun had simply died.

I need a plan, she told herself: something to hang on to when the going gets rough, as it will. She wrote on the pad: *one – re-establish your life as far as possible as it was before – by doing that the difficulties will be easier to isolate and deal with; two – identify your real friends and use them sparingly, as they may not be over-keen to help; three – try, if you can, to keep Mark happy as you'll need to keep him; four – find things to do to keep yourself busy; five – try to put out of your mind what happened – what's done is done and recriminations will not help.*

She found herself chewing the end of her pen. Five was not right. She knew from her days as a houseman that patients who pushed disasters from their minds later regretted it. Okay, *five – face up to it and consider counselling only as a long stop if you really need it; but only if.*

Mark rang as she was reading through the list again.

'Mark, dear. The dinner we cancelled. I want it to be on again.'

'Sarah-Jane, don't be ridiculous. You're not yet up to it.'

'I'm fine, really.'

'We'll talk about it when I get back.'

It was a start. She would surprise him with her determination and resolve. But she would come to find she had underestimated his resistance.

At the car park near the shops she drove without thinking to the far end where there were fewer vehicles, and sat there agonising for having already allowed her behaviour to be dictated by fear of embarrassment. So she took a deep breath, straightened a few stray wisps of hair with her fingers and drove back along the row of cars. Having parked, she walked towards the shops with her head erect.

There were five people in the gift shop. With each the first response was the same: a stare, a momentary engaging of the eyes and then a furtive looking-away. From two of them, not quite strangers, the usual smile of recognition was not there. The third, stricken with guilt and pity, approached her. 'Mrs Preston, I'm so sorry.' Then she paid at the counter with cash and was gone.

Sarah-Jane bought two packets of the most expensive invitation cards, each with an elaborate floral design surrounding the words 'At Home'. The counter assistant's eyes flicked from her face to the cards and back again. A rush of anger, and Sarah-Jane said, 'You don't think I should be entertaining, do you?' But she had misjudged. 'Oh, Mrs Preston, I just hope you will be brave enough.' The hand that passed her the change paused to pat her wrist. There was some hope, then.

But no-one asked her about the attack, or how she felt, or whether she could cope. That reluctance to engage would be the cruellest of the barriers she would face in the weeks to come.

With petrol low her next stop was the garage at the end of the road. This time she would do it herself rather than, as was usual, ask one of the gardeners.

She could see Ann Fowler's car by one of the islands. She drew alongside with the pumps between. Ann's three-year-old daughter was climbing out of the car as Sarah-Jane unscrewed her filler cap. The child liked Sarah-Jane and always greeted her. At the level of her legs the child said, 'Hello, Sarah-Jane.'

'Hello, Arabella.' She bent to pick up the child, as she'd done twice before. The response was electric and terrible. As their faces closed the child shrieked, squirming out of Sarah-Jane's grasp. She ran in terror towards the door of the kiosk from which her mother had just emerged, tripping on the rough concrete and flying headlong into the woman's legs. Ann Fowler looked at the child's grazed knees, then, witheringly, at Sarah-Jane. The child's head remained buried in her mother's skirts and no amount of coaxing would make her look around. The grim countenance said, I was prepared to pity you, Mrs Preston, but frightening my child has deprived you of that; I want no more to do with you. 'Good morning, Mrs Preston,' she said, sweeping up Arabella and marching away.

Sarah-Jane had been home only five minutes when Alice rang.

'I've been trying to get you all morning. Brian and I wondered if you'd like to come to supper tomorrow. Bring Mark if he'll come. Whatever.'

'No thanks, Alice. Ask me in a week's time when the honeymoon's over and I'm really going to need it.'

'As bad as that?'

'It was this morning. You can't imagine.'

'There are some good people about, Sarah. In time you'll become good at spotting them. You won't be alone for ever.'

She had no appetite for lunch, but forced some soup down. Where was that bloody girl, for heaven's sake? She hunted for the Sinatra tape that Mark had given her before they were married. There seemed to be something wrong with the equipment – the magic voice had lost its sparkle.

Writing the invitation cards took her the whole afternoon. She followed the original guest list to the letter. No matter what their responses had been at the time – or what had been her thoughts towards them – it was to be as it was to have been. Whatever proved otherwise she would come to terms with, if necessary through sheer force of will.

On the day the stitches came out Sarah-Jane accepted Alice's invitation to a barbeque the following Saturday evening.

She had been to the Davisons' Putney house twice in darkness and once in desperation. This time she was better able to appreciate the white Georgian façade, perfect in its symmetry, unspoilt by the conservatory on one side and the new extension on the other that she rightly guessed housed Brian's private consulting rooms. The bow of the drive rose to the front door, then fell away towards the second entrance, reminding her of a sensuous upper lip. She switched off the engine at the door, where Brian, dressed in check shirt and white flannel trousers, was waiting for her.

'You see, we've observed your request to be casual,' he said, adding, 'May I see?' She could feel him mentally rearranging the stitch marks on her face.

'When did they come out?'

'A week ago. Your Dr Ransome was awfully kind.'

He ran his finger down the line of the scar. The corrugations were horribly apparent under his touch. Pride prevented her asking for a prognosis, even though her need to know was almost uncontainable.

'It won't be quite so obvious when the swelling subsides.'

What might have been an opportunity for further explanation was destroyed by Alice emerging from the doorway. 'You're a naughty girl for leaving it so long before coming to see us!'

The words jarred. They were of a kind she associated with a perverse love of scolding children. Had, then, her vulnerability reduced her to the status of a mindless delinquent?

'I needed to think things out,' Sarah-Jane said flatly.

'To us you're still the same old Sarah. Isn't she Brian?'

'Not quite the same, Alice. If anything more dignified, almost regal. It's given you a presence, Sarah, that didn't show before. Or if it did it wasn't obvious to me.'

Alice looked at him critically. 'That's just despair, Brian, so don't go glamorising it. Why don't we all go in?'

The hall extended to the back of the house, where a pair of lightly etched glass doors with Aesculapian snake motifs opened directly onto the terrace. A dozen or so people were gathered outside, all but one men, casually dressed, each with a glass. They were talking quietly; almost expectantly, Sarah-Jane thought.

'I suppose they've all been forewarned?' she said.

'Well, no, actually they haven't. Most don't even know, so it's quite a test for you.'

Some of the faces seemed familiar. It took her a while to realise that they must have been at the opening of Brian's plastics unit at Beckenham. Perhaps they were other consultants or, more likely, benefactors. She thought about her resolutions and set herself the task of determining this for each of them; but at the end of the evening she would have to admit she'd largely failed. The difficulty seemed to lie in their peculiar reticence, but that was at odds with their charm. These, it seemed, were the discreetly rich of the type that Mark's organisation preyed upon. She reflected on how far Brian had come in the six years or so she had known him: his work, his house, his garden, his… his wife? She looked across to where Alice was being ignored by a diminutive and vociferous Arab and trying, in defence, to make conversation with his strikingly beautiful female companion. What she had long suspected was true: Alice did not quite fit.

Sarah-Jane walked to the edge of the terrace. Beyond the balustrade of weathered sandstone stretched a garden whose conceptual perfection was matched only by the palette of colour from the masses of rhododendrons and azaleas, and the velvet closeness of the turf. Beside the terrace an immaculate swimming pool was tucked in close to the house. Her own garden, larger by far and tended by two gardeners, could not rival it.

She felt the light pressure of a hand against the small of her back. It was the man who had been avoiding Alice.

'Your friend Brian has exquisite taste, has he not? In all that he does, I believe. *Mirabile visu*. It is an honour to meet you, Mrs Preston. I am Imran Khasoni.' He came only to her shoulder. Licking his lower lip before each utterance, only the choicest words were allowed to flow.

'Brian? A perfectionist, yes.' She would try her luck. 'Are you a doctor too?'

'Shall we say an associate with a particular interest in surgery.' The same reticence channelled the conversation away from himself. 'You will forgive my impertinence, Mrs Preston, which I fear is a failing of my race, but you have had a recent accident. May I ask as to its origin?'

Had the questioner been more to her liking the answer would have tumbled out, for she was aching to give it to someone; she told him all the same.

'Then you are a woman of great fortitude. I truly wish for the miracle that will restore your beauty.'

Sarah-Jane was mildly amused. 'You believe in miracles?'

'As a devout Muslim I must believe in them.' He gave her the most subtle of winks. 'But I happen also to believe in the refinement of human skill and technological innovation – and their promise for the future. Your face will not always be so, Mrs Preston. You have my word on it.'

'Mr Khasoni, I'm grateful for you reassurance.'

He answered only with a slight bow, as if a piece of business had been successfully transacted, then withdrew into the gathering.

When darkness fell a score of soft yellow lights turned the garden into a fairyland of arching boughs and dark cushion-like shrubs. Sizzling animal juices from the barbeque, exotically spiced, were carried in the gentle breeze.

They had all been kind, these people. Without knowing her, they had asked and listened; none had turned away. Then, gradually, one by one, they left the garden and the terrace. She noted with pleasure that all took the trouble to say goodbye. Curiously, Alice did not seem to command the same respect. To her, as hostess, their farewells were perfunctory.

But then, Sarah-Jane thought, that was how it had always been with Alice.

The garden was deserted. Alice appeared with two mugs of coffee and they sat at one of the tables on the terrace.

'Please don't turn the lights off yet,' Sarah-Jane said. 'I want to squeeze the last drop from this evening.' Suddenly she was puzzled. 'By the way, where were all their cars?'

Alice laughed. 'I don't know much about them, but

I do know they don't drive themselves. Their chauffeurs arrive at agreed times and off they go, back to their pleasure fortresses, or whatever.'

'You know, Alice, if I didn't know better I would say this evening has been arranged just for me.'

Brian, overhearing, sat beside her on her good side. 'I have to admit you're partly right about that. We'd planned to have it for some while but brought it forward a bit when we knew… well… that you were likely to come. We felt it would help you to mix with people who weren't – how shall we say – influenced by appearances.'

'That's a bit odd. I would say they were people who cared very much about appearances.' She thought she saw Brian give a little shrug. 'And they really didn't know?'

'They didn't know. Oh, except one.'

She pinched her arm for not thinking to ask before. 'Not your friend the psychologist?'

'Astute of you. He thought it was neither time nor place to dwell on such a dismal subject. Tonight we look forward, not back.' He reached for a bottle of wine and placed it on the table. Uncharacteristically he began to fumble with a corkscrew. He was holding something back.

'Brian, if there's something I should know you must tell me.'

'Not tonight, Brian,' Alice said. 'Don't spoil it.'

'Look, you two. If you know something, you're going to tell me.' Sarah-Jane's hollow laugh was nothing if not threatening.

'Shit, Brian, now you have to.'

'Okay, Sarah. It was a chance discovery, out of the blue. And nothing to do with our psychologist friend – in fact he doesn't know. I've been going through the correspondence on the new unit at Beckenham, mainly to check that there weren't people we'd forgotten to thank.' Sarah sensed a pause for effect. 'Amongst the letters were some from fundraisers.'

'From one fundraiser in particular, Brian means!'

'Alice, please! The typeface – and indeed the paper – was the same as for your letter.'

'There's no particular significance in that, surely. Typewriters are common enough objects.'

'Correct. But I had the texts compared by an expert, under a microscope. The flaws in the print matched exactly. It was the same typewriter, Sarah. There can be no doubt about that.'

Sarah-Jane's heart beat faster. It was information she needed badly but was afraid to hear. 'Tell me where.'

'The fundraising office. The Adams' house. Jack Adams' house.'

'I don't believe it!' She was withering under their searching eyes, then rallied. 'What must I do?'

'Perhaps if I were to speak to Mark. I don't think it's a good idea for you to worry about it. Leave it to us.' Brian's eyes narrowed in a way that reminded her of their very first encounter on the wards at Catherine's. 'And you're quite sure there have been no others?'

'Who would want to harm me now?'

Alice saw her to the car; Brian had unaccountably disappeared.

'By the way,' Sarah said, as she climbed in, 'who was the glamorous female with the greasy Arab? She seemed rather... well... distant from the proceedings.'

'Her name's Nicole. Beyond that I really have no idea. I presume one of the companions.'

'Companions?'

'Surely you haven't forgotten the Massingham Tower? Your husband runs it!'

Driving home, Sarah-Jane thought of Maia, standing

by the fire in her diaphanous white gown, waiting for an opportunity to please. For a brief moment she regretted that her parting with Edwin had been so final.

By the time she drove into the Dell the conflict in her head had taken control. There was a mismatch, somewhere. If nothing else, it told her she must look further afield than Jack Adams, whatever he might have said to her. But what else was there? Only the dubious sighting of a stranger on the golf course by a hostile neighbour. A painfully considered hundred metres past her own gateway she turned into the driveway leading to the clubhouse.

In the failing light she noticed three cars parked suggestively close at the perimeter of the tarmac. The movements within were barely discernible, but enough, for a few seconds, to divert her thoughts. She parked away from them, picked up a magazine and stared at it, not seeing, while she summoned courage to walk onto the fairway. Others did with their dogs at odd hours, so that was no big deal. She rummaged in the glove compartment for the field glasses that had been a present from Mark two years before when he had tried, unsuccessfully, to interest her in racing. She had no plan, but there was a compulsion to take them.

The path along the trees climbed steeply, then levelled out to follow the same contour as that occupied by the houses on the opposite side of the Dell. Most of them were visible now only as confections of twinkling lights sporadically visible through the trees. Even in moonlight she had no difficulty in locating the place where Mrs Fowler had claimed to have seen the man with the binoculars.

The clarity of the only lighted window visible was unnerving. Her hands trembled as she raised the field-glasses to her eyes.

There were figures within the uncurtained frame. One was low down, a head just visible above the sill in the position of someone sitting before her dressing table mirror. The other, muscular and powerful, towered above. The first rose and seemed to turn, and the two became an amalgam of passionate life-surging flesh. The mass rotated and heaved, then fell below the level of the sill.

She was not surprised, but it was not what she had expected, or sought. The hurt was that the two of them – for the lesser was certainly Marguerite – could not have cared much about her return.

One of the two policemen at the gate began to tell about the security measures. He seemed to be spinning it out and she became impatient. Then, in her wing mirror, she saw the other slowly retreat into the bushes. She thought she heard his voice, speaking as if into a telephone. An explanation was not difficult to imagine.

'Officer,' she said casually, 'who could your companion possibly be phoning at this hour of the night?'

In his position she too might have handled it as a joke. 'That would be telling now, wouldn't it? Good night, Mrs Preston.'

He was standing at the top of the stairs with the same bland and – as she now knew – concealing smile with which he had once charmed her on the terrace above the blue lagoon.

'You're back early, darling.'

'It got quite chilly outside and everyone left early.'

'By the way, Brian rang.'

'About Jack? So he doesn't trust me to tell you myself.'

'It's not that, Sarah-Jane. He just thinks you are not ready for a mental assault so soon after the physical one.'

'But you'll have me in the witness box all the same, won't you?'

'I think it's inevitable, whatever we do. You want him punished, don't you?'

'I want the man who did it caught. That could be a different matter.'

'I don't quite follow. Anyway, I've already told the police. They'll be round again in the morning.'

'So for the moment we can all relax?'

The sarcasm was lost upon him. 'Then let me get you something. Scotch?'

'Maybe, but not just yet.' She passed him in the doorway, brushing his cheek with her hand, and went directly to the dressing table. 'That's funny. My pots seem to have been moved.' It was a lie, but worth telling.

'That's not possible.'

'Why ever not? Marguerite might have been tidying up. Except that she's no inclination to tidy anything unless she's asked.'

'I wouldn't know. I don't even know whether she's about.'

Sarah-Jane walked to the bed and sat on the edge, stroking the coverlet. 'You know what I'd really like?'

'What?'

'For you to make love to me. Now. Just like before my accident, as if it hadn't happened.'

'Sarah-Jane, it's a lovely thought, but I'm tired. I've had a tough day.' He put his arm around her shoulders. 'This business has taken it out of me too, you know.'

'It's not because of my appearance?'

'Sarah-Jane, no. Good lord no.'

'That's all right then, isn't it?' She got up abruptly from the bed and left the room. From the corridor she called back, her voice shrill and cracking. 'When you next lie to me, try opening the window. Then the smell won't give you away!'

She was already beginning to break the rules she had set herself.

Marguerite found her in the kitchen brooding over a mug of Ovaltine. Milky drinks were less painful in her mouth than tea or coffee.

'I'm sorry, Miss.'

'So he told you I'd found out?'

'I couldn't help it. It wasn't to hurt you.'

'He's an attractive man. Don't worry. I understand.' She patted the seat beside her. 'Here, sit with me for a moment.'

Marguerite looked on incredulously as Sarah-Jane spooned some of the grey-brown powder into another cup.

'Have you tried this?'

The girl flicked her black hair aside in disgust and laughed. 'I shouldn't think so!'

'Marguerite, listen carefully. When the man who did this to me passed you on the stairs did he remind you of anyone we know?'

'No. Well, no.'

'No? Then would you say he knew where he was going.'

'Oh yes.'

'So might have known the layout of the house. Perhaps have been here before?'

'Yes. I suppose.'

'Can you ever remember Jack Adams coming to the house?'

'Once or twice, never upstairs.'

'That's what I think too.'

It was the first time Sarah-Jane had slept in the guest bedroom. Of all the rooms this was the most cosily decorated: a kind of museum in miniature dedicated to the cult of Laura Ashley. The soft furnishings had the substance of puff-balls. The quilted bed invited diving and engulfment.

Was it the girl's naivety that stopped her from being angry? Or was there something deeper in this developing ménage à trois that had begun to excite her more than it repelled. No, Sarah-Jane, she told herself, it's that your authority in this household has become assailable and you are beginning to accept your position can be compromised. Yet, had either one of them – Mark or Marguerite – appeared in the doorway at that moment she knew that her spirits would have soared.

The sound of a television somewhere in the house suddenly ceased. The chimes of two longcase clocks called midnight in unison, as Mark had fixed them to do. She set her alarm clock, forgetting that bleak grey mornings were never a time for invited wakefulness. Then she turned off the light.

Her thoughts dwelt on the events of the early evening. She tried to place the characters that had peopled the Putney garden in an intelligible context. They seemed hardly real friends of Brian, still less of Alice. They reminded her of a Francis Ford Coppola film in which the warring Mafia factions might come together at a brief moment in time, like at a funeral, to recognise a bond that was greater than the urge to kill one another. Was the real clue Khasoni's beautiful companion, singled out by her looks and her composure, and because all the other guests were men? If I were not so charitably disposed, she told herself, I would think that the girl had been put there to humiliate me: as my mirror image, but in a perfect form. That was not quite right though, for no-one had shown the slightest inclination to slight her. Quite the contrary in fact, and to a surprising degree. No, the girl must have been there by chance, as a companion – in the true Massingham sense – of the Arab.

It was right what Alice had snidely hinted at: she was not party to her husband's business. She wondered as to its origin. He had never concealed his work from her exactly; rather, she had rarely been interested enough to ask him. Yet, at first, there had been an overwhelming fascination, and she had nearly sacrificed herself upon Edwin's desecrated altar to satisfy her curiosity. That first prying visit to the Tower had been followed by only one other, when, as Mark's new girlfriend, she had gone in the guise of a companion. 'You will enjoy yourself,' he had said with his usual worldly laugh, 'but keep your wits about you, don't drink too much… and keep your nightie tied firmly to your toes.'

The mask, she remembered, had been offered in advance, for faces were not allowed to show during the entire evening. She had chosen one of a faun that was neither threatening to others nor constructed so that it required more than a simple adjustment to allow her to eat and drink. Over her scant underwear she had worn a white gown edged in silk the colour of her hair. And under the indiscernible dome that passed from the deep blue of evening to the speckled blackness of night they cavorted and danced around the indigo lagoon. It did not concern her that clothes were shed, or that flesh touched flesh without discrimination or favour.

At one point she had approached the rock face at the end of the lagoon, and peered through one of the apertures giving access. Behind there was another cavernous space, but darker and occupied by less frenzied and more engrossed figures. A girl clad in the same white gown that Maia had once worn emerged from the shadows and led her gently away with a smile that told her she was not permitted there, or at least not yet. Back in the throng she was suddenly bored. She looked for Maia and could not find her; then, at that moment, the fascination ended. 'You know why it was, Sarah-Jane,' Mark said afterwards. 'It's because without your face to complement it your body could be rivalled by some of those other women. Can you imagine what it means to them, the ones without faces that unlock doors? It's like being pitched into paradise.' He'd drained his brandy glass and got up to go. 'But I'm not surprised you didn't enjoy it.' There, as she now realised, the chapter had closed.

Mark's voice from the corridor asked if she were asleep.

'Not asleep Mark, just thinking.'

'Can I come in?'

'Of course.'

He pulled aside the crumpled coverlet and ran the back of his had along her spine under the single tortured sheet. 'Why are you on your tummy?' he asked.

'It's better that way,' she replied, raising herself onto knees and elbows. 'You chose the time. For once let me choose the position.' He must have seen that the pillow where her head had rested was wet with tears.

13

Her face was not healing properly and the local press were coming to interview her. She wondered how they'd been held at bay for so long. Months later she would realise the extent of Mark's hand in that.

Brian had telephoned at nine to say that the *Echo* and the *Shirley Chronicle* had the story and would she be ready by ten. She filled an hour in front of the mirror, dabbing on an array of creams and lotions – all with flesh-like hues – and wiping them off again. Nothing seemed to work. She wrinkled her nose at her reflection, as if her failed quest were a putrid fish, then cleaned her face with soap and water. When she looked again there was an irregular reddish band along the line of the scar. It was angry and its discovery caused her heart to sink, because all along she had been expecting it.

Brian arrived early and sat with her in the conservatory, reassuring her with the low bedside voice he had cultivated for his patients. When he took her hand she did not remove it; and not doing so was one of the signs that the attention of others, on which her life-blood had depended, was steadily and surely being withdrawn. It hurt her that Brian did not once look at her face.

'You realise, Sarah, that they will only be able to publish the facts as they are known, not opinions that might prejudice a jury.'

'As I see it the facts are rather few and far between, Brian.'

'That's because there's one more piece of evidence I've still to tell you about.' Was this, then, why he was here?

'Oh?'

'The signatures on your two letters. Quite indecipherable, of course, and deliberately so, but the ink has been traced.'

'To Jack Adams' pen, no doubt.'

'Exactly. Absolutely right. The police searched the house again. They expect to pick him up when he gets back tomorrow.'

She raised a thin smile. 'Then I owe you an apology. I really thought you were on the wrong track – all of you. I guess I've not been thinking straight lately.' A warmth dredged up from somewhere deep within made her confide in him. 'There were other possibilities, you see.'

'Oh really? Who?'

She laughed. 'Well, they belong to closed chapters steadily gathering dust. Forget I said it. But Brian...'

'Yes?'

'Thank you. I don't deserve your help. I know I haven't always been as nice to you as I might have been.'

Brian's response, which would have been illuminating, was cut short by Marguerite ushering in the two reporters.

Jack Adams was apprehended at Gatwick as he cleared customs – and before he'd had time to see the local papers. His mother was hysterical. The customs officers were said to have marvelled at the protestations of innocence.

The case came before the Crawley magistrates later that morning and by the end of the afternoon he was on bail. His only consolation, apparently, was an offer of help from his only contact of stature in the legal world, an ageing QC called Fairburn, the father of an old school friend once on drugs and, with Jack's help, hauled back from the brink.

For Sarah-Jane it was an opportunity to take stock. The easing of the pressure had allowed in a little of the creative energy – admittedly never much – that had lain dormant since childhood. In a chance comment to Mark she had suggested painting, and he had bought her a splendid box of acrylics with boards and an easel. She set the easel up in the conservatory and was sitting in front of it, trying to make aesthetic sense of the labyrinthine backcloth of ivies and ferns, when Marguerite came in.

'There's a Thomas Sharp at the door, Miss. He says he knows you and wants to come in.'

So he hadn't taken notice of her letter, nor heeded her advice to stay away.

'I don't want to see him. Tell him to go away.'

But Tom, uninvited, had followed Marguerite. From outside the conservatory door he had heard Sarah-Jane's remark, and showed it by stamping his feet in mock impatience. He did not bother to remove his cap.

'Sarah – or should I say Sarah-Jane. Oh my, how the mighty have risen – that's not a very nice way to greet an old friend.'

'Hardly that, Tom. Why have you come, now of all times?'

'Simplicity itself. Business in Croydon, saw the local rag. Local beauty gets her come-uppance – or words to that effect. I still come this way, see. Not often though, so it was lucky, wasn't it?'

'Not for me.'

'Forgive and forget. That's what I always say. But you were never much good at that, were you Sarah?'

'I never had cause to be. Tell me what you want, then go.'

All the while he had been studying her face, intently, as a lepidopterist might have squinted at one of the rare butterflies that from time to time alighted around them. 'My goodness me, you've certainly copped it. You must have upset someone real good and proper.'

'If it doesn't boost your ego too much I can tell you the first in the frame was you.'

'You might just have been right to think that, Sarah. I owed it you. But there we go, someone's beat me to it.' Sarah-Jane felt, as much as heard, an inexplicable depth of malice she had never encountered in him before. 'Haven't they, my proud beauty?'

Marguerite, until now hovering in indecision, reluctantly positioned herself between them. 'Shall I get help, Miss?'

'No. First I want to hear what he has to say.' She glared at Tom. 'Go on, you bastard, get it over with.'

Tom slapped Marguerite's bottom. 'How about making us a nice cup of tea, eh?'

Marguerite looked beseechingly at her mistress. But Sarah-Jane had no thought now for her sensibilities. 'Do as he says, Marguerite.'

'But, Miss…'

'Do it!'

The girl took one uncomprehending look at each of them and fled.

'Let's go back to basics, shall we?' Tom said. 'What you owe me. You remember that much?'

'Go on.'

'A debt that could have been repaid without harm to anyone, except a bit of hurt pride.'

'You're referring to my mother's will.'

'Right. Betty's will. But you weren't satisfied with that solution, were you?'

'You tricked her! You had no bloody right to involve her!'

'It was what she wanted. Perhaps still does. Or would if she knew half of what we know.' The raised eyebrows above the thin cruel smile invited complicity or denial. 'Not the other half, mind! But that's by the way.' He lunged forward and grasped her knee, his voice chillingly serious. 'I want it settled Sarah. Two hundred grand you lost me, give or take a few quid. I want it. Now.'

Sarah-Jane felt the blood drain from her face. She imagined the inflamed band crawling down her pale cheek like an exotic caterpillar, red with rage.

'Then tell me just one thing,' she hissed. 'When the cards are so obviously stacked against you – that letter of mine could do you great harm – what gives you the impudence to bargain for anything?'

'Like in all such cases, Sarah. Because of something I know.'

'Nothing you know can hurt me. My life's an open book, except for what's past history.'

'It's not about your life, Sarah. It's about your face.'

'My *face*?'

'I mean, I know who did it to you. And I can tell you one thing now, for free. It wasn't Jack Adams and he wasn't involved.'

Sarah-Jane lay back in her chair and laughed. 'If you'd told me that yesterday I might just have believed you. Now I know you're bluffing. I'm sorry, Tom, you'll have to try harder.' She squeezed her eyes in contempt. 'Now get out!'

Tom rose to his feet and bent over her. Without concern for her damaged cheek he grasped her face between fingers and thumb and shook it from side to side. But realising he couldn't expunge the scorn in her eyes he thrust it away. Taking a step backwards he wagged his forefinger at her.

Neither of them had heard Mark enter. Without seeking an explanation he gripped Tom by his collar and the seat of his pants, dragged him struggling to the front door and threw him head first onto the gravel.

Tom scrambled to a safe distance, then shouted back: 'You tell that bitch of a wife she knows where to find me.' In the grinding chase on the gravel Tom, lighter than Mark and with greater cause, reached the gate – and the freedom of a waiting car – with inches to spare.

If Sarah-Jane had been unnerved by Tom Sharp's appearance it was less on account of his threats than on Mark's reaction to the intrusion. It was Mark's first intimation that something he might not be prepared to contemplate had existed prior to their relationship. His usual laissez-faire attitude towards her had become inquisitorial in the space of hours.

'For the last time, Sarah-Jane. What did he want?'

'I've told you. Just a dispute we had way back in the past. It doesn't concern you.' Then a forlorn gambit: 'Have you forgotten our agreement?'

'I find a man assaulting my wife in my own home and it's not my concern?' Mark's face was slowly turning crimson.

'Mark, just stop bothering me. It's giving me a headache.'

'When women get headaches men sometimes seek alternatives.'

'Meaning what?'

'Meaning, Sarah-Jane, that you're no longer in a bargaining position.'

Marguerite, frozen in the doorway, was surprised to see Sarah-Jane's eyes fill with tears. She moved protectively towards her mistress.

'Don't touch her!' In frustration Mark brought his fist crashing down on a butterfly that had alighted on his other hand. It was an act against his nature, making the two women recoil in surprise. The muscles around his mouth twitched with remorse. 'I'm sorry,' he mumbled, 'I never thought you'd see me do a thing like that.' He took the wings of the mangled insect between finger and thumb and transferred it gently to a leaf. 'Marguerite, you talk to Sarah-Jane. See if you can convince her we're only concerned for her welfare.'

He left the two women with their arms about each other, not speaking, and making no move to disengage.

Brian found Sarah-Jane on her knees surrounded by a dozen balls of screwed-up paper.

'They're not coming. Not a single bloody one is coming!'

'Who's not coming?'

'The cretins we invited to dinner. Listen to this.' She unscrewed one of the balls. 'We're really sorry, Sarah-Jane, but Friday is the night Percy goes to pottery! And here's another. Bertie is flying off to Moscow next week, so we're sure you'll understand if… Christ, Brian, am I a leper or something?'

'If it's any consolation, we might come.'

'Not much point now, is there?'

'Why ever not? You seemed pleased enough last time when you got your painting.'

'Brian, I'm sorry. I didn't mean it that way.'

'Of course you didn't. You never do. So let's change the subject.'

'But you'll come?'

'Perhaps. Now listen carefully. By some means Adams has got a top man to represent him. So we're going to have to work doubly hard. You do want that, don't you?'

She bit her lip. 'I want to see justice done.'

'Exactly. So Mark and I have leant a bit on the crown prosecution. We think now we can better them. But we must have the wherewithal, Sarah.'

'But you say the case is watertight.'

'Of course. That's right. But remember, there were no independent witnesses. Convincing though it is, the evidence is still circumstantial. For a start we thought that Marguerite might be a shade more positive about your attacker's features – his walk, his height, shape of the face under the stocking, that sort of thing.'

'We are determined, aren't we?'

'Why do you ridicule, you of all people?' A little pallid ring was extending like a fungus over each cheekbone.

'Who gains?'

'I beg your pardon.'

'Who gains? In a single sentence.'

'From convicting Adams? No-one in particular, besides yourself. But a debt has to be paid to society. That's what justice is about.'

'Thank you. I did wonder.'

'Mr Throgmorton arrives at two. Let's run through it all once more, then get Marguerite in. Hopefully there'll be a time for a little lunch before he gets here.'

Mark arrived home early, and paced in the hall before ascending the stairs. Sarah-Jane was still in her evening clothes, glaring into her dressing table mirror. 'You had a hand in it, didn't you?' she said viciously.

'In what, Sarah-Jane?'

'Sabotaging my – our – dinner party.'

'I don't know what you mean.'

'You rang around, didn't you, to put them off.'

'Nonsense!'

'They told me!'

'Oh, who?'

'The Peters, the Wellboroughs, the…'

'As an incidental remark I might have mentioned that the size of the gathering was likely to be too much for you. I didn't expect them to take it personally or act upon it. The Davisons are coming though.'

'I asked them not to. Or rather it's been postponed to the evening after the trial, whenever that will be. If you're free, that is.'

Jack Adams' appearance at the crown court on a charge of causing Sarah Preston grievous bodily harm commenced on a Monday; it was all over by the Thursday afternoon. To the public and jury alike there was a singular lack of evidence and a questionable motive; almost from the beginning it was obvious that an acquittal was inevitable.

Years later Mr Justice Hobson would confide to Sarah-Jane that he could never quite understand why the prosecution had embarked upon their brief with such apparent confidence; and she, for her part, could not bring herself to tell of the undercurrents concerning the trial that only afterwards had come to light. She had kept a copy of the transcript of the summing up, parts of which she had highlighted: …*whether you are safe to convict on the basis of the factual evidence before you. No-one questions that the threatening letters to Mrs Preston emanated from the fund-raising office – that is to say the defendant's home – but you must consider who might have had access to the stationery and the typewriter, and even the defendant's pen. The answer must be many people, for it was a very busy office at that time… nor can we be sure that the letters were intended to be anything other than intimidating, as distinct from predictive, for there is no absolute link with the deed that was actually perpetrated… we see a possible motive in the hurt that the defendant sustained, but in taking account of his former*

*unblemished character you should also ask yourselves whether he
would not, were he the perpetrator of the act, have realised that the
finger of suspicion would assuredly be pointed at him... you may
then ask yourselves on whom, if not the defendant, might suspicion
otherwise fall. Both the prosecution and the defence probed deeply
into this question and neither could identify any person who might
have had sufficient grudge against Mrs Preston to contemplate this
violent act...*

'What I don't understand,' Sarah-Jane said that evening
at dinner, 'is why I got off so lightly. Surely, if the defence
had wanted to divert suspicion away from Jack Adams they
would have taken me apart looking for someone with a
better motive. Why didn't they?'

'Perhaps because they didn't need to.' Brian folded his
arms and momentarily raised his left eyebrow. It was a new
mannerism that told her the point scored was significant
but unlikely to be explained.

'You seem remarkably sanguine, Brian, about the result,'
Mark said. 'It looked to me as if you were the one most
anxious to see Adams put away.'

Was there a whiff of complicity about her husband's
reply?

'Brought to trial, Mark, brought to trial. There's a
substantial difference.'

'But the result's hardly satisfactory, is it? I for one am no
wiser.'

'Oh, I wouldn't say that,' Brian said. 'We had to take it as
far as it would go. Surely you can see that.' He leaned back
in his chair, inhaled deeply on his cigar and blew smoke
rings into the air.

Try as she might, Sarah-Jane could not see why he
seemed so satisfied with himself.

Mark was right, though: the whole wretched business
was unsatisfactory. The only conceivable benefit was that it

had served to occupy her mind. Now the waiting was over another terrible void was becoming filled with brooding and contemplation of her ravaged face.

If anything the red band along the scar had widened. Worse, the surface of the skin was becoming increasingly irregular, reminding her of an abandoned and slowly desiccating beetroot. It was worst of all at the junction of the lips and the surrounding skin; and it was no longer possible to disguise the puffiness with lipstick, a cosmetic of which, in any case, she was not particularly fond. When it all settles down and stabilises, Brian had told her, only then start worrying about what you should do next.

But it didn't stabilise. She went back to St Thomas', first with a staphylococcal problem which was quickly dealt with and then a herpes virus infection that was not. Still Brian refused her as a patient, in spite of Mark's telephone entreaties. Patience, he would say, it will come right in the end.

Her visits to the local shops became less frequent. Eventually they stopped. Her only regular contacts were her two gardeners – she could have sworn they pulled their hats down to shade their feelings – and Marguerite, who was gradually assuming the role of nurse. Day by day the house was coming to resemble a sanatorium in its patterns of activity. She might have been a tubercular patient of a generation back. She had not seen Brian or Alice since the dinner at Hightower after Jack Adams' acquittal.

Her enthusiasm for painting became an embarrassment with the – to her surprising – realisation that she had no talent. The crudity of the few daubed canvasses she did produce only reminded her of her condition. The ones that were not punched through or slashed quickly found their way to a cupboard in the tack room, away from critical eyes. The others, the majority, were cut up, bagged and taken to the council tip. Fits of frustration habitually resulted in her lying supine on the sofa with the curtains half-drawn, willing Marguerite to attend to her then scolding her when she did. She still read avidly, but with less and less concentration, for her thoughts were always on her face.

Once, with her face veiled, she visited the medical library at the hospital and for the whole day read through surgical texts on facial repair. Afterwards she sat in the cafeteria and confided to her teacup that the conclusion was inescapable: she could hope for an improvement but a return to her former state lay only in the realm of fantasy.

From beneath her veil she studied the faces around her. Most seemed to be patients. She tried to guess the conditions from which they were suffering. From somewhere within came the same pangs of pity she had once felt for her own patients. Then the pointer swung back: such sentiments were irrelevant. What she had lost was more important to her even than a healthy body, so long as it was in an intact frame. If she could barter days of her life for the restoration of her face where would the bottom line lie? She would be satisfied, she knew, with a residuum of almost anything: two years, a year, anything.

At the next table a young mother sat with her two infant children, the younger on her lap, reaching up to explore her face. She wore a white pleated dress and had her long fair hair tied back in a pony-tail which switched shoulders as she spoke with another mother at the table behind. She was a treat for some young paediatrician; and it would be a treat for her to display her youth and prettiness in this awesome and exciting place.

Sarah-Jane watched as the older child reached across the table towards his sibling's glass of dark red juice. But instead of grasping the glass he pulled at the straw, tipping it over. A fan of the bright liquid advanced across the table and over the his mother's spotless white dress.

With the woman's scream Sarah-Jane felt a surge of resentment towards the child. It came like a rogue wave, from nowhere, inexplicably. *Why don't you punish him?* she demanded of the mother in her head, for blemishing something that had been perfect. But in that brief second she found the mission that until now she had entrusted only to others – and they had let her down. Culpability should not go unpunished. It was now up to her, and no-one else, to seek out and deal with her own assailant. The pursuit of Jack Adams had been a ridiculous escapade, against her better judgement, despite the pointing finger of possibility. And clinching it was the information Tom Sharp had given her. He was an exploiter and a persecutor, but hardly a liar, and she believed him.

It happened coming back from town, somewhere south of Westminster Bridge. A church bell rang out, from no place she could see, but incisive and clear through the din of the traffic. She looked in the mirror, and for an instant the face there was her father's. Into her head came his words, *It tolls for thee.* At the Elephant and Castle roundabout it was hardly a conscious decision, just an impulse to turn back. Re-crossing the bridge she found herself passing the palace, then Mayfair and on to the Edgware Road. Even when she joined the M40 she had no plan. But to confront Tom was now an overwhelming urge, against which nothing else mattered.

It was still early evening. She had no wish to frighten her mother with her appearance, which she had trivialised in their few telephone conversations since the attack. So she drove into Oxford and walked the streets for a couple of hours, returning to Peverell Hessett just after ten. The wind had got up and the branches of the uncut laurel hedge in the lane brushed against the car. She parked at the bottom of the drive and walked on the grass to the door. At the foot of the stairs she stood listening for the regularity of her mother's breathing. Satisfied, she tiptoed to her father's study, still as it was when she had tried to sleep there curled up in the chair. From the small wall safe which she had installed secretly while her mother was on a shopping trip she took a small pistol that had once belonged to her father, on what authority she neither knew nor cared. She toyed with the cartridges, then put them back in their box: a threat was one thing, a possible murder quite another. Then she left the house and walked in the darkness to the Sharps' home near the church.

Pauline opened the door. 'Oh my God, Sarah. Tom told me he'd seen you but I didn't know it was quite like that. You poor girl. Come on in.'

'Is Tom about?'

'Funny you should say that. He's in your neck of the woods today. Wouldn't be surprised if he'd tried to call on you. Said he had something to tell you.'

'Pauline, you wouldn't happen to know what it was?'

'Well, not exactly. I'm sure you know how interested he's been in your case. Got all the local papers religiously. I don't know who it is but I think he suspects a former colleague of yours, but who and on what grounds I wouldn't know.'

'A doctor, you mean?'

'Yes, I believe so. But you'll have to ask him yourself. I'd hate to mislead you.'

'Pauline, may I ask a favour?'

'Of course.'

'Don't tell my mother I called. I don't want to alarm her with my face, you see. I'll see her when it's healed a little more.'

The door closed and the street assumed the mantle of silence that Sarah-Jane had known in her distant childhood years, before cars had come to dominate the village (although later some would be siphoned off by the by-pass.) To the west the mass of Beacon Hill and, nearer, the lesser bulk of the church, obscured most of what remained of the night sky. Never before, it seemed to her, had the synthesis of silence and darkness been more perfect. The walk back to her car would be difficult, but there was pleasure to be had in the cold tingle at the base of her neck, bearable through anticipation of the warm security of her car.

She had walked only a few yards when the twin headlights of a vehicle appeared in the far distance. Slowly the lights penetrated the oblivion from which her sense of disfigurement had been banished. Once again, in spite of the darkness, she became conscious of her face, and experienced the now familiar urge to creep into the shadows and hide herself away.

She was, at that moment, level with a gate in the hedge at the extremity of the Sharps' garden, visible only because of its white paint. She estimated that the car had just passed the turning into Tippett's Lane and within seconds she would be glaringly and uncompromisingly visible. She groped for the latch and, finding it, opened the gate and crept through into the blackness beyond.

It seemed at first that the driver must have seen her for the car slowed almost to a halt. But it passed the gate and drew up outside the Sharps' door. It confirmed what had been spinning in her mind these past few seconds: it was Tom's car.

Whatever desire she had had to confront him had been dispelled by what Pauline had told her. In its place had come an intense curiosity, without obvious origin. There was more, significantly more, to be gained from the situation in which she now found herself but she could not fathom what it was. Except... except... that it had to do with the darkness and the place where she was standing.

He would surely come looking for her. Five minutes after the front door had closed she heard it open again. Then the engine sprang to life. With a grating of gears the car executed a rapid three-point turn and headed in the direction from which it had come. Leaning over the white gate Sarah-Jane watched the tail lights disappear into Tippett's Lane. She was confident he would not find her car, which she had parked round the bend beyond her mother's house, and would assume she was well on the road back to London. But for the moment it would be unwise to re-enter the street.

Her eyes had become accustomed to the darkness. She was at the top of a short flight of stone steps leading down to a path between two hedges, so overgrown as to be almost touching. One of these, the lower, bordered the Sharps' vegetable garden. Although she remembered the gate, she had no recollection of what was beyond. Yet, somehow, it was familiar. But then, she told herself, there must, even in this small village, be other paths between tall hedges; so a sense of *déjà vu* was at least explicable.

The path led her to a squat rectangular building, brick-built and probably old. It might once have been a stable or coach house, modified over time, but there appeared to be no route by which a vehicle, or even a horse, could have gained access. The structure was separated from the Sharps' back garden by a bank of shrubs so thick that the lights of the house were barely pinpoint stars merging with the night sky. On the opposite side of the building there was dense undergrowth and beyond that a belt of trees. She tried to walk around it, but nettles stung her legs and brambles drove her back. Rounding a corner into hazy moonlight the sense of familiarity so palpable at the gate now, inexplicably, returned. Why do I know but do not recognise this place? she asked herself.

The squeal of brakes and slamming of a door announced

the return of Tom's car. She heard him berating Pauline, angry at having missed her. At least he had not found her car, for that would have prompted a search. She wondered later why it didn't occur to her to call again at the house; fear, maybe, outweighed any advantage. The earlier motivation, then so strong, had been replaced by a deeper, more subtle, urge that seemed not to require immediate action.

With trembling fingers she lifted the latch and dabbed at the gate to avoid the squeal of its hinges. Keeping close to the hedgerow she walked with feline stealth along the pavement. Then, for the first time in years, she ran, and didn't stop running until she saw the red glint of her car's reflectors in Tippett's Lane. She didn't think to look at her mother's house as she sped by.

The following morning Sarah-Jane called on Mrs Fowler. When she left she was less sure that the man seen on the golf course had been Tom Sharp. But, try as she might, she couldn't explain away the gut feeling that he had played some part in her demise.

She drove to the clubhouse and sat for several minutes staring down the fairway. There were two possibilities, both medically qualified men who could, perhaps would, wish her harm. One was Edwin, but he was old and would have acted long before if he was to act at all; and besides, he had that wonderful capacity to resign himself to adversity. No, the more likely candidate by far was the disturbed Alan Murphy. Could a cut face alone expunge the pain of three deaths? She had to concede that, if anything, it offered too small a measure of revenge. Sarah-Jane was beginning to see her own disfigurement in a wider – and perhaps more threatening – context.

She still had Alice's letter concerning Alan in her pocket and drove straight to Jeff's flat in Bermondsey.

'I can give you five minutes of my time,' he said. 'Then I've a busy clinic.'

'Then let me ask you one question, which you'll answer because you will have no wish to involve your friend if he's innocent.' She stared into his face until his eyes reluctantly engaged. 'Where was Alan Murphy when my face was cut?'

'Alan Murphy returned to Australia the week before. In fact I had a card posted on the very day it happened.' He walked to his desk and returned with a postcard showing the Sydney Opera House. 'There's no possibility, Sarah, believe me.'

'Just one more question, then.'

'Yes? Be quick.'

'Why were you so sure about the date?'

He laughed. 'Because at the time we all thought he'd done it! I must go. Goodbye, Sarah'

14

It was becoming clear to all that Mark's overt affection for his wife was waning. What was going on behind the stone-set mask was anyone's guess.

'He always did treat you like a piece of crystal,' Brian said. 'Preening himself in its reflected light but dropping it once the flaw was obvious.'

'That's not true. Why do you say that about your friend?'

'You have to be realistic, Sarah'.

She lay awake for nights in succession with the subject of her anger shifting between Mark for causing the hurt and Brian for revealing it. The truth was the stark emptiness of the bed beside her until midnight and why twice within recent days he had not even returned home until the early hours and once not at all. 'When did he last make love to you?' Alice asked. Sarah-Jane turned away, afraid she might see her fear. 'Don't worry, Sarah, you don't have to answer. That's what I live with all the time. One gets used to it.'

Sarah-Jane told herself she had no intention of living with it. For a while Alice's analysis of her predicament had led her to exploit new ways of concealing her disfigurement. In company she learnt to mingle with people so that they were kept as far as possible on her 'good' side; and sometimes strangers walked away from a conversation without suspecting anything was amiss. She sat on unfamiliar chairs because the lighting happened to be more favourable. She chose to shop where waiting at counters or in queues exposed only her intact face. She took to wearing hats, provided it suited the weather, and sometimes even wore a head scarf, until she heard Mark mutter 'fish wife' to Marguerite under his breath. But most of all she simply kept out of people's way, becoming more and more a recluse.

It was difficult to gauge the depth and nature of Mark's antipathy towards her. She rightly suspected that re-adjustment was almost as difficult for him as for her. She knew now that her role in the partnership had largely been an extension of his ego. Previously content not to face the issue, she had accepted it because of the advantages it conferred. Thus there was a loss to both of them. But the rejection was not total and from time to time there would be little acts of kindness – a box of chocolates here, or a new novel there – but it was much as she might bring home a bone for the dog, or a bag of carrots for the horses.

Marguerite's position was equivocal. Was it better that her husband should satisfy his lust with someone incapable of snatching him away? Strangely, it did not hurt her that much to think that the girl was disloyal. One reason was that there was no deliberate attempt to deceive. If Sarah-Jane had asked how many times or what positions they used she would have been told, with a shrug of the shoulders that said, I'm sorry, Miss, I don't have a choice. The other reason was, for the moment, less easy to define.

The bright summer days had led Sarah-Jane to set up her easel in the guest room where, through Venetian blinds, the high windows still admitted abundant light. The room overlooked the twinkling blue water of the swimming pool. In parting the slats one morning it came as no surprise to see Marguerite sunning herself on the terrace. It amused Sarah-Jane that the gardeners had chosen that morning to skim a handful of leaves from the surface of the pool, no doubt having thrown them in the night before. The girl preserved her modesty by lying for most of the time with her back to the sun.

Sarah-Jane knew that Marguerite was nothing if not a creature of habit, and on top of that the weather held. The following morning she dealt with the gardeners by sending them to a farm near Godstone to collect hay for the horses. For the winter, she said with tongue in cheek when they protested that the hay loft was still a third full.

By the time Marguerite appeared, Sarah-Jane was stretched out on a beach towel on the grass of one of the green bays on the far side of the pool. It was one of a number of enclaves on the lawn separated from each other by shrubs or low hedges to give privacy to guests at the house parties that she and Mark had long contemplated but never actually held. The vegetation had grown lush, and each now afforded almost total seclusion, being visible only from the upper floors of the house.

Marguerite nearly tripped over her. 'I'm sorry, Miss. I didn't see you there.'

'I'd be pleased if you'd join me.'

'Well I…'

'I had something to tell you.' Sarah-Jane thought fast. 'I'm sorry I forgot. Jed and Abel are going for hay. If you're quick you could go with them.'

'I'd rather stay with you, Miss.'

Sarah-Jane patted the ground beside her. Marguerite laid out her towel. For a moment she remained standing, embarrassed, not knowing what to do next.

'Come and talk to me,' Sarah-Jane said, still lying on her stomach, the damaged part of her face tucked away towards the bushes and invisible.

'If you don't mind.'

The girl's jeans crumpled around her ankles. Sarah-Jane held them while she freed her feet. Instead of the bikini bottom of the day before the girl wore the skimpiest of panties that Sarah-Jane had already noted, from their occasional appearance in the laundry, tended to be reserved for special occasions. As she lowered herself onto the towel her ample breasts were barely restrained by the tied front of her shirt.

'You won't get much of a tan if you keep that on,' Sarah-Jane observed.

No longer supported, the breasts swung free. Sarah-Jane saw that the nipples were erect.

Suddenly Marguerite raised herself up and made to go, as if a door through which she must escape was rapidly closing. 'I forgot my sun cream,' she said.

'You can share mine. If you like I'll put some on.'

The girl settled back uneasily onto her towel.

Sarah-Jane worked the oil into the girl's back with long, lazy movements of her forearm and hand. The delicate fingers carried the white liquid over her shoulders and under the shining black hair that parted to reveal the olive-white skin of her neck. Then down from the shoulders to the armpits, which Sarah-Jane noted with pleasure were for once devoid of hair. And on down each side of the body, negotiating the ribs and the small of the back, until the fingertips encountered the hem of the panties. For each woman there was a pause: for Marguerite a faint wiggle of the body, a token protest; for Sarah-Jane a momentary catching of the breath. The tips of Sarah-Jane's fingers traversed the skin under the hem, separating the rough from the smooth, but no more, before withdrawing.

'And now the other side.'

Marguerite made no reply but slowly and obediently rolled over onto her back. The sun in her eyes made her blink and Sarah-Jane took off her own sunglasses and put them on the girl's face. 'Perhaps it's better if you don't see too much.'

'Miss, I think you should...'

'Begin at the shoulders like before?'

'Oh.'

It was the first time Sarah-Jane had sought to give pleasure to another woman. She had once caressed Maia's small but perfect breasts; but on that momentous occasion she had been the novice and recipient, her involvement responsive, not active. Then, the doors had opened onto a world undreamed of, and, in its context, whole and undefiled. If it could not be so with Marguerite there would be no pleasure, no purpose in continuing.

The oil glistened on the flawless skin. What a pity, Sarah-Jane thought, that it was not real cream, or jam, or yoghurt, or anything that would let her legitimately lick it away. She replenished her palm and the hand descended with slow and deliberate excursions over the ribs and the convexity of the abdomen to dwell in the trimmed black hair below.

'Does he treat you well, Marguerite? I mean gently.'

'Yes, he's kind. But sometimes, well, he's… he's…'

It was an excuse to separate the hair and advance her three middle fingers further and further until their tips were able to flex to enter the soft moist vacuity.

An observer from the guest room – had here been one – might have wondered why the two figures, until that point in subtle motion, had suddenly become quite still.

Without warning Marguerite grasped Sarah-Jane's still-exploring hand and laid it forcibly by her side. In a single continuous movement she jumped up and flicked the towel about her body, then ran crying into the house.

Sarah-Jane found her in her bedroom at the top of the stairs, sobbing into a pillow. She knelt by the bed and tried to turn the girl's body towards her. But each time she grasped the shoulder it sprang back like a bent sapling.

'Tell me what I've done, for goodness' sake!'

'It's wrong, all wrong!'

Sarah-Jane tried hard to suppress her agitation. 'Marguerite, it was a new experience. Life is full of new experiences. You have to be able to cope with them, that's all.'

The girl rolled over to face her, angry now. 'That's all it meant to you?'

'No, since you ask it wasn't. It gave me pleasure because I thought I was doing the same for you.'

'That's the trouble!'

With her forefinger Sarah-Jane raised the girl's chin, barely touching the flawless skin. 'You mean it's something you've experienced before?'

'No. Yes. I don't know.'

'Then you'd better tell me.' Sarah-Jane handed her the edge of the quilt to dry her eyes. Marguerite sat upright and sniffed into it, while Sarah-Jane put her arm around her shoulders.

'If you want to, that is. Only if you want to.'

'At home… in Marseille… I had a cousine. My aunt's girl. All the family lived nearby, you see. It was very large, our family. We saw each other all the time.'

'And you felt something for her?'

'Yes.'

'And what was wrong with that?'

'She died.'

'That's sad. I'm sorry. But how does that affect us?'

Marguerite ignored the question. 'They found out. Not with me, with another girl. They caught them, my brothers, and my cousins. It was only to be a lesson.' She began to cry again and the blubbering morphed into a long drawn out wail.

'They took her to the park… it was dark by then… to the piscine.' She looked out of the window. 'Just like down there. Then they threw her in… to teach her.'

'And she couldn't swim?'

'No.'

'Weren't they punished?'

'They took her to the sea. Five days she wasn't found. An accident, that's what everyone wanted to believe.'

'And you've had to live with that?' It was Sarah-Jane's turn to cry and she turned her head away. 'I feel so ashamed. It was so selfish. Forgive me.'

'Miss?'

'No-one saw us, Marguerite. You must put it from your mind, not think about it anymore.'

'That will be difficult.'

'Why, because it was so bad?'

'Because it was so wonderful till I spoilt it.'

By teatime the two women had outwardly resumed normal relations. Shielded from the sun under a green striped awning they sipped Cinzano and lemonade on the terrace beside the pool. Each had come independently in a long summer dress, as if to protect from temptations they both knew would never come again. They must have recognised this, for at the same moment they began to laugh.

'Miss, that's the first time you've done that since your face got…'

For once the reference did not dampen Sarah-Jane's spirits. 'And that's the first time you've mentioned it and looked me in the eye at the same time. Or anyone else has for that matter.'

A crunch of gravel beyond the house signalled a vehicle coming up the drive.

'The men returning,' Sarah-Jane said. 'See, you should have gone with them.'

'They wanted to stay near the pool.'

'That might have been fun, too, but let's not go there.'

The phone on the nearby wall started to ring. Sarah-Jane answered it and pulled a face, mouthing 'Alice.' 'Funny thing,' she said, replacing the receiver, 'she asked if Brian could come round this evening and photograph his – or rather my – painting. What do you make of that?'

'What do you mean?'

'For starters he never asks if he can come round and for another he doesn't usually trust Alice to do anything.'

'Then you'll have to ask him.'

Sarah-Jane told herself not to bother.

The women were still beside the pool an hour later, when Mark appeared. His grin was as broad as the mystery surrounding the black box under his arm. He beckoned and they followed him into the house. Once inside, he closed the doors and windows. With their noses nearly touching they peered into the box.

'It looks more like a moth, but actually it's a butterfly. It's for you, Sarah-Jane, to keep in the conservatory. A sort of companion. They say these big ones actually recognise people and come to them to feed if they're given time.'

It was no ordinary insect, this. Larger by far than anything they had ever seen, it dwarfed those already in the conservatory. Its wings quivered, as if already it could sense their admiration.

'Put your hand in.'

'Ooh, should I?'

'It won't hurt you.'

The insect climbed onto Sarah-Jane's hand and fluttered its wings, showing no fear.

'It's lovely!'

'It's unique. Apart from the half-dozen in the Tower there are no others in the world. It was engineered, you see, genetically. In effect it's a new species.'

'Why would anyone want to do that?'

'For you, Sarah-Jane.'

'For me? How can that be?'

Mark spelt it out slowly. 'I mean that one of the friends had it made, for you. Just for you. The others are there only to keep the line going. For no other reason.'

'That's lovely. But who would want to do... who did... that?'

'I could only tell you that on pain of death.' He sniffed and turned away from them at the apparent unreasonableness of what he had said. 'Well, almost. Let's just say you have an admirer.'

'But you made it possible, let it happen?'

'I suppose I can take credit for that much.'

Neither Sarah-Jane nor Mark saw Marguerite slip quietly from the room, having no part in this transaction. She did not go with them to the conservatory to release the insect and when Sarah-Jane returned to the pool she found her gazing far into the distance, tears coursing down her face.

'What's the matter, Marguerite?'

'I'm just happy for you, Miss.' She got up and ran into the hall.

Sarah-Jane assumed she'd gone to her room to hide her embarrassment. And indeed, she thought, things might just have taken a turn for the better.

The telephone rang inside the house. She heard Mark shouting into it. A minute later he emerged onto the terrace, wild-eyed and gesticulating. 'There's a fire at the Tower. I have to go back. Fuck!'

229

'Who was that on the phone?'

'The police. Sorry, Sarah-Jane, I have to go.'

Seconds later she heard gravel striking the windows and the car tyres scream as they hit the road. It was lucky for Brian he did not drive into the gate a minute sooner.

'Want a drink, Brian, before you start? Marguerite can get you one.' Sarah-Jane called up the stairs. There was no answer.

'It seems very quiet. I would say we're alone,' Brian said.

'She must have gone with Mark, on the spur of the moment. The whole thing was too dramatic for them to have planned it.'

'Why would they want to?'

'What do you think?'

'I'm sorry. I didn't know.'

'Well, you do now.'

'I seem to have touched a nerve.'

'One has to adjust, that's all.' She saw his mouth tighten as he struggled to break the silence. 'Why do you want to photograph the painting? I thought you'd done that already.'

'I'm not saying anything about the painting. It didn't help last time.'

'Things might have changed.'

He must have thought she was being facetious. Then his face lit up, as if from the crows-nest he'd sighted land after months at sea. She decided to take her chance.

'Brian, tell me honestly, as a friend, what do you see ahead for me?'

'Physically, you mean? Let's be frank, Sarah. The infections were unexpected and they've taken their toll. Scar tissue's still forming and there'll be a little more distortion, particularly around the mouth. As I said before, until it's stabilised it would be premature to make a judgement.'

'But then, assuming the worst scenario?'

'There's always hope in medicine. New techniques come along all the time. I'll advise you when the time comes.'

'You promise?'

'Let's look at the painting.'

Sarah-Jane followed him meekly into the dining room. 'It's a travesty, isn't it? An image so beautiful pretending to represent something so... hideous.' She stopped herself short, recognising that such self-denigration was new. She could not guess where it had come from; nor why now, when only an hour before Marguerite was telling her how well she was rallying. It reminded her of how a paper aeroplane rises precipitously, only to stall to a much lower level, and again until...

Brian was watching her through half-closed eyes, as if reading her thoughts. Perhaps his destiny for her, generating that self-satisfied smile, at last accorded with her own dream for the restoration of her face.

'Stand by it Sarah. Good side towards me and smile.'

The flash of the gun hurt her eyes. It annoyed her because of the fatuity of it all. 'Oh, for God's sake Brian.' She sat on the end of the table, despair taking possession. Brian had moved around her and suddenly the flash illuminated her bad side.

'What are you doing?' she screamed. 'Are you a bloody sadist?'

Suddenly his arms were about her shoulders, with his mouth pressed against her neck and his head buried between her jaw and shoulder. 'Sarah, Sarah, nothing changed for me. You still hold the key in your hands. You just...'

She pushed him away just in time. Neither of them had heard Mark return. He stood in the doorway glowering at them. 'What are you two doing?'

'I'm afraid I upset Sarah with my photography. I think it brought back memories of happier times. It was thoughtless of me.'

'Never mind that now.'

'Was there much damage?' Sarah-Jane asked, regaining her composure.

'There was no damage. No fire, nothing. It was a hoax. No-one knew anything. The police knew nothing.'

'Well, thank goodness for that.'

'I looked a complete fool, Sarah-Jane, and someone's going to answer for it. My guess is that it was that little rat I caught in here the other day.'

'Tom Sharp? No, that's not his style.'

'We'll see!' Mark thundered down the corridor to his study and slammed the door. They heard the chink of glass.

Sarah-Jane lowered herself into a chair and sat brooding with her chin in cupped hands. Then she spoke, more brightly than Brian was expecting. 'Let me show you my new friend.' She held out her hand for him to take.

Even in the sepulchral gloom of the unlit conservatory the luminosity of the creature was impossible to miss. The wings, with their reticulate patterns, were miniature stained glass windows on the most sunlit of days. High against the dark vegetation it shifted its position with measured deliberation.

'Don't put the light on, Sarah. It's exquisite. I've never seen anything so beautiful. May I photograph it?'

'Go ahead.'

'With you?'

Sarah-Jane laughed. 'If you wish!' She stood beneath the overhanging leaves, her good side towards him. Suddenly she stopped laughing. 'Brian, did you see Marguerite come back?'

'No.'

In desperation she brushed past him and ran into the house. She banged on Mark's door and went in uninvited. But he had not taken Marguerite with him to the Tower, or seen her since they had looked into the black box. She followed her thoughts up the stairs to the girl's room. The family photograph and the enamel alarm clock with the little brass bells had gone from the bedside table. The wash-basin was stripped of the usual myriad toiletries. Gone too was the jumble of clothes that always littered the floor. Worst of all, the bed had been made. She had left.

Sarah-Jane looked everywhere for a note or message of some kind, but there was none.

For all his dynamism in business and play there was a streak of introversion in Mark that was hidden from all but his nearest acquaintances. Not friends, because he didn't have any real friends, Brian apart, at least to Sarah-Jane's knowledge. Rather the sort of people – business people usually – who would stay at the house for one night, get drunk and never be seen again. Those were the people who might get a glimpse of that side of him.

Once in a while, in the early hours of the morning when there was nothing next to her to offer satisfaction, Sarah-Jane would find him sitting downstairs with the hi-fi playing something low and melancholy, a scotch in his hand, staring into a burnt out fire. In these instances she had always left him quietly alone to become his usual self the following day. Now she was beginning to see that her reluctance to intrude into his personal thoughts was one of the reasons he, in turn, could not relate to her present predicament. He might have recognised it, though perhaps not consciously, as a failed trade-off, something akin to one of his less successful business deals.

This time he didn't ignore her.

'Your boyfriend gone?'

'Brian? Two hours ago. Anyway, he's your friend, not mine.'

Mark grimaced, but said nothing.

'Mark, Marguerite's gone.'

'I know.'

'How?'

'Because she left a note.'

'May I see it?'

'Not really.'

'Mark, I want to see it. Please, where is it?'

'It's about somewhere. Tomorrow, perhaps.'

'Now!'

He turned in his seat and looked her up and down, contemptuously, she thought, letting his eyes dwell on her face; then he continued staring into the fireplace. He took a large swig from his glass.

She decided that only by making a concession could she break through. She said seductively, 'If you show me perhaps I can help find her.'

'Hardly.'

'Why?'

'Because by now she'll be on the Paris train.'

Only then did she realise that the loss to her husband, whatever its nature, was as keen as her own. Perhaps their positions were not so different. Was this not, therefore, a reason for them to come together, to commiserate? 'Mark,' she said, 'I know how you must feel.'

'You can't know that, Sarah-Jane. You thought it was all physical, didn't you.' He lowered his eyes. 'I can assure you it wasn't.'

They didn't speak for several minutes. There was a question burning its way to the surface, needing the hand of courage to grab it as it emerged. The moment came.

'Mark, if it was not just physical, what was it that gave her an advantage over me?' She pointed to her face. 'Before this happened?'

'It's a fair question. I'm not sure I can answer it. I think it's because she was open, Sarah-Jane. You know, nothing deep. Like me really. I laugh when something's funny. I cry when something's sad. I don't mix them. Because there's nothing else there to complicate it.'

'Do I? Complicate it, I mean?'

'Not obviously. But there's something there, Sarah-Jane, all the time, behind all that you do and say. I don't know what. I don't hear anything or see anything in particular, but I feel it. It's like looking at something you're afraid of through frosted glass. A little demon there that prompts you when you say something – not what you say but how you say it. It was there on the terrace by the lagoon, when we first met. It's still there now.'

'That's about the longest speech I've heard you make. I wish I knew what you were talking about.'

'I believe that. I wish I could tell you. I even think it would help you if I could.'

She hid her alarm behind a wall of sarcasm. 'Then perhaps you can recommend a good exorcist!' Mark flinched, as if the idea had already occurred to him.

'Sarah-Jane, let me be honest with you. You know why we've stayed together?'

'Tell me.'

'Because you were beautiful, and sensuous, and desirable; and on top of that I liked you and still do.' He paused. 'I venture to suggest that your reasons were much the same as mine.' He chuckled to himself. 'With the advantage of a little cash thrown in!'

'So where's the difference?'

'I don't know. But here's what I have to tell you, Sarah-Jane, and please don't be offended. I don't care anymore. I only know we can't go on as we are.'

'Not even with Marguerite out of the way?' she whispered.

'Come on, you know there will be others. Just as there were for you. You don't imagine I didn't know?'

'No.'

'Well then.'

Sarah-Jane turned and walked slowly along the corridor and up the stairs to the bedroom. She stood in front of the dressing table mirror, staring at her face, not realising that Mark had followed and was standing in the doorway. She gave a little start when she saw his reflection, but feared to turn her head. 'So what are you suggesting? We give up?'

'Not necessarily. Just go our own ways, until something else turns up.'

'Then what is there for me?'

'Medicine, Sarah-Jane. Brian has never stopped chastising me for leading you into the wilderness. I think the time has come to go back.'

'And frighten a few more people with this?' She pointed to her scar.

'Think it over. No need to act prematurely. Talk to Brian.'

'I see. Mark, I have just one wish at this moment.'

'What's that?'

'From now on I'm Sarah. I think that mythical creature Sarah-Jane died this evening.' She took her nightdress from under her pillow and a couple of token items from the dressing table. 'If you don't mind I think I'll go and bury the body.'

Without turning on the light she tossed the few items she carried onto the bed in the guest bedroom. In the darkness she nearly missed it, the plain envelope, whiter even than the pillow, bearing just her name. Her heart beat faster. She had not been left out. Here must be that last expression of affection, that sharing of a common loss. 'Oh, Marguerite,' she whispered, 'at least there's one worthwhile thing left, even if it's just a memory.'

All the envelope contained was a card, not personalised in any way, inviting the bearer to the next masked entertainment at the Massingham Tower. In disgust she threw it into the bin amongst torn-up scraps of canvass bearing still-fresh paint. Surely Marguerite had not left her that. Yet...

From the window the pool and the lawn beyond were dark rectangles under a sullen sky. She searched with her eyes as if hoping for a movement that might tell her the girl had not taken offence, or fright; had reconsidered so that tomorrow could be yet another in the chain of days that had no end.

What little breeze there had been to rustle the leaves and send ghostly ripples across the pool died. She closed the curtains. Drained of all feeling, she backed away into the cloying darkness of the room and fell onto her bed, grateful for the insidious onset of sleep.

A butterfly appeared at the window. Not a large butterfly like the one in the conservatory but in its way, when you looked closely, just as beautiful. The eyes – for it was a kind of peacock – held her in a feline stare. The wings closed, so that the hold was broken, and then opened again, just as quickly; and then the fascination became stronger still, until it had extracted an unsaid promise that they would meet again.

The house was empty as she passed through, but when she entered the garden there was the butterfly circling around Moffat's – surely it was Moffat's? – head; and he, with the agility of a ballet dancer, just failed to catch it with each leap he made. She with her arms wide, protecting, the threesome progressed down the lawn.

The laurels were young then and you could pass between, and buddleias grew in the spaces they didn't yet need. The honeyed scent from the long purple racemes overcame the butterfly's sense of caution and in a second Moffat had it in his mouth, using the same incomplete snatching movements of the jaw that in other circumstances could crush the sturdiest of bones. She walked away thinking it was dead and returned disconsolate to her room.

Then once again the butterfly alighted at the window and engaged her with the magnetism of its wings. She saw that one wing had a notch in it and an antenna was missing.

Then a question occurred to her: what would happen if the sequence were repeated? She knew that the butterfly must be weakened by what it had endured, but that did not stop her and she went down again to the garden.

This time the progression was more formal, more predictable. The wings of the butterfly no longer trembled as it encountered the heady pollen scents. It flew quite voluntarily to settle on the dog's nose. And Moffat, for his part, did not this time snap at it, but held it lightly in his mouth.

Again she withdrew to her room and again the butterfly appeared at the window, continuing in a relentless cycle, until one day it was no longer there.

Like counting sheep, it led to a profound, fathomless slumber.

15

The worst thing was that the house was empty. Each day Sarah awoke with a feeling of remorse that – although she did not recognise it – was guiding her steadily along a path of humility and self-examination. That path skirted medicine – that is to say brushed with it because of its humanitarian content; and it kindled memories that were not wholly bad. But it passed medicine by and led her to the belief – realisation would not be factually accurate – that redemption lay in service to others.

First she tried the Croydon public library, and scanned the notice boards: Samaritans, Corcoran Trust, Shelter, Help the Aged – all possible. She went home clutching a notebook full of contacts and telephone numbers. She scoured the local papers for evidence of good deeds that she might emulate. She even travelled to town in her now familiar black hat and veil – there was no confusion with mourning – to buy a copy of the *Big Issue* at Victoria Station. More practical approaches hadn't yet occurred to her.

Once home, an afternoon spent on the telephone convinced her of one thing: what these contacts expected was money, not service. They had hands enough, but funding? That was a different matter. Somehow, none of it appealed.

She lay, exhausted, on the drawing room sofa, streaks of

shuttered sunlight playing across her thin form. Gingerly, she allowed her fingertips to explore the scar; it hovered around three on her self-devised healing scale of one to ten. Not much progress, then. The piped edges of the cushions jabbed and poked at her body, however much she tried to adjust them. Forced to get up, she thrust her bare feet into her slippers and crossed the carpet to the chair opposite, then looked back to where she had been lying. The image in her head was seared by the vicious sword-thrust she had delivered to Jack Adams, someone more damaged, even, than she was now. What is better, she asked: to turn the blade upon herself or bathe the wound, making it as best she could with the talents she had? The pain of her hurtful eyes dissolved; a new self-awareness took its place. Be careful, she told herself, it may be just illusion.

It was an unwise decision to contact Brian, because he had, of his own volition, distanced himself irrevocably from the man. She knew immediately that she had judged wrongly. On the other hand some follow-through seemed unavoidable.

'You haven't come round to thinking Jack Adams wasn't responsible, Sarah. What's happened to your intelligence?'

'I don't believe he did it.'

'Not did it, Sarah, was instrumental in having it done. Was that so difficult for him? That's what you must ask yourself.'

'I've nothing to lose, Brian. By talking to him about charitable work I might just learn the truth about my face.' She turned away from him and added quietly, 'But that's not the reason.'

There was no response. Or, if there was one, it was to light a cigar and surround her with a halo of smoke. That seemed to defile her face even more.

An attitude of mind in some individuals blessed with intelligence and affluence can manifest itself as pity for others less comfortably endowed. Superficially it can resemble the public school mentality of superiority, where the same factors can be instrumental. In Sarah's case there was little connection: stemming from a generosity of spirit, hers was quite unlike the ostentation of the other.

Yet it was a twinge of the first kind that Sarah experienced on Jack Adams' doorstep. And it was augmented by shame because she had never been there before. The reason, she knew, was her previously unquestioned assumption that when Mrs Adams' fund-raisers for her husband's and Brian's cause had sought her assistance she had always expected them to come to her own house. That might have been why she had seen so little of Jack Adams, who had been more of a publicist than a collector of funds.

The semi-detached house might have suggested 'council' were it not for the attention to shrubs and the creative artistry of the front garden. Neat rows of salvias flanked the path to the front door and meticulously pruned standard roses were precisely centred in weed-free circles in the grass.

She hadn't really expected Jack to be in. She had prepared what she would say to Mrs Adams to lay the foundations for a meeting. But it was Jack, in his shirtsleeves, who opened the door. If he was not pleased to see her, he was not noticeably hostile either.

'Mrs Preston, this is unexpected. You'd better come in.'

'Mr Adams. I have to begin with an apology.'

'There's no need. You must have believed it all to have gone through with it.'

'No… no. I didn't mean that. I meant the things I said to you… well… about Clare. You can't have forgotten.'

'No, nor will I.' He flapped his loose sleeves and she

saw his hands were dirty. 'I've just pulled the last of the King Edwards. You've come at the right time. Tea?'

Even in making tea there was a brisk practicality about the man. No wasted movements, not a trace of affectation. He would have behaved the same way talking over his shoulder to his dog or to his member of parliament. She felt strangely relaxed.

'Now,' he said, putting the cups on the table, 'let's start by being truthful with one another. Do you still think me guilty?'

'I never did really. It was just… well… the evidence seemed so compelling. And I suppose I had a grudge against the world.'

'Not the whole world, Sarah-Jane, only some of us in it.'

'Call me Sarah, Jack. It's plainer and simpler.'

'It is. Plain Sarah you might be, but hardly a plain Jane. Milk, sugar… no?' He helped himself liberally. 'You know, Sarah, you're right about the evidence – the letters and the ink – but a shade too incriminating if you ask me. I've racked my brains to explain it. Lots of people had access to the office, but my pen… that was always with me. Not only that but I've checked out everyone who came here – no one comes close.' He glanced at her face and she could tell he was sorry for her. 'But that's not why you've come, is it?'

'If I went now it would have been worth coming, Jack. But no, you're right.'

'So how can I help you?'

'By finding me something worthwhile to do. That helps others. I'm tired of helping myself. Really.'

'And you're not ready for medicine?'

'In time, maybe.'

'Then I'll think about it.'

A key was turning in the lock of the front door.

'Lord,' he said, 'I didn't expect her back that soon. You'd better prepare yourself for fireworks, Sarah. And I apologise in advance.' To her surprise his fingers closed reassuringly over her wrist. Then he straightened up to face his mother. There was something military about his erect bearing. Something to find out about, Sarah thought.

Sarah had always been fascinated by how dramatically Mrs Adams' expression could change without apparently moving a muscle of her face. The wide horizontal mouth, one moment a smile, became a deletion mark of hate when she recognised Sarah. 'Jack! How could you let that woman in?' Two paces and she was close to Sarah's face. 'What harm are you plotting now, you hussy. Weren't you content to kill my Clare, then try to lock up my son, when all he had in his heart was forgiveness? My God, you're not welcome in my house, Mrs Preston, and I'll thank you to get out as fast as those treacherous little feet will take you.'

'Mrs Adams, please let me…'

'Out, out, out!' She rushed out of the kitchen and returned with a broom. Jack, anticipating violence, leapt across to take it from her.

Sarah, frightened, saw no purpose in remaining. She looked back once to see Jack and his mother fighting for possession.

Minutes later she lay trembling in a hot bath, in an unwelcoming house in which the only sounds were of distant clocks ticking away unspent and useless minutes. It hurt her to realise, only now, that after the acquittal some restitution to the Adams family had been necessary; and not giving it accounted for, and justified, the vitriol in Margery Adams' tirade against her. She understood at last how her indifference to people, preserved as a facet of her character since her student days, had led to all this. I've been a cow, she told herself. A useless demanding cow languishing in undeservedly lush pastures.

Her naked body in the bathroom mirror repulsed her. She draped a towel across her face to hide the scar, turning her head this way and that until it was right, and squinting at the now perfect image with one eye. If only Marguerite could have stayed, got to know her that little bit better, so they could have stood together like this. So close they'd come, hadn't they? But, thinking rationally, wasn't their relationship only a tiny segment of her sexuality, enlarged and distorted through the lens of her damaged state. Otherwise might it not have passed her by? Well, not quite, but left unexploited at any rate. As for men, there were now no takers, nor prospect of any. Not even Abel or Jed would get much pleasure from kissing that mouth. Yet if they could see her with the towel draped so…

In the litter bin the Massingham invitation was lying, message uppermost, where she had thrown it. Get the thought out of your head, she told herself, it's not for you.

But while she slept the thought took root. In insidious wakefulness, with grey light and bird song filtering through the curtains, bodies cavorted by an indigo lagoon beneath ethereal lights and sounds. Pervading everything was an indifference to identity. Then the image and its invitation faded.

On the doormat was an envelope, in familiar handwriting, with a postmark she recognised. Her fingers trembled as she opened it. It read: *If you were serious in what you said – and I believe you were – you could try contacting Marcus Repton at 11 Avalon Road, Bermondsey. Good luck, Sarah.* At least not local, she thought to herself.

It scarcely mattered that Mark had not been home.

She parked at East Croydon station, retrieved her hat and veil from the back seat and put them on. The journey to

London Bridge was a trial, but on the bus going eastwards no-one looked towards her. She removed her hat and veil and pulled her collar lower with a twist of her hand that was almost coquettish.

Eleven Avalon Road was not a terrace house, as she had imagined, but a reclaimed derelict church – or rather gospel hall. Faint pre-first world war advertisements for *Pear's Soap* and *Sloan's Liniment* were still visible on a side wall above the level where bouncing footballs had turned the brickwork a uniform grey. She found Marcus Repton sitting behind a trestle table and joined the queue in front of it. The first thing she noted was that he didn't suffer fools gladly; the second was that he was tired, with the kind of fatigue that comes with giving excessively of oneself. The exchanges across the desk were lively: sound advice demanded commitments in return. Already she felt nervous.

Then it was her turn.

'I've come to help.'

'So you have. Jack told me.'

When the last of the pavement dwellers had gone he closed the massive door and locked it. 'You wouldn't believe that anyone would want to come in here to steal, but they do.' He made her coffee with powder from an unlabelled jar and water from a thermos flask. 'Milk?' She wasn't given the choice of sugar.

'The first thing you have to remember, Sarah, is that you're part of a family. In all families there are people you like, and some you don't like but respect – and a few that you just can't abide at any price. But because you belong yourself you have a special relationship with them – all of them – and whatever else they might think about you, in time they'll come to trust you. Then you can help them, but only then. It will be difficult for you, Sarah. You'll need to forget you were a doctor, or rich housewife or whatever you were – and you've got to stop feeling sorry for yourself. God knows, all of them are worse off than you, although that's not the way you've got to look at it. What I'm saying is try not to take refuge in what you were.'

My God, Sarah thought, what has Jack Adams told him? Has he deliberately set me a challenge I can't possibly meet, so that he and his fearsome mother can watch me plummet still further? It didn't seem likely.

'When are you free?'

'Anytime.'

'No commitments at all?' He looked at her in disbelief, then pity, as he saw from her expression that it was true. She had not, until then, realised just how sterile her world had become.

'We'll start you in here for a few days. Help with the food. Get to know the regulars. That way they'll know you – or at least some of them will – when you start on the streets.'

She found she was not alone in the disfigurement stakes. Chris, a reformed alcoholic lawyer who appeared every day at four to help serve tea, had lost an ear on the Northern Line one Saturday when he had been slow to hand over his wallet. Then there was Samantha, who had herself walked the streets before coming over. She had a deformed nose from an infection caused by a ring through the septum. There were others Sarah had yet to meet.

The first few days stretched her to the limit. 'First it's your patience, then your intelligence. Let them go,' Marcus had told her. 'Then it's down to basic humanitarian instincts and that's the make or break situation.'

At the end of her second week he grinned at her as he closed and bolted the door. 'Congratulations,' he said. 'The first real hurdle is to stay with us. Not many pass that test.'

She saw little of Mark during those early days. It had

seemed at first that continence was a natural consequence of – and sustained by – the work she was engaged in; and in some ways was even an advantage of what she was doing. Sexual matters were rendered trivial in the face of the greater issues that now dominated her life. She thought she could appreciate how nuns, for example, could divest themselves of such feelings through the assumptions of their faith. But as the days passed it became clear that things were not that simple. The more she came to terms with the work and felt comfortable in it, the more persistent the ache became, and the more intense the frustration of not being noticed by men. Worst of all was when, on being introduced to a young and attractive male, he first set eyes on her ravaged cheek.

In the house her frustration had been compounded by a new discovery: the finding of semen stains in Mark's bed when she searched there after he had left for work. Once there was a faint tinge of red. Obviously he had a mistress. It pained her that he would not tell; when she asked he just shrugged and walked away.

Once, on her way home after dark, she stopped off at Tottenham Court Road station and went into the Ann Summers shop in Charing Cross Road. Every customer seemed to be an acquaintance in disguise who knew her intimately but whom she couldn't quite place. She left hurriedly without buying anything; but it was not the last of her visits there.

After a while she saw that there was no real conflict between her private thoughts and her new-found work. There was no one standard of conduct that an individual had to observe. More than that, no-one else seemed to think it relevant. You could still do good and enjoy your thoughts as best you might, even if you did from time to time feel guilty about it.

A nip in the air and dew on the car windows signalled the end of summer. Marcus had told her that what might have seemed a pleasant exercise in sociology would now turn into a worsening inventory of hardship and deprivation. 'By next spring a lot of faces will have gone,' he had said, 'and not through emigration. You must be prepared for that, Sarah – assuming you're still with us.'

On the Monday morning of her third week the hall was more packed than she had ever seen it. It had rained and the floor was a slurry of London grime, cigarette ends and spilt food, though not too much of the latter because it tended to be retrieved as soon as it fell. The smell was at odds with the greater stench of unwashed bodies.

Sarah was needed behind the tables. When Marcus came up she was wielding a soup ladle.

'Don't stop now, but when you do be sure to introduce yourself to Mr Fadil, who's just come in. I'll ask him to take you around the streets tomorrow. Nice lad. Had some medical background but not too sure what. You'll like him.'

For all her involvement and satisfaction with the work, Sarah had to admit that the clang of the great door as it closed after the mid-day meal was the single most welcome event of the day, if not of her entire existence during this period. She liked the way Marcus would turn and stand with his back to it, as if the last intruders had been expelled from a city under siege. For a few minutes the team would slump down at one of the tables and drink coffee, saying little, bracing themselves for the afternoon's onslaught.

Sarah, near the point of exhaustion and cradling her mug, was startled by a familiar voice from behind her chair.

'Is it you, Dr Potter? I truly didn't dare believe when Marcus told me. Potter is after all a common name.'

'Ali? Is it Ali?'

'And your face? That story too I did not believe!' He peered at her without embarrassment. 'Alas it is true.'

'It doesn't matter anymore, really.'

'Then you are a very brave woman. But then that does not surprise me.' He pulled up a chair and sat beside her. 'So tomorrow you come with me, yes? Then we can really talk.'

'I'm looking forward to it.'

'Ah, but it won't be so much fun. You will be shamed by being part of a so-called civilised society.'

It seemed to Sarah that he had aged. The black hair had become peppered with grey. But there was a brightness in his eyes that she could not remember.

'What brings you here, Ali?'

'I lost my job when the hospitals merged. At one point I lost everything. And then, you see, I became one of these people – for a while.'

'It was a close-run thing, Sarah,' Marcus said, overhearing as he passed. Then he turned to Ali. 'I'm sure you won't mind me saying that?'

'Dr Potter knows much about me already.'

'Sarah, Ali. Sarah, please.'

For a brief moment she would come to treasure she was overwhelmed by a desire to cry. It was the same feeling she had experienced one day alone on Beacon Hill when the clouds were driven off by the evening sun to show her the golden carpet that was Oxford. It was moving because it was splendid and unexpected and new. And what was wonderful now was that for the first time in many years she knew what it was like to be amongst friends.

The morning ended as it had begun, with rain. They were sitting under the rear awning of a hamburger stall on Jamaica Road. Ali took her paper cup and put it inside his own, then tossed them both into a nearby bin. 'What did you think, then?' he asked.

'To be honest it seems an intrusion into their private life when we have to lift the polythene to talk to them.'

'They don't mind – most of them.'

'And the others?'

'Almost gone from this world. I think it's brightening. Let's press on.'

By mid-afternoon they had reached a large gap between two faceless office blocks fenced off from the pavement by plywood boarding. The place was inert and silent. The permanence of the long defunct cigarette advertisements rearing up from behind the fence suggested a locked battle between mighty and anonymous commercial concerns for the right to develop the site. Perhaps they had lost interest and given up the struggle, each defeated by the bleakness of it all.

Ali put his hand through a hole in the boards. With a click a short length creaked open on a rusty hinge.

The ground within had been excavated to a depth of several feet and then left, with only an abandoned digger remaining to guard it. The hole had exposed the foundations of a former building, leaving a ring of caves and crevices that had once been cellars. Sarah was surprised to see that each was occupied, although the openings were obscured by patchworks of plastic bags and old curtaining. The whole resembled a bitten sandwich with the most unsavoury of fillings. No-one was to be seen.

'The police clear them out now and again, but it's a token gesture. However many times they did it they would always come back. There's too much on offer.'

'A concrete slab over your head?'

'Better than a sodden cardboard box, or being dripping wet with condensation under a bin liner. This is a prime site, Sarah, and there is – how shall we say – competition for it.' She saw from his expression that the inhabitants of this grim place did not always live in harmony.

Ali climbed down some steps improvised from the wooden detritus that still littered the site. At the bottom he held out his hand for her to grasp. 'Who's at home?' he called.

Three of the makeshift curtains were lifted and then allowed to fall, giving Sarah only momentary glimpses of the haggard faces behind. But a fourth was held high while the occupant stepped out onto the orange London clay. There was still pride in his bearing.

'Sheikh Ali, welcome! Had'st thou forsaken me, I kept asking myself, all those aeons ago. How did you fare in the pleasure palaces of Kubla Khan?'

'I sought them in vain, Excellency, but what I saw was far from delighting the eye and the ear.'

'How so?' He was suddenly serious and attentive.

'What you have here, Hassan, is paradise on earth compared with those people.'

'Ah, I believe, I believe. And Jazreel, you saw her?'

Sarah's ears pricked up. This was not idle banter after all.

'She's working under great strain, Hassan. Little help, less food, few medicines, and now there's fear of cholera. There are many sick, many deaths.'

'Aah, poor, poor country.' He appeared to wipe away a tear. Sarah could not decide if it was imaginary or real. 'Poor, sad country. When will you return?'

'Soon, when I have saved the fare.'

'They will not give you that?' His voice resonated with deep indignation. 'Not even that? Devils!'

'They don't want us there. The government.'

'Devils, devils, devils.' He turned and walked back into

his hideaway, his concentration wavering, then giving way completely. They heard him muttering 'devils' under his breath until the sheet fell. Then there was silence.

'A junior diplomat in Iran,' Ali explained. 'Taught at the university in Terhan for a while before he fled here. Then he flipped. Sometimes he can be quite lucid, other times you can't make contact.'

'He seemed a nice old man. Can't we do something for him?'

'Sarah, let me tell you something. Nice is not a word we use. It has no meaning. For these people niceness was left behind before they became what they are.'

'Ali, I want to ask you some questions.'

'About Jazreel?'

'About both of you. And life.'

'Then let's have some tea.'

They walked along the street and turned down an alley between two featureless warehouse walls. It led down to the river where water lapped around a tiny fenced concrete platform with a white painted seat. In the water two wooden dinghies bobbed and plopped like conversing turtles.

'And the tea?'

'Look behind you.'

Sarah saw a tiny pub, little more from the front than a lattice window and a door, and a sign saying *The Mary Rose*. A slate board on the pavement listed the most basic of London fare.

'Some jellied eels, no?'

'No!'

He returned carrying a tray with two mugs.

'You want to know about Jazreel because you are still just a little bit guilty. Am I right?'

'In a way.' She felt uncomfortable, then realised he was teasing her.

'She recovered, but it took a long time. Almost until now. Then one day she was confident again and, you know, once more a real doctor. You heard me say that she runs a hospital, for the refugees. Well, not really a hospital because it has little a hospital should have. But the skill, the dedication, of those people! Ah, you should see what they can do.'

'I would like to.'

'Would you? Maybe you should. They told me you had that skill, once.'

'They?'

'People in the hospital spoke about you. The lovely lady in the white coat, always with a smile.'

'And what do you see now?'

Ali thought hard, reluctant to answer. 'A child becoming a woman again and having to learn a little more the second time round.'

'Learning what, Ali? What do you mean? Give me an example.'

'That in a camp like that nobody notices faces.'

'So there's hope for me?'

'Hope in abundance!'

Sarah looked at the two bobbing boats, each with the same excursion, in the same perfect rhythm and with the same mutual indifference to time and tides and weather.

Ali would have sensed that she could not turn her head back to look at him. So it was unlikely he caught her faltering, whispered words. 'It seems that Jazreel has everything.'

There were several cars on the drive so she sped past the house and parked in front of the stables. It was a rash decision. As soon as the first head appeared she felt guilty. When all three were looking at her, with exactly the same expression of resentful neglect, she felt terrible. I'll find you all better homes, she promised them. I don't deserve you any longer. She didn't notice Jed had joined her until he spoke.

'There's a riding school t'other side of the golf course, Miss. They'll take 'em off yer 'ands.'

'Will you find out for me?'

'Right you are, Miss.'

She went first to the conservatory, to see her butterfly. She'd called it Esmeralda because somehow the name seemed to reflect the splendour of its wings. Whether the gender was right she had never thought to find out. It was amongst the other butterflies, near a bowl of sweet things she'd left there the day before, but aloof from them, like a swan amongst ducks, there only because it was hungry. When she offered her hand it crawled onto it and rested there, facing her.

'Esme – Ali and Marcus – can it really be true that I now have two friends?'

The butterfly shrugged its wings and rotated its body on its six legs so that it was pointing away from her. She expected it to re-join the others but it did not, and in the end she had to put it there against its wishes.

There was something menacing about the cars stationed outside the house. They had a dark severity about them that suggested work and purpose, not recreation. There was hierarchy, too, in the way they were parked. It was interesting that Mark had put his own car at a distance to make room for them. That was quite out of character.

Her slamming of the conservatory door was followed within seconds by the opening of the door to the dining room where, from the low, intense voices, she deduced they were gathered. It would be interesting to see who was there. But Mark intercepted her in the corridor. His voice was jovial, but his expression brutal.

'Sarah-Jane, my dear, have you had a good day in town? There's something I have to tell you.' He took her roughly by the shoulders and ushered her away. She couldn't understand the incrimination in his voice. 'I think it's better if you don't meet them, don't you think, Sarah?'

'Why ever not. What's upset you?'

'Never mind, but I'd be grateful if you'd leave us undisturbed. You understand?'

'No, and if that's how you feel you can get stuffed, all of you.' She spotted a weakness in his attack. 'You want me to shout that down the corridor?' She opened her mouth, as if to execute the threat.

Mark agonised between silencing her by force and appeasement, wisely settling for the latter. 'Sarah, go and have a lie down – you must be tired after tramping the London streets – and I'll bring you something when they've gone. How's that?'

'Brilliant if you stick to it. Pathetic if you don't.'

He turned and left her crying in the corridor.

She climbed the stairs, slowly, with no purpose but to lie flat on her back and close her eyes against the world. So promising the day had been but now, here she was, jealous of a person she hardly knew for whom she had once felt only contempt. The woman had not been the only recipient of that. No. Perhaps they should get together and start a club. The Jack and Jazreel mutual protection society. You've been a bloody fool, she thought to herself.

It was an absorbing line of thought. But as the minutes, then an hour, passed, it gave way to a deeper longing that she had now come to accept would not go away. Then, just as her hand moved to her lower abdomen, the phone rang. She could not have guessed when she picked up the receiver that the call would seem an answer to her prayers.

It was a female voice, business-like and well used

to dealing with people; above all it was an anonymous voice.

'Mrs Preston, I'm glad to have caught you. Is this a convenient time to speak?'

'As good as any other. Speak away.'

'That's good. I have a note here to say that you might be coming to tomorrow's function at the Massingham Tower. Would you confirm that, please?'

Sarah's thoughts raced. But in her mind the answer had long been prepared and rehearsed. Her response was immediate and mechanical. 'Naturally, if the arrangements are acceptable I shall be pleased to attend.' She had no idea what she was asking.

'Splendid! I have already arranged for a car to pick you up tomorrow evening at seven precisely – that is to say to the second – at your gate. You will find the chauffeur well able to take care of all your requirements. You need do nothing more.'

'Thank you for your trouble.'

'No trouble at all. Goodnight, Mrs Preston.'

She stood at the window, thrust back the curtains and raised her arms to the night. She was a caged bird being shown the open door to the sky. She felt a desperate need to tell someone, if not the truth, then at least to convey to them her excitement and gain a response. She thought first of Alice and Brian, yet somehow they were not right. Then Jack Adams, but – my goodness – that would never do. Then it came: Ali.

There were gangs of youths on the street where she parked: white, black, a few Asians; in threes, fours, fives or more. In spite of their coarse banter they were uneasy, with the alertness of game on an African plain, ever mindful of attack. She suspected that each would know where to run, where to hide, when the signal came; and, more ominously, when to make a stand.

She chose her moment carefully, looked all around, and walked swiftly across the pavement to the door. The red brick portico was cavernous and dank – as much a place of danger as of refuge. There had been businesses here, but the brass plates alongside the bell buttons were covered in crude labels; one was a piece of Elastoplast, but whether used or not she could not tell. Ali's – no surname – was at the top.

His voice crackled from the speaker. 'Close the door as soon as you're in. Fourth floor, on the right.' Then the catch clicked open.

There had once been luxury of a kind: smart offices and waiting rooms with plush furniture and pin boards belonging to long-legged secretaries in tight skirts and high heels. Now paper peeled from the walls under its burden of green mould. Fragments of lino and carpet remained only because they were beyond salvage. Another floor up he was waiting for her.

'Sarah, you should not have come.'

'Why?'

He went to the window and pulled back the pieces of sheet that served as a curtain.

'You see them outside, like pariah dogs.'

'Yes, I saw.' Ali was as much a hostage to his surroundings as any of the vagrants he had befriended on the streets.

'Last week there were two knifings, one white, one black. They always seem to go together. How do you say, tit for tat? The most dangerous are the mixed gangs – they hate everybody.'

He suddenly realised she was still standing and was ashamed. 'Please, come and sit. Forgive me.'

'You live alone?' From his expression she saw that the

question had been spurious and unnecessary; but why, she wondered, had it hurt him?

'I have only one other person, as you know.'

'Then why are you not with her?'

'Because I have business here to complete. Then I go.'

'What sort of business?'

'Bad business. You wouldn't be interested.'

'I might. If you want to tell me.'

He reached across the table for a cigarette packet. Not to take one out but to rap the packet repeatedly on the table top to release some inner tension. It was an effort of will to tell her.

'It's simple. I got into debt.'

'Because of the baby?'

'The doctors' bills. That was the beginning. Then, after Jazreel became sick, we couldn't live off what we earned. Where we lived, it wasn't difficult to make money. In certain ways.'

'Drugs?'

'But then Jazreel found out. In her temper she destroyed what I had without realising its value. It was a lot.'

'And then?'

'I owed the dealers. I've been paying them ever since. There's interest, you see.' He took out a cigarette and lit it. 'I'm sorry, I shouldn't have told you.'

'Ali, can you tell me how much is involved?'

'No, Sarah! That's not what I want!' He tapped the table again in frustration. 'Why did you come?'

Sarah smiled at his anger. There was time enough to help without embarrassing him now. But the smile pulled at her lips like little guy ropes. Her face clouded over as in her mind the subject of her attention shifted. Then it became a wry half-smile.

'First – the easy one – to tell you that I can't come with

you tomorrow. Just a social thing I'm going to. There are so few of them for me these days.'

'That's a pity. Hassan was not well today. I was hoping you could look at him. But the next day will do. What's the other?'

'That's more difficult. You told me once that Jazreel hated Edwin – you know, Stricker, the surgeon. Did she ever tell you why?'

'No. It's the only thing she will not share.'

Sarah wanted desperately to ask about the baby, but did not dare. 'Then does she hate me too?' There was no particular purpose in the question. It was just something to say.

'No, she was just scared for you.'

'And you told her she needn't have been?'

'I told her about your face.'

Something in his voice alarmed her. It caught her breath and she felt her eyes widen. Why in heaven's name had he responded with a reference to her face?

'What's that got to do with it?'

'I'm sure nothing. Please forget it.'

'Then what made you say it?'

'At first she thought there might be a connection. I told her no. She doesn't think so now. It was a silly remark. Please put it from your mind. Do you want to see some photos?' He took a packet from the mantelpiece and sat on the makeshift sofa. He patted the seat for her to join him. Sarah doubted whether he really wanted to show her; it was probably only a way of changing the subject.

'They're all mixed up and some are quite old. I'm not a photographer.'

Most were of Jazreel, looking woodenly at the camera, against many different backgrounds: cities, mountains, desert even.

'She is really beautiful now,' Sarah said.

'Yes, yes, beautiful again. And here's the camp… and the hospital. See how primitive it is! And these are the children… and the patients.

'Well, at least some of them can smile.'

'For the camera, I think.'

'And where's this? Not the Middle East, surely?'

'It's Oxford.'

'Oxford?'

'On our last day together in England! I treasure it.'

'Why Oxford?'

'She had not been there, she said. We drove through the countryside. The hills and the trees. The real England, here see.'

The print was of a church and, in the background, a hill, dome-like, green with vegetation and bald on top like a monk's head. Sarah looked at it in disbelief. Then she looked at Ali. But in his face she read only the splendour of a last evening shared by two lovers.

'Ali, I know this place!'

'Do you? That's interesting. Jazreel had a friend there to say goodbye to. Near the church.'

'Did you see… this friend?'

'No. I stayed with the car and looked at the church.'

'Do you know who it was?'

'No. Just a friend.'

'Then what happened?'

'She came back and we drove to London.' He seemed to be searching his memory. 'She seemed very tired. Didn't speak much. She was still not well, you see.'

'And the next day?'

'Gone. It was two years before I saw her again.'

Their thighs were firm together on the seat, the warmth flowing between. By chance her damaged face was away from him. She sensed the fierce conflict within that was making his hand tremble, its excursions magnified by the photograph he still held.

She touched his stubbled cheek with the back of her hand, uncertain what to do, knowing that something precious could be shattered by the slightest misjudgement. The urge would have been uncontainable if the prospect of the following evening had not come to her rescue. She was grateful when he spoke.

'I cannot, Sarah. My feelings do not count against these things that hold me in chains. Just accept it. Please.'

He walked her to the car and she left him on the pavement, looking about him with the feral anxiety affecting all who lived in the squalor of that street.

But it was Jazreel's association with Peverell Hessett that occupied her mind for the duration of the drive home.

16

Precisely meant just that. Sarah left her room with a minute
to spare, ten seconds of which she spent mouthing to Mark,
who was arguing on the telephone, that she was going
out. She had her usual coat over the white dress she had
worn before, with it tucked up around her midriff so he
couldn't see it. It seemed curious that he didn't know her
purpose, but evidently he did not. He was, if nothing else,
transparent.

As she stepped into the road the car, sleek and black,
glided to her side. She walked with it for a few steps until
both were out of sight of the house. The rear door opened
automatically and she got in. She wondered if the timing
would have been as precise had there been anyone in the
road to witness it. Was that, too, just coincidence?

To her surprise the driver neither turned around nor
spoke. By the time her seat belt had fastened itself around
her – for that too was automatic – they were already travelling
at speed. A glass panel separated her from the driver and it
seemed pointless to speak. Yet this was no taxi. It was the
most opulently furnished car she had ever been in.

The car turned into a narrow lane, unknown to her
even though they were still within a mile of the house. It
skirted the edge of a field and pulled onto a bare platform of
concrete for the temporary holding of root crops and farm

waste. The partition descended to reveal a tanned face, with a neatly trimmed black beard and lips held sufficiently apart to show a perfect set of teeth.

'Mrs Preston. Firstly, my apologies for the brusque manner of the rendezvous. Secondly, may I extend a most hearty welcome on behalf of the Massingham Foundation.'

Sarah began to speak but he silenced her with a slight motion of his hand that suggested a profound capacity for persuasion.

'Before we go further there is one thing I have to ask. Is your husband in any way aware of your adventure this evening; by that I mean through your own agency?'

'No, I am sure he is not. Why do you ask?'

'To assure you of a splendid evening uncompromised by thoughts of a… domestic kind. There is no need for him to know, nor will he, I assure you. Now, my name is Pierre, and I shall be at your service whenever you need it, for whatever reason. Or discreetly absent if you do not.'

He passed across the seat a small flat box in fine leather. It contained a simple gold amulet bearing a single ruby. 'You must wear it all the time. Under the stone is a tiny transmitter. If you need my help simply press it and I will come. But remember that, once in the Tower, until you press it I will not be able to locate you. Like everyone else, you will not be recognisable from your appearance.'

He was about her own age, but with a worldly assurance that suggested greater maturity. The face under the dark hair was malleable, and the goodwill it now radiated seemed of the kind that could be supplanted in an instant by derision or cruelty. There was also charm and power, the latter suggesting that he was an employee only because it was to his advantage. It seemed he was trying hard to disguise a raw Gallic sexuality that had Sarah sitting upright in her seat with her head turned away to hide her disfigurement.

'When we get to the Tower – that is to say park beneath it – I will direct you to your personal dressing room where you will find a variety of forms of attire. It is for you to choose. There is one rule only: under no circumstances must your mask be removed. It is this rule that ensures enjoyment for everyone. I know you already understand that. Then you may enjoy the evening in whatever way you wish. When you want to be taken home return to your dressing room, press the stone and I will be waiting by the car within five minutes. Is all that clear?'

'Perfectly. Thank you.'

'Then we'll drive on. I shall not speak again, so as not to be guilty of spoiling your enjoyment.' He brushed aside her protest with the now familiar twist of the hand. 'There is a switch in front of you, if you would like to be occupied during the journey.'

No passenger could have resisted that simple gold switch, which Sarah saw was in the form of a butterfly. She pressed the uppermost segment and a screen that until then she had not noticed burst into vibrant colour. At first the images were blurred, beautiful only because of the motion of their abstract shapes. But as she watched there appeared recognisable forms that had meaning, expressing themselves for a moment only before becoming lost in the swirling cavalcade. The effect was to intrigue and fascinate and she began to search in the screen for greater clarity of understanding. Gradually, she became aware that what she was seeing were images of the most erotic and suggestive kind, so discreet that it was impossible to be offended, though at the same time so powerful and sensuous that she felt her body begin to writhe in pleasure and sympathy. And the whole was ever-changing, devoid of the numbing of the senses of even the most subtle of the few erotic films she had seen. This was pornography turned upon itself in the hands of a master film-maker.

Then – oh my God, could that possibly be? – she was in the picture herself, with the most intimate parts of her own face and figure in juxtaposition, heightening the sensations that gripped her body. How was that possible? Who had filmed her? And when? But it had been done with such consummate taste that offence was far from her mind.

She did not notice when the car entered the tunnel. Once in darkness Pierre switched on the interior lights. For a moment it seemed that there was a second person sitting in the passenger seat beside him. Then he twisted his arm and she realised he had been holding up, like a monstrous glove puppet, a mask in the form of a bull's head. Then the light was off again. Had he allowed her to see – she suspected against his instructions – how she might identify him?

When he opened her door she was relieved that he did not fall short of the promise of his face and demeanour. The only thing to set against him was that he was not particularly tall. Such a point of detail might once have mattered; it didn't count now.

He pressed a numbered disc into her hand and motioned her through a door next to the car. Concrete, glass, the Massingham monogram faded almost beyond recognition; she was momentarily disappointed. Then she realised they were still in the world of the uninitiated, the drabness of the barrier intentional. The door closed immediately. She found herself in an upholstered cell which, from its slight vibration, was clearly an elevator. The door opened again and she was in a carpeted gallery with doors each with a unique pattern in inlaid wood. She chose the one bearing her number and went inside.

To this point she had not seen another person. Later she would learn that the lift door would only open when the gallery was empty.

The closest it came was to a first class cabin of an ocean liner. There were flowers and baskets of exotic fruits, some she did not recognise; and on one wall a large screen that reminded her of the source of her fascination in the car. It would be possible, she thought, to spend a whole evening here without going a step further. Perhaps some companions did just that. That was not why she had come.

It amused her to find a white gown similar to the one she was shedding, but of finer quality. In the mirror she could just make out the detail of her own body, but over the breasts and pubis the material was imperceptibly more dense, so that the effect was tantalising rather than obvious. Even if she had wanted to, there was no chance of wearing anything underneath. Of the choice of masks, that of a faun seemed the most benign.

A watch seemed inappropriate and she left it behind. The cautionary red light of her amulet was a reassuring substitute. Then and throughout the evening she could not stop herself looking at it.

The first surprise came as she passed from the gallery linking the personal rooms to the dome. Before, in spite of the absurd extravagance of the setting, there had been conventional elements: in the decor, the music, the conversation even. And light: enough, at least, to put a brake on the more extreme forms of self-abandonment. It had been a wild party, but one conducted within an envelope of sobriety and decorum.

Now, there was purple-blackness under the vast dome.

She heard the lapping of water around the quaint quays and inlets before they became visible. A network of faintly luminous paths within the vegetation encompassing the lagoon had the form – yet, strangely, not the menace – of a coiled serpent. She weaved her way to the water's edge to take stock. There was no hurry to go where the guests were more densely clustered.

So fine was the construction of her mask that she was scarcely aware of it. For the first time since the attack she felt whole again – yes, that was the word that kept circulating in her head – and at... at peace? No, not peace, because the carnal stirrings that had been suppressed with such difficulty during all these weeks had been re-awakened by the stimulus of her journey and the suave attentiveness of Pierre.

She stared across the dimly lit space beneath the dome. Where before there had been a wall of limestone there was now continuity with a greater darkness beyond. She looked instinctively for her watch to scale her progress, but the red eye of the amulet returned the message that time here had no meaning. The evening would end when she was replete, or exhausted.

How many others, she wondered, were guests like herself rather than companions or friends. There was no answer to that. The sexes seemed balanced, but that was no guide. The whole performance might be for her benefit alone; or, just as easily, her role and that of the other women could be the sole gratification of the friends, and they merely gullible stooges hired for free. Not knowing these things lent piquancy to the proceedings.

She was approached by a woman dressed in a similar gown to her own and sporting a lamb mask. Looking around, it seemed the common choice. Perhaps the innocence of white enhanced the potential for transgression.

'Is this your first time?'

'My second,' Sarah said. She should have added, but not like this. But it did not come.

A figure in black they had not noticed joined them silently out of the shadows. 'Perhaps I can offer guidance, dear ladies. The amusements and delights' – he nodded towards the black vacuity – 'are arranged in sequences, rather like the branches of a tree, with diversions on each theme to suit all tastes. How you progress is entirely at your discretion, but I should add that not many guests would wish to experience all that is on offer, or even pass to the extremity of any one branch.' His small chuckle, intended to be reassuring, carried the merest hint of warning. 'But first,' he continued, 'please enjoy some refreshment.'

From the demeanour of those around her Sarah decided that they were still on neutral ground: an unmarked haven where to do other than remain in conventional behavioural mode would have been bad form. Attendants in the same white garb as her own came and went with trays of food and drink. They seemed adept at being close only when needed, at other times receding unobtrusively into the shadows.

'Why don't we start off together?' the woman said, 'then go our own ways as soon as we feel like it.'

'That's a civilised approach. Yes, let's.'

'Civilised, yes. That's what it is. Our base natures in a respectable and enlightening frame.' She sounded like an academic. Sarah resolved to find out more about her before the evening was out.

They entered a dimly lit, rectilinear landscape. It resembled the contents of a warehouse in which all the crates of goods and all else visible were encased in fine black velvet. But there the resemblance ended. For the rest the effect was sumptuous and splendid. Here and there little oases of light illuminated clusters of people gathered in rapt attention. And around and beyond each of these, diverse routes and passages led into deeper recesses where activity was evident only from the glow of distant and subdued lights.

'A rabbit warren,' Sarah said.

'I would say it's more that we're spoilt for choice.'

There was simplicity and directness about everything she saw, presented without embarrassment or shame. They entered between two near-motionless groups of figures: on their left twins, hardly more than girls, clasping each other tightly and writhing with the slow deliberation of serpents, their golden tresses alive against the blackness of the velvet podium; on the right a single brooding male wearing only a translucent waistcoat extending to the bottom of his rib cage. It was like entering the statuary garden of a Palladian villa, except that here was promise of fulfilment, not parody.

'I know where my talents lie,' whispered Sarah's companion, with a knowing glance towards the girls.

Sarah was surprised because they showed no reaction when their hair and skin were caressed, and their bodies explored. They were signposts only, there merely to hint at what lay beyond.

She, for her part, stood undecided. The male figure turned his head slowly towards her, with a fleeting smile; but she was more cautious than her companion, who had already moved on.

Words alone, as Sarah would one day find, could not do justice to what she saw that evening. There were images that would remain lodged in her memory, as much for their grace and beauty as their licence. Like when, by chance, she looked up and saw suspended above her a couple linked together with their only aid the single rope passing between their naked bodies. There were postures and contortions beyond the reach and imagination of ordinary lovers; and extremes of physical development interlocked in the manner of Chinese puzzles, for contemplation and exploration.

She chose a path on the theme of solitary masculinity and found herself in a group admiring the phallic splendour of three youthful Apollos competing with one another for the accolades of elevation, turgescence and rigidity. She laid her forearm alongside one and found herself wanting in each dimension. 'You've priced yourself out of a market,' she told him. But a squirrel-faced woman beside them took the remark as a challenge. Sarah looked back in amusement to see the pair in earnest contemplation of the impossible.

There was further development of this theme, in which the devotees no longer enjoyed the right of choice, or even the option to move freely. And beyond that were devices that gave pain, or situations where the willing participant – the guest – was able to couple her own pleasure with the humiliation of her victim. Sarah's body language must have revealed her feelings for when, out of curiosity, she peeped to see what was beyond, a figure emerged from the shadows to ask if that was truly what she wanted.

Up to that moment she had been a passive, if fascinated, observer. No medical training could have prepared her for human behaviours such as these. But it was not what she sought and she made her way back to the relative sanctity of the first few tableaux. She tried another route where bisexual combinations and numbers held the key. And beyond that was the exploitation of age: youths enjoying the attentions of older women, women still teenagers subjected to the aesthetic equivalent of gang rape. Again she was politely but effectively barred. 'For you there would be no pleasure in going on. Have you not already passed what you came for?'

But something here had caught her attention. She brushed aside the well-meaning attendant. The girl, passive and moaning beneath a convulsing scrum of male lust, engendered a sense of pity that welled up from some deep, hidden and unstoppable source. The pity was not for what was being done, but for the willingness of the girl to let it happen, oblivious of the consequences – for herself, her violators and those sick enough to watch.

Sarah stepped closer, the better to see the girl's expression. The force of the penetration caused the resigned face to contort in pain. Sarah turned angrily to the attendant. 'Why do you let this happen to her? Can't you stop it, for God's sake!' She could not see the face behind the mask, only the embarrassed hunching of the shoulders, admitting to a situation that should not have been allowed to develop. The explanation was not what Sarah expected to hear. 'But that's the purpose of it. It's what some guests want to see. Come away now, please.'

She sought refuge near the lagoon, away from people. What had moved her? Why this concern for a waif evidently willing in spite of the degradation and pain, and who no doubt would be paid fabulously. There was an answer, she was sure, but it was so deep within her as to be quite inaccessible.

She needed a drink badly. Across the floor an attendant in a red gown stood holding a tray. Rather than wait for the attention that would be offered within seconds if she remained where she was, she walked across and helped herself to a glass. There was no remonstration, but she had the feeling she shouldn't have done it.

The unidentifiable yellow liquid was cool and refreshing, and faintly familiar. Within seconds the depression that gradually had been gaining ground was dispelled. No longer was there indignation; instead her thoughts regressed to the delicious expectation she had experienced in the car, and the surge of desire when Pierre had opened the door for her. She looked around for the bull mask. But why should he be there? He was probably in a bar somewhere, loudly ridiculing the crass stupidity of it all.

There was one avenue, more central than the others, that she had still to explore. It stretched more visibly into the distance or, rather, into the far darkness, for the end could not be seen. Here were no set pieces, but people interested only in one another: discarding gowns, stroking, probing, penetrating. Sarah found herself looking at a sea of disembodied animal heads tossing about on a white-cream froth of convulsing flesh. Thankfully the shrieks and groans were reduced by the all-embracing velvet to the level of low vulpine howls.

More out of curiosity than in expectation, Sarah negotiated her way through the seething mass, careful not to touch. A fascinating anomaly caught her eye: the physical perfection of the women against the less impressive endowments of the men. Were they here just as objects of gratification, selected for their bodies alone? And what did that say about their faces? As to her own face – until now she had not thought of it.

Unlike most of the others, she had not shed her gown. She realised she was singled out by it. She might become, if she were not careful, a target of attention, and began to move away. She felt faint; but something else was gaining possession in her head, telling her it did not matter.

Her last tottering steps were towards a velvet wall, high enough to keep the revellers in but low enough to see into the blackness beyond. And there, as if suspended in space like a brown balloon, she saw Pierre's bull mask.

'Hello, Sarah, how do you feel?'

The voice was indistinct; she was no longer in control. Her legs felt weak and her mind was quietly numb. She became aware of a delightful throbbing in her lower abdomen. It seemed wrong that he should have known her name. Surely he couldn't have known the mask she would be wearing.

'How did you recognise me?'

He pointed at her amulet.

'I didn't need to press it?'

'No.'

The drug was taking hold now. The bull's head was beside her, somehow having come through the wall. She could not see clearly. Images assumed the undulating motion of chocolate being layered onto biscuits in a television advert. Then – horror – she was sinking to her knees.

Her upper arms were gripped by hands that appeared from nowhere, turning her body so that she was looking upwards. She worried that the dragging of her heels on the soft carpet might leave marks that would not go away. As her head lolled from side to side she could see back down the long, dark tunnel, over the masses of cavorting flesh, to the silence of the of the lagoon under its black dome. Then the movement stopped and there was only darkness.

Was it you, Elizabeth, who told me this, so vividly that I've usurped your own memory and see it all now as if with my own eyes? Looking first far out over the blackness of the vale of Oxford and then below to the lesser darkness of the churchyard and all around. So cold it is, up here, with the wind biting at my chapped knees and blowing hair about my face. It's a savage place, isn't it, until the wind lessens and becomes still; like the silence of an audience before the curtain rises.

We used to signal to one another, didn't we, you and I. From here, on this old bench. So that light – that distant pin-point star – should not have surprised me. What is your word? Meandering? Rivers do that, not lights, Elizabeth, but I know what you mean: that it's the path and not the light that meanders. And it's not difficult to trace its course through the ancient oaks of Tippett's Wood to the churchyard; and then away again through more trees until it's joined by the greater light of doors opening and milling grey figures melting into it. But who held it, that coursing, purposeful light, and what did it signify?

She was looking upwards now, with near sightless eyes, sensing, not feeling, the weight that bore down upon her. There was still the other image: the face of the raped girl. But, try as she might, she could not identify with it. And that was because there was no violence here, external to her, that is; such violence as there was came only from the rhythmic aching of her own responsive body.

Pulses of brilliant light came at her through the window as they sped through the streets. As she closed her eyes against them her stomach began to turn. She needed to keep control because there was no way to communicate through the glass screen, and the consequences could be severe if she were sick on the carpet. So she tried to hold herself in a state of semi-consciousness that hovered between grasping for reason and planning resistance. If she remembered anything it was the car stopping where there were trees above and fewer lights, and the door quietly opening.

A voice, presumably Pierre's, said something like, 'five minutes and I'll bring her in.' Then the car prowled noiselessly about the streets. It stopped again and once more the door opened; but she could hear only fragments in low whispers. 'He's out there now. You know it, Tom, you've been there. You go ahead.' Then: 'Okay, take her over your shoulder, but no touching, know what I mean?' It was a serious threat and the tenor of the reply did not disguise an unconvincing bravado. 'As if I'd do such a thing!' 'Wait though,' the other said, 'give her another shot first.'

It seemed she was being carried to a party. There were people shouting, and more lights; but it was all further into the distance than they would go. There was gravel underfoot, but over his shoulder all she could see were imprints from their combined weight. Then something else took hold of her mind: a scything, numbing assault that demanded sleep.

It came again, Elizabeth's voice. Look now, Sarah, through the crack in the curtain. What can you see?

She wanted to tell her sister that the pain was too much, that her little body could take no more. But she was just able to turn her head. She could almost reach out and touch it, so bright it was. And for a second – but only a second – there was relief from the pain and the shame.

Elizabeth! Elizabeth! They've lit the fire on Beacon Hill.

Then someone took hold of her face and wrenched it back. After that there was nothing left to remember.

17

Mark was shaking her violently by the shoulders. 'Jesus, Sarah, won't you ever wake up?'

'What time is it?'

'That doesn't matter. Where the hell were you?'

'What do you mean?'

'You didn't hear anything, see anything? Christ! Get your skates on. You've got a shock coming, young lady.'

She still had on her white dress, but Mark would not have seen that under the sheets. She waited for him to go, then tore it off. She dragged on her dressing gown and coaxed her feet into her slippers, then followed him down the stairs and out of the back door in the direction of the stables.

A kinder man would have prepared her better for what she saw.

Steam was still rising from the piles of ash and charred wood. Steam because they had doused it so thoroughly that the ground was covered with oil-brown rivulets of excreta and blackened straw, with deeper pools where the fire engine had stood. Figures in rubber boots prodded and probed amongst he remains. One was a policeman.

'Apparently it was ablaze before anyone noticed,' Mark said. 'We tried to wake you but couldn't. Heaven knows what you'd taken.'

'My horses! Are my horses alright?' she screamed.

He pointed to two heaps amongst the charred fallen rafters, like gigantic overdone steaks on a barbeque griddle. A man in wellingtons was attaching ropes to the nearer one. She followed their line to the winch in a recovery vehicle, then paced up and down on the periphery of the mess until her slippers were sodden. Suddenly she stopped and looked up sharply. 'Where's the third one?'

'Broke loose, apparently. Not been found yet.'

She recognised the policeman as one of Guthrie's men who had guarded their gate.

'Constable Waverley, Mrs Preston. Not having much luck these days, are we?' He called to the others, 'Can we go inside now, please, to talk it through.'

They gathered around the kitchen table. Sarah tried to determine whether Mark's agitated glances towards her were of sympathy or exasperation.

'You see Miss, there's a problem,' Waverley explained. 'Mr Preston here says he woke up at three when Mrs Fowler down the road telephoned to say she could see flames. That's correct, isn't it, Sir?'

'Get on with it.'

'Mr Preston says he called by your room on his way to investigate.' He lowered his voice. 'I... um... understand you have separate bedrooms now. You weren't there then, but twenty minutes later you were sound asleep in bed. I'm sure there's nothing amiss, but you see the problem.'

Sarah saw the problem only too clearly. Indirectly she was being accused of arson. She needed desperately to bring her intelligence to bear. Her head ached and she felt terribly alone. She realised her response had to be a bold one.

'I wouldn't know about the time, officer, but I was unwell during the night and couldn't sleep. It's possible I was in the loo.'

'You weren't, Sarah. I checked the bathroom.'

'Would that be next to the bedroom, Sir?'

'Yes'

'That's because I went downstairs,' Sarah said. 'To get water from the fridge – for my sleeping pills. She hated lying, but what was the alternative? The consequences of divulging the truth needed evaluating. 'There was a noise while I was sitting there, but I'm afraid I wasn't in a position to investigate. Probably that was you, Mark.'

'And soon after that you found Mrs Preston in bed, Sir?'

'Yes. It was impossible to wake her. That was bloody frustrating, Sarah.'

Sarah's brain was clearing now. 'Maybe two tablets were too many – on top of the others.'

'Mr Preston also said you were out last evening. May I ask where?'

'Is that really relevant, officer? Why is all this necessary? It was my stable, and my horses.' Her anger was genuine, but she could see Constable Waverley sensed a deeper fear.

'I know that, Miss, but there's something else to consider.'

'What?'

'That if it was deliberate – I say if, mind – there could be a cruelty charge. One of the men out there is from the RSPCA, here because of the escaped horse.'

Sarah leapt to her feet. 'You're actually suggesting I deliberately set fire to… killed my own horses? I loved those animals!'

'Jed said you wanted to get rid of them,' Mark said.

'To good homes, because I couldn't cope!' Sarah was crying bitterly now. This was reality, no longer subterfuge.

'So you see, Miss, I have to ask you about last night.'

Sarah wiped her eyes on a tea towel. It became an artist's palette with spent make-up from her face. 'Of course you do, officer, I understand that. But before we go on would you mind if I cleaned up my face? Help yourself to more coffee.'

She went slowly up the stairs, but once out of sight sprinted to her room. Closing the door she lifted the receiver of the bedside phone and dialled furiously.

'Alice? Thank God. Listen Alice, I need help. Please don't ask me to explain now but I need an alibi, desperately – yes, a man, quite right. Alice, is there any reason I was not with you until late last night, and you brought me back around two?' There was a pause of several seconds. 'Alice?' Then, 'Bless you, Alice. Bless you, bless you, bless you. I'll ring later to explain.'

Mark was angry. 'What kept you?'

Sarah looked away from them, speaking in an urgent whisper as if only to her husband. 'You know how my face embarrasses me.'

'Don't be hard on her, Sir. Now, your movements last night?'

'Yes, of course, officer, that's not a problem. I had dinner with Mr and Mrs Davison, our friends in Putney. Mrs Davison drove me home, about two, I think.'

'You never told me,' Mark said.

'My policy these days. You've only yourself to blame for that.'

Constable Waverley was no further forward. He would check Mrs Preston's account but saw no reason to doubt it. He also needed to consult with colleagues on the possible causes of fire in stables.

For the rest of the morning Sarah quietly mourned the loss of her horses. Then, around lunch time, it occurred to her, with a sudden tingle in her spine that was not unpleasurable, that things were moving forward. Just what those things were she couldn't begin to guess.

Brian's unexpected arrival at five was an assault on Sarah's weakened defences. She didn't know what, if anything, Alice had told him. Mark was still at home, having cancelled a business meeting with bad grace, ready to take it out on Sarah at the slightest provocation.

The relationship between the two men had grown cool. As Sarah's demise was the only factor that seemed to have changed in past months she believed it was linked to herself, but she could not explain it. But there was no doubt that Mark's dwelling on her situation was influencing his behaviour towards her. An evening with the Davisons without his knowledge would just confirm the suspicions that seemed to be churning in his mind.

Sarah was in the conservatory having tea. They found her playing with Esmeralda, rotating her wrist back and forth so that the butterfly walked first one way and then the other, reluctant to leave her. Mark must have caught the apprehension in her eyes when she saw Brian.

'Sarah tells me she enjoyed her evening with you, Brian,' Mark said. 'Good of you to entertain her.'

'A real pleasure, Mark.' Obviously he couldn't resist returning the sarcasm. 'I just hope the day will come when it will be both of you together. But there we go.' He turned to Sarah, who was blowing gently at Esmeralda's wings, so that the colours flashed like distant fireworks. 'Sarah, we were devastated to hear about the horses. The police telephoned Alice this morning. I imagine they thought you might be too distressed to speak to them. I gather you told them you'd been with us. Unusual for them to act considerately for once.' He began to rummage in his briefcase. 'But I haven't come just to commiserate. I meant to give you this last night, but it slipped my mind.' He handed her an envelope.

She drew out a photograph of herself and Esmeralda

that he had taken on his previous visit. 'Look Mark, isn't it beautiful?'

'Fantastic. Now if you'll both excuse me I have a call to make.'

'He seems under some sort of pressure,' Brian said, after Mark had left.

'Me probably. Since his image of the perfect wife was shattered.'

Brian went to the window and looked thoughtfully into the distance. 'I have… er… been intending to talk to you about that, Sarah.'

He was not prepared for her reaction. Something snapped. She could not speak fast enough to get the message out.

'Look, Brian, I think we've reached a watershed, don't you? You paint my picture, you bring me this beautiful photograph, but the help you can really give you refuse me. You have the skill and the knowledge that I desperately need – desperately, Brian, remember I said that – yet you continue to pretend that it's something trivial, that I don't really have a problem. Well, I've reached the end. I've very little left now to live for. So my advice is, if it's just more of your platitudes and excuses you can leave now and I never want to see you again.'

Esmeralda flew off in alarm and Sarah brought her forehead down heavily on her vacant forearm.

'Sarah, Sarah, I understand, I understand. Listen, I'll be frank with you. The truth is that since your accident – and quite contrary to your accusations – I've kept a watchful eye on you. The injury you sustained was actually more serious than you or anyone else suspected – the knife was blunt and there were infections afterwards. Now, at last, I think it's possible to give an accurate prognosis.'

'Go on.'

'The bottom line is that current treatments would improve it but there would always be – how shall we say – a defect.'

'Surely that's better than what I have, for Christ's sake?'

'But maybe – just maybe – it wouldn't be for the best. My colleagues at Northwick Park and at the Blond-McIndoe at East Grinstead have been working on a new technique. Instead of replacing the skin, which would show, they use cultured skin cells which, in time, would not. I'm trying it out right now.'

'Why not on me?'

'Because I need to perfect it first. Isn't that worth waiting for? Sarah, isn't it?

'Then you'll do it for me?'

'I promise I'll do it.'

'I haven't always been kind to you, have I?'

'It doesn't matter. Anyway, that's irrelevant.' He seemed to slip into bedside mode. 'It's a matter of professional judgement.'

'Brian.'

'Yes?'

'Don't be too long. I really can't go on much longer.'

'I understand.' He returned from the window, as if business had been satisfactorily transacted. 'Now you must show me what happened to the stables.'

They were surprised to hear Mark walking swiftly behind them. 'Your horse has been found. Jed says to tell you it's at the riding school. Oh, and by the way, the police want to see you tomorrow morning.'

Sarah slept soundly that night, exhausted, understanding nothing.

The great door at Avalon Road creaked open.

'Well, Mrs Preston, this is unexpected. I thought you'd given us up.'

'Don't be sarcastic, Marcus, please. There were reasons why I didn't telephone yesterday. I haven't given up.'

'Sarah, you look awful. I mean worse than usual… sorry, how clumsy… let me start again. Sarah, you look as if I should be concerned about you.'

Sarah laughed. You know, you're the only one who can talk to me like that and get away with it.'

She joined the volunteers drinking coffee at the table. 'Where's Ali?'

'Well, word came that Mr Hassan was not well again. Ali looked for you. Said to follow if you did turn up.'

'I promised to give an opinion.'

'But remember that your role here is not as a doctor, Sarah. Second thing is take care of yourself in that place.'

She finished her coffee and left. After the door had closed with a thud she realised she had offered Marcus no explanation for her absence.

First she tried the Mary Rose. Yes, he had been there half an hour before. 'Did he mention where he was going? Anyone hear? Yes, George, to that fucking pit – quite likely. Well, lady, if I was you I'd wait for him to come back. That's no place for you.'

But she didn't listen.

It took her a minute or so to locate the hole in the fence and then the catch wouldn't budge. Perhaps it was her fumblings that alerted them. Gave them time to think. Put ideas into their heads. Possibly.

It had rained and the wooden steps were caked with clay and slippery. Twice she fell and her skirt – skirt in a place like this? – was yellow with mud. She regretted her decision to come but pride would not let her go back. The polythene sheet of Hassan's makeshift shelter was down and held there by two bricks.

'Mr Hassan?' No response. She called again. Still no answer.

'You lookin' for the Arab?' He must have trodden carefully to have reached her shoulder unheard. She didn't recognise him. He took a swig from a green gin bottle and wiped his mouth on a tattered and grubby sleeve. He called behind. 'You seen the Arab, Charlie?'

Another figure – they might have been brothers – jumped down into the pit. 'They took him away, Sammy, 'smornin' in the amb'lance.'

'How'd I miss that, Charlie?'

'Don't believe you did, Sammy, seein' as you're wearin' his coat.'

Sarah saw that this was true. The coat had a distinctive oriental cut that was unmistakable.

'And that's not all, Charlie. Look 'ere.' With a deft pull of the string at his waist the trousers fell to around his knees, revealing a respectable pair of underpants.

'Don't you go gettin' excited now,' Charlie said, giving Sarah a push. 'And don't you go exciting him neither. He's known for that, ain't you Sammy?'

'A real stud, Charlie. Hey, look at this. Bet you've seen nothin' to match this, have you lady. Good thing you're past it, Charlie, else we'd be fightin' over 'er.'

'You go ahead, Sammy. I'll have a quick feel afterwards.'

'You won't, my boy!'

'Not you! 'Er!'

Sarah was unsure how to interpret this exchange. She knew nothing about these people. She had always assumed moral laxity resided in the higher strata of society; at the bottom of the pile deprivation simply made sexual excess an irrelevance. That assumption was being severely tested.

The men began to perform little marching jigs in step with their ribaldry. Then Charlie was behind her, she in the middle. She looked around frantically for a means of escape. All she could see were sullen windowless walls and an impenetrable wooden fence high above where the location of the door was lost in the uniform drabness. She couldn't think of anything useful to say.

Had she known the histories of these two – as Ali would have done and she would come to do – it would not have surprised her that Charlie went straight for her neck, pressing with his fingers into the jugular furrows. She felt her body bend backwards over a pile of clay where the crater edge had fallen in. The small of her back was ice-cold and wet. Perhaps, in his haste, the fingers at her throat had loosened their grip, for she could still hear.

'Do it 'ere, Sammy, but be quick about it.'

Then the pressure at her throat must have increased again.

The blackness was penetrated by her own name, in a searing arc of a shout that seemed to scour the pit. Such relief as it brought was short-lived. She looked up to see Ali flying through the air towards Sammy, hitting him with a resounding blow to the head as he landed. The pair fell to the ground and rolled over and over in the mud. From the violence of his expletives it seemed to Sarah that Ali's intention was nothing less than to kill. She tried to raise herself to intervene, but her strength had gone.

She saw Charlie emerge from his hovel, clutching something hidden in a cloth. He stood poised over the struggling pair, casually enjoying the action, with all the time in the world to choose his target. He winked at her. 'I used to be a butcher, lady, in my younger days. Think I've lost my touch? Course you don't.' Then he plunged the knife into Ali's back, somewhat to the right of the spine. 'Don't want to blunt it, do we,' he said, withdrawing the blade and wiping it on Ali's jacket. 'And now, Sammy boy, it's time to scarper, as fast as our little legs will carry us.'

Sarah felt horribly guilty because the paramedics had

underestimated the seriousness of Ali's wound while tending to her. Ali had not helped himself either, by minimising his injury so that they could look after her. When they got him into the light of the ambulance his face was already pale and a teardrop of blood had appeared at the corner of his mouth. His speech became slurred and his thoughts began to wander.

'Can you hear me, Ali?' she said, against the wail of the siren.

'Don't talk to him, Miss. Let him lie still.'

'He said something. What did he say? Tell me what he said.'

'I think what he said was to go there and not let him down.'

A minute passed. Neither spoke. The wail of the siren intensified as the vehicle gouged its way through the congested streets.

'Has he said anything more?' Sarah asked.

'I think he's gone, Miss. I'm sorry.'

Sarah rolled on her side to face the lifeless body. The paramedic shrank back at the force of her voice.

'Then that's what I'll bloody well do,' she shouted.

They took her first to casualty, but after a day of intensive screening and being pushed around in a trolley they gave her a bed in a general ward. Its familiarity frightened her, until she remembered being in a similar ward with Nurse Trubshaw the night before Debbie died. It seemed fitting it should be so. She had heard Ali talk of predestination and of wheels that brought you back to where you'd once been, almost, except that the pitch of the screw had advanced by one infinitesimal place in the grand order of things. And who better than Ali to have known that?

But for Sarah there was no reason to think that the wheel had stopped. She knew now that all it had encompassed was in the past and behind her and therefore of no further relevance. When her visitors came – and there were many of them – she impressed them with her cool and dispassionate philosophy, which they equated with recovery in the sense of a return to the Sarah they had previously known. How wrong they all were.

Well, not quite all. On the third day – the day before her discharge – they brought the mobile phone trolley to her bed.

'It's Marcus.'

'You've already been to see me today. Why telephone?'

'There's someone else who would like to see you. Can we come round? It's important that we're not disturbed. Can you get yourself into a quieter ward temporarily?'

'This is the NHS – you don't know what you're asking.' But the staff wheeled her away for an hour and persuaded the ward sister that something important was afoot.

Marcus and Jack Adams sat on opposite sides of the trolley. Jack apologised for having been a link in the chain that had dragged her here. Marcus told him not to be so sentimental. 'Sarah doesn't think that way.' Jack raised his hands in resignation. 'I know, I know.'

'Why we're here,' Marcus said, 'is to give you this.' He handed her a brown envelope.

She withdrew a bundle of banknotes, mainly tens and twenties.

'I don't need money, Marcus. It's about the only thing I've got.'

'It's not just money, Sarah. It's Ali's money. To be precise the money he saved to get back to Jazreel's hospital, left with me for safe keeping. You see, I think he would have wanted you to have it. To use it as he would have done.'

Sarah lay back and contemplated the patchwork of tiles on the ceiling, glowing pink in the late afternoon light that permeated the ward.

'Jack here has been kind – and clever – enough to make some arrangements. Reservations, permits, that sort of thing. There are no real obstacles, if it's what you want to do. Think about it carefully and we'll talk again when you've made a decision.'

'That decision's already been made,' Sarah said. 'It was made a long time ago.'

After the bleak affair of Ali's funeral there were only three matters to attend to before she left. Well, two really, because the third was a kind of indulgence, but as important to her as the others in its way.

The first was a visit to Peverell Hessett. She went via Wycombe to collect Graham Carruthers and then to the medical centre to pick up Dr Hislop. By the time they reached Laurel Cottage they had planned for every eventuality that might befall her mother, should anything happen to Sarah.

'I won't be gone long, Mum, and I promise I'll write.'

'More often than you visited, I hope. But Dr Hislop will look after me.'

For some reason Mark was reluctant to part with Esmeralda but Sarah insisted and grudgingly he found her one of the original boxes for the transfer. 'It will not travel well, Sarah,' he said, not knowing that its destination was no more distant than Jack Adams' greenhouse.

She refused his offer of a lift to the airport.

'I can manage. As I'll have to from now on.'

'Come back to me, Sarah. This is still your home.'

'Yes it is.' She kissed him goodbye. Seeing that his eyes were moist she felt sorry for him for the first time in their relationship.

The taxi driver had never heard of the Mary Rose. Nor had he ever been asked to wait for anyone while they sat for five minutes doing nothing except stare at a solitary boat bobbing in the water.

HATOMI CAMP

September – December 1987

18

Irmkutz was the end of the line, where civilisation of sorts ended and the wasteland began. There were already patches of rock-strewn plain, devoid of life, visible between the mutilated dwellings.

Jefferies, from the region's consulate, had travelled with her from Ankara. He was pacing up and down on the platform beside the waiting carriages of the returning train. He glanced at his watch and frowned at the end of each excursion.

'Look, Mr Jefferies,' Sarah said, 'they've obviously got held up. You need to get back on the train and I'm quite happy to wait here. I can always get the next one back if nothing happens.'

'The day after tomorrow?'

'If need be. There'll be a hotel in town.'

'Well then, if you're sure. I do have a dinner with the minister that I can't really miss.' He relaxed a little and held out his hand. 'I do wish you good fortune, Dr Potter. I think you will need it but I also have the feeling that you'll manage. You have my number – use it if you have to.'

The train resolved into a tiny dot that suddenly was no longer there. On the empty platform she felt the kind of loneliness that can bite the most hardened travellers, when all ahead is unknown and previous human contacts have been severed – worse now that evening was approaching. She shivered, in spite of the still searing heat. She was not, she now realised, adventurous.

The few remaining taxis were leaving the patch of earth that was the station's forecourt. There was nothing left for them, the unlucky ones. The last reversed back to her in a swirl of dust that hurt her eyes. She waved it away; there was no place she could think of to be taken to.

How about a real rebirth, she thought. If I were to toss my bag into that bin over there and tear up my passport, just start walking, and pretend amnesia, what then? The idea appealed. But it was the old Sarah thinking. Her face would put paid to any real thought of survival, except as a beggar.

Across the road a defunct neon light with cable ends dangling suggested a moribund café. She walked towards it, hopeful of a flicker of life. No English anywhere, not even a cola ad, but a smell of frying onions seeped through the boarded windows. She pushed at the door, releasing a dose of animated male menace, like a fart.

It was a mistake to enter. Just like the figure-hugging jeans and the blouse were mistakes. This was a place where women had either one use or one purpose. That was conjecture, but she read it in their eyes, all score pairs of them, and none directed at her face. It was confirmed in the brazen photos pinned haphazardly on the walls. The barman, with a glass and a cloth, froze to a statue, then slowly put them down

'Deutsch?'

'English.'

'English? Better, better! Ha! Ha, ha! Ha, ha, ha! The cackle was taken up all around the room. All the grinning, chanting mouths seemed to be missing teeth.

'You want food?'

'A drink would be nice. You have juice?'

'Ha, ha! Ha, ha, ha!'

Already Sarah could see one of the men feeling her bag. Then he tested its weight and lifted it onto a table. 'You pay for drink?'

Her body was expendable, maybe, but the few instruments and books she had brought were not. They meant lives, and were not negotiable. She had to keep her head and her nerve.

'Put it back on the floor.'

The man played drunk, his face contorting into an idiot's grin.

'On the floor,' she repeated, glaring at him and pointing. The returned stare was that of a Rottweiler, unblinking, savage against the background titters.

His fingertips pushed sharply into her shoulder. One of the others had got on his hands and knees behind her and she cursed herself for not realising the cause of the premonitory laughter. She collapsed backwards onto the floor, her head narrowly missing the edge of the bar. No one moved. They were waiting to see what she would do next.

Sammy's attentions were all too recent to allow a trace of inaction. She sprang to her feet and rushed to the bag, intending to grab it and make a run for the door. Its new custodian snatched it away and danced with it to the far end of the room.

One of the men gripped her arms from behind, bringing the elbows together, forcing her to watch while the contents of her bag were displayed, one by one, on the table. It was a rape of her mind, and a pointer to what might follow.

The ophthalmoscope brought an outburst of mirth.

'Vibrator, brmm brmm.' He licked it and put the black head in his mouth.

Then, suddenly, they realised what she was.

'Doctor? You doctor?'

'Doctor'.

'You go to camp? Help at camp?'

'I go to camp.'

'You no look like doctor!'

'You no look like man,' she replied, imitating him. 'More like animal.'

He took no notice, then jabbed his hand towards the others 'We… have brothers there. From across border. Need help very bad.'

'Then why do you stop them getting it?'

They stopped playing with her bag and backed away from the table. She went to it and with slow deliberation repacked the contents. The man who had pushed her over appeared at her shoulder.

'We…' This time he restrained the jabbing fingers. 'We… are sorry.'

'And I am sorry. I hope your brothers have better manners.'

They let her go. A shrill voice behind her called, 'Your juice!' She ignored it. At the door someone was coming in. She almost collided with him. Without thinking she accepted the hand that was thrust towards her.

'Dr Potter? Andrew Plumpton, Red Cross liaison. Well, congratulations! Not many women come here and emerge unscathed. That kind of resilience… could be useful to us. Here, let me take your bag.'

She let him have it without a murmur, unquestioningly. Not because she trusted him but because her powers of resistance had simply ebbed away.

The jeep was parked outside and she got in. She didn't look at him and didn't speak, just stared in front towards the expanse of plain dotted with rock clusters ochre-pink in the dying sun. It seemed to promise a future that was as barren as the past. She blinked back tears.

'You appreciate this is highly irregular, Dr Potter. Red Cross jeeps don't usually pick up doctors from rival organisations.' He must have seen she didn't care. 'Only joking,' he added coyly. 'Fact is, I passed your chap on the road – broken axle – and promised to fetch you. If it's mended I'll hand you over. If not I'll take you all the way.'

'That's kind of you.'

She watched him choose his words.

'They give you trouble in there?'

'Sort of.'

'Harmless, but bloody annoying. Sums up most of them. Touch you, did they?'

'No… not in that way.'

'Don't let it get to you.' He hadn't misread the situation after all. His concern made her look at him again: young, early thirties probably, but sounded older; fair hair, clean shaven and rimless lenses that don't detract from good looks.

'You're a doctor too?'

'Good lord, no. Field director. We just boss them around.'

A few hundred metres further on the metalled road stopped. Suddenly she was being flung from side to side as the tyres clutched and grasped their way forward over the rock-strewn track. In daylight the journey might have held some interest; in darkness it became an interminable assault, not only on her senses, but on what little remained of her physical stamina.

Probe as she might, her memory of what she had left behind offered no refuge; far from yielding niches of comfort, it repelled her. She felt hot, as she had during the day, but inexplicably now given the cool of the evening. The sweat on her body was cold, clammy and unnatural. At one point the vehicle stopped and Andrew jumped down to remove some obstacle on the road. But the swaying continued in her head, to be joined by waves of nausea. Then she was out of the vehicle, retching over the rocks. She had never felt more vulnerable, or so willing to be kicked aside and left to die.

She remembered her mouth and face being wiped and something – probably a blanket – being put around her shoulders; then, as it all became indistinct, of being lifted and carried back towards the vehicle.

Which side of her face was towards him? she wondered. No, no, no, that was past.

She had been lying on her side, so they told her, which is why, when she opened her eyes, the first thing she saw was a silhouette of heads at the window, featureless against the sunlight. A faint tremor, a response to her own, produced a row of flashing teeth – children's teeth – and the whites of widening eyes. Then hands appeared above the sill to wave to her.

An adult voice said, 'Welcome to Hatomi Hospital, Dr Potter.'

Her thoughts, which had channelled themselves rapidly to receive the welcome at the window, now became confused again, as if, with these words, a damp mist had fallen across her bed. It was a shadow not of the speaker's making, but of her own distant guilt. She struggled to turn her body to see but the sheets held her. In that brief moment her spirits descended from elation to misery. What's bugging you, Sarah? she asked herself.

'Dr Potter, Sarah, it's Jazreel. You're safe now.'

Jazreel's smiling face glided into view as she rounded the end of the bed to sit beside her.

Sarah looked at her with eyes filled with tears of apology. 'I'm sorry, Jazreel, forgive me.'

'For taking ill? You couldn't help that.'

What Sarah had meant could not be explained, not yet. 'Was I ill?'

'Unconscious for two days. And a little delirious. Your Red Cross friends – whom you don't even know yet – think it's a virus. Maybe they're right, I'm not so sure.'

'I've been so much trouble to you. I only wanted to help.'

'You shall – all too soon, I'm afraid, my dear. Things are not so good here, as you will see. But first some food, then proper sleep. After that we can talk.'

A black bubble of ungraspable information was growing in Sarah's mind. There was a name there, but it wouldn't come. She started to speak, hoping that the act of doing so would bring it forth. 'I want to…'

'If you're thinking of Ali,' Jazreel said kindly, 'it's okay. I know what happened. Marcus wrote to me. You don't have to be anxious on my account.'

When Sarah woke again there was a candle burning, and soap and a towel on the chair beside her, with clothes neatly folded across its back. She found water – so little of it! – in a bowl on the table. She dressed and opened the door.

Voices, serious and concerned, echoed down the corridor. She traced them to a door like her own and knocked. There was a response in a language she did not recognise. She entered.

Apart from Jazreel, all were men, a mix of colours and nationalities. They rose to welcome her.

'Perfect timing, Sarah,' Andrew said, shaking her hand, which he retained long enough to whisper, 'Thank me later for getting you here in one piece.'

From the head of the table Jazreel said, 'Let me introduce Dr Farouqi, Dr Al Esben, Mr Sirivan, the hospital manager, and Mr Kempis, Camp Director. Dr Nuru, who takes over from me next week, has been held up by bad weather and is still in Ankara.

'Replaces you?' Sarah said. 'Are you leaving?'

'For a short while only,' Jazreel replied, 'but I may return to another hospital, Sarah, not necessarily this one.'

'Jazreel is returning home to get married,' Farouqi said. 'Her – how do you say it in English? – honeymoon? We all hope it will be a well-deserved vacation.' He looked at Jazreel, hoping he had not spoken out of turn. Sarah thought that perhaps he had.

'Gentlemen, back to business,' Jazreel continued. 'Mr Kempis was starting to tell us that from tomorrow we can expect the next influx from across the border. Apparently there are many sick this time, including some with gunshot wounds and, as you might guess, rather more with less conventional injuries. Exposure too, if the weather doesn't break. Saddam's merry men seem to have excelled themselves this time.'

'On past performance that means a hundred beds,' Sirivan said. 'We can make available fifteen at most.'

'We can help with a few tents and blankets,' Andrew said, 'but that's all this time.'

'For that we need more ground,' Jazreel said.

'We can let you have that,' Kempis said, 'but not where you would like it. You'd have to fetch your own water.'

'And antibiotics, dressings, halothane?'

'Afraid not this time,' Andrew said. 'I'm sorry.'

'Then we'll have to raid the clothes store and tear up a few more shirts,' Jazreel said.

'We'll need all we've got to clothe them,' Kempis replied. Impatience and frustration were surfacing in his voice. 'So you'd better think of something else.'

Sarah watched in disbelief as the bartering became more heated. It reminded her of travellers at the council tip near home, fighting for choice pickings amongst the refuse.

298

Jazreel's engagement and intended departure had unnerved her, perhaps because she was the last link with the world Sarah knew. Or was there another reason for it? Had Ali known of Jazreel's plans? If not, why hadn't she told him? It seemed that Sarah had about a week to get some answers.

Breakfast was taken in an airless box of a room with windows above eye level and a scratched, formica-topped table surrounded by an assortment of chairs, none matching. It was only seven-thirty, but from the soiled clothes and anxious expressions, the work of the day had already begun. Sarah sat down next to a pretty nurse with spots of blood on the back of each elbow which, being invisible to her, she'd failed to wash off. She was of Marguerite's age and not unlike her; except that Marguerite seemed one of nature's innocents compared with this girl.

'Dr Potter, hello. I'm Allison. If you're wondering, coffee is in the flask next to the cereal – that's cereal in the cardboard box. There might be bread there and something to put on it, but I don't know what they've given us this morning.'

Sarah was about to ask for guidance, but the girl anticipated it.

'For meals the principle is to help yourself to what the textbooks say is a healthy diet. Enough to keep you active, but that's all. There's a chart on the wall. All you have to do is know your weight – and make sure it stays the same.'

Sarah got up to study it. A spoonful of this, a slice of that, all given values, and a grand total to be exceeded at one's peril. It seemed pitifully meagre.

'It's fair. It's of no help to anyone if we go sick,' Allison said, getting up. 'I have to go, I can hear the next lot coming in.' She turned at the door. 'Good luck, Dr Potter.'

'Sarah!'

'Sarah.'

Jazreel appeared in a white coat with a stethoscope at her neck. 'I'm sorry, Sarah. I'll have to throw you in at the deep end and leave the sightseeing till later.' She rested her hand on Sarah's shoulder. 'Believe me, it's the easiest way. Like diving into a cold sea.'

Sarah found herself seated beside a small table in a makeshift cabin. She looked out through a wide, open door into an homogenous, grey mist. The ground was visible for about twenty paces and would have been a morass of brown mud if someone had not thrown down a load of rubble to create a path. She got up for a better look and was surprised to find another figure standing just outside under the awning.

'Karim, Dr Potter. I help you this morning.'

They came. In ones, twos or small groups, young and old, sometimes with others helping but usually unaided, hobbling, clutching at one another, many weeping. Sarah realised that Karim had been posted there to segregate them so that the more needy cases were seen by Farouqi or Jazreel in an adjacent hut. For her it was a luxury that was to last only that day.

Allison came in with a box of improvised dressings which she placed on the table. Then she stood beside Sarah.

At first Sarah was more of an observer, lost without the accoutrements of modern medicine. She remembered, ruefully, what it was like to be a mere houseman under the patronage of a ward sister. She was awed by the movements of Allison's deft hands as they probed, dressed and bandaged. But when she had established the limits of the nurse's competence the pair began to function as a team. Most important of all, Sarah learnt from her where to place the shifting line between admission and contested discharge into the heaving squalor of the camp.

Allison seemed relaxed. Around mid-morning there were a few minutes respite when she fetched coffee in cracked mugs. 'You're okay,' she told Sarah, with a hint of a smile. Praise never came sweeter than that.

There was another break around midday, before the theatres swung properly into action. By then the mist had begun to disperse; soon the remaining wisps of vapour were carried up and away on the strengthening breeze. All around were mountain peaks, crisp and bright in the sunlight. Sarah's attention was caught by the snow-flecked ridge to the south. 'They crossed that,' Allison said. Then she looked down. 'Well, most did.'

The scene now revealed reminded Sarah of the beginning of an operetta, when the curtain rises on a stage packed with peasants cheerfully busy with themselves: a human ferment from which leading players would soon emerge. Here, just the same, people fetched and carried, idled away the time and passed things from hand to hand that Sarah could not identify. The difference was that nothing remotely interesting seemed likely to happen; except that, from the mass, life itself would gradually seep away.

The camp was on a kind of plateau halfway up the mountain. To the north the land fell away again into yellow-green pastures. In the distance were villages, and far, far away a small town, and beyond that more mountains. 'They're not so aware of us up here,' Allison said. 'Some don't even know we're here. It depends a bit on whether you're an Armenian or a Kurd.'

'What made you come?' Sarah asked.

'To this camp? Simple really. My parents worked in Iraq, until the trouble began. With the Americans I mean. There's always been trouble of other kinds. Eventually they left. By then I knew what was happening to the Kurds, what had been happening – except that we were never told. I had

to come, you see. I keep looking for faces I might know.'
She sighed deeply. 'But there are so many.'

'And they gave you training?'

'About as much as you had this morning. But then, it's
not much to do with medicine really, is it? Oh yes, the bullet
holes and the diarrhoea. But the rest? Well it's in the mind,
isn't it. When everyone important to you has gone, you go
too, that's how it seems to work. How it seems to me.'

'Can we give them hope?'

Allison looked directly into Sarah's eyes. 'You can. You
have it, whatever 'it' is. I could tell that from the start.'

Sarah lay still, trying to sleep, trying to fend off the
encroaching images of the day. There were two that would
not go away. The first, indelible, the faces as they came
out of the mist: deluded winners in a gamble with death
who had still to cast the dice again. The other was slowly
crystallising out of the last dregs of consciousness.

She was blinking into the sunlight, admiring the
glistening caps of the distant blue-green peaks. Allison was
walking ahead of her between the rows of tents, then turned
and was lost from sight. Beside the path a group of children
was playing – some sort of hop, skip and jump – except that
not all could join in. One, a girl of about nine, had her eyes
fixed on the other children, who were calling to her, but
the fingers of her left hand still toyed with the strings of
the tent-flap behind her back. Her neck was bent, or rather
the head was held to one side, at odds with the lustre of the
intelligent eyes. Moving closer Sarah saw the wasting of her
leg and arm on the right side.

One of the older children called out: 'Irina, come and
say hello to the new doctor.'

The girl hopped towards them like a winged bird,
an unintended but perfect parody of the game she was

watching. Her eyes met Sarah's. There was familiarity there: not unkind, not critical, but gently probing.

'Irina,' the older child explained, 'was wounded in the head. We think the bullet touched the side of her brain. We're very proud of her.'

The girl performed a little bow of the head to acknowledge the praise. Her questing eyes gave way to a welcoming smile.

'Can she speak,' Sarah asked?

'Irina, say something to Dr Potter.'

'Hello, Sarah Jane Potter.'

'Why, that's remarkable,' Sarah said, pleased and impressed. She bent towards the girl. 'What have you to show me, Irina? You have some toys for me perhaps?'

The older child held back the flap of the tent. Sarah had to stoop to enter. It took her a long time to adapt to the darkness. At first, she thought there was no light at all. Then, one by one, lights like tiny candle flames flickered into life, dimly illuminating the tent. Sarah was surprised by its vastness. A small hand forced its way between her fingers and palm. On her other side the same thing happened. Staring ahead, she could see neither child.

'Watch, Sarah Jane!'

The days sped by. If pleasure hastens time, what then was happening here, where there was little else around but pain and despair? Sarah asked herself if it were possible that such things were actually pleasing to her. Not consciously, perhaps, but indirectly, as facets of a trade that satisfied. She had seen it in magnified form in certain of her colleagues at the hospital back home. Alan Murphy for instance.

Her hand went instinctively towards her face. So positive was this train of thought that she got up from her bunk to look in the mirror. It was the first time she had examined herself in that way since she arrived at the camp.

Allison, lying on the next bunk, became alarmed. 'Sarah, I thought you'd put that out of your mind.'

'I have, honestly. Something from my past just confronted me.' She grinned and flopped backwards on to her bunk with her arms behind her head. 'It's gone now.'

'You're sure you're not working too hard?'

'No. I love it.'

There. There it was again. What was it about the work that she loved? What right had she to take advantage of people in that way, if it was just for self-gratification? She plucked up courage to ask.

'Do you think it's immoral to get satisfaction from the work we do?'

'Well, if you didn't you wouldn't do it; then everyone would lose. Listen. I asked my father a similar thing once. Only I was accusing him of milking the local markets for cash.'

'What did he say?'

'That to question one's motives all the time was a selfish indulgence. It was much better and more honest to accept yourself as you were. Then everyone knew where they stood. If you were a villain and didn't try to hide it at least people had a chance of avoiding you.'

'A villain? I'm not a villain!'

Allison grinned, pleased with herself. 'Sorry, I thought that's what you were leading up to.'

They hadn't heard Jazreel enter.

'I agree with Allison,' Jazreel said. 'You can't be a philosopher in a place like this. There are too many conflicting values.' Then she turned to Allison, 'Would you mind if I spoke to Sarah alone? About something back in England, not here. It won't take a moment.'

When the nurse had gone she sat beside Sarah on the bunk.

'We've not really had a chance to talk and tomorrow morning Nuru arrives and then in the afternoon Adnam comes to carry me off.'

'So soon?'

'I'm ashamed to say I deliberately didn't tell you.'

'Why?'

'Because I didn't want you to dwell on problems back home when you were getting on so well here. To be frank I considered clearing off this evening after surgery, but you would have hated me for the insult.'

Sarah knew that the opportunity to learn things – about the Massingham Foundation, Edwin, Jazreel's baby – might never come again. It didn't matter. They were part of something left behind by the roadside, soiled memorabilia, unworthy to be touched ever again.

'Like me you may want to let sleeping dogs lie.' Jazreel said quietly.

'If I asked you, you would tell me?'

'Yes.'

'Then that I've had it in my power to know is enough. Let it rest, as you say. Except…'

'Yes?'

Sarah pulled a blanket around her shoulders to hide a shiver. 'It was something that Ali said to me once – that you'd both visited a little village in Oxfordshire called Peverell Hessett.'

'That's difficult to remember, but yes, we did.'

'Why was that?'

'Oh, just to say goodbye to an old school chum who happened to be staying there with friends. I can't remember their name.'

'Does the name Sharp – Tom Sharp – mean anything to you?'

'No, not at all. Should it?'

'No.'

They walked out into the evening sunlight to look for Allison. There was a damp chill in the air that Sarah hadn't noticed before. Because of it the camp had become subdued. Now people scurried around outside only if there was a purpose. The children playing were fewer and moved more slowly. It was like the effect of smoke on a hive of bees.

'You haven't asked me about Ali,' Jazreel said.

'He was devoted to you.'

'He was obsessed with a dream.'

'He could have been of great help.'

'I told him long ago it could not work.'

The following morning an expectant buzz among the staff signalled the imminent arrival of Dr Nuru. In another situation flags might have been lowered and raised as one incumbent was replaced by another, except that there was no flagpole, other than the one flying the permanent red pennant of the organisation. He swept in by Land Rover about eleven while Sarah was in the theatre. He was still with Jazreel and Kempis when the rest broke for lunch.

More spectacular was the arrival of Jazreel's fiancé. A thousand pairs of eyes had followed the serene progress of the beige Mercedes as it climbed ever upwards towards the camp. Sarah was sitting in her familiar place on the veranda when the car drew up in front. The descending dust sparkled in the sunlight. When it had settled the driver got out and walked around the car to open the rear door.

A chauffeur opening a door for a passenger in a refugee camp! Sarah wanted to scream out at the indelicacy, the sheer arrogant stupidity of it. Where was Jazreel to counter and reprimand, to strike a balance and lessen the offence? When she emerged, in a chic white dress to mid-calf and top to match, Sarah's understanding of values was sent crashing. There was a glass of water beside her. To throw it would give her…

She found Andrew sitting beside her, riding the waves of disapprobation crashing around him and laughing openly at her. 'It's a pity my own entry didn't cause even a hundredth of the impression that that's made on you. Calm down, Sarah! Consider the situation.'

She turned on him. 'It's obscene!'

'Sarah, before he gets out, listen to me. Without him and his support for Jazreel this camp wouldn't exist, financially or politically. Lives saved, sick cured; people sent home otherwise than in coffins. So do you have the right to weigh ostentation against philanthropy?'

'But what must they think?' She waved her hand vaguely towards the camp. 'These people, think?'

'They think it's a bloody long time since they've seen good clothes, still longer a Mercedes that wasn't a politician's. It might just remind them there's hope yet. So bury it, Sarah. Please.'

Adnam Hussein was mounting the steps with a wide grin, a bejewelled hand extended towards her.

'Bloody well take it,' Andrew hissed into her ear.

'My dear Sarah, you will not understand my pleasure in meeting you, but please accept that it is heartfelt. I have heard so much, and all of it to your very great credit.'

'Jazreel has exaggerated.'

'No, please don't misunderstand me. I wasn't referring to Jazreel. To Jazreel you are just a fellow doctor.'

Sarah wanted to ask, who then? But the warmth of the man was making an impression, and weakened her. She was pitched into that middle ground of indecision where churlish resistance was fighting sensible acceptance of undeniable fact. She took the proffered hand and returned the squeeze. Suddenly she felt good about it.

'I've heard good things too – that without you this camp might not exist.'

'Well, shall we say I enjoy manipulating people, especially lazy politicians, so that wasn't such a hardship. What I can't buy are people like you, with willingness to give of their skills, and themselves.'

Adnam was greeting Andrew. They obviously knew each other well. 'Are you prepared for winter? Be honest now.'

'As ready as we can be.'

'That's good. Let me know if the situation changes.' He stepped back towards Sarah and sat beside her. 'Now, Sarah, let me have your impressions of the camp.' She sensed, rightly, that he was seeking praise.

'We're lacking basic essentials. Drugs, dressings, spares for pieces of equipment.'

'Really. I was told you had most things.'

'No, far from it.'

Andrew had turned away in embarrassment, knowing when it is diplomatic to milk a benefactor no further. Sarah withdrew her legs, to avoid her shins being kicked. But in this instance her judgement of the man was the keener.

'I truly did not know that.' He drew a gilded leather notebook from his breast pocket and opened it for her. 'Write there what you need.'

They sat in silence while Sarah thought hard and wrote in the book. Then she handed it back to him, still open, with the sweetest smile that control of her face could command.

He snapped the book shut. 'It will be done.' Then he looked around for Jazreel. 'My lady, we must go. We have a long drive before nightfall.' For the last time he looked at Sarah, and returned her smile with a wave of his forefinger towards her face. 'You will not always be like this, Sarah. When the time comes, remember what it means to be humble.'

The words had a familiar ring, but she couldn't place them.

'You bloody nearly disgraced us,' Andrew said when the shifting plume of dust had at last settled in the valley. But by the following Wednesday Sarah had her drugs and her dressings, and enough over to give some to Andrew.

19

The door was ajar. Sarah quietly pushed at it for a better view of him before she went in. Dr Nuru sat writing at his desk with the crown of his head towards her. There was silver in the grizzled hair that fitted his reputation as a wise greybeard with considerable diplomatic skill. With the evening sunlight behind him his face was in deep shade.

Sarah made for the further of the two vacant chairs so that she could see him more clearly.

'Good evening, Dr Nuru. You wanted to see me?'

'No, I was looking forward to meeting you, Sarah, and that's a different thing.' From the quick flash of gleaming teeth Sarah deduced that he was laughing at her. 'I guess it's difficult to know which of us should be welcoming the other. The resident fledgling against the old migratory bird. Why don't we just shake hands at the same time?' He rose to take her hand.

At the same level, their eyes fell upon each other's face. Nuru had been told all about Sarah, but Sarah knew little about African tribal markings. When she saw the deep symmetrical lines carved into his cheeks her alarm must have showed. The humour of the situation struck them at the same time.

'This is a very exclusive club we belong to, Sarah,' he said, grasping his lapels with mock gravity. My father had to own thousands of cattle before he could get me these. How did you get in?'

'Oh, strictly on the recommendation of a friend – who's been discreet enough to stay anonymous.'

'When you'd really like to have thanked him. I know. But that's how it goes.'

Nuru had a total disregard for the niceties of meeting a stranger; but it was balanced by a professional charm that made offence impossible. He placed a finger under Sarah's chin and turned her face into the light. 'Has no-one ever offered to help you?' he asked with surprise.

'Well, not quite offered. They tell me it's very difficult to get a good result. Better to wait.'

'Nonsense, I've been into it myself.'

'Then why didn't you go ahead?'

'I'll tell you.' He drew his chair up to hers as if about to confide a personal secret of some magnitude. 'Because I've kind of grown to like them,' he said, peeling away from her with a loud guffaw.

In the days that followed she came to respect him as a capable doctor as well as a gifted administrator.

The influx of refugees over the mountains had dried to a trickle, giving everyone time to breathe. Aided by Adnam's supplies the hospital actually began to flourish. The evening meal was no longer taken on the run, but offered opportunities to reflect with the others on wider issues. Profound things were said in the light of the exotic candles that Nuru had smuggled into the camp. One issue began to dominate all others.

A few days earlier Sarah had woken to the popping of distant gunfire, although it was only when the sounds were heard again two days later that she admitted to herself what it was. 'It's the army flushing out the PKK,' Karim explained.

The shots signalled a plunge in morale within the camp. The gloom that Sarah had at first attributed to the closing weather she now realised might have another component: fear. Walking between the tents she would come upon faces that did not quite belong. Surly expressions shielded fierce prides that had not been expunged by the rigours of flight. One day Karim said, 'The camp's been infiltrated. It's now only a matter of time.'

Kempis doubled the guard on the perimeter fence at night. That seemed to have little effect. The camp guards rounded up a few suspects, but had to release them when their stories were corroborated. Curiously, though, they were not seen again after these encounters. One day the tents were searched systematically, and guns were found and confiscated. Nuru said someone must have informed the government forces, because at dawn the following morning a convoy of armoured vehicles roared through the gates. Once inside the soldiers fanned out, leaving few – apart from in the hospital enclave – unmolested.

Sarah was unprepared for the brutality. The search seemed to have no purpose except to provide opportunities for physical hurt. People were clubbed, regardless of what account they gave of themselves. The soldiers, she noted, were particularly adept with the butts of their rifles. Worst of all, the children were not spared. The clinics were especially busy that afternoon.

About three the mist rolled in, its ethereal tentacles groping the tracks between the tents. The fine drizzle it contained gave it a tangible quality, so that one could almost imagine gathering it in handfuls. Inside the hospital it crept along the main corridor and seeped into the wards. It seemed to move with a purpose, as if seeking out unfinished business.

In the children's ward there were a dozen new cases. The most frightening thing was the silence, broken only by the occasional crash of trolleys or equipment. Sarah had noticed that for the children of the camp the learning process seemed to involve taking from adults, not exchanges amongst themselves. Their eyes were adult eyes, not the eyes of children in a London hospital where enquiry was almost the last thing to be stifled. Why hadn't she put toys on Adnam's list? She was really beginning to learn.

'There's one here you should see first,' Allison said. 'She's had a blow to the head – could even be that her neck's broken. Look at that bruise! Who could do that to a child? Bastards!'

'I know this child,' Sarah said.

'I shouldn't think so.'

'Yes, we saw her once when we were touring the camp.' She knelt beside the bed. 'Irina, can you talk to me?'

'Sarah, she can't even speak English! I've never seen this child before.'

The girl looked at Sarah with vacant eyes.

'Karim,' Allison called down the corridor, 'come and help us.' When he came she asked, 'Do you know this child?'

'I've seen her about, playing with the others.'

'Playing?' Sarah said. 'You don't mean normally?'

'Well, no. There's always been something wrong with her.' He went across the floor to another child. 'Who's that little girl over there?'

'That's Irina,' came the reply in Kurdish.

After supper, Sarah went to the ward and sat beside the child's silent body. It was too early to say if the blow had caused more lasting damage than she had already sustained. At least she was stable.

Allison was surprised to find her sitting there in the darkness. 'What are you doing?'

'Waiting.'

313

'Nothing's going to happen.'

'No. But I'll sit with her for a little longer.'

'Watch, Sarah Jane!'

'Is this a tent? It seems so dark.'

'It doesn't matter. Can you feel our hands?'

'Warm and cosy!'

'Do you remember it now? Where you are?'

'It's too dark to remember.'

'Yes, it is very dark. For you it has been dark for a very long time. Now watch.'

There were muffled taps to the side and then movements within but still nothing could be seen. Shuffling feet, invisible, passed in front of them; then a whispered response, and the sound of a door being unbolted.

As the door opened, yellow light flooded in. Not solid wholesome light but the restless beam of a torch, randomly illuminating the bodies and faces of those outside and the one inside that she seemed to recognise. There was commonness of expression and grim lascivious purpose as they manipulated the burden through the door.

'Is this a funeral?' Sarah whispered.

'In a way it is,' came the reply, 'but that's for you to judge.'

There was progression forward into the soft black interior. The lights – those little glittering specks that Sarah remembered – now seemed to fuse into a pale yellow luminosity. And suddenly Sarah could see that they were not real lights but a device against which the movements of the figures could be seen in abstract motion. Was there purpose, then, in hiding the images from her and showing the actions only by implication and suggestion? Did it spare her sensibility or was it that her memory, if confronted with it openly, risked being snuffed out like a candle flame, never to reignite?

Sarah felt a gentle tug on each of her hands and allowed herself to be pulled forward into the swirl of light and shadow.

'Closer, Sarah. You still have far to go.'

The little body was raised under the playing black shadows but she could not see its detail. There were noises: faint whimpers from a half-open mouth that, from its gasps, seemed to repel, then survive, transient and repeated exploitation.

Closer, and she was now a part, a kindred spirit to the figure lying there, beginning to feel with it, beginning to understand. Her face was alongside but, try as she might, she could not get the eyes to engage. Her hands were released and she felt herself lifted. Her pain and fear were incandescent around her like swarms of fireflies.

Consciousness was returning now, dissolving the image but leaving just enough of it for her to move her head towards the window, where the thin curtain held out against the night sky. Elizabeth, Elizabeth, where are you?

Then someone gently took hold of her chin and eased it back.

She woke to find Allison's torch playing into her eyes. 'Sarah, Sarah! It's three o'clock in the morning!'

'The one rule in a place like this,' Allison said, 'is that patients are treated equally. There's no room for favourites.'

'Just show me one I've neglected.' The scar down her face nestled precociously in the raw anger of her flushed cheeks.

'Sarah, I'm sorry. I didn't mean it that way.'

But Allison was not alone in noticing the depth of Sarah's involvement with the child.

After supper Sarah wrapped one of Jazreel's abandoned coats around her shoulders and slipped outside. The closeness of the stars, pin-sharp in the absolute stillness, threatened with an intensity she had not felt before. She wondered if it were an instruction to go back inside, into the warm, and forget what it was that she had no permit to explore. If it was, it didn't succeed. She continued along one path after another, between silent tents flapping in the wind, trying to remember the crude numbers on pegs at each junction to find her way there. She looked desperately for the spot where the children had played and Irina had limped towards her with knowing eyes. But Allison was right. There would be no yellow earth churned by children's feet; no tent-flap with cords to occupy a child's fingers. These things, then, had come from within, surely. And yet…

Cradled in its pillow the sleeping head was no different from that of any other sleeping child. Against the white linen the bruise from that calamitous blow shone green in the lamplight. Her forehead was cool to the touch, not damp as before.

Sarah had an intense desire to watch the child, to get her to look and say her name. And then again she remembered Allison's reproving finger which said, you are asking the child for something it cannot give. Be content that she can smile and hold your hand and recognise you as a friend. Isn't that enough?

How could she know!

There was a letter from Mark in an envelope the colour of bone china that reminded her of the invitation to the evening at the Massingham Tower. How far away that seemed; how beautifully irrelevant.

'What will you do, Sarah, when the camp closes?' Nuru asked.

'Closes?'

'It won't last for ever. Already some of our clients are beginning to leave.'

'Back across the mountains?'

'The Iraqis have withdrawn – for the moment. The planes you hear are the Americans and British patrolling the skies. It won't last, of course. Next they'll be flushing out the remnants of the PPK. But for us it's weeks rather than months, I would say.'

Allison was more interested in the letter. Instinctively she knew whom it was from. 'What does he say, Sarah? You haven't even unfolded it yet.'

When she did read the letter, it was in the privacy of Nuru's office, and he'd quietly left her to it.

My dear Sarah,

I got your letter today and it saddened this wretched soul when it should have cheered him to know you were safe and well. It's curious how we see more clearly when the things that matter most are taken from us – or should I say pushed away? How one can be locked into the pursuit of some dubious agenda when all around is crying out for common sense to prevail. You would not believe the people that have shunned me for rejecting you, Sarah. But perfection was everything – job, money, wife. And so I let you go your own way. I wouldn't know whether, having pulled away that particular skin, what is left is the real genuine me – but I would like to think so, and believe so. Just as we need protection, so we need someone to protect and care for. I have no-one else Sarah – in my life, in my bed or in my mind. It's God's truth. Perhaps, at thirty-five, I'm growing old. Perhaps, too, it's not a bad thing.

If this picture I'm painting seems calculated to put you off ever coming home, it's all I deserve, but not what I want. For myself I don't really care if Brian manages to patch you up. But that is selfish and for your sake I hope he can. I've put all your pots and potions back on the dressing table, and the bear on the bed. You've no idea what a comfort that creature has been to me. Think about it, Sarah. You could do better, I know, but there's always a risk. But I do know you could do worse.

Working for MF is rapidly becoming a nightmare. The machinations at the top – which I can barely see now – are like great rolling thunder clouds, spitting fire and destruction. One wonders how the pursuit of absolute pleasure can be upheld with such goings-on. But, remarkably, it still is, and probably will continue to be. Humiliating, though, considering how I built it up, the profitable bits at least.

You know now how it is between us. I can only ask: come home.

Affectionately,
Mark

Sarah tracked Allison down to the dispensary. The nurse stood with a half-filled bag of syringes limp in her hand, gazing out of the window that overlooked the mountains to the north. Sarah stood beside her to watch vast banks of grey cloud pressing hard into the higher slopes and rolling upwards to obscure the snow-tipped summits.

'They'll be completely white by morning, if it clears,' Allison said. 'You can already feel the temperature dropping.'

'Before supper, do you want to come and play with the children for half an hour?'

'You go. I may have a period starting. Take Karim if you can find him – they adore him.'

For Sarah, concern for such personal matters had become displaced by altruism. A period. Were women here still troubled by such old-fashioned things? And if they weren't, wasn't it because of the hardship, and the stress, and the diet?

Somehow none of that was relevant to her. She was not

stressed. In fact she was at ease with herself in a way that had transcended the shock of being pitched into this alien, harrowing place.

Karim came in and the thought passed.

The next morning, when Sarah had swallowed her tea and crushed oats more compulsively than usual, and the light from the whitening mountains swept the children's ward like a new broom, Irina had gone.

By the end of the week the camp was beginning to look depleted. Rumours were rife that Saddam was shifting his attention to the Marsh Arabs in the south. Or at least pounding them that bit harder.

Sarah and Allison were enjoying the rare luxury of a pot of tea on the hospital veranda when Andrew's jeep swung round the corner. He got out clutching a sheaf of letters, while they skimmed the dust in their tea with their fingers.

'Two for Sarah and three for Allison.'

It seemed to amuse Andrew to compare their responses. Allison fell greedily upon her letters, relishing the indecision of which to open first and hovering over them with a spoon handle as an improvised paperknife. Sarah glanced at the handwriting on her envelopes, then pushed them to one side while she finished her tea. She noticed Andrew's look of concern.

'You wonder why I'm not more interested in my friends?'

'I'm more concerned that life-before-Hatomi can have been so barren.'

Sarah cocked her head to one side and stared at him through half-closed lids. 'Barren? No, not barren, if by that you mean uneventful. No, rather the reverse – just not very pleasant. Still, no point in delaying the moment of truth.' She took Alice's letter and opened it methodically with Allison's spoon.

'What does she say?' Allison asked impatiently. She had already digested her own news and was in the mood for more personal revelations.

Sarah scanned Alice's spidery handwriting. 'The usual greetings. My husband Mark still not well, but we'll let him tell his own story in a moment.'

From their expressions they must have seen the colour drain from her face. She began to read out loud: '*Now for the big one, the moment you've been waiting for has arrived! Brian says he thinks he can patch you up at last. Hooray! I believe what he says, Sarah. He's suddenly become quite enthusiastic about the idea whereas before he was always, well, so guarded. It's your golden opportunity, take it. There should be a note from him enclosed with this letter.*'

Sarah fumbled with the remaining sheets. 'Here it is. *Dear Sarah. Alice will have passed on all the gossip, so let me just repeat what I am sure she has already told you, that I am now confident I can achieve a worthwhile result with your face – if you are still willing to let me. There is only one difficulty, which is that I have a visiting professorship in the States beginning in a month's time. I would like, if possible, to do it before I go. If you agree would you please arrange dates and times with my secretary at the above address. Yours, Brian.*'

'Sarah, that's wonderful news,' Andrew said, beaming delightedly.

'I'm so pleased for you. Sarah.' Allison squeezed her arm. 'You have to go.'

'Do I? Why do I?'

'Why ever would you question it?' Andrew asked.

'Because it will bring to an end the only real happiness I've known. That's why.'

'You mean in this camp?' Allison's eyes widened. 'That's ridiculous.'

Andrew gestured to Allison to be cautious. 'The camp is

not a happy place, Sarah. It may be that you achieve fulfilment here, just as I do further along the mountain. And Allison too, I suspect. But it can never be a substitute for being at peace with yourself and those of your own kind.'

'And what kind is that?' Sarah asked.

'Well I…'

'I'll tell you. It's the kind that does this to you.' She pointed a trembling finger at her face. 'And wrecks your marriage and kills your horses, and drives off your real friends.' She brushed away a tear. 'I know where the truth lies.'

Allison, realising she was out of her depth, got up to go. 'I've got to prepare the theatre. I'll see you in there.'

'She doesn't understand you,' Andrew said, 'and neither do I.'

'There's no reason why you should.'

'Look, what time do you finish in theatre?'

'Are you asking me for a date?'

'In a way. There's something I want to show you. While the weather holds and before it gets dark.'

'About four. It's quiet today.'

'Meet here at a quarter past, then – and bring some stout shoes.'

'That does send my expectations soaring.'

'You won't be disappointed, I promise you.'

The track from the camp led down to the floor of the valley where it joined a metalled road. They drove through sparse scrub and ruined stone dwellings for a mile or so before taking another track to the right leading back up into the mountains. Over her shoulder Sarah saw the camp appear, brown and dirty on its rocky pedestal. Soon they were looking down on it. It reminded her of a putrescent fungus about to discharge its spores. Andrew had to reassure her that this was not the purpose of their journey.

Sarah's spirits rose as each turn of the rock-strewn track opened up a new vista of increased splendour. She forgot the dilemma of her face. 'You know, Andrew, this is the second time I've climbed into this vehicle without the slightest guarantee of safety. Why is it that I trust you above all others?' She had said it lightly, not intending to be provocative, but that was the effect it had.

Andrew looked back at her sadly. 'It's not a question of trust, Sarah. It's a matter of unconscious perception.'

'Of what?'

'Can't you guess? What would make you safe with me?'

'That you're gay? No, I hadn't guessed. Neither do I give a damn – although in another way perhaps I do. But if it's any consolation I don't believe there's any such thing as absolute sexuality – hetero, homo or whatever.'

It must have seemed a strange remark. She could see questions in his expression but not read them. Perhaps he wanted to ask if she spoke from personal experience, but was too shy.

The track ended in a tiny turning circle against a near-vertical wall of black rock. The site anticipated visitors, but clearly never more than one or two vehicles at a time. The air was thinner now, the relief of the landscape more delineated. In the pale evening sunlight each ridge glowed like the edge of a honed knife. Involuntarily Sarah inspired deeply with the pleasure of it, then looked guiltily to see if Andrew had noticed.

Andrew rummaged in the back of the jeep, emerging with a neatly coiled rope. 'Arms up!'

She obliged meekly while he tied one end around her waist.

'Just in case.'

The climb was not difficult, but sufficiently obscure to deter anyone without knowledge of the exact route.

'Jefferies showed it to me,' Andrew explained. 'About the only useful thing he's ever done.'

They were breathing hard when they reached the top. Andrew said, 'Keep your eyes fixed on the ground until you get your breath back. You can look only when I tell you.' He took her shoulders and shuffled her into a new position. 'Now!'

Her eyes opened to see a tiny cone of ice and snow, far distant and isolated in a great plain beyond the jagged escarpments of the middle ground. Everything was touched by the glow of evening. It was a calendar view, with all the ingredients in place, shining and perfect.

Andrew cast her an anxious glance, knowing that the association with Jefferies would re-enter her mind. 'We're both mountaineers, you see.'

She took his arm. 'It's all right. Really.'

There was a small horizontal rock slab, natural but so appropriately placed that there was no option but to sit there. He had brought a rug and spread it out for her.

'You recognise it?'

'Ararat?'

'I'm told so. Seventy miles, yet you can almost touch it. Some would say it's the centre of the world.'

'You believe the legend?'

'Of the ark? I believe it has substance, but not here. Even legends must conform to physical laws. But yes, I believe in a Noah and his ark.'

'Tell me what you believe.'

'Noah was a small-time farmer on the outskirts of Nineveh – today's Mosul. There's an account of the flood preserved on clay tablets found there. He had a few livestock – cattle, pigs, chickens and the like – more members of the family than commodities. When the waters began to rise he had the gumption to pack them into a converted boat he happened to keep on the river. The rise was of only a few feet and didn't last, but it spelt death to his neighbours' animals. So he became a local celebrity. It had all the elements for a legend.'

'But why Ararat?'

'In the early Chaldean form the legend placed the grounding of the ark on mountains much closer to home. Mountains were needed, you see, to give the story dramatic appeal. Those early chroniclers wouldn't have known that the peaks to the north were actually higher. When that was realised, Ararat had to be the prime candidate.'

'So what does the story tell us?'

'More than you might think. The modern version has lost its meaning in becoming fantastic. The message, Sarah, is that you take judicious advantage of what's available, so that you can restore the good things to how they were.'

'That's the message for me, you think?'

'It might be.'

'About whether I should go back?'

'Ah, now you're putting me in a position of great responsibility. If you stay as you are – and there's something inside you that wants to do that – someone once called it the Streisand nose syndrome…'

'She's beautiful!' Sarah protested, 'I'm not having that!'

'And so, scar and all, are you.'

She felt the warmth of his body through the course cotton of her jacket and shivered. Had the wind risen and become more chill, or was she feeling once again the glimmer of a dimly remembered teenage passion?'

'If you stay as you are,' he said, picking up the thread again, 'you will be a great gain for humankind. You have compassion without sentimentality – leaving Irina aside for the moment.'

'I'm no Livingstone or Schweitzer.'

'I believe you could be.'

'You're sweet to me, but what you can't know is that I'm really a simple girl, rather hurt in ways I don't yet fully understand, quite kind, I suppose, and incredibly lazy. What can you make of that?'

'If you go back you'll need a strong will to resist the temptations of the good life. What makes it difficult for me is that I believe you can. So you could still become a Mother Theresa, even with a perfect face.'

'Streisand? Theresa?'

'Different, worthwhile, something substantial that won't blow away in the wind.'

'So you're telling me to go.'

'Yes, reluctantly. Very reluctantly.'

'Am I allowed five more minutes here?'

'Yes.'

There was no sun now, and no distant peak beyond their capsule of suffused twilight. Tiny snatches of human voice wafted up from the camp far away: disembodied spirits, restless, dissipated. What they signified was no longer an influence.

'This little seat we're on,' Andrew said. 'I think God made it with a purpose.'

'Can you forget what you told me just now? About being…'

'I'm remembering what you said about nothing being absolute, nothing so exclusive that you can't make a dive for the apple when it falls from the tree.'

How those last few exquisite moments contrasted with the final cruel recollection: of the white rope against the immutable black rock, lowering her back into the cauldron of everyday life, to sink or swim as best she might.

After her last days at the camp Sarah had decided to spend her final weekend in Istanbul. 'You'll need to acclimatise yourself to western culture, sort of,' Allison had told her in her worldly-wise way. In the event the pull of going home was too great. She changed her Sunday ticket for a Friday flight, then telephoned Alice to meet her at Heathrow. She thought the reception was cool. Then she remembered that Alice was always a bit like that where she was concerned.

She went to the kiosk to collect the photographs taken during that last hour of hectic activity at the camp when everything had to be recorded. Looking at them now, spread out on the seats in the departure lounge, great bubbles of sadness welled up within her. Smiles, tears, gifts squeezed from resources of almost nothing, her gratitude greater than they could have known. And Andrew, waiting by his jeep, the saddest thing of all.

Boarding the plane would be the cut-off. At that point the recent past would become encapsulated and stored, to be savoured when she felt herself worthy enough to look back. That, she thought, might be a long way off.

Already, as she climbed the steps, she was fingering the envelope that Nuru had given her with his final handshake. 'It's from Jazreel. I promised to give it to you only when you'd decided unequivocally to go. Very odd. You know, we met in Ankara just so she could give it to me. Most mysterious.'

The flight attendant at the cabin door looked at her for a moment longer than she should have done. There must have been things about Sarah's expression that she couldn't quite reconcile.

SUBURBIA

December 1987 – July 1988

20

The decision to return to Shirley Hills had been easier than its acceptance when the time finally came. Even as she wheeled her trolley out of baggage reclaim it was in her mind to avoid Alice and go somewhere where she could hide up for a while, to think things out and prepare herself for Brian's knife. In the event two things prevented it.

In the first place it was Christmas; if, that is, Christmas can be brought forward three weeks to include the manic urge to buy that seemed to prevail – at least at Heathrow – at the time of her arrival. Howard Blake's *Snowman* extended a metaphorical hand as she walked out of customs. Once through the gate the cacophony was almost unbearable. But for a delicious moment it brought back the wonder of being a child.

In the second place Mark was waiting there with Alice. His features were drawn, as if all confidence had been sucked out, leaving him dry and wrinkled, like an ageing balloon. The smile, touched now by self-consciousness and apprehension, was as welcoming as it was honest. She could not recall a time when he had been so pleased – really, truly pleased – to see her. Perhaps there had been only one skin after all.

Alice, by contrast, seemed to have flourished. Her cheeks glowed within the frame of a fur-lined bonnet, giving her the warm cosiness of a children's book character. It was a wonder that the extravagant sardonyx cameo at her neck had not tempted some passer-by to pluck it off and run. Perhaps it was Alice who had sucked Mark dry.

They drove to Shirley Hills in Alice's car, which was odd as Mark usually got into a car only if he was king. She screeched to a halt, sending gravel spattering against the front steps. Sarah was surprised that Mark had not become angry. But, looking at him, he had not even noticed.

'Wakey, wakey, we're here,' Alice shouted over her shoulder. With a sudden realisation of lost manners Mark jumped out to open Sarah's door at the front.

'You see, the man still cares,' Alice said. Then she relented. 'Sorry, Mark, that was a bit forward of me.'

Mark had not taken offence. 'No, not at all. It was astute of you to remind me.'

They sat drinking coffee at a kitchen table longing, in its bareness, to share some of the plates piled up at the sink. 'A woman comes in,' Mark explained, 'but not until Monday.'

Sarah was itching to tell of her adventures and had her photographs ready in her bag. But no-one asked. Alice boasted of the dinner she had to attend that evening at the Surgeons' Hall. 'They were lucky to get Brian to speak before he leaves for the States,' she said, adding brightly, 'A bit like you, Sarah.' Mark sat watching them, quietly waiting for Alice to go.

'That woman is trying to score over you, Sarah. I think she's trying to make the most of it before Brian puts you right.' Then the corners of his mouth twitched and he chuckled to himself. 'I had to work on Brian for weeks to get him to agree to it. You know what he said to me? I will only do it if I think I can get it absolutely right; otherwise someone else can. He's an odd-ball, Sarah, but underneath a good friend I think.'

'I can't believe I've only five more days of this,' Sarah said, touching her face.

The first thing she looked for upstairs was her bear, Alfonso. He sat presiding over an ice-flat counterpane, defiantly daring the most nymphoid of potential concubines to disturb its pristine surface. His raised arm pointed to the pots on the dressing table. There, he said, just as they always were. 'You're a good, loyal bear,' she told him, whisking him into the air and hugging him tightly.

Her gyrations around the room stopped abruptly as she passed the window on her third rotation. Before, the leaves of the chestnuts in the Dell had been russet, defiant in the wind and impenetrable. Now, wet tarmac shone through the dark lattice of boughs and twigs. What she saw froze her heart: a for-sale notice posted at the perimeter hedge. She shouted to Mark down the stairs. He came sheepishly towards her, knowing what was coming.

'Tell me it's just land you're selling.'

'I'm afraid it's the house. I'm sorry.'

'Why?'

'I couldn't tell you in the letter. Or on the way here with Alice around, although – God knows – she's aware of it. The fact is I lost the battle at Massingham and haven't managed to find anything since.'

'But you're a businessman, for heaven's sake. You weren't tied to their apron strings.'

'I didn't think so – then. Please let me tell you in my own time. You wouldn't believe how far their tentacles spread, and how tight the grip.'

'I think I might.'

'Sarah.'

'Yes?'

'Lie down with me. To talk.'

There was a long silence as they lay side by side,

uncertain what to do. Eventually he put his arm beneath her neck and she rolled towards him. Then she said, 'There's something else, isn't there? That you haven't told me yet.'

'I think I'm being poisoned.'

'Mark, that's ridiculous!' She thought for a moment. 'What does Brian say?'

'With your problem, I haven't bothered him.'

'He must have noticed.'

'He's… well… very selective in what he sees.'

'I thought he saw everything.'

'Anyway, there are headaches and nausea, and cramps in the morning and evening. I'm steadily losing weight.'

'Cancer?'

'That's what I thought. Then I had it checked out. It isn't. Nor AIDS. Nor anything else in the text-book, apparently. They're baffled, Sarah, and frankly so am I. And frightened.' She watched his eyes playing on the ceiling like twin searchlights. 'Surely, if they'd wanted revenge – and I can't think why they would – they'd have had their pound of flesh by now.' He laughed bitterly. 'It's the sort of subtlety I used to practice, remember, in a more benign way.'

'That could be why you're jumping to the wrong conclusion now.'

'Not this time.'

Can Christmas really have meaning – even as an escape from the mockery of living – when your face hurts like hell beneath the grip of bandages?

It was a struggle to think so, this Christmas eve. Sarah had wanted to put sprigs of holly above each of the pictures in the drawing room, as her parents had done when they – the two sisters – were young. But the etiquette of the Dell forced them instead into crystal vases where they simply looked spiky and menacing. Mark had lit a fire and was prodding at blackening chestnuts on the grate against regular belches of smoke from the unswept, barely breathing chimney. It could have been the set of a Hammer film, with two ghoulish figures facing each other across a cheerless hearth.

It was an apt setting in which to throw the impressions of the event about in her mind. Those words of Brian's: 'It's the beginning of a new life, Sarah, better even than before.' Were they said before or after the surgery? The hand that held hers as the anaesthetic coursing through her veins expunged all fear: was that the same hand that had stroked her forehead – and more than once – before her eyes opened? She did not know. Most vivid of all was the feeling of having at last escaped, but from what exactly? It had made her cry dry tears.

'Sarah, you're dreaming again.'

'Sorry. Do you want another tape on?'

'No.'

With difficulty Mark got down on his knees to harvest the chestnuts. The white oval at his crown was no natural balding. Suddenly he began to laugh, compulsively, in quick snatches, as if he were trying to imitate a donkey. 'From now on you go up and I go down, isn't that how it is?'

'They'll sort you out next week. They wanted to admit you before Christmas, remember? Next week do as they say.'

'And you? When the bandages come off? I bloody well wish Brian was here.'

'He said he'd fly back if there were problems. He meant it. He's got complete faith in Dr Ransome, who reports daily.'

'I wanted to be first to see it.'

'And you shall!'

There was no question of dinner. But after its normal

time Alice arrived with presents, though they had nothing to exchange. There was also an envelope with a Christmas card inside and another which Sarah immediately recognised. 'It was on the floor of the car,' Alice explained, 'after I collected you from the airport. Sorry I forgot to give it to you.' It was Jazreel's letter, which Sarah thought she had lost on the aircraft. She put it on her desk without opening it.

'Don't you want to see who it's from?'

'I know what's in it,' Sarah lied. 'I'll open it later.' She hoped she had concealed her agitation and spent the rest of the evening willing Alice to leave. If there was success in that, it took a long time to achieve.

'Any message for Brian?' Alice asked at the door.

'Tell him there will be when I know the result. Oh, and happy Christmas.'

There were sounds of footsteps from the corridor upstairs.

'What's that?' Alice was alarmed.

'My mother. Didn't I tell you? She's staying with us for Christmas. She's not very sociable these days and a bit shy with visitors.'

'I see.'

That night Sarah slid in beside her husband and pulled the sheets over her face. He made no move, but she knew he was awake. When at last his breathing was regular Sarah crept downstairs to read Jazreel's letter.

As Mark faced her across the breakfast table he could not have failed to notice the anger in her eyes that was still there.

When the bandages came off, Sarah was neither pleased nor disappointed. There was something of a ripe Victoria plum about the blotched purple of the bruising that remained. Had she not known better, she would have seen it as a change for the worse. It was, in fact, precisely what Brian had told her to expect.

The effect was that the problem of her face now gave way to a more pressing matter: the secret that had been a constant companion since before her return and which she had dared not share.

A blast of cold air caught her vulnerable cheek as she stepped out of St John's Wood tube station, forcing her back inside to adjust her scarf and straighten her dark glasses. The local map on the wall told her that Bidwell Street was only two blocks away.

A luxury private clinic with fine views over the city, the brochure had said. Who in their right mind, having their womb scraped and the contents sucked out, would care about the view. More likely, for some, the drop to the ground would be the greater attraction. You'll like it there, the counsellor had told her, and Mr Prandesh gets very good results. She wondered if a not-so-good result meant a continuing pregnancy.

The fact of the pregnancy had been less of a problem than the identity of the foetus. Did it have to be Sammy's? Wasn't there just a possibility that Mark had slipped quietly into her bed before the shutters against love and respect had finally come down? She couldn't remember. Should she take more time, perhaps, to consider? After all, if she had the mind for it the timings could probably be checked more precisely. And, for her of all people, weren't children's lives now precious?

She knew already in her heart that Mark, in his demise, would have no space for an unborn child; so the question was academic. Another bitter gust caught her cheek where the scarf had slipped, like a spiteful friend pinching her when she told a lie. Yet it was no lie, this thing that held Mark in its grasp and would not – she was sure of that now

– ever let him go. It was cowardice, of a kind, that stopped her questioning deeply enough. Perhaps, in a vague way, she already knew the 'how'; what she could not fathom was the 'why'. She set off wearily along the pavement.

The receptionist had that prim early-twenties hauteur that could comfortably accommodate whoever approached her desk. Whether delight that the client had had the wisdom to choose Rosedale Clinic, or sympathy with an aggrieved relative whose loved-one had died unexpectedly overnight, the versatile red mouth worked independently against the same expressionless face. It was one of the drawbacks of private medicine, this hypocrisy at reception. What she had seen in embryo in the NHS flowered with vigour in this rarefied atmosphere. Why, Sarah wondered, in an abortion clinic of all places, did they have to choose a girl whose fulsome blouse-and-skirt, no-nonsense sensuality seemed only to belittle the unfortunates passing through: they for whom that decision – that wretched decision signifying the ultimate in waste – is nothing if not the renunciation of the essence of womanhood.

'You will have the rest of the morning to relax in comfort and Mr Prandesh will examine you at twelve. If all is well the procedure is scheduled for four-thirty. There's a room available should you wish to stay an extra night, but I'm afraid payment will be required in advance.' She lowered her voice. 'Please sign this form.'

No memory could match the loneliness of that cold white room. Why didn't she bring Alfonso, to share her tears and remind her how glorious the new beginning was going to be. She would have given anything to be in a ward with other women, to see her plight in a human, not dishonourable, perspective. And they would have known about Mr Prandesh through the eternal grapevine. She, silly creature, had not even looked him up in the Medical Register. And why, in the cause of anonymity, had she thrown away the advantage her own medical qualification might have given her.

Prandesh reminded her of the barman in Irmkutz. Having examined her, he stood at the sink washing his hands, lazily resolving Chinese puzzles with his soapy fingers. He paused with towel raised to ask if the father would be visiting.

'You can't have a father if there's no child.' It was a stupid remark, but what prompted it – the identity of the foetus – was still important to her.

'No, quite. Then – how shall we say – the person responsible for your condition.' He smiled serenely, obviously having been here before.

'I don't know who it is.'

'But you're married, are you not, Mrs Macdonald. That's what I was told.'

'In a manner of speaking.'

'And you don't wish to know? Who this person is?'

'I expressly forbid the retention of any sample that might make that possible.'

'I see. Well, of course, that wish will be honoured.'

'Thank you, Dr Prandesh.'

'Mr Prandesh.' Again the serene smile that he must have practised with the receptionist. 'Until four-thirty then.'

Sarah buried her head in the pillow as the door closed. She had already begun to hate her own kind.

She woke the following morning feeling wretched. There was a nurse in uniform beside the bed with a tray in her hand.

'It's a good thing you're staying another night, Mrs Macdonald. You lost a little blood yesterday so we need to build you up a bit.'

'You did destroy it, didn't you?'

The girl was puzzled and looked around the room for guidance. 'Destroyed what, Mrs Macdonald?'

'The foetus, of course.'

'Of course, if that was your wish. Look, I'll pull the curtains. See, the sun's shining. If you look outside you'll see the ducks playing on the pond. That'll cheer you up.'

Staying away the extra day had made her apprehensive. One night allegedly spent with her mother had been a safe excuse; two offered scope for being found out. Having called a taxi, she telephoned Betty Potter.

'Mum, you haven't tried to contact me, have you?'

'No dear, why?'

'Oh, only that our phone's been out of order. So you haven't heard from Mark either?'

'No. But someone called Alice rang.'

'You know Alice is… Did she say what she wanted?'

'No.' There was a pause. 'But Tom asked after you yesterday. He said he was surprised he hadn't seen you lately. He was pleased to hear your face will be alright again.'

Sarah put the phone down. 'Jesus Christ!'

She redirected the taxi to Putney, parked outside the front door and walked through the silent house to the terrace. The sour smell of an unsuccessful bonfire hung in the air.

Alice was sweeping leaves and loading them into a wheelbarrow. 'Bitter isn't it,' she said, banging the palms of her gloves together and stamping with her boots on the flagstones. 'Don't let it get to your cheek, Sarah. I must say it doesn't look too good. Come to think of it, neither do you.'

'I'm all right, really. Mum told me you phoned.'

'I tried you at home first. Mark said that's where you were.'

'Did you let him know I wasn't?'

'Would I do such a thing?' Alice's giggle was suppressed

by something she seemed to have on her mind. 'You don't exactly look as if you've been enjoying yourself.'

'I needed to get away to think. So why did you ring?'

'I suppose I shouldn't have. But Brian's back and wants to see you.' She paused, not knowing what to say next.

'Yes, go on.'

Alice was fighting with herself now. And with something that was too difficult for her to handle, because it was too big for her to comprehend. She blurted out, 'I don't like what's happening to Mark.'

'Yes, it's a puzzle.'

'Is it? Sarah, while you were abroad they put him through hell.'

'It was stressful, but he's getting treatment now.'

'Yes... well. The point is it hasn't stopped, has it? I may not be as intelligent as you, Sarah, but I'm not blind. I've no evidence, but Brian has passed odd remarks. They saw each other regularly before you got back. I wouldn't be surprised if he wasn't at your place now.'

'Because he's concerned?'

'They're supposed to be friends, aren't they?'

'Then you'd better come with me,' Sarah said.

Can a desperate act shed an aura of malice that persists after the event? It seemed the only way to explain how Alice and Sarah looked at one another as the car drove into the Dell.

'I just know something's wrong,' Alice said. Sarah stared at her, her mouth set, not doubting.

The scene as they turned into the gate was familiar. To Sarah, it seemed only weeks had passed since her own trauma. An ambulance backed to the door and a police car – its blue light still flashing – parked a respectful distance away.

They found Brian first, sitting at the dining room table with head in hands, a policeman opposite. He looked up sharply. There was no doubting the pain of loss in his expression. 'They think it's an overdose. There's nothing you can do, Sarah. It was a shock for me to find him.'

The stretcher was coming down the corridor. Mark's face was ashen and still under the oxygen mask. She held his hand and walked with them to the ambulance. 'It'll be the Beckenham hospital, Miss,' the paramedic said.

Sarah returned to Brian. 'You found him?'

'In the conservatory. I looked around because the car was outside.'

'He seldom went to the conservatory.'

'Elephants will travel to die.'

'That's facetious!'

'It wasn't intended.'

'I feel so guilty,' Sarah said. 'Leaving him alone.'

'You needn't. I doubt whether you could have influenced him.'

'Why not? He still had everything to live for.'

'Perhaps he didn't see it that way.'

Brian rose and placed his arm around her shoulders. 'Come. I'll take you to the hospital.'

She struggled free, but not in an unkind way. 'Take Alice, I'll follow in a moment.'

Believing herself alone, Sarah went first to the conservatory. The chair by the fountain – the one in which she had so often played with Esmeralda – was still on its side where it had fallen. Beside it, fragments of a broken tumbler lay in a drying pool of spilt liquid. She dipped her finger into it and tasted alcohol. There was nothing else unusual.

'If it's the pills you're looking for, Mrs Preston, we've already searched everywhere.' Guthrie must have been watching her from the shadows. He was oblivious of the butterfly landing on his hair.

'It's a sad house, isn't it Inspector?'

'An unfortunate house, Mrs Preston. There could be a difference.' He came up to her. 'Before you go would you mind showing me where your husband kept his sleeping tablets?'

'He didn't take sleeping tablets.'

'He must have, though. Mustn't he?'

'He used to say that he rowed himself to sleep on a river of scotch. I was never aware of anything else and I got rid of mine before I went abroad.'

Guthrie looked at her long and hard. Then he pursed his lips and sniffed. Only the twinkle in his eye showed he had exonerated her. 'Now you'd better be after them.'

But while Guthrie went ahead, Sarah hesitated, held back by a distant memory from happier times. But Guthrie was holding the door open for her, and the moment passed.

Brian was sitting on a low wall beside the hospital steps, staring at the ground, waiting for her. From the depth of the tragedy in his face she had underestimated the strength of his relationship with her husband. His eyes seemed withdrawn into their orbits. The doves inside – how they must be fighting to escape!

'It's over, Sarah. He died in the ambulance. Do you want me to come with you?'

'No… no, thank you.'

'Shall I wait for you? Alice was too upset to stay. I sent her back with a driver.'

'Yes, wait for me.'

When she emerged an hour later he was still there, in the same position. She doubted if he had moved.

Guthrie called later to question them both, and would leave no wiser.

'I found him exactly as you saw him,' Brian repeated. 'There's nothing more I can add.'

'I'm grateful for your involvement in this matter, Sir.'

That night Sarah lay awake trying to decide if she had been right in sensing irony in Guthrie's remark.

Eventually Mark's same healing river carried her away, still not knowing.

It was a delight to find that Esmeralda had survived the winter. She alighted on Sarah's arm, resplendent as ever, coquettishly rotating, and opening and closing her wings.

Being in here is the only treat I looked forward to, you know, when I was... well... away.' Sarah brought her arm to Jack's to transfer the butterfly. It clamped its wings shut, reluctant to move, then slowly obeyed. 'It's difficult for you all to understand, isn't it? – why I've avoided my friends until now.'

Jack preferred to transfer his attention to the insect. 'Don't worry about it,' he mumbled.

There was a tap on the glass and Marcus Repton's head appeared around the door. 'Your mother's sent me to tell you tea is on the table. My goodness!'

'What?'

He drew closer, searching her face. 'That's incredible. It looks as if your Brian's made a rather good job of it. You really are beautiful, Sarah. I'd never really appreciated that. Somehow it was always...'

'... hidden behind a veil of laziness, arrogance and downright bitchiness. Right?'

'Not right!'

'Don't contradict the lady,' Jack said.

'Oh, I almost forgot,' Marcus said. 'Congratulations on your new appointment at the hospital.'

Sarah was content, or so she told herself. Mark, against all expectation, had left her financially secure and the severe debts she supposed had hung over him had not materialised. To her relief the for-sale sign had gone from the roadside. Her face was restored, almost, and she had a job, a proper job bringing with it interaction with real people amongst whom she was only mildly exalted. Those close to her, like Marcus and Brian, were accessible, but generally at a comfortable distance. Only Jack was nearer; but there was still that thin barrier of mutual shyness there that she considered prudent to leave intact for the moment. In a nutshell life was bland. She wondered seriously if she could live with it. At least she knew she had to try.

Funny how, positioned in this same spot on the sofa, knees in the foetal position, aimlessly staring at the ceiling, she seemed once again to be inviting the hand of providence to point a finger. In her state of do-nothingness, it took no thought to reach out to the button of the CD player, Mark's last gift to her and not touched since he died. It didn't matter what it was, classics or pop. She would take what came, like someone else's juke-box choice in the pub of her teens.

She smiled to herself, hearing the first few bars. *Three Coins in the Fountain.* One of Mark's. She could hear him telling her: one for me, one for you and one for good fortune. That was in happier times, when together they'd contemplated that perfect, enclosing, concealing film of water. Which even the police, with all their experience, had not thought to violate.

Alone in the house, the beat of the longcase clocks sounding louder than ever, as if driving her on, Sarah entered the conservatory and quietly closed the door. In a gloom scarcely relieved by the shifting moonlight the fountain glowed white under its dark canopy of vegetation. It was how, as a child, she had imagined a magician's cave holding a secret for which she must find a key. She sat next to the quiet luminescent dome, which no-one had thought to turn off. She thought back to that bright and wonderful morning when she had committed herself to Mark and to this house – and to her retrieval of his ring from within the cascade. The message of his music became clear. She placed her hand horizontally into the flow and felt with her other hand deeper inside. The empty pill bottle was expected and for a moment she was inclined to leave it there. But then her fingers touched the edge of the paper wrapped around it, secured with a rubber band. She withdrew them carefully, so as not to wet the paper. The light from the dome was just sufficient to make out Mark's message.

My dearest Sarah

If you are reading his alone, I thank God for it. Not seeing you for one last time is now my biggest hurt. I hoped and believed that we would meet last night, but you were not to be found. I wanted desperately to say goodbye. But not only that, you deserve an explanation for what I am about to do.

You have witnessed my demise since your return from Hatomi. It's not your fault if, with your poor face – and this may not even have been the case – it has taken second place in our scheme of things. It's become clear to me that without knowing the cause of my plight, its progress is unstoppable. And this in spite of the best medical attention – or what I have supposed it to be. Yesterday came new signs which I will not burden you with, except to say that new and horrific things are happening in my head and my vision is beginning to go. This decided me. Reason enough, I think.

I do not know what has been behind it all but I have little doubt that MF has had a hand in it. Besides yourself, only our domestic lady has had regular access to me, but that is so far-fetched as to be unbelievable. It could be in the air, or in the water – or even in my mind. Brian has been a great support but, as he says, he is not a medical man and has never been able to throw light on it. I called him to come for one last talk, but got only a recorded message. In the end I decided not to wait.

Try to be kinder to my memory than I have been to you.

Your loving

Mark

21

A well-meaning receptionist in the undertakers' office had told Sarah that you only finally got to know someone when you saw how they were mourned. The remark was intended to be comforting. It had the opposite effect because the handful of distant relatives in the crematorium chapel only confirmed the truth of the assertion. But that much had been expected: besides herself Mark had had no real friends, unless Brian could be counted as one.

Alice was unwell, so it was only Brian approaching the chapel steps. She watched him, with his thoughts elsewhere, skipping delicately between puddles to avoid soiling the polished uppers of his fashionable black shoes. The performance smelt of clients in waiting. As he drew level they exchanged smiles that held back stacked-up thoughts best left unspoken. Sarah took his arm and led him towards the seats at the front. She counted twelve grey heads – all female and few recognised – and one young man towards the back, kneeling, his dark head bent as if in prayer. All were on the left side of the aisle; the seats on the other side were empty and unlit.

The undertakers had assured her that the priest was one who could overlook any lack of religious conviction on the part of the deceased. After two mumbled hymns, cheerless prayers and a regurgitation of the notes she had given him over coffee at Hightower the red curtains finally parted. With a click that suggested slipping into gear the coffin lurched forward into the glimpsed flames and the curtains closed. Brian looked at his watch. 'Twenty minutes, not bad.' She imagined him saying much the same thing to theatre staff after a particularly slick surgical procedure.

Approaching the rear of the chapel she looked again at the figure still seated there, willing him not to open old wounds by raising his face. But there was no doubt it was the Massingham driver, Pierre. She looked back at Brian for signs of recognition, but none came. On the steps outside he asked, 'Who was that young man? He looked awfully out of place.' 'Probably just a business acquaintance,' she replied. But for once it seemed better to secure the lie. 'I really don't know,' she added.

There were many more wreaths against the chapel wall than there were mourners. Most were expensive, each no doubt an appeasement of a guilty conscience. But one, the largest – a confection of white lilies against a background of subtly pink dendrobium orchids – bore no card. Stepping closer, Sarah was just able to make out the letters MF within the arrangement of the flowers.

No-one accepted the invitation to return to Hightower for refreshments and Brian offered his usual patients-needing-me excuse. Perhaps, she thought, it was to avoid giving a prognosis on her still-healing face, now devoid of bandages but still criss-crossed by delicate pink suture lines that made her feel like an expiring fish in a net. Since he arrived she had not once seen him look at it.

The last of the vehicles sped from the car park, throwing up clouds of spray. Sarah stared after it. Now, she realised, came the test: to follow it, go home and let the chapter close or… Or what? Succumb to a wilful curiosity that even Bermondsey and Hatomi had failed to expunge? She

347

glanced at her watch, mindful of her recklessness, then stood immobile, eyes fixed on the ground. Two minutes passed: the invitation could not have been more plain. She didn't turn even when the footsteps stopped behind her.

'Well, Mrs Preston, my compliments for such a clear signal.' Pierre's voice carried no trace of a French accent, but there was another inflection, barely discernible but still foreign, that she could not place.

'I'm surprised you came.'

'Someone had to deliver the wreath and we were hardly likely to use Interflora.' Their eyes engaged. 'I see they've all deserted you. Shall we travel separately or together? I can have your car delivered to your home should you…'

'I think separately, don't you?'

'As you wish.'

She sped towards the arc of a rainbow that encompassed Shirley Hills like callipers. By the time she reached home Hightower was bathed in clear winter light. A flight of Canada geese circling overhead descended like stones behind the house. Against all logic her spirits soared. To her surprise the familiar black limousine was already parked discreetly under the trees.

They sat in the drawing room across the spread of unwanted food.

'I catered for twenty. So you see, Pierre, I can still get nothing right in my life.'

'Sarah-Jane…'

'Sarah.'

She caught him smiling to himself. 'In that case I'm Peter.'

'I wasn't really fooled.'

'Of course you weren't. Sarah, you have questions, but I must tell you I am not here to answer them.'

'Why, then?'

He shrugged. 'But I can tell you that my association – my contract – with the Massingham Foundation terminates today – and with it this assignment.'

'Me? An assignment?'

'Your visit to the Massingham Tower – remember – raised… resulted in… concerns for your welfare.'

Sarah realised, with a flush to her cheeks, that they had usurped the basis of their meeting. '*My* welfare? What about Mark, my husband? Was that part of your assignment too?'

'Mark was never part of my remit. The principle at Massingham is to compartmentalise. Mutual ignorance, believe it or not, is the cement that binds the organisation together.' He put down the prawn sandwich that moments before he had selected carefully. 'Look, we have an hour of daylight and I have never properly explored your garden.'

'Have you not? Alright then, you shall.'

They went by way of the conservatory.

'Your butterflies?'

'All dead.'

'All of them?'

'Except one.'

'Ah.'

The path from the terrace skirted the swimming pool and led up to the seat overlooking the lake, where the geese had congregated on the grass. It was an inevitable place to sit.

'My guess is that this is where your husband proposed to you. Am I right?'

Sarah looked up sharply. 'Why would you want to be right?'

'Up there…' He pointed at a spot midway up the trunk of a silver birch about twenty yards from them. '…used to be a tiny surveillance camera. Be assured it was taken down a while ago.'

'My husband put…'

'No, not your husband. He would not have known. It was… for the owner before him.'

'The one killed by the elephant?'

'You have to give them credit for imagination!'

'For Christ's sake, does this nightmare never end?'

Realising he had said too much he was suddenly humble. For the first time a look of concern replaced the defensive shield that belonged to Massingham. 'It will, Sarah. For both of us, if…'

'Right. Then tell me about yourself. What seems to be coming across is a person, not a henchman in thrall to your bloody organisation. Can I cope with that? Or is this just more delusion?'

'Gently, gently, Sarah. Let me tell you.' She could see that confiding in someone did not come easily. 'Can you believe I was once an academic – a lecturer in linguistics at the Technical Institute in Beirut?'

'Not easily.'

'It happened during the troubles of 1980. My family were killed by a bomb thrown through the door. Not an uncommon occurrence, then.' He paused. 'You see, our local militia managed to capture one of those believed to be responsible.'

'And brought him to justice?'

'Maybe, maybe not. I was invited to participate in the… interrogation. And a barrier was crossed. Do you know what I mean? So easily done, with all the provocation in the world confronting you; now, with hindsight – I mean now Sarah, not just last week, or yesterday – incomprehensible. If Massingham has taught me anything, it's that violence is within all of us. Anyway, I had a brother in London and fled here. When I was recruited by Massingham – for a certain kind of job, you understand – my moral numbness was – how shall I say – an asset. It has taken your…'

'So now?'

'So now, shackles released, I'll return and find the man's grave, and pray to whatever deities I can think of to grant me forgiveness… and peace.'

'And I'm part of that journey?'

'I believe you have been…' He looked away, letting his eyes wander across the lake, and over the lawns to the blackened ground where the stables had once stood. 'You never rebuilt them?'

'My needs changed.'

He must have sensed the question that was building in Sarah's mind. It seemed he wanted to say something but caution prevailed and he nodded his head slowly from side to side. 'Sarah, try not to look back, still less to reason why. Look only to the future and to your own welfare, no-one else's. Move from here, get new friends, let no-one influence you. One day you'll understand.'

'And you won't tell me more?'

'That's more than my life is worth, even now.' For several seconds he sat in silence, scrutinising the geese, which had drawn closer. Then he leant across and stroked her damaged face with his forefinger, and she moved her head closer to him. 'You'll get there, eventually. Wish the same for me.' She did not flinch when he kissed her cheek.

As if a matter of public business had been transacted the geese became suddenly restless, shook their feathers and waddled back to the edge of the lake. As they did so Sarah caught sight of Jack Adams walking slowly towards them from the conservatory. He was clutching a small cardboard box. She knew instantly from his long face what it contained.

'I'm sorry, Sarah. I found her on the floor next to the fountain.'

Sarah took the box. At first she was undecided what to do, then she said, 'I'll look by myself if you don't mind, Jack. Why don't you two men introduce yourselves over a cup of tea? It should still be warm. Give me a minute of two and I'll join you both in the house.'

As soon as the conservatory door clicked shut behind them she lifted the lid and peered inside. The colours were as brilliant as they had been in life. But it was the integrity of the wings and antennae that drew her gaze. Smiling wistfully she snapped the lid shut. Whether it was because of that or something else, the geese, as if mindful of the significance of the moment, lifted themselves as a body into the air and disappeared over the rooftop.

Sarah looked once more into the box, then followed the men into the house.

22

Could she sense a difference in the air as she drove through the Davison's white gates, this second time of facing such a gathering, months after the trauma to her cheek and many weeks after Brian's repair? That was irrational and she thought not, but by the time she had reached the front door she was less sure. Some things were similar, like Brian coming down the steps with Alice a pace behind, and the warm sunshine – although that was at odds with the still bare trees. No, it was rather a tension in the atmosphere, an expectation – not necessarily threatening – where before there had been sympathetic concern.

'I'm glad you could come early, Sarah. There are a few friends I'd like you to meet before the hordes arrive.' Brian's eyelids flickered nervously.

'Twenty-five are hardly hordes, Brian.'

He ignored Alice's remark.

In the hall outside the drawing room a young woman, slim, with long black hair, was contemplating a framed photograph on the wall. Sarah thought she was more interested in her reflection in the glass.

'Sarah, you remember Nicole from last year?' Alice said.

Sarah had never quite forgotten the pushy Arab's seductive companion. So here was an opportunity for a real comparison: today's pride against yesterday's abject misery.

Sarah thought momentarily that she herself might have the edge, then pushed the thought aside as unworthy of her new-found status. To her surprise Nicole grasped her hand and squeezed it.

'I'm so, so pleased for you, Sarah. Brian's done a magnificent job.'

'I'll never be able to thank him enough.'

It was not intended for Brian's ears, but he had moved silently behind them.

'One day I'll put that to the test, my dear Sarah.' He took their arms and led them into the drawing room.

As if a control button had been pressed, the room was suddenly in motion. Glasses tinkled, the French windows to the garden opened, someone sat at the piano and began to play *Summertime*. It could have been a theatrical stage. Only later would Sarah realise that the pushed button was her own presence there.

Sarah counted twelve men gathered in the room. The dress was uniformly casual – slacks and jackets – but the faces belonged to bodies that were more at home in charcoal grey. Bankers, were they, or lawyers? There was warmth in their handshakes. Perhaps success in business segregated with benevolence. She could recall meeting none of them before.

It didn't seem odd that the men should want to charm them, she and Nicole; the strangeness was in the measured doses, reminding her of seabirds diving to take fish and just as quickly veering away. No-one complimented them directly, yet the interest in both women seemed concentrated and focused, in contrast with the snatched conversations.

The attention must have lasted only eight or nine minutes before Brian re-appeared. Sarah glanced at Nicole to see if she had found the experience unusual, but there was no evidence of it in her bright open face.

Brian said, 'You must forgive me for being a little jealous of the attention. Let me demonstrate that beauty is not exclusively in your keeping. Come with me.' He led them into a long gallery at the back of the house that Sarah could not remember from her previous visits. Nicole was already ahead, pecking at each of the paintings with her eyes like a chicken thrown corn. 'Brian, they're magnificent! Sarah, isn't he just a genius?'

'A craftsman, that's all.' Brian's attempts at modesty were always ill-concealed.

Sarah stood back to take a longer, harder look. Already, in those few seconds, she had an agenda to work through. While Nicole enthused and Brian demurred, she was asking herself how this man, if friend he was, could have concealed the extent of his talent from them. Why hadn't she – or Mark for that matter – been invited to witness these paintings being brought to life on his easel. What was his motivation? But was that so difficult to grasp, looking at him now with Nicole, imbibing praise?

No, this was a superficial and simplistic analysis. This was not at all the joy of a kissed footballer or a prima donna parrying flowers after a performance. It was more the achievement of one more step towards a goal, and the accomplishment of it followed the exercise of will and conscious expectation in which pleasure – as she knew it – had no part. Now she understood why, against almost universal medical prognostication, her face was perfect.

Her thoughts had never quite left the group of men remaining behind in the drawing room; which was why, when the music stopped, she heard the distant cries of celebration, of glasses raised and contents downed.

One of them – the pianist – appeared beside them, exuding benevolence. 'Brian, we'd appreciate your attention for just one moment, if you two good ladies can spare him.'

Brian followed him with a measured tread that reminded Sarah of when they came to fetch her from the common room for her first interview at St Catherine's. What had made the man suddenly humble, in the twinkling of an eye?

'Where's your companion?' Sarah asked Nicole, with as much indifference as she could muster.

'Mr Khasoni?'

'Yes.'

'He's coming. About now I should think, with all the others. It's just that I came early.'

As she said it, from the front of the house came that peculiar muted closing of doors that typifies cars belonging to the rich.

Now comfortable in Nicole's company, Sarah began to enjoy the evening. They went into the garden together with an admiring entourage which grasped at glasses and canapés and fanned out on the lawn with the purposeful precision of soccer players taking up their positions.

The images slipped into focus. It was as it had been all those months before, except that now there were faces besides those at the previous gathering. The same juicy aromas from the barbeque wafted around the same clipped bushes and over the blue water of the swimming pool. Exactly as it had been, except for the group of men they had met earlier, now standing apart with Alice. Then it was clear that everyone was waiting.

Conversations died as attention shifted to the French windows of the drawing room. A moment later Khasoni was standing there, beaming, with his arms raised. Then, as if someone had rewound his spring, he minced across the flagstones followed by a bevy of girls in white tops and short black skirts carrying trays of glasses pink with champagne. He clapped his little brown hands with the delight of a child, calling them to order.

'Friends, colleagues. Do I scent victory in the air? A triumph perhaps? What would our friend call it?' The corners of his mouth turned down in the manner of a clown. 'Let us see. He would say, a job which on this occasion happens to have been well done. Is that not how he would express himself? No?' He looked directly at Sarah. 'And indeed well done it was, as you all can see. Perfection restored by rigorous discipline and perfect technique.' He stared hard at her. 'And you, young lady, *vulnerata non victa*, the subject of all this attention. How would you describe it? Come, tell us.' He extended his cupped hands towards her, as a conductor of an orchestra might to extract the last drop of sentiment from his players.

Something curious was happening here. She had come to the party as one guest amongst many. Suddenly she had become the focus of patronising attention. She felt anxious, and damp under her blouse. She glanced sideways at her companion, but Nicole was looking hard at Khasoni. She had to stay calm. 'The result is more perfect than I imagined possible, Mr Khasoni. So I am pleased to join with you in acknowledging Brian's skill.'

She saw Brian's forehead crease into a deep frown, but for what reason she could not imagine. He came forward and stood beside her. 'The point is, Sarah, the technique we used is of interest to a number of people here, so you must forgive them if they appear inquisitive.' He glared hard at Khasoni, then spoke to the wider circle. 'It was a great relief to me that the exercise was brought to a satisfactory conclusion for all concerned. I am most appreciative of Mr Khasoni's kind words.'

It seemed an odd remark to make. But stranger still was the collective raising of glasses, led by Khasoni. 'To future accomplishments,' he said. 'To future accomplishments,' they all replied. Sarah, still facing the group that had remained apart, noticed their puzzlement in joining in the toast. One of them whispered something to Alice, but she only shrugged her shoulders.

'I think I owe you an explanation and an apology,' Brian said to Sarah afterwards. 'Let's get out of earshot.' He led the two women to the end of the terrace and pointed to a rose growing just beyond the balustrade. He said loudly, 'That's the one named after me – one of the most fragrant in the garden, but you must judge for yourselves.' Then he lowered his voice. 'The fact is, some of my friends didn't think a perfect result was possible. I'm afraid Khasoni went a little over the top, don't you agree, Nicole?'

'Sarah coped very well,' Nicole said. 'Now, Brian. While you attend to your guests Sarah and I will finish the debate we were having over your paintings. Definitely not for your ears, if you'll excuse us.'

'Of course. You can be as frank as you like.'

'What debate, Nicole?' Sarah asked when they were back in the gallery. 'I thought we were agreed about them.'

'I don't give a shit about the crappy paintings. I'm concerned for you. Do two things. First get out of this house and away as soon as you can make a convincing excuse. Second, if you ever need to contact me use this number.' She squeezed a fragment of paper into Sarah's hand. 'Ask for Nicole, but never give your real name. Macdonald will do.' Looking at her watch, she said loudly, 'These could occupy me for hours, but it will have to be another time. It was lovely to meet you again, Sarah, and I'm really pleased for you.'

Sarah stood, mystified and alone, in the centre of the gallery. Christ, why did Nicole choose that name?

There were footsteps behind, and Brian's voice. 'I'm really flattered that you can't drag yourself away, Sarah, but won't you re-join the party?'

358

'The excitement's given me an awful headache. Would you mind terribly if I didn't stay?'

'No, not at all. I understand. I'll walk you to the car.'

Nicole's car was already speeding down the drive. It entered the stream of passing traffic without stopping.

'Nice girl. A real foil for Khasoni. I dread to think what it costs him to keep her.'

Brian seemed reluctant to let her go. As she climbed into her seat she noticed the nervous pattern of his feet on the gravel.

'Please say it. Don't be embarrassed,' she joked.

'Well, actually it's something I've been meaning to say for a long time, even though it's none of my business.'

'I'm intrigued!'

'It's simply to congratulate you on your pregnancy. Don't look shocked. It came up quite by chance when we ran a hormone profile before your op. Mark would have been delighted. In a way I wish he could have known, but it seemed to me he didn't.'

Sarah felt the flush of her cheeks. Not knowing how to react she played for time. The record could always be put straight later.

'No, he didn't. I felt it would have added another complication to his life. But it's easy to be wise after the event.'

'Is everything, well, okay?'

'Quite okay, thanks. It's just that I'm still a bit shy about it.'

He tapped the bonnet of the car with his knuckles, releasing her. 'Look after yourself, Sarah.'

At the gate she looked into her mirror and was surprised to see him still standing there.

Sarah had been back for only an hour when the phone rang. Already she'd downed two generous whiskies and was propped up in bed reading to Alfonso from an Orange-shortlisted novel. It was about a girl who loses her memory and then finds it again only to discover what a trollop she'd been in her previous existence, and was becoming again. She'd started it the previous evening and picked it up whenever she had moments to spare; but there was something about her fascination with it that made her uncomfortable. She put the book down reluctantly and lifted the receiver.

'Sarah, it's Nicole.'

'So soon?'

'Sarah, something terrible's happened. Alice has been killed.'

Even with her head beginning to swim this seemed an odd expression. Surely one died, unless there were suspicious circumstances. 'My God, what's happened?'

'She fell from the balcony above the swimming pool, just as the last guests were leaving. Drunk, apparently. It seems she hit her head on the edge of the pool and drowned before they could reach her.'

Sarah's head cleared miraculously. 'Did anyone see?'

'No, I don't think so. But several heard the scream.'

'And Brian?'

'He's distraught. After the police left he locked himself away.'

'Nicole.'

'Yes.'

'How do you know all this?'

'He telephoned Khasoni and we went back together.'

'Why Khasoni?'

'I can't tell you that. I'm not sure I know.'

'And why are you telling me?'

'Look, who else is there, apart from Brian? Alice was your friend, wasn't she?'

'Yes, yes, she was. Nicole?'

'Yes?'

'Was this what you were warning me of?'

'Sorry, Sarah. The line's very bad and I can't hear. I have to go. Don't forget that you have my number. Goodnight, Sarah.'

Sarah picked up her book again and addressed the bear. 'Alfonso, Alice was my friend, wasn't she? And if she was, why aren't I crying buckets of tears for her? It's like Mark over again, isn't it? Something way back drained me of sympathy. But that's not how it was at Hatomi. No. You would have thought me a sentimental fool if you'd seen me crying over those people and their children. What do you say, Alfonso? You want to whisper it?' She raised the bear to her ear, rocking backwards and forwards and nodding. 'A common factor? Yes, there is, isn't there? And you think we should investigate? Well, you're a braver bear than I took you for. My apologies. And where do you suppose we start? At the beginning? Right, that makes sense. But where is the beginning? Where is it, Alfonso? Alfonso, don't go to sleep on me. Alfonso!'

Sarah's telephone calls to Brian that night and the following morning found only an answering machine telling her he had gone away for a day or so. Two deaths each: a wife and a friend for him against a husband and a friend for her. So why was she back in bed with a cup of tea and the paper while he… She got up and for the next two hours sat at her desk scribbling on a writing pad, trying to harness her thoughts into a plan of action.

Two deaths each. No, that wasn't right. In the turmoil had she already forgotten the unborn child? Could she be that callous? For the rest of the day waves of remorse flooded in as through breached defences, confusing everything.

Why hadn't Brian tried to contact her? That was causing her more distress than she might have imagined. Each day she tried his number and always the message was the same. Each morning she sped to the front door as soon as the post fell to the floor. She tried to analyse her feelings for him and couldn't decide whether the motivation was affection or pity. Maybe the potency lay in the combination of the two.

The emptiness of her days was forcing her thoughts into wilder territory. Her waste paper bin was full of crumpled up sheets from her pad. She had not yet followed Alfonso's advice to take action, but his idea had taken root. Wherever she went, whatever she did, she could never escape the feeling that around her was some vast ordering of events – a force that picked up people's lives and dashed them down according to a programme that could not be glimpsed and had no discernible purpose.

One morning she looked at herself squarely in the mirror. For the first time she saw in the shadows under her eyes that fear had replaced bewilderment. Ignorance, she decided, was no longer a defence. One thing was clear: she could not go about it alone. When Jack Adams telephoned to check on her well-being she decided to grasp the opportunity.

From the deepest recess of her desk she withdrew Jazreel's letter.

My dear Sarah,

It would be churlish not to begin by thanking you for your efforts at Hatomi. Without your dedication we would have been stretched beyond the point at which people needlessly die. You know that already. And you know also that this is not my purpose in writing.

I once told you – and meant it – that I would answer whatever questions you had about the Massingham business. I was truly thankful you did not press me because, for me, it

would have brought back much pain (remember my child!).
You then caught me unawares with what might have been no
more than harmless interest. I have to confess that I lied to you.

I had no friends or acquaintances in that village in
Oxfordshire, whose name even I have forgotten. It was
simply where I thought I would find Tom Sharp, to exact a
revenge I could only contemplate knowing that I would be
out of the country the following day. Perhaps luckily for me
it failed, because with hindsight I see now that the hook of
Massingham (yes, that expression is actually used) might
well have found me.

Let me just warn you against having anything to do with
the man, on any terms. Ignore this at your peril. Promise me!

Married life is so-so and Adnam sends you his best
regards, as do I.

Jazreel

P.S. No, no, this is not enough. I believed my child to be
Edwin's, but could not be sure. The circumstances are still too
painful to relate. I have never forgiven him for keeping the
truth from me. J.

Sarah telephoned Tom Sharp that same evening. It took the courage of a couple of scotches before she could dial his number. The relief on hearing Pauline's voice was overwhelming.

'Pauline, it's Sarah Preston.'

'Tom's away Sarah, on business.'

'Do you have his diary there?'

'Yes.'

'I need to speak to him. Also… I was thinking… as it's so long since I've seen you both, I wondered if you might like to come over for a meal. If you feel like it – but only if – you could bring my mother along. What do you think?'

'Sarah, that's a marvellous idea! We've been so concerned about you.'

'How about Thursday week, say about eight? Nothing special, just casual dress.'

'Lovely. Tom will be pleased.'

'Oh, and Pauline.'

'Yes?'

'Does Tom have a car phone?'

'Why yes, I'll get you the number.'

As a precaution, Sarah invited Jack to the dinner. He confided to her later that he had been surprised his own mother, who was now on reasonable terms with Sarah, had been excluded, but had been too polite to say anything.

It was a week to the day that Brian telephoned.

'Sarah, I need to talk to you.'

'I've lived with that feeling for days.'

'I'm sorry. There were all kinds of things to be sorted.'

'I could have helped.'

'I know. And perhaps you still can. Did you know the police are regarding Alice's death as accidental? They'll take no further action, they said.'

'I'm relieved.'

'Oh? Why do you say that?'

'Because there was something about it all that belonged in a movie, not in real life. Did she fall or was she pushed? Oh, I'm sorry, that wasn't very tactfully put, was it?'

'I think I can see your point. However, the funeral's at Mortlake crematorium on Friday. There'll be refreshments afterwards at Putney. I thought we could talk after everyone has gone.'

'Is that quite proper?'

There was a barely audible clicking of the tongue that fell just short of a chuckle. 'I think I'd better come clean, then. I was intending to ask if you would like to come and work for me. To help run the Beckenham unit.'

Sarah walked slowly up the stairs to consult Alphonso.

Jack Adams rang. 'Sarah, are you sure you want to go ahead with this dinner tonight, with Alice's funeral tomorrow?'

'Quite sure. You're not going to let me down, are you Jack?'

'It makes no odds to me. No, that's not quite true. I'd be disappointed if we cancelled. Though heaven knows why.'

'Good. Look. There's something I need your help with beforehand. It's difficult to explain over the phone. Could I pick you up by car around five? I promise to run you home afterwards.'

'Do you want me to bring old clothes?'

Sarah barely recognised it as a joke. 'I hadn't thought about it, but now you mention it, yes please. But bring your posh gear too, you can change later.'

The timing was crucial because of the uncertainty of the rush-hour traffic. She waited at the corner of his road, then arrived at two minutes to five.

'A new car, Sarah?'

'Mine's playing up. This one's hired for the day.'

Instead of returning to Shirley Hills, Sarah drove southwards. On the slip-road onto the M25 Jack leaned back in his seat and groaned. 'I just knew this wouldn't be straightforward.'

'In fairness to you, you'd better read this.' She rummaged in the door pocket and handed him Jazreel's letter.'

'This Tom Sharp – you know him well?'

'People not knowing better might call him a family friend. That's how my mother sees him – and Pauline, his wife. But it's not how it is for me. What's interesting is the alleged link with the Massingham Foundation.'

'Mark's employers.'

'The truth is, Jack, I'm scared out of my wits. Which is

partly why I invited you to dinner. You need take no active part – just hold my hand, please.'

Jack twisted in his seat to look at her. She returned a fleeting smile. Their speed had crept up to above eighty.

'Better keep your attention on the road.'

'Sorry.'

At the exit for the M40 Jack asked, 'If the Sharps and your mother are supposed to arrive at eight, what are we doing driving away from London?'

'You'll see. Just trust me.'

'Sarah, you're not being fair.'

'They would need to leave by six-thirty at the latest to be sure of reaching Shirley Hills by eight. That gives us about an hour before we need to make contact.'

'What do you mean?'

'Telephone them in their car to say we're delayed.'

'You've lost me.'

Sarah drove past the first turning to Peverell Hessett and took the next, entering the village from the direction of Oxford to avoid the possibility of passing the Sharps' car coming in the opposite direction. The village street was deserted. Apart from the porch light there was no sign of life at the Sharps' house, and no car in the driveway. She stopped in the car park next to the church.

'Six-thirty.' Sarah got out her new hand-held phone and called the Sharps' home number. There was no reply. 'I really enjoy looking up old friends, don't you Jack? Come on, time is short.' She walked close to him, with her arm through his, slowing him to appear casual. Still there was no-one in the street.

'Not this gate, the next.'

He followed her down the stone steps. The hedges on either side had got higher and the stinging nettles more vicious. Brambles horizontal like fishing rods clutched at their clothes,

366

and he went ahead to hold them back for her. Behind them the road was already out of sight. In front loomed the squat brick structure, dark and threatening. She felt her heart pounding, just as it had done the first time she had seen it.

'This building is of particular interest to me, Jack. We need to get inside.'

He pulled at the door handle; it wouldn't budge. The windows were tight shut, and covered on the inside with black fabric. 'You'll need proper tools to get in there.'

Sarah opened her handbag and held it for him to see.

'Tools! Gee whizz. You're serious about this, aren't you?'

'More serious than you could possibly imagine.'

'Then let's not waste time. The window first I think. Let's have a crack at that.'

Jack told her later that what he remembered most vividly was how she had entered the building. She'd waited for him to unlock the door and came in as a child in a fairy-tale might enter a magic kingdom. Even in the fading light through the door he'd seen her eyes widen; but it had taken him a few seconds longer to realise that they blazed with anger, not wonder.

'You've been here before,' Jack said.

'I believe so, yes.'

The bizarre interior was incomprehensible to Jack, but not to Sarah. The rich black velvet coverings were familiar from the vastly different setting she remembered from the night of her visit to the Massingham Tower. She knelt at the foot of the podium with its austere table and rested her head against the soft material that accorded with her dreams. She paced the room, looking for enlightenment, but none came.

'Can you imagine, Jack, what this is used for?'

'Cult worship? Satanic rituals? I don't know.'

'Could be. I only know about the function, not the

background.' She shuddered. 'I think I've seen enough. Let's go home.'

He could not know the depth of her despondency. He became absorbed in examining the rest of the room in minute detail.

'What's behind this door?'

'I've no idea and I don't care. Let's go.'

'I'd like to take a look.'

'Please!'

But with a sharp kick he already had the door open. Inside were clothes, dark and musty, billowing from pegs. Beyond, wooden steps led down into a black void. Reluctantly Sarah searched for the torch in her bag.

They were in an empty stone cellar the same size as the room above. They found a door within a low arch; it would not budge and Jack kicked it open. There was no choice but to follow the tunnel that lead directly towards the house. Then they were in another cellar and mounting another flight of steps.

Curiously, the door at the top was not locked. It did not take long to discover why. The room they were in was itself separated from the rest of the house by a formidable array of locking devices. There was no window. The interior was comfortably, if simply, furnished: two upholstered chairs stood either side of a wooden table bearing a projector pointing towards a screen on the wall. Shelves around the walls were laden with books, photograph albums and a library of videotapes identified only by serial letters and numbers on the spines.

Without any plan Sarah began to leaf through one of the photograph albums. At the first page she threw it down in disgust. Jack picked it up and looked at it. 'This is terrible, Sarah. What in God's name have you got us into? This one's for the police. Let's get out.'

Sarah sank into one of the chairs, fighting to regain her composure. 'Jack, bear with me for a minute longer.'

With trembling hands she picked up the album again and leafed slowly through its pages; then another volume and another, while Jack replaced them carefully on the shelves.

'Jack!' She was distraught and crying. 'Jack, look. Please look.'

His voice cracked. 'What fiend would allow a kid to endure that?'

'My father, Jack, and others. That's Elizabeth in the picture. That's my sister you're looking at.'

They covered their tracks as best they could. In the car they hardly spoke, sharing the remaining question that neither was brave enough to raise. The M25, looming up again, seemed to return them to a saner, more hospitable world. For Sarah the bonds were released enough for her to say, 'I don't know, Jack. I really don't know.' He didn't reply, so she said in a whisper, 'Maybe I was just too young to remember.' She wondered if he believed her.

They stopped briefly at a service centre. While Sarah telephoned the Sharps to say that they'd been delayed by a flat tyre, Jack took it upon himself to telephone the police from a call box.

When they pulled into the drive Tom's black Mondeo was shining in the lamplight beneath the trees. Pauline was the first to get out.

Sarah kissed her lightly on the cheek. 'Pauline, I'm so sorry. I had no idea the RAC would take so long.'

'Sarah, it's okay. We've only just arrived. Thanks for letting us know, though. Lucky I gave you the phone number.'

'Lucky I had it on me.'

At the Sharp's car a titanic struggle was underway as Tom tried to extricate Sarah's mother.

'You managed to bring Mum. That's wonderful,' Sarah said.

Betty Potter hobbled up to them and laid a hand on her daughter's arm. 'Sarah, I'm so pleased we've all been able to make up. Please let's try to keep it that way.'

'Bygones be bygones, eh Sarah?' Tom held out his hand.

Sarah hesitated for only a moment, then grasped it. 'Oh, what the hell. Why not? Who was it who said the past is nothing and the future everything?'

'I don't know,' Tom said, 'but I'll drink to it.'

'Come on in then.'

Throughout the dinner Jack looked on in wonderment, finding it difficult to stay detached and act out his part.

'Your friend's the strong silent type, I think, Sarah.'

'Yes,' Sarah said, 'that's why he's my friend.'

After that Jack was even more at a loss for words. He could only watch as Sarah – who was harbouring the most intense feelings of resentment – forced herself to assume the role of relaxed and dedicated hostess.

'You've really done us proud,' Betty Potter said as they got up to go.

'Next time it's Tom's place,' Sarah said.

Tom appeared not to hear. He was staring intently at Brian's painting of Sarah draped over a chair contemplating roses in a silver bowl.

'That doctor friend of yours did this?'

'Yes. Good, isn't it.'

Tom peered more closely. 'Remarkable, I'd say. Ever studied the detail?'

'I usually admire it from a distance!' She blushed. 'As a picture, I mean, not me.'

'Well, look at it carefully when you get a minute. You might find it more interesting than you think.' He took the cap that Pauline was waving in front of him. 'Goodnight, one and all. Thanks for a very satisfying evening.'

Ten minutes later Sarah was still standing in front of the painting. 'Jack, this is killing me. See if you can make out what the bastard was getting at.'

Jack took out his reading glasses and peered at the canvass.

'It was the rose bowl he seemed to be looking at, Sarah. The reflection, perhaps. Ah, I think I see.'

'Then for God's sake tell me!'

'Well, although your damaged cheek's not visible, there's a reflection of it in the rose bowl. You can see the line quite distinctly – faint, but it's there. I'd say he's painted your scar, or the suture line. Weird he should want to do that. But why, now, would Tom find that interesting?'

'Sarah felt as if her legs were giving way. She slumped into a chair.

'You know?'

'You really can't guess?'

'No idea.'

'Jack, the picture was painted before it happened.'

'Then either it's been added since, or...'

23

At Mortlake crematorium – Alice's funeral – the stabbing recollection of Mark's bleak cremation made her look at the faces more closely. There were many more of them, and in their midst was the kernel of family. They were known to Sarah only as distant figures hovering on the periphery during their early student days who had since receded into nothingness. Yet here they were, mother, father and two sisters and a bevy of others, large as life, sharing a silent, potent grief.

Dr Pardoe, Alice's father, had to introduce himself to her. She felt ashamed; what kind of friend had she been? Well, she knew the answer to that. He stood around two metres tall and his shape reminded her of Alfonso. Mrs Pardoe might have been a child at his side, were it not for the greying hair.

'My daughter always spoke highly of you, Dr Preston... Sarah. I hope you won't think me impertinent, but latterly she became very concerned about you. She never said why. We've – and please don't take this the wrong way – wondered sometimes if there was a connection... you know, with her accident.' He lowered his voice, as if shielding the two women from eavesdroppers with his bulk. 'You see, we were never quite convinced it was just an accident.'

'Dr Pardoe, there's no reason at all to think otherwise.'

She felt the force of his penetrating stare, difficult for someone soft by nature to maintain. Sarah hoped he could not read the doubt of Nicole's warning in what he saw. 'If I ever hear anything to the contrary I promise I'll tell you.'

The couple's two faces, separated only by distance, brightened in unison. 'That's all we ask, Sarah.' He patted her arm. 'Take care of yourself, now. We wouldn't want the same thing to happen again.'

That warning of Nicole's, so ambivalent, grew in her mind as she drove back to Putney alone. She needed time to think and for an hour cruised the dismal streets. Some of the mourners were already leaving when she arrived. Inside the house a few gluttons were still attacking the remains of a spread too lavish for the occasion. She looked for faces that had been at Brian's party the evening Alice died, but there were none. They had not been at the funeral either. Somehow that seemed significant.

Brian was waiting for her on the terrace. Already he had changed into grey trousers and a sports jacket. He might have been leaving a wedding reception for his honeymoon.

'Shall we go inside?'

'It's nice out here.'

'Better inside. More private.'

The house was empty, as if her arrival had sent the last of the mourners scuttling away. She wondered if the echoing corridors made any impression on Brian. If so, he did not show it. Outside the music room she thought she heard faint fleeting fragments of conversation and wisps of syncopated piano. But once she was inside they resolved into the twangy, metronomic beat of a single grandfather clock.

'Drink?'

'Tea would be nice.'

'A bit later perhaps. Nothing cold?'

'No.'

'Sarah, I have an admission.'

She laughed. 'Let me guess. There's no job.'

'No. Well, yes, there could be, but that's immaterial.'

'You can be straight with me, Brian.'

'You don't find that difficult, under the circumstances? With Alice…'

'The truth is I'm drained of sentiment. That was so even before Mark died. You can say what you like.'

He poured himself some something from a decanter on the piano.

'You remember an evening at Rotherhithe, on the balcony overlooking the river, just after your finals?'

'It holds special memories for me.'

'And how you looked at me when I was too shy to talk to you. As if I was the wettest thing next to the river?'

'Yes, I remember thinking just that.'

'Which explains why I'm being direct with you now, though God knows, it's difficult.'

'You want us to have a relationship?'

'Yes.'

'But why so soon? After losing Alice?'

'Because I see you taking up with another crowd. Like Jack Adams and Marcus Repton, of which I'm not a part.'

'They're friends! I can't exclude them!'

'I'm not asking that. I need someone to share a common purpose – and I desperately need you, Sarah. Not having you has caused me much pain. Lately I've felt… well… am I right in thinking things might have changed between us? For the better perhaps?'

'I'm eternally…'

'Not that.'

'Then yes, I suppose they have.'

Brian crossed the room to sit beside her. 'And there's

something else. This is really difficult and you must count to ten before you make any response. Will you promise me that? I hope it will be joyful news!'

Something of terrible significance was coming. Sarah was upright in her seat, her tired eyes wide open. Nothing could have prepared her.

'You're expecting my child.'

'Brian, stop fantasising!' She pointed at his glass. 'How many of those have you had?'

'I told you to wait. Listen. One night you came to the Tower, remember? I behaved badly towards you, I'm afraid when you were in no position to resist. I can only apologise for it, but, God knows, I've never for one moment regretted it.'

'Then you were the beast – in the bull mask? Not Pierre?'

'It was me.' The raised eyebrows over the thin smile reminded her of a chess player confident of check-mate.

'But you claimed not to know Pierre – in the chapel.

'There were others… involved.

'Then you'd better pour yourself another brandy, and one for me. Brian, there is no child. Why do you think I've kept my figure?'

'But the tests…'

'It was aborted, weeks ago. I couldn't tell anyone about that. Only you knew about the pregnancy.'

'Then why didn't you…'

The telephone rang. Brian leapt on it and viciously lifted the receiver. The crackle of the distant voice was angry and threatening. The words were unintelligible but they had a familiar ring about them. Before her eyes Brian's face began to age. He put the receiver down slowly and thoughtfully.

'There's been an accident at the Tower. They think it's Khasoni. I'm sorry, Sarah, I have to go.' He got up and made for the door, then turned back to her. 'Look, why don't you follow in an hour. I'll treat you to dinner there. Just go to reception. I'll leave a message. They'll direct you.'

The engine roared. Dust flew. She was alone in Brian's house.

There was an obligation that overrode her more basic inclination to explore. And in any case most of the downstairs rooms were locked. So she climbed the stairs and made her way to the first floor, towards Alice's room and the balcony from which she was alleged to have fallen.

Had Brian been so friendless that there was no-one to help clear away Alice's things? The police would not have wanted them moved, but their interest had been short-lived, apparently. Was his regard for Alice so low that even in death he saw no obligation to guard her privacy? If he had wished simply to forget, why had he not just locked the door, instead of leaving it open to the corridor?

There was something familiar about the way the clothes were scattered and the chaos of the dressing table surface. Choices were being made, under pressure of time. What to wear, what shades of make-up to choose, what jewellery would match. There was sadness here, because it was the room of someone trying desperately to get things right, to please against the odds. It was the room of a single woman on her first date with a new man. The familiarity that had so struck Sarah on entering was not hard to explain: she had seen this room before, many times before when they were students together.

Why, then, hadn't the police asked her opinion, as Alice's friend? Who of all people could have interpreted this scene better than she? Could she not have told them that no guest would have been invited here during the party for mere social intercourse, in spite of the evidence of the three champagne glasses on the dressing table? There was nothing innocent about that close grouping. May I take your glass, Alice, because with you still holding it, it will be difficult for us to throw you over? Sarah opened the door to the balcony to get air, and the door to the corridor banged shut. She turned violently to protect herself. For God's sake, Sarah, you're letting your imagination run away with you.

Trembling, she looked over the edge, into the... But beneath her were the flagstones of the pool surround; the water's edge was several feet away. Only a deliberate and desperate leap could have carried her that far. But if there had been others...

The faint chimes of the music room clock carried up from the floor below. She looked at her watch. It said six. If she were to follow Brian she would have to fly – if that was still her intention.

The three glasses again caught her attention. Could the police seriously have overlooked taking fingerprints? She ran downstairs, fighting to remember. In the drinks cabinet the patterns were different. But in the kitchen there were lots the same. She ran back upstairs and carefully replaced the ones on the dressing table, putting the originals in her bag.

Her last stop was at the telephone in the hall. There was an answering machine on Nicole's line. The message was to the point: Miss Macdonald will be at the Tower around six-thirty and would appreciate Nicole's company if she is free. Then she telephoned Jack.

Even in front of the towering building she could cut and run. But what was the point? The influences emanating from this malevolent mass so circumscribed her life that it was difficult to envisage an existence apart.

This time there was no security man to distract from his copy of the *Sun*. Instead a white-clad girl of Maia's clone stood waiting by the lift. She held a small device which seemed to generate the click from the main doors behind Sarah's back. 'Why is there no security guard?' she asked. The girl simply smiled and followed her into the lift.

They reached a corridor giving access to rooms that overlooked the lagoon through windows framed by red and purple bougainvillea. From her previous experience she would not have suspected their existence, so well were they hidden. Between the gently swaying fronds she glimpsed boats on the water and intense human activity that suggested preparation for an event of some kind. In contrast, the decor within replicated the cool tranquillity of a tropical interior. The girl's knock on one of the doors was gruffly acknowledged. She opened it and stood back for Sarah to enter. From the paintings on the walls there was no doubting whose office it was; but Brian was not alone.

Sarah had half-expected to see Edwin, but was unprepared for the third figure, back towards her, looking out over the lagoon, foot tapping in irritation on the teak floor. There was no doubt, even before he turned. It was difficult to reconcile the pin-stripe suit with the casual jacket of the evening before. He, a butcher? But, as she now knew, one could assume nothing.

He joined the others, who had moved to seat themselves behind the desk. The atmosphere was inquisitorial.

'Hello Sarah,' Tom said. 'Are you here for tonight's fireworks? I see they've started preparing.'

'I came to talk to Brian,' Sarah said sharply. 'I would like to do so now.'

'Would you now? Well, Sarah, that's an option you've just deprived yourself of. Do you know how that is?'

'I don't know what you're talking about.'

'Well, you're not exactly a respecter of privacy yourself, are you? You and your boyfriend.' He looked across to

Brian to see if the jibe had taken effect. Brian's face was grey and desperate. 'The point is, did you enjoy the family photographs, Sarah? Enough to share them with the police anyway. Sorry there were no later ones of your sis – they would have enjoyed those more. But, come to think of it, they did take the videos, so they'll not be too disappointed.'

'The police raided Tom's house at dawn this morning, Sarah,' Edwin said. 'It's difficult – indeed impossible – not to connect it with your intrusion last night.'

'Hard on Pauline, who's now under arrest, rightly protesting her innocence, as it happens.' Tom's chuckle became a scream of anger. 'And bloody hard on me. You've buggered everything, haven't you?' The crackling anger that had escaped from Brian's telephone was no longer a mystery. That call had changed everything.

'Then you'll get what you deserve, won't you? For God's sake, haven't you had your pound of flesh from me many times over?'

'Listen, Sarah. Last night at your place I reckoned to call it quits. To forget that debt of your father's, and what's still owing. That's being generous, I told myself, but at last the trollop's seen sense. So it seemed, mug that I was.'

Sarah remained silent, biting her lip.

'Tom, is this leading us anywhere?' Edwin asked wearily.

'Shut up, Edwin. It seems she's got to be reminded. Sarah, if you don't recall – and that I strongly doubt – then let me enlighten you. When you were a kid your father owed me two hundred grand, give or take a few, and would have gone bust if he'd paid. So I let him pay the interest in kind. It's as simple as that.'

'With sexual favours courtesy of his children?'

'A little harmless fun, Sarah. No harm done to anybody. Except to your sis when she stopped co-operating.' Tom glanced nervously at Edwin, seeing his error.

'You killed my sister?'

'The bitch would have told.'

Sarah, until now standing, slipped uninvited into a chair.

'Enough, Tom.' Edwin said. 'All this detail is in the past and is irrelevant. We have decisions to make and time is short.'

Tom took no notice. He had risen to his feet and was pointing at Brian. 'And what about his dealings, then?'

'You're right about that, Tom,' Edwin said. 'Sarah should know about it now there are no secrets between us, apparently. Tell her, Brian.'

'I'd rather tell her alone.'

'Very well, then I will. Or better, illustrate it for her.' He looked at Sarah over his glasses. 'Turn your head, my dear, and look at that screen.' Edwin might have been at a case conference with his medical colleagues. 'You see, Sarah, we like to keep a record of all our projects. That way our library is a source of interest for years to come.'

The credits meant nothing, except to confirm the professional touch of the film-maker. There was a dinner, a lavish, refined, all-male affair, like up-market Masons or Rotary. Faces were flushed, voices animated, polarised across a table seen end-on. Khasoni was on his feet. 'This man,' he said, pointing across the table, 'taxes my credulity. I propose to call his bluff. I propose to make him eat his words. *Verba vorare!*' Conversation died as abruptly as when knights once lowered their lances to charge. 'I wager the building of one new research centre to five million pounds against his achieving what he claims.' The camera panned to Brian, who rose shakily to his feet. He was boxed in, humiliated; he had no choice. 'I stand by what I said. I accept the wager.' Hands shook limply across the table. Conversation resumed like a kick-started engine.

A voice-over explained the terms: a face, as perfect as possible, to be disfigured and then restored within a year. It was followed by a monologue in legalese, formalising the proposed obscenity.

'Turn it off now,' Brian pleaded.

'Certainly not, Brian,' Tom said. 'She has a right to know.'

'Do you want to see more, Sarah?' Edwin asked.

'Yes,' Sarah said, 'you can't hurt me anymore.'

Suddenly she was looking at her own face coming rapidly towards the camera, then falling down and sideways as the blade bit. For a moment everything was still. There was no blood, just a black pencil line subtly changing in thickness. Then it filled red.

'You'll appreciate this bit,' Tom said.

They were at her gateway at Shirley Hills. A black shape, just identifiable as a car, entered from the right. The rear door opened and the scene faded. Then the sequence was repeated, but from the car's perspective, with Sarah getting in. She could even see her dress hitched up under her coat.

'Nice detail that, Tom,' Edwin said.

Now they were in the Massingham Tower, immersed in the dark extravagance of a companions' evening. Sarah dressing, her hands caressing her body under the satin-white gown, the mask of the faun in bizarre sexual contexts, the prostration before the figure in the bull mask; it was all there. And then, in what seemed to be a hotel room, the impregnation itself and Brian's flushed, triumphant face.

Brian jumped to his feet. 'You had no authority to film that!'

'But we did, didn't we,' Tom said.

Edwin was waving an admonishing finger. 'It was the sweetener you wanted, Brian. Not to renege on the face deal, remember?'

For a moment the screen divided: on the left figures milling on the terrace of Brian's Putney home, Sarah, with her ravaged face, in their midst beside Nicole; on the right virtually the same scene, again with both of them, but this time with Sarah restored and happy.

'That was the test, you see, Sarah,' Edwin explained. 'Whether the adjudicators – who were quite independent, I assure you – could tell which of you had undergone the surgery. In the event they couldn't and Brian won. Khasoni was livid.'

'I've seen enough,' Sarah said. 'Switch it off, please.' No-one moved. The film continued to run: more cars, people moving in darkness. They seemed of no interest, but then something caught her attention: the name *Hightower* on the entrance pillar of her house. The troubled darkness of the screen exploded into a fiery orange glow.

'So my stables were your handiwork too?'

'We needed a diversion, Sarah, to get you back indoors. Surely you can appreciate that?' The malice of Tom's stare was concentrated into two rigid black pupils. 'Anything else we can help you with?'

'If you would be so kind.'

'Feel free to ask.'

'Why did you have to kill Mark and Alice?'

Brian, who had kept his face buried in his hands, rose in his seat, glaring at them furiously. 'Don't answer. Let me tell her.'

'Shut up!' Tom pushed him roughly back into his seat.

Edwin was rotating the palms of his hands and contemplating the tips of his fingers. It seemed to say that the proceedings were drawing to a close. 'They too were sweeteners, of a kind. You see, to put it crudely, Brian still fancied you, Sarah. As, indeed, we've all done at one time or another. We simply wanted to ease the way. Isn't that so, Brian?'

'I love her. I adore her. Now I can give her the world if she asks.'

'Could have, Brian, could have. We're not talking the same language as yesterday. Things have changed. You took from her. Now, stupidly, you've let her take from you.'

Edwin looked up above her head and nodded towards the door.

Pride prevented Sarah from turning around. She was aware only of someone approaching and the prick in her arm, and Edwin and Tom filing past.

'She's all yours, Brian,' Tom called from the door. I'd say you've got about three minutes of coherence. Make the most of it.'

Sarah had begun toying with the ashtray on the desk. Suddenly it slipped from her grasp. She tried to pick it up but her hands drifted uncontrollably above it and she gave up. 'Brian, what was it?'

'What they gave you? *Somonaril* – a potent sedative.'

'Why? What will happen to me?'

'I don't know. I'm sure they'll salvage something from the situation.'

'To what purpose?'

'To entertain. For profit. Those fireworks over the lagoon this evening, that may offer opportunities.'

Her pity was not for herself and she wanted to reach out to him. 'I might have given in to you, you know, if you'd let me have half the chance. I think at last I'd come to terms with the downside.'

'It's unkind to tell me that now. Why not when it might have meant something?'

'Unkind? I've never been unkind. I was always the target for any unkindness around. Something in my nature seemed to invite it. I wanted to be loved, just that, without strings. I see now how my whole life has been... manipulated.'

'The hook of Massingham.'

Sarah's head would have jerked towards him if the muscles had worked. Instead it rotated with robotic smoothness. 'Not at first, Brian. Surely it was only Tom then.'

'You're certain about that?'

'What do you mean?'

'Those photographs of Tom's. You didn't see?'

Sarah's brow puckered in frustration. 'Tell me.'

'Edwin was one of your sister's first – how shall we say – admirers. He'd assumed you'd seen the photographs of himself, you see. You must have been a very small child when Tom started procuring for Edwin.'

'Then why was I spared? Why only Elizabeth?' The patterns on the ceiling began to undulate. Something vital was still missing. A kaleidoscope of images circled in her head: black velvet, Irina in Irmkutz, torchlight, taps on windows. 'Why do I know these things?'

'Elizabeth must have…'

'But she never did! We never spoke about it, ever. Me, her close sister!'

'Sarah, I beg you, put it from your mind.'

'And why was that building familiar, if I'd never been there? But I had been there, hadn't I? Hadn't I?'

'I… was told it stopped before you were old enough to remember. Obviously that was not quite true.'

'So why didn't it continue?' Her weakened voice became a sarcastic snarl. 'Wasn't I desirable enough?'

'It's… it's because your sister would have told. You were left alone because she allowed herself to be… That was the deal: her submission in return for your safety.'

'Then why did she have to die?'

'Because you'd reached an age to question, to seek out the truth. And then, in a strange way, you began to take her place. How else do you think you got a place at Catherine's, and joined the surgical team?' The words left his mouth twisted in derision: 'For Edwin's gratification.'

'Brian, I can't keep my head straight anymore.'

'Lean against me.' He was on his knees now, tears running down his cheeks.

'Brian,' she whispered, 'there's only one more thing: my face. Who did it to me?'

'I don't know.'

'You must know! It was Tom, wasn't it?'

'It was… Massingham. Keeping me in ignorance was part of the wager.'

'And you were never interested enough to find out? You must know something.'

His response was defensive, he resentful of being asked. 'I was told he left the country, so I don't think it was Tom.

She heard the sound of the door opening as Brian crumpled to the floor and sensed hands roughly grasping her shoulders. Her eyelids were already closed.

Was this the stuff of dreams? To be pulled across the surface of the dark lagoon, the light reflected from the vast dome touching with silver the ripples made by her dragging hand. Those left behind on the shore, so attentive to her progress: how concerned they'd looked, those two gentle girls in white, more beautiful even than Maia, who had helped her onto the raft. The tender kisses on her cheek: surely a promise, not a parting.

But why should she fear? Here was another craft coming out, weaving its way through the water. Would it not people her raft, to while away the evening. She rocked backwards in her seat, a light contented jelly under an indigo sky.

An expanding point of light was tracing its slow, paraboloid course towards her. A dull thud, then a crackle of combustion near her hand. Then heat: sudden, aggressive and focused, like a dozen suns emerging together from behind black clouds. Yet surely this was night?

Light was all around now, the shore and the sky just blurs through the spitting orange palisade. If only her head would clear and she could rise, to separate the dazzling beauty from the awful reality.

Through the concentrating colours something distant was changing: black shapes seemed to be engaging in some primeval ballet. She heard her name twice over in different pitches, and other voices in conflict with the plunging and splashing of water. Then a movement of the raft so abrupt that suddenly here was the wooden floor against her cheek. Above, the canopy turned orange.

With skin insensate, there were no such constraints on her nostrils. The singeing of hair – like at cremations at Hatomi – could only be of her own. Her mind at last began to wake to the proximity of death, panic countering the depth of her sedation.

A jolt of still greater violence, wood against wood, and desperate footfalls crunching the ash on the deck around her face. Hands pulled and arms hooked under her back and knees, releasing stabs of pain from the smouldering clothes. A greater splash and water closed momentarily over her head, but the hands did not let go. And out again, her body scraping over rough edges and shingle.

A sudden pause, her back propped against knees, as a vast billow of flame seared upwards from the point she had just left. There were two of them, a man and a woman, helping her, bearing her away.

She recognised the terrace where there had once been a table and chairs, and geraniums. 'Stop, please, just for a moment!' 'Next time, sweetheart!' The rock stairs hurt her arms and legs. Then, oh, the relief of open corridors and an elevator that still worked. Why did it have to be so rushed, when all was now quiet? If only her legs would support her weight.

'Look up, Sarah. Can you see who we are?'

'Jack? Nicole?'

'Good girl!'

'I'm going to break the glass.'

The glittering shower crashed onto the pavement. They dragged her over to the waiting car.

'Hospital, I think,' Jack said.

'No, I'll be okay.'

'Where then?'

'I'm trying to remember.'

'Just drive, Jack,' Nicole said.

'Greenwich.'

'Greenwich?'

'You're confused. But do it Jack and think about it afterwards. She's not hurt physically, apart from a few grazes.'

'Are we being followed?'

'No, I don't think so.'

'Go up to the observatory.' Sarah said. 'As close as you can get.'

They nestled under the stone wall where, to an observer with only cursory knowledge, the story might just have begun. Already, in the direction of the city, there was a match-flame of light more intense than anything around or beyond it.

'Look how it's growing, Sarah, Nicole! To think we were in that. I've got binoculars in the car. I'll get them.'

'No telescope?' Sarah asked.

'Afraid not,' Jack replied, puzzled by the question.

The explosion came about eight, that is to say about thirty minutes after their escape. In spite of the flames it was quite unexpected, and even after weeks of investigation by the police and a miscellany of other agencies, the cause, like the fire itself, was never properly explained in the absence of witnesses.

'The answer's in the psychology,' Nicole told them, the day the house at Shirley Hills went up for sale and they were sitting on the terrace waiting for the first of the summer flush of potential buyers. 'It's natural that if you create something evil and are capable of recognising it, then it would be second nature to build in a means of its destruction if it were ever needed. That's my theory, anyway.'

'What does Khasoni say?' Jack asked.

'Khasoni, sensibly, is keeping silent,' Nicole explained. Then she brought her hand involuntarily to her mouth. 'Oh, I nearly forgot. He asked me to give you something, Sarah. I'll get it from the car.'

The pink silk ribbon that encompassed the small black box slid silently to the floor.

'It can only be a Fabergé egg!'

Nicole was already peering inside. With a little foreknowledge she said, 'I think you'll find it's more exquisite even than that.'

Sarah withdrew a butterfly in pure gold encrusted with jewels. It bore a simple inscription on its base:

ESMERALDA PULCHERRIMA
REQUIESCAT IN PACE

PEVERELL HESSETT

June 1993

24

No-one could remember quite so many cars fighting to enter the church car park and spilling out in indignation onto the road. That was because the village had seldom produced a son or daughter worthy of the public eye.

Emerging into the sunlight, Sarah's first impression was of a flock of birds twittering in approbation. They might have been disappointed by her modest white two-piece suit; but, as they told her over and over afterwards, she herself more than made up for it. The showers of confetti seemed as much tokens of affection as of tradition.

A wheelchair carrying Betty Potter trundled out of the church behind her.

'It's good of you to do this, Dr Hislop.'

'Not at all, Sarah. Your mother and I are as inseparable as Paulo and Francesca. Isn't that so, Betty?'

'He's a good man, Sarah.'

Andrew had wanted a low-key reception in the village hall but Jack and Nicole had advised Laurel Cottage and won the day, although strictly it was none of their business. Given the sunshine it was the right decision. The grand marquee dominated a manicured lawn patched with life and colour.

Sarah and Andrew placed themselves inside the garden gate, just in time to see Carruthers and Bentley wheel into sight. 'Look at your watch, in case they charge us for their time,' Sarah whispered, intending to be overheard.

Marguerite followed with a little boy who was torn between clutching her leg and dragging a toy rabbit on a lead. Her wide smile was fixed and wouldn't break because of the pent-up emotion after five years of separation.

'At least I got rid of the horses,' Sarah whispered in her ear, and the ice was broken.

'Oh, Miss.' Her arms were around Sarah's neck in an instant.

The boy removed a thumb from his mouth in quiet contemplation of a new phenomenon, then replaced it when he realised there was nothing on offer. Seeing him begin to wander away Nicole tried to pick him up and was rewarded with a plaintive wail.

Jack was getting impatient. 'Put that child down, Nicole, and help me get them all inside.'

Volunteers from Sarah's contingent of medics and researchers from the Davison Institute and Andrew's cohort of Red Cross workers helped push Betty Potter's chair up the slope to the marquee.

Eventually the lawn was quiet again. Inside the marquee they made resolutions for the future, to spirited applause. Outside the sun still shone. But not everything was harmonious in this seemingly idyllic garden.

There is a kind of collective boredom that sets in somewhere around the time of cutting the cake. Jokes are done, insults hurled, embarrassments survived. People that have not seen each other for years begin to realise why. There is an intense urge to get up and wander, constrained to the limits of endurance by not being able to leave before the bride.

Children, of course, are affected in a similar way but at a much earlier stage. They fan out like Indian scouts, secreting themselves into holes and crevices in the landscape. For that, this garden, with its perfection and neglect in equal measure, spelt paradise. For Marguerite's boy the adventure was doubled, because it was foreign and therefore mysterious. The threat of the unfamiliar language might just have driven him a little further than the others.

At first – as she would tell Sarah afterwards – Marguerite asked the other children if they had seen him. Then she went off by herself to search. She crawled under the bizarrely twisted laurels, possible only because they were old and bare near the ground. The light was beginning to fade and her heart pounded as only a mother's can. She struck what remained of an ancient fence and welcomed it like a lifeline. After a few paces there was an opening to a narrow strip of grass and low vegetation dappled in the sunlight that was once a path. It was there she found them, chatting in a French that was as child-like on the one side as on the other. Hearing her name was more than just a surprise, because even when she looked again she hardly recognised him.

It was not easy for Marguerite to catch Sarah's eye, discreetly, to say what she had been told to say. There was a jug on a nearby table. She made it fall, causing it to shatter, its contents soaking the matting floor. It was enough to draw attention from Sarah.

'Miss, there's someone in the garden who wants to see you.'

'Oh, who?'

'I promised not to say.'

'Then why should I want to see them?'

'Him. Someone you know.'

'A friend.'

'Oh, yes.' She hesitated. 'But changed.'

'Stop being mysterious!'

'He asks you to go alone and not tell anyone. I'll take you.'

The path had changed since she had walked that way to Beacon Hill a decade before. The trunks of the laurels were more twisted, the undergrowth – where there were gaps – was more exuberant. The way to it would have been obliterated had not one of the gardeners preparing for the reception ridden with his mower a little way along it. What it signified sent a bitter chill through her body. She stood for a moment to let the feeling pass.

'Are you alright, Miss?

'I'm fine. Are we nearly there?'

He stepped out from the shadows in front of them.

'Hello, Sarah.'

She had not meant to stare, and it had only lasted a second. When she turned in confusion for support Marguerite had gone.

'Brian? Are you Brian?'

'Unhappily, yes.'

There were so many thoughts and questions. A sensible response was impossible. She turned and grasped the bough of an ancient laurel with both her hands and rested her forehead against them.

'Brian, it's been five years!'

'And two months. I've kept count.'

'It's wonderful you're alive. We all thought…'

'… that I died in the blaze? Well nearly, as you will see. Sarah, time is short and it's getting dark down here.'

'Brian, I'm supposed to be changing. The car comes for us in an hour.'

'Sarah, I have things to tell you and show you.'

The brambles and nettles worked on their legs as they had a decade before. It seemed to Sarah he was trying not to go ahead of her when he should have led the way. The top of the hill was still bathed in the yellow light of the evening sun while all around was a muted sea of dark green and grey. The wooden seat was still there, miraculously unchanged. They sat.

'There are facts, Sarah, you need to know.'

She realised he had been keeping the left side of his face from her. Now he turned his head deliberately so that the light fell directly upon it. She recoiled in horror. Momentarily his expression was of an animal at bay, broken and hopeless. Then, slowly, he turned the damaged side of his face away.

'It was the first blast of flame, when all the fireworks accidentally went off, after the raft had beached at the jetty and your friends had spirited you away. Edwin was standing by me. He was more fortunate.'

'He's alive?'

'He died that night – of his burns.'

Sarah walked to where she could see the lights of Oxford beginning to twinkle in the darkening expanse around them. She turned and looked back at him.

'And Tom?'

'I... killed Tom.'

'What?'

'Please don't ask. It was between us two, no-one else.'

She thought for a moment, then said quietly, 'Why?'

'To get an answer to your question... your face... who did it.'

'And?'

'A teacher in Lebanon, he said...'

'It was Pierre then.' She whispered it to herself, having known, yet still reluctant to believe. She doubted that he had heard.

'It was all he would say.' His voice rose in remorse. 'It meant nothing. It was not enough to stop me...' He raised his hand to stifle any further discussion. 'Then I escaped and went to ground, but all that need not concern you. Khasoni helped arrange treatment and the papers. Eventually, with a new identity, I reached the States. As you might imagine, there was a market for my skills. I did well. Very well, in fact, considering that all sense of purpose had gone.'

'Why didn't you let me know, for heaven's sake?'

'After the things I did? You wouldn't have wanted that. But I've followed your progress, Sarah. I've watched you at meetings and conferences. Read your research papers. I've even visited the Institute, and your own office and – please forgive me – sat at your desk. But always alone, always in disguise. Anyway, I can tell you I'm pleased that my ill-gotten money wasn't wasted. It's fortunate that Khasoni is a decent man at heart and honoured the bargain.

Sarah's hand went instinctively to her cheek. 'I still wonder about that.'

'It was to have been for both of us, you see. My dream.'

'That's still not impossible.'

'It's quite impossible. And when I heard what was to happen today. Well, somehow the door finally closed. This time, Sarah, I intend to allow myself no escape. You understand now why I had to see you.' His head was bent forward, almost to his knees. Sarah felt a faint tremor of the wooden seat. 'The funny thing is I hadn't bargained for what's come flooding back to me now. You didn't realise, of course. This hill once seemed like a stairway to the stars.'

Sarah drew herself closer to him and gripped his hand. 'Brian, I'm sorry. So very sorry.'

'Don't be. Everything is complete. In spite of the evil that was done it gladdens me to think that in the end only one of us was scarred by it. Stay as you are, Sarah. Never go back to what you were.'

Brian stood up and looked towards the faint carpet

of light in the distance. 'Oxford! It once beckoned to me too you know, after London. Who knows what effect a cloistered college existence might have had? Anyway… ' He slapped the palms of his hands against his thighs as a gesture of closure. 'You mustn't look for word of me or ever dream of investigating. It would be pointless. All the arrangements have already been taken care of. Don't be surprised if you find a little money coming your way – just accept it with grace. At least it will ensure the future of the Institute for your lifetime, if that is what you want. Oh, and there may be a few paintings. I would like to think you would wish to keep them yourself.'

'Thank you. It's all I can think of to say.'

'Just one other thing.' She thought she caught a fleeting smile. 'You can thank Jack Adams for that brief loan of his pen. I'm sure he'll understand.'

'So long ago! But I'll tell him.'

'Then goodbye, Sarah.'

She had turned away from him to hide her tears and choose her words. But when she looked back there was only an empty seat and nothing left for her but fleeting memories from years before.

It was really dark now. Down below voices were calling for her. There was agitation there, and a little anger. But it was within the bounds of business of ordinary people living ordinary lives. For a few more minutes, surely, she could remain apart. It was so little to ask when set against the greater canvass.

Her drawn-up legs grew cold in the wind. The hair caressing her bare knees seemed to be trying to dry the wetness there. The dampness of the bench was beginning to seep through the thinness of her dress.

She turned her back on the brightening lights of the distant city. Something impelled her to look down into the black well in which the memory of her sister was still contained. A minute passed, then two. The stars dimmed.

For the last time she followed in her mind the progress of that faint processional light along the hidden path until it was received and the doors finally closed upon it.